JUNE '88

TAMMY LANE,

YOU'RE ABOUT TO EMBARK ON ANOTHER ONE OF LIFES MANY ADVENTURES. I KNOW YOU'LL ENJOY & MAKE THE MOST OF THIS ONE AS YOU DO OF EVERY CHALLANGE YOU MEET. YOU'RE ABOUT TO LEAVE HOME AND BE ON YOUR OWN AND MEET THE WORLD HEAD ON. WE'LL THINK OF YOU OFTEN. GO AHEAD AND LIVE YOUR LIFE TO ITS FULLEST. ENJOY EACH OF THESE STORIES FOR THEY ARE YOUR KIND OF ENJOYMENT.

LOVE
DAD.

50
Great Horror
Stories

50
Great Horror
Stories

EDITED BY
JOHN CANNING

BONANZA BOOKS
NEW YORK

This 1987 edition is published by Bonanza Books, distributed by
Crown Publishers, Inc., 225 Park Avenue South, New York,
New York 10003, by arrangement with Souvenir Press, Ltd.

Printed and Bound in the United States of America

Library of Congress Cataloging-in-Publication Data
50 great horror stories.
    1. Horror tales, English. I. Canning, John, 1913–
II. Title: Fifty great horror stories.
PR1309.H6A128   1987   823'.0872'08   87-21214
ISBN 0-517-13671-6
n   m   l   k   j   i   h

Contents

		Page
Acknowledgments		
Editor's Note		
THE RUFF	*Michael and Mollie Hardwick*	15
THE WEREWOLF OF ST-CLAUDE	*Ronald Seth*	23
THE HAND OF FATHER ARROWSMITH	*Michael and Mollie Hardwick*	31
THE MAN WHO TURNED INTO A CAT	*J. Wentworth Day*	42
THE DEAD KILLED HIM IN HIS OWN GRAVE	*J. Wentworth Day*	52
THE DEVIL IN THE FLESH	*Ronald Seth*	62
THE BO'SUN'S BODY	*Michael and Mollie Hardwick*	69
A WARNING TO SCEPTICS	*Michael and Mollie Hardwick*	80
DOUBLE DAMNATION	*Michael and Mollie Hardwick*	95
THE TONGUELESS WOMAN OF GLAMIS CASTLE	*J. Wentworth Day*	105
TRAPPED IN A FLOODED TUNNEL	*Geoffrey Williamson*	113
THE GIRL IN THE FLAME-RED DRESS	*Ian Fellowes-Gordon*	120
WITH THIS RING	*Michael and Mollie Hardwick*	131
THE VAMPIRE OF CROGLIN	*Michael and Mollie Hardwick*	142
DONOVAN'S DROP	*Ian Fellowes-Gordon*	148

CONTENTS

Page

THE BEAKED HORROR WHICH SANK A SHIP
J. Wentworth Day 158

THE DOG-MAN HORROR OF THE VALLEY
J. Wentworth Day 163

THEY ATE THEIR YOUNG SHIPMATE
Geoffrey Williamson 169

THE MATE OF THE *SQUANDO*
Michael and Mollie Hardwick 179

RIPE STILTON *Michael and Mollie Hardwick* 188

THE PRINCESS OF THEBES
Michael and Mollie Hardwick 197

DEATH TAKES VENGEANCE *Vida Derry* 208

A DATE WITH A SPIDER *Vida Derry* 218

OLE ROCKIN' CHAIR *Michael and Mollie Hardwick* 229

THE FRIGHTENED CORPSE *Vida Derry* 241

THE VAMPIRE OF CASTLE FURSTENSTEIN
J. Wentworth Day 250

THE GREAT WHITE BAT *Frank Usher* 258

LET SLEEPING BONES LIE *Michael and Mollie Hardwick* 267

SUNG TO HIS DEATH BY DEAD MEN
J. Wentworth Day 274

THE MAN WHO HATED CATS
Michael and Mollie Hardwick 282

ACCUSING EYES OF VENGEANCE
Geoffrey Williamson 288

THE WALKING DEAD *Frank Usher* 298

VISIT FROM A VAMPIRE *Ronald Seth* 307

THE EXORCISING OF THE RESTLESS MONK
Ronald Seth 320

THE RECLUSE OF KOTKA VESKI *Ronald Seth* 328

THE SECRET AGENTS AND THE CORPSE
Ronald Seth 341

CONTENTS

		Page
THE BATH OF ACID	*Frank Usher*	353
THE GIRL IN THE TRAIN	*Ian Fellowes-Gordon*	364
THE BLACK DAHLIA	*Frank Usher*	374
SCENT OF DEATH	*Ronald Seth*	383
THE FACE OF MRS CARTWRIGHT	*Ian Fellowes-Gordon*	397
THE EVENTS AT SCHLOSS HEIDIGER	*Ian Fellowes-Gordon*	408
THE BIRTHDAY GIFT	*Ian Fellowes-Gordon*	418
THE ATTIC ROOM	*Ian Fellowes-Gordon*	427
FOOTPRINTS IN THE DUST	*Ronald Seth*	438
AMAZONIAN HORRORS	*Frank Usher*	444
THE IMAGE OF FEAR	*Vida Derry*	453
LULLABY FOR THE DEAD	*Michael and Mollie Hardwick*	464
ROSE: A GOTHICK TALE	*Michael and Mollie Hardwick*	470
THE EYES OF THOMAS BOLTER	*Michael and Mollie Hardwick*	481
INDEX		491

Acknowledgments

The editor expresses his acknowledgments to publishers for their courtesy in permitting condensations from the following books:

Hutchinson and Co. (Publishers) Ltd., *True Ghost Stories* by Townshend and Foulkes; Geoffrey Bles, Ltd., *Lord Halifax's Ghost Book*; A. Watkins, Inc., *The Magic Island* by William Seabrook.

Editor's Note

I have described the collection of tales gathered together in this volume as "horror" stories. By this word I mean to convey not the horrible (in the sense of the outpouring of blood and the heaping-up of mayhem), but the horrific—those weird, macabre, unnatural happenings which seem to defy a rational explanation.

A small minority of the tales, however, do not yield to this classification, and these I have included because each of them combines a strangeness and rarity which makes one wonder at the incongruous paths that men have sometimes trodden.

All of them, however, have in common the fact that they are either true, have been recorded in contemporary documents as fact, or have become such a prevailing folk myth as to suggest some evidence of actual occurrence.

But why produce a book of horror stories? Because people are made up of feelings and passions as well as of reason, and find refreshment and entertainment on those levels. Also there is a strong dream-like quality about many of these stories which gives them a quite startling vividness and persistence in the memory.

Emily Brontë makes Catherine say in *Wuthering Heights*: "I've dreamt in my life dreams that have stayed with me ever after, and changed my ideas: they've gone through and through me, like wine through water, and altered the colour of my mind."

It would perhaps be too much to claim that this book is likely to change its readers to this degree, but I'm sure that for everyone who browses within its covers there will be something that will remain in his mind long after many other memories are forgotten.

JOHN CANNING

The Ruff

Anna Vermeylen leant forward to examine her image more closely in the mirror. The light was poor, filtering through small panes of greenish bottle-glass, in a window half-hidden by rich heavy curtains. Anna clapped her hands and imperiously demanded a candle-branch to be lit, though it was barely three o'clock in the afternoon.

Elisabeth, her maid, made a face behind Anna's back, but obediently did as she was bidden. It did not do to oppose her mistress's commands, however extravagant or unreasonable. Candles in the daytime, when they cost so dearly, and the poorer streets of Antwerp were crammed with people who could barely afford a rushlight after dark! But if you were the spoilt only daughter of one of the richest merchants in the city you could afford as many candles as the image of the Virgin Mary in the Cathedral. You could also afford a bit of charity to the poor: but catch this one throwing any coins from her coach, or even passing on a gown she was tired of to her maid, that had but one to her name! No, thought Elisabeth bitterly, she'd hoard them in a chest for the moths to fatten on, rather than see another girl look handsomer in them than herself.

Elisabeth did her mistress a certain injustice, for Anna Vermeylen was beautiful, by the standards of her time. She resembled somewhat the Queen of England in youth, having the same pointed oval structure of face, high-bridged nose and small mouth. Her hair was of the rare true golden, naturally curling, so that when washed it snapped back into a multitude of ringlets like small watch-springs. Her eyes were cold in expression, but of a striking speedwell blue, her skin as white as the flower of the privet. At the age of twenty she still possessed all her teeth (a remarkable achievement in 1582) and the terrible hand of smallpox had not touched her. She was small-statured and slender to the point of thinness, in delicate contrast to the sturdy Flemish build which was more usual among the maids of Antwerp. The late King of England had not been at all pleased to find himself matrimonially yoked with that other Anna whom he unchivalrously described as a great Flanders mare. It was a pity, Anna thought, that she herself had not been My Lady of Cleves. The English succession would certainly have turned out very differently.

However, no king had yet offered for Anna's hand in marriage. More disquietingly, no commoner had done so. Neither her looks nor her riches could lure the young men of Antwerp into a proposal. Merchant society was a small world. In the families of Ryswyck, Willems, Claes—all moneyed, all blessed with sons—it was well known that Anna's eligibility was offset by her notorious bad temper, hauteur and meanness. Shrews were not popular. Erasmus of Holland had written a "colloquy" against them, which, translated, may have inspired a very young man in Warwickshire to write a certain famous play: but that was in the future. He was not yet wed to his own shrew. Nobody wanted a curst wife, and it was pretty clear that Anna would be one.

Her father was in despair. He had let it be known that a rich endowment would go with his daughter; he had held splendid routs to show her off. The young men came, enjoyed his food and drink, were polite to Anna, but went away uncommitted. He could understand it only too well, having lived with her for twenty years, but that made it no better. He wanted grandsons to carry on his business and inherit his money; he also wanted (and this he would admit only to himself) to be rid of Anna.

It was not surprising that Mynheer Vermeylen seldom looked cheerful. When he entered Anna's room on this April afternoon, smiling broadly, Anna raised her eyebrows, that were plucked and arched into small cupid's bows. Her father waved a letter at her.

"This will please you, Anna! Only to think you were complaining this morning that there was no gaiety in Antwerp."

She extended her hand for the letter. "What's all this coil? A wedding? Why should I want to go to a wedding?" She laughed bitterly. "Unless it were my own, and I see no sign of that."

"But this is no ordinary wedding, Anna!" said her father eagerly. "Jan Claes and Margriet Willems are to be married in the Cathedral, and there will be a splendid breakfast. Guests will come from far and near—from Bruges and Ghent, perhaps from London, even! You know how wide is Claes's trade, and Jan is his eldest boy. You will meet every likely young man in the world of commerce. Surely, among them . . ."

A speculative look came into Anna's eyes. "I shall need new clothes, of course. I've nothing to wear, not a rag to my back."

Mynheer Vermeylen mentally reviewed the array of dresses, cloaks, shifts and accessories his daughter had ordered for Christmas, but decided that it would not be politic to refer to them. "By all means, my dear," he said. "Anything you fancy."

"And grandmother's jewels. You must take them out of the chest and have them cleaned. At once."

Her father's brow furrowed. "Would it be wise, my dear, to go through the streets in them? The cabochon emerald—the collar of pearls and rubies—what with the rogues there are about, and all these infernal Spaniards from the Duke of Anjou's household, just waiting to massacre us as they did in '76 . . ."

Anna thumped her dressing-table with a small fist. "I said I wanted them and I'll have them. See to it!" She whirled round to face the mirror and began to push the front waves of her hair this way and that, admiring the effect. Her father watched her, his face worried and sad. He laid a hand gently on her shoulder.

"Anna. You will be good, my little girl—this time, when it might mean so much?"

Anna tossed her head. "I don't know what you mean."

"Child, you know very well. Speak gently and softly, as a woman should. Conduct yourself modestly. Pride goeth before destruction, and an haughty spirit before a fall, says the Scripture."

"Don't preach to me, father! We get enough of that on Sundays. And I hope I know how to conduct myself without advice from you."

Her father sighed as he turned to leave the room. "Your tongue is your worst enemy, daughter," he said. From the antechamber his little dog, an aged griffon, trotted in, hearing its master's voice. It approached Anna's skirts and sniffed them interestedly: some pleasant-smelling morsel of food had fallen from the table at dinner, and still clung to the fabric. Anna aimed her sharp-pointed slipper at the dog in a kick that sent it sprawling across the room with a shriek of pain.

"Anna! You wicked girl!" Her father picked the small creature up and fondled it. "You have hurt his side. You might have killed him."

"A good thing too. Stinking cur. Keep it out of my chamber, or I'll have it hanged." She began to polish her already pink and shining nails. Mynheer Vermcylen left her without a word, the dog cradled in his arms, and went to his own room, where he knelt and prayed.

"Wherefore is light given to him that is in misery, and life unto the bitter in soul?"

The weeks that lay between the arrival of the wedding invitation and the wedding-day were a foretaste of purgatory for Anna's servants. She sent to dressmakers, milliners, glove-makers, to prepare for her the best possible toilette for the great day. Her maids were ordered to rise at dawn and gather herbs from which to make whitening lotions for her skin. The already golden hair was coloured even brighter with an infusion of the flowers of camomile; the slender waist compressed almost to vanishing point by that ingenious instrument of torture, an iron corset. The finest leather in Antwerp was sought out to make her new shoes, and dyed to the exact colour of her dress, a celestial blue embroidered thickly with artificial pearls and semi-precious stones. Her slender neck, like the stamen of a flower, was to be shown off against the background of the very newest and most glorious of ruffs.

The old-fashioned concertina type of ruff had given way to the wired lace collar, more comfortable, becoming and spectacular than its predecessor. Fan-shaped, it backed the head, descending to points at the junction of the sleeves and bodice. As a maiden, Anna was entitled to display her bosom, adorned with the necklace of rubies and pearls which had been her grandmother's most precious ornament, as well as by a triple-twined rope of larger pearls. She chose for it a Genoese lace design edged with gold and supported on golden wires arranged in triple layers. So elaborate was the pattern that the ruff took as long to make as the rest of her wardrobe put together. Day after day an apologetic servant would be dispatched to the lace-maker's cottage to inquire about its progress. He dared not, for shame, deliver his mistress's threats, so abusive were they.

For though it might have been supposed that the acquisition of so much finery would improve Anna's temper, the reverse was the case. Never had she abused her servants so savagely. Elisabeth, Greta and Johanna went in hourly fear that she would do them some serious mischief. When her father's little dog died from a growth which had resulted from the kick she had given it, she laughed and vowed she would serve another the same. Riding through the streets in her coach one day, she encountered the admiring gaze of a young Spanish soldier belonging to the train of the Duke of Anjou, who had moved into Antwerp that spring in the hope of taking over the rule of the city. Another girl might have blushed or smiled, or merely returned his looks coldly. Anna leant from her coach window and loosed at him such a torrent of invective, calling him a foreign dog, smircher of womankind, and the like, that a crowd gathered to listen, and Anna's coachman feared for his life, seeing the young man's hand on his dagger.

"The Devil will claim her for his own, one of these days," said an old woman who stood by.

"Nay, she'd be the death of him," answered her neighbour. "He'll dispatch her to lead apes in hell, and so keep her out of his way."

At last, on the eve of the wedding-day, all the finery was ready. Except for the ruff, which now had to be starched and set in place. When she saw it, after the household laundress had dealt with it, she threw it on the floor and seized the woman by the throat, shaking her like a terrier with a rat and beating her. The terrified woman managed to escape and ran to the kitchens, hysterical with fright, saying that she would never venture near her mistress again. Two more laundresses were sent for, but their efforts at starching pleased Anna no better. As the old story says, "then fell she to swear and to tear, to curse and ban, casting the ruffe under feete, and wishing that the devil might take her when she wore the neckerchers again".

But at last the ruff was starched to something like her satisfaction. On the morning of the wedding-day, the 27th of May, she rose at dawn and called up her maids. They dressed her from head to foot in her new clothes, so that when the sun rose she was a glorious sight to see. Her spreading blue gown was the colour of the May skies, gems and pearls glittered on it and set off the fair skin of her bosom and neck. Her hair was dressed in a tower of curls and crowned with a pearl circlet, from which a pendant hung on her brow. Two long rolled ringlets graced her shoulders.

Only the ruff remained. Elisabeth and Johanna took it carefully from its wrappings and set it about Anna's neck, tier ranged behind delicate tier, and prepared to secure it.

"That's not the way, you dolts!" their mistress shouted. "You have set it all amiss!" and she wrenched the laces apart.

"But, madam . . ." began Johanna. Anna slapped her face. The girl put her hand to the scarlet mark, and her eyes met those of Elisabeth in a long look. Then she went to the window and opened the casement, standing before it with her back to the room, a white kerchief in her hand.

"What are you about, wench?" demanded Anna. "Get on with your work!"

"I am not well, madam," replied the maid, in a faint voice. "I must have air for a moment."

Anna frowned impatiently. "Megrims! You, Lisa, see if you can do it better than this fool."

There was a timid knock at the door, and Greta, the youngest maid, entered. "If you please, madam, there is one to see you," she said. Anna spun round.

"On this of all days? I can see no one. Tell them to go about their business."

"Madam, he will take no denial . . ." began Greta. She was pushed aside by the caller, and there stood before Anna a remarkably handsome young man. Dark-complexioned and red-lipped, he appeared to be no Flamand. His doublet was of the finest black velvet, his trunks slashed with scarlet, his hose of black silk. A short cloak of rich leather swung gracefully from his shoulders. The plumed velvet cap he swept off revealed black, closely curling hair. Anna's eyes widened with admiration, but she began to rail at him out of custom.

"God's body, sir, how dare you invade my chamber? I'll have you thrown into the street!"

He darted forward, knelt at her feet, and snatching one of the white hands clenched at her side, kissed it. His voice, when he spoke, was soft and heavily foreign. Anna could not identify the country, but she listened fascinated to his speech.

"Fair madam, forgive my intrusion. The blaze of your beauty has drawn me here, as a lamp the poor moth. Since I saw you enter your house yesterday I have waited impatiently to approach you and beg you to pity me!"

Anna was flattered and impressed, but determined not to show it.

"You would do better to approach my father, sir, if you mean honourably. And it is no time to woo now, for I must leave within the half-hour—if these thick-fingered ninnies will finish their work. Look what a havoc they have made!" She snatched up a hand-mirror and surveyed disgustedly the crooked, drooping frills of lace. The stranger rose swiftly and bowed.

"Your maids do not set your ruff to your liking, madam? It happens that I have great cunning in the art, for in my country these new collars are much worn. If it will please you to dismiss your women I will take their place."

Anna hesitated, then yielded. "You can do no worse than they, I suppose. Go to the antechamber, both of you, and wait until I call." Silently the two girls left, shutting Anna in with the unconventional visitor. Standing behind her chair, and bidding her face the mirror, he deftly pulled and tweaked the ruff into shape, straightening bent wires, smoothing out crumpled folds of lace, arranging the highest tier to form a snowy background to the glittering curls. Anna, for once, was silent. His hands, touching her skin, seemed to burn her, and there was dark fire in the eyes that met hers in the mirror. She was excited, charmed. Her reflected eyes and his exchanged looks that questioned and answered, challenged and yielded. She would willingly have prolonged the operation, but now the ties were fastened and the ruff perfectly set.

"It is exactly to my liking!" she said.

"And my reward?"

He bent over her, his long hands caressing the white stem of her throat, and gently tilted up her chin. Their lips met in a long kiss. He raised his face from hers, and as she sighed with satisfaction fastened his hands about her throat in a vicious grip, and squeezed it tightly. Her choking cries and convulsive struggles were short, for the hands that were strangling her had demoniac strength and knew no mercy.

A moment later the door to the antechamber opened and a black figure strode past the two waiting girls, vanishing down the stairs. When they re-entered their mistress's room their screams brought the rest of the household running. Something like a broken doll lay on the floor, limp as sawdust in the blue begemmed dress. The neck had been wrung like a chicken's. The eyes started horribly from their sockets. The face was livid—"most ugglesome to behold," says the old document. The tongue which protruded from that once pretty mouth was silenced for ever.

So the Devil had taken her at last, said the old women; for the murdering visitor had been no mortal man, it was clear. None in Antwerp had seen him before, none recognized him from the girls' description. Eerie stories were told of Anna's funeral: how the four bearers were unable to lift her coffin, so heavy was it, so that from curiosity they opened it, and found within "a black catte, very leane and deformed, sitting in the coffin, setting of great ruffes, and frizzling of haire, to the great fear and wonder of all the beholders".

Elisabeth and Johanna said very little of their mistress's death, to each other or to the world; which was curious, for Johanna had hated her deeply and had once been heard to swear that she would stop at nothing to be even with her. There had been another who had sworn the same: a certain young Spaniard of the Duke of Anjou's household, whom Anna had so vilely insulted in the street, wounding his pride beyond endurance. When Johanna left her new mistress's service, some months later, married the Spaniard and returned with him to France, the gossips expressed only surprise that she should have wed an enemy of her country. The Devil, they said, must have seduced her to his own purposes.

And they were nearer the truth than they knew.

The Werewolf of St-Claude

Lycanthropy—the ability of a man or woman to change into a wolf—is a very ancient belief. Now rejected as a hallucination, throughout the history of witchcraft it is a constantly recurring theme, but at no time did it occur so frequently as during the classical period of the persecution of witchcraft as a heresy: that is, from 1450 to 1750.

Though there are accounts of werewolves ranging the English countryside, such accounts are more numerous in the annals of continental witchcraft. But there, again, there were certain regions which suffered in particular, one of which was the Jura, in eastern central France. Here among the mountains and valleys between the Rhine and the Rhône, some of the most horrifying lycanthrope cases were brought to book.

In 1521, for example, Father Jean Boin, Inquisitor-General of Besançon, tried three men of Poligny, Michel Verdung, Pierre Bourgot and Philibert Mentot, for their alleged werewolf activities. These had first been brought to the attention of the authorities by a traveller who, defending himself against an attack by a wolf, wounded it. He followed the trail of blood that it left, intending to dispatch it, but the trail led to a cottage where he found Michel Verdung, whose wife was dressing wounds he had acquired, so he said, while hunting for food.

The traveller was unconvinced by Verdung's explanation and reported his suspicions to the authorities in Poligny, who arrested the wounded man for questioning as a possible werewolf. Under the inevitable torture, Verdung confessed that he did possess the power to turn himself into a wolf, and named two companions who from time to time accompanied him on his lupine expeditions.

The two men, Bourgot and Mentot, were forthwith arrested and charged with lycanthropy. Bourgot described how he had entered the service of the Devil, who had endowed him with the power to change himself into a wolf. A great storm, he said, had scattered his flocks some twenty years earlier, and while he was out looking for them he had encountered three horsemen dressed in black, who civilly asked him what he was searching for. When he told them, one of the horsemen, whom he later identified as Philibert Mentot, promised to help him on condition that he would become his servant "in everything he demanded". Bourgot consented, and within a very short time found his sheep.

Not long afterwards Bourgot met Mentot again, and from their conversation learned that the horseman had himself made a compact with the Devil. At Mentot's suggestion, Bourgot also made a compact, denying his Christian faith and kissing Mentot's hand.

Bourgot's heart was not really in witchcraft, however, and within a couple of years he embarked on a slow process of reconversion. This did not meet with Mentot's approval and he ordered Verdung, who was also under his influence, to keep Bourgot up to the mark. One of his measures to effect this was to promise Bourgot money, provided he remained faithful to the Devil.

Bourgot was persuaded, and before very long he agreed to attend his first sabbat. At some point during the ceremonies Verdung ordered Bourgot to strip naked, and when he had done so he rubbed him all over with a magic ointment. As soon as he was completely covered with the ointment Bourgot found that he had been transformed into a wolf.

Next, Verdung and Mentot stripped and anointed one another with the ointment. They, too, became wolves and together with Bourgot went on a foraging expedition. When they returned, they applied another ointment to one another and regained their human shape.

Henceforward the three men met regularly and practised lycanthropy. Under torture Bourgot made a full confession of his and his companions' werewolf activities. As wolves, he said, the three men sometimes ran with a pack of real wolves, and from time to time mated with the females, when, he declared, "they had as much pleasure in the act as if they had copulated with their wives". Bourgot also told his inquisitors of his killing and eating children. One, he said, was a four-year-old girl whose flesh he found particularly savoury. He also described how he had once almost been caught. He attacked a boy of seven, but the child screamed so much that people came running, and he only got away by scrambling into his clothes and returning to his human shape.

This Poligny case caused widespread consternation at the time, and it entered the record of classical witchcraft when Johan Weyer, one of the earliest witchcraft sceptics, recounted it in a book which had an extensive circulation in the mid-sixteenth century, *De Praestigiis Daemonum*, published in 1563. (The book won continuing fame as a result of the attack made on it by King James VI and I in his own book, *Demonologie*.) Weyer had told the story to demonstrate that lycanthropy was, in fact, a delusion; but a later demonologist, Grand Juge Henri Boguet, repeated it in his great work on witchcraft, *Discours des sorciers*, to prove the exact opposite of Weyer's contention.

Henri Boguet was the principal judge of St-Claude, one of the chief towns in the Jura, and his over-all fame rests as much on his record as a witch-trial judge as it does on his *Discours*, which is almost totally based on his personal experiences, for it was he who instituted one of the most extensive witch-hunts in the Jura. Among the cases he recounts one relates to a family living in St-Claude called Gandillon, consisting of two sisters, their brother and his son, three of whom were brought before him in 1593, accused of lycanthropy. The fourth member of the family, Perrenette, met a death perhaps even more horrible than the burning to which Henri Boguet condemned her brother, her sister and her nephew.

One sunny September morning in 1593, Madame Bidel, who lived at Naizan, a small village nor far from St-Claude, was once more in labour. The child soon to be born was her ninth, but only three of her children now survived—Benoît, aged sixteen, Maria, aged twelve, and Anne, aged four.

Maria, on her mother's instructions, had already gone to fetch the neighbour who had agreed to help her, and the neighbour's bustling about the kitchen had frightened the four-year-old Anne, who had in any case been made apprehensive by her mother's contortions and moans. Though not comprehending what was happening, with childish intuition the little girl had understood that her mother was not the calm, loving mother she usually was, and had gone to comfort her, only to be rebuffed. This, too, she had not understood, and had begun to sob. The loud voice of the neighbour and her self-important fussing had increased her uneasiness and the sobs had turned to bellows, which a direct scolding did nothing to soothe.

"What can we do with the child?" the woman demanded.

"Shall I take her into the orchard?" Maria asked.

"No, I shall want you here! Ah, there's Benoît. Benoît!" she called. "Come here."

The youth put down the pail he was carrying and crossed to the cottage door.

"Madame?" he said.

"Your mother—her time has come, and this naughty child bellows so loudly one cannot hear oneself speak," she told him. "Maria must stay to help. Take the little one and keep her amused for an hour."

"But I am helping my father," Benoît protested.

"Now you must help your mother!" the woman exclaimed, and thrusting Anne out of the door, shut it in their faces.

Benoît picked up the little girl and kissed her.

"There, there!" he soothed. "Don't cry!"

"Maman!" the child cried.

"Maman will be all right. Come now, dry your tears and we will see if we can find you a nice ripe juicy apple, and then we will go and look at the pigs. You like the pigs, don't you?"

Between sobs the child nodded and presently, as her brother carried her towards the orchard, talking quietly to her, and now and again nuzzling his lips against her cheek, she quietened.

In the orchard, Benoît walked from tree to tree testing the fruit, but found none sweet enough for a little girl to eat without getting the belly-gripes.

"I know!" he exclaimed, and began to run through the trees with her until he came to the edge of the orchard and the wood beyond.

Here he stopped before a giant apple-tree which ought to have been pruned years since. Because of this oversight, fruit now grew only on the topmost branches, where the newer growth was, but they were the earliest apples to mature and were crisp and sweet and rosy-cheeked even now.

Putting his baby sister on the ground at the foot of the tree, he swung himself up into the branches.

"Don't move!" he called down to Anne, "and I'll bring you a beautiful apple directly, but I shan't unless you stay there until I come again."

Laughing, the child assured him, "I stay here."

The foliage thickened as he mounted. It was so thick by the time he was half-way up that on looking down he could not see the ground. So it was that he did not observe a large animal emerge from the wood and stand, its right front paw poised in mid-air, its muzzle delicately raised.

For a moment it stood, and then, half-cowering, slowly and silently it began to stalk towards the apple-tree.

Though she did not recognize it for the wolf it was, Anne was instinctively afraid, and began to scream with all the force of her lungs. In response, the animal bared its fangs and set up an angry snarling.

From both screams and snarls Benoît realized that there was something very amiss at the foot of the tree, and half-scrambling, half-falling, he began to descend with all speed. On reaching the ground he saw with relief that the animal had not yet attacked the child and that immediately it had caught sight of him it had turned its attention to him.

Seizing the knife from his belt, half-crouching, he taunted the wolf to attack him, moving all the while so as to draw it away from his sister, who, as soon as she had seen him, had stopped her yells and was now laughing and chattering with excitement. He hoped the wolf would decide not to join combat, for it was a large female and females were reputed to be more courageous than males, except when hunting in packs. In a moment or two, however, he realized that the animal was hungry and that it meant to be satisfied.

Doubtful of his ability to deal single-handed with it, he began to shout for help, praying that there might be workers in the nearby field who would hear him and come to his aid. At the sound of his voice the wolf seemed to sense that if it did not attack at once its prey would escape it, and with a cry, half-bark, half-howl, it suddenly leaped on the boy. The noise it made and the suddenness of its movement once more frightened Anne, and as wolf and boy struggled on the ground she began to scream again.

As the boy fought desperately to keep his assailant from his throat and to reach its throat with his knife, he heard vaguely the shouts of men and women. The wolf heard them too, and increased its efforts.

With a strength which sprang from hopelessness, Benoît managed to draw back the hand holding the knife, but as he was about to plunge it into the wolf the beast seized his wrist, wrenched the knife away and plunged it into his throat.

But even in the split second that the attack had taken the boy saw something that took away all his strength.

The paw that seized his wrist and the paw that wrenched the knife from his hand were not pads of an animal at all—they were human hands!

The wolf had time to make only one jab at him, for at that very moment seven or eight men and two or three women came running on to the scene. Dropping the knife, the animal leapt away, making for the shelter of the wood.

While the men pursued it, the women rushed to the aid of the little girl and wounded boy. There was nothing they could do to help Benoît but make his last moments comfortable.

As one of them knelt beside him cradling his head in her lap, for a brief moment he opened his eyes and spoke clearly and loudly.

"It had hands for paws!" he said, then, choking on the spurt of blood which gushed from his mouth, he died.

When the women had crossed themselves, one of them said, "Did you hear?"

"Yes," the others replied. " 'It had hands for paws'."

"Run after the men," the first woman said to the horrified girl staring down at Benoît's blood-sodden shirt, "and tell them what he said. Quick, quick! It's not a wolf they are searching for."

When the girl caught up with the men, they were already beginning to fear that the wolf had escaped them and that they were wasting their time carrying on with their search. But on hearing what she had to tell them, with angry shouts they beat through the tangled undergrowth of the wood.

And presently one of them found, cowering under a bush, a frightened, gibbering, demented woman, seemingly old before her time.

When his cries of discovery brought the others running, one of them immediately recognized her.

"It's Perrenette Gandillon from St-Claude!" he exclaimed. "What are you doing here, so far from home?"

Her lips moved, but no recognizable sounds came from them, as she cowered in the grip of the young peasant who held her.

"Look, her hands have blood on them!" another exclaimed, seizing her hands and regarding them closely. "But they have no wounds on them."

"Did you do it? Did you kill Benoît Bidel?" another demanded.

At the question the woman's attitude changed. Drawing herself up she said, proudly, "Yes, I killed him."

"You are a werewolf?"

"I am a werewolf."

"You admit it?"

"I am a werewolf," she repeated.

For a moment there was stunned silence. Then, with a cry of rage, the young man holding her ripped at her clothes and in no time she stood naked and haughty before them.

The men were struck immobile and speechless at the sight that confronted them. In contrast with the greying hair and the age-creases of her forehead, cheeks and throat they beheld the body of a beautiful young girl. The curves of the milk-white shoulders, the firm, round, up-tilted breasts, the waist tapering to sleek hips, were such as they had never seen before, and for a brief time they were spellbound by what they saw.

It was the girl who had brought the message who broke the spell.

"Witch!" she shrieked, and hurled herself on Perrenette Gandillon, tearing at face and body with her work-roughened fingers.

With cries rivalling the girl's shrieks, the young men in the party, as though maddened by the beauty that because of witchcraft they could not possess, flung themselves upon the woman. As they tore and clawed at her, helped by the older men, who should have restrained them, she shrieked with the pain of what they were doing to her.

Presently, they were a heap of flailing, jerking bodies on the ground. Then there came silence broken only by their panting and the moans of their exertions.

One by one they pulled themselves away and stood up, and there was not one of them who was not spattered with his victim's blood.

They looked down and saw the result of their emotions. What had once been a beautiful body made in the image of Mother Eve, as she emerged in pristine beauty from Adam's rib, was now a heap of mangled flesh and distorted bones without life.

A young man leant against a tree and retched.

Above them in the trees a thrush trilled out his twice-repeated song.

The Hand of Father Arrowsmith

Of all horrors in the history of religious persecution, carried out in the name of a loving Saviour, there is none to equal the terrible ritual of human vivisection known as hanging, drawing and quartering. It shamed the great age of Elizabeth, and lingered on into the days of the Stuarts. Charles II, renowned for elegance, tolerance and good humour, could watch calmly the execution by this means of ten of his subjects at Charing Cross. In his father's reign their fate had been suffered by many Roman Catholic priests. The penal laws of the time were particularly savage, enforced against the King's wishes by a Puritan parliament; besides, Charles I had too much interest in the "Anglican Papacy" controlled by himself and Bishop Laud to make any concessions to the Pope of Rome. Priests who persisted in the practice of their Faith and the celebration of its rites knew the risk they ran. They schemed, hid, and disguised themselves with a resource surpassing that of political spies: and they died with a courage above that of soldiers.

So it was that on 28 August, 1628, Father Edmund Arrowsmith, of the Society of Jesus, was to die at Lancaster. He was forty-three, born into an old English Roman Catholic family at Haydock, a small town near the Cheshire border of Lancashire. In 1605 he had left his home, Bryn Hall, to enter the Jesuit College at Douai, where he was ordained priest. It was his natural destiny. As a little boy he had seen his parents dragged off to prison by Elizabeth's agents in the middle of the night, himself and his small brothers and sisters left alone and terrified. A kindly priest brought Edmund up and sent him to Douai where his Uncle Edmund was a professor.

For years he had pursued his mission with the high intelligence characteristic of the Jesuits, allied to immense zeal. Beloved and welcome in every secretly Catholic manor or cottage, he acquired a reputation for saintliness. It was said that he had the divine art of healing. Before long his fame came to the ears of Government spies. A close watch was kept on his activities, and in 1628 proof was obtained that the sedate gentleman who dressed so quietly and had so many friends was a secret priest. He was arrested, denounced and taken to a cell in Lancaster Castle, then used as a gaol: a grim place where sixteen years earlier the Lancashire Witches had lain in fetters, waiting for the flames.

His refusal to take the Oath of Allegiance sealed his fate. Two days later they dragged him on a hurdle from the gaol to Gallows Hill, the plot on the green before the Castle where executions were held. The entire population of the town seemed to have turned out to watch him die. They thronged the green and the edge of the moat; they were massed as thick as flies on the hill crowned by the Castle. It was a grand entertainment they had come to see. Mothers nursed their children, boys played games. Those who had nothing to do watched the antics of jugglers and paid their pence for a ballad-sheet telling in doggerel verse of *The Papist's Last Dying Confession*.

Then a murmur of excitement spread. He was there, on the scaffold, being unbound from the hurdle: a pale-faced man in a black robe which the hangman would tear from him in a moment. He stood up, stiff from his bondage and confinement in a cell which was icy-cold even in August, and he took his last look at the world. Around Castle Hill and the grey stone town seven counties spread their colours: to the north, the hills of Lakeland rose in majesty; to the east, the Pennines marked the boundary of Yorkshire; westward, Morecambe Bay glittered in the August sunshine like a silver mirror; to the south were the Wyredale Hills and his distant home. "*Levavi oculos ad montes*," he said to himself: "I will lift up mine eyes unto the hills, from whence cometh my help." He turned his gaze to the tower of the Priory Church, serene against the blue sky; once it had been called the Church of the Blessed Mary of Lancaster. "*In te speravi, Domine,*" he said aloud, and crossed himself. Then he turned to the hangman with a smile.

When it was all over the crowd edged away, sated with excitement, pleasurably shocked. But there were some who had neither chattered nor cheered; who now went home to weep and pray. For in Lancashire there still flourished a strong Catholic element, unquelled by persecution, dogged and uncompromising as the county character, but schooled in secrecy. The night after the execution a man entered the Castle by an unwatched window; skulked along dark passages dripping with damp, flattening himself against the wall every now and then as the distant voices of sentries and gaolers floated to his ears and the thought of what would happen to him if he were discovered turned him cold beyond the coldness of that place.

Luck and swift silence brought him at last to a wooden door. He pushed it gently, found it unlocked, and crept in. The fading light, filtering through a high slit window, showed him a small room used as a storage-place. On a slab by the wall lay something covered by a sheet. The sheet was of coarse fabric, like sailcloth; but the blood that had poured from Father Arrowsmith's butchered body had soaked through and stained it a rusty brown. Joseph Barlow pulled it aside and looked down at the mangled remains that lay beneath. The long intellectual face was calm again, unmarked by agony; somebody had closed the eyes. There were tears in Joseph Barlow's own eyes as he knelt and prayed that the bitterness of his soul might be relieved. He took from round his neck a small crucifix on a chain, and placed it reverently round that of the dead man, hiding it beneath the robe they had thrown round the terribly mutilated body to hide its nakedness. Tomorrow it would be bundled into a rough coffin and shovelled into an unblessed plot of earth: they would not bother to search it for valuables.

Then Joseph Barlow did what he had come to do: with a sharp dagger he cut off the right hand of the corpse. The thin wrist was quickly severed, and there followed no blood. Joseph wrapped it in a handkerchief and put it in the pouch at his belt. Then he gently replaced the sheet over the face of his master, for whom he had so often served Mass, and left the Castle as he had entered it, but this time without fear, for he felt himself protected by the sacred relic for which he had risked death. His promise to Father Arrowsmith was fulfilled.

The dead hand was embalmed with spices, enclosed in a bag of white silk, and taken to Bryn Hall. Soon the Hall became a place of secret pilgrimage. The man who had worked miracles during his life continued to work them after death, it was said. One touch of the withered hand and your ailment was cured, be it a troublesome rheum or the dreaded consumption that ate the lungs; most of all, tumours and cancers were susceptible to its powers. The dying—even the dead—had been revived by its touch. Not since the Shrine of Thomas of Canterbury had drawn sufferers to its bourne had a holy relic been so renowned in England. The authorities grinned and turned a blind eye, for not only Catholics were seeking miraculous cures: many a Protestant stole by night to the back door of Bryn Hall to beg for a touch of the Hand.

Charles I went to his death in Whitehall, Cromwell tyrannized and departed; throughout the reigns of Charles II, his brother James, and Queen Anne, measures against Roman Catholics continued. They were excluded from corporate offices, from Parliament, from the throne, forbidden to possess arms or to marry Protestants. Yet the hand of Father Arrowsmith, a century dead, continued to exercise its powers with sublime impartiality.

One of the great families of the parish of Winwick, near Father Arrowsmith's birthplace, was that of the Gerards. They had come to England soon after the Conquest, and lived at Ince Hall, near Wigan, a stately Jacobean house standing in its own park. Rich and respected, Gilbert Gerard was one of the most affluent of Georgian squires. But neither land nor money could protect him against the approach of death. He lay pain-gripped in a silk-hung bed, his eyes roving restlessly from bright windows to painted ceiling. Outside, beyond the rebuilt classical front of the Hall, deer grazed on the lawns and peacocks strolled, trailing their jewelled tails on the velvety grass. By the sick man's bed sat William Townley, his servant and companion. Gerard was a widower, his son Richard and daughter Ellen married and gone away.

"William . . ." Gerard turned his head slowly on the pillow. "I shall not recover from this, William. Within a week I shall be dead."

William Townley tried to throw some conviction into his voice.

"Nay, sir, never talk like that. You're mendin' a cake at a meal, as they say."

Gerard shook his head slowly, as if it hurt him to do so.

"I shall be glad to go. But there's one thing that troubles me, William. I have provided for my children in my will, and for my household. Each of my servants will receive a sufficient legacy—except one—yourself, William."

"Me, sir?"

"Yes. I have left you something—but I want to increase it, William, for you have served me most faithfully and nursed me tenderly. You shall have twice the sum I had meant for you when I made my will, and a cottage besides."

Townley's face worked with emotion. "I don't want it, master. I want nowt for serving thee."

Gerard feebly patted his arm. "Don't wrangle with me, Will, but send to Wigan for Mr Philipson and his clerk. Tell him I want to draw up a codicil. And tell him"—a spasm of pain distorted Gerard's face—"tell him to make haste!"

But though Philipson rode briskly to Ince Hall on receiving the summons, the Rider on the Pale Horse rode faster. When the lawyer and his clerk arrived, a weeping maidservant answered the door.

"He's dead, sir—the master's dead!" she sobbed. "Gone as sudden as blow out a candle."

Philipson uttered the conventional regrets, but his thoughts were sour. So much for his fee and supper. As he was about to leave, William Townley appeared, and invited him in, leaving the clerk to mind their horses. Townley was white and worn: he had hardly slept for the past week, and the shock of Gerard's death had brought him almost to a state of collapse. He began to apologize for Philipson's being left standing on the threshold.

"We're all at sixes and sevens, sir. It's nobbut just happened. I went to take him a posset, and found him . . . found him . . ." his voice broke.

"Yes, yes." The lawyer was embarrassed. "But his end was expected, surely—he had a cancer, I believe?"

"Aye. But we thought he'd linger on a bit. There weren't even time to send for the doctor, or Master Richard and Mistress Ellen."

"Sit down, Townley," said Philipson briskly. "You need a glass of wine, and you can offer me one while you're about it." He pushed Townley into a chair and helped them both to a generous glass from a decanter that stood invitingly on a small pier-table, noting as he did so the diamond-brilliance of the cut glass and the chestnut glow of the wood. Mahogany: very fashionable, very expensive. Very little escaped the sharp eye of Lawyer Philipson, when it concerned money or possessions. Lowering his bulk on to a delicate chair, he surveyed the handsome room, the harpsichord, the alabaster table brought from Italy by a Gerard who had made the Grand Tour. He tested with his foot the rich softness of the Turkey carpet; caressed with one fat hand the surface of an embroidered cushion, heavy with gold thread.

Townley, after two glasses of wine, was drooping from his chair. Philipson helped himself to another bumper: a pity to waste a good bottle. It was after the third brimming glass that the idea came to him. At first he rejected it as fantastic: this was, after all, the eighteenth century, the Age of Reason. And yet, superstitions die hard, and there had been some convincing tales. Within the brain of the lawyer of Wigan a wild and daring plan sprang to birth. If it failed, nothing would be lost; if it succeeded—the small eyes brightened with infinite calculation.

"When did your master expire, Will?" he inquired casually. Townley raised his head and muttered: "Half an hour sin'. I mun go and lay him out, decent."

"Do nothing of the kind, man. You're exhausted, I can see that. Take a nap, or you'll be ill yourself. I'll send some of the women upstairs."

But Townley was already asleep, slumped forward on the table. Philipson rose swiftly for so heavy a man, and went lightly from the room. He knew the way to Gerard's bedroom, where he had taken instructions for various pieces of legal business. Up the broad stairs he sped, along the galleried landing. A brief listening pause outside the bedroom door, and he entered.

Inside the death-chamber he wasted no time on sentiment or prayer. Hurrying to the bedside, he noted the still-open eyes of the corpse, not yet glazed in death, and felt the wrist. No pulse-beat, but some warmth still lingered in the flesh. He nodded with satisfaction, and bustled out again.

Roger, his clerk, walking the horses up and down in the cold night air, was surprised to receive an order to ride at once to Bryn

Hall at full speed. Within half an hour he returned, bearing the object of his mission. Philipson was keeping vigil by the corpse. He had locked out the wondering maidservants and the protesting Townley, now awake and anxious to get back to his dead master.

"Within this hour a miracle may be performed," declared the lawyer. "I must have absolute quiet within the room." He relocked the door, and took from Roger the white silk bag which the clerk held nervously at arm's length. From it he extracted the withered hand of the martyr.

"They said you weren't to take it out," Roger said. "It's wearing away with folk touching it."

Philipson ignored him. Bending over the corpse, he stroked with the relic Gerard's forehead, eyes and lips repeatedly. Finally he laid the spidery claw on the breast, and stood back, his fat face as pale as that of the body on the bed. For within the space of a minute the miracle he had hoped for occurred. The death-film began to clear from the eyes, the lips moved, a tinge of colour stole back into the waxen cheeks. Then, slowly, like one awaking from a heavy sleep, Gerard sat up and looked about him.

Roger fell on his knees, gabbling a prayer. But Philipson, though himself in a sweat of fear, was not to be turned aside from his purpose. He snatched up a document from the bedside and put it before Gerard, backed with a Bible. In the fumbling right hand he placed a pen, himself holding the inkhorn.

"You were about to sign this, sir, when you swooned just now," he said rapidly. "Pray do so, and I will call your attendant."

Gerard moved his head from side to side, uncomprehending. "A swoon? I thought . . . I seemed . . ."

"Sign, sir—sign!"

The new Lazarus was too weak and dazed to disobey. His hand guided by the lawyer's, he scrawled his signature in the spot indicated by a plump finger.

"That—is all?" he asked feebly. "I need do no more?"

"You need do no more," grimly echoed Philipson. Before the terrified Roger could move or protest, he had snatched a pillow from the bed and pressed it with all his force over Gerard's face. The clerk rushed upon him, crying "Murderer!" and tried to drag away the cruel hands. But he was too late. The life that had revisited Gerard was already ebbing away. In a moment his feeble struggles were over; once more the long, wasted body lay still in death.

Philipson turned to the half-hysterical clerk.

"If ever you breathe a word of what has passed here, I swear I'll serve you as I served him. You understand, you dog?" He shook Roger from side to side. "Hold your noise, or they'll hear you outside." He replaced the pillow, carefully arranged the corpse in the same attitude as before, and put back in the white silk bag the withered hand which had fallen among the bedclothes. Then, carrying it, he went to the door, unlocked it, and called to the cluster of whispering servants to come closer.

"You may return this useless bag of bones to Bryn Hall," he told them. "The priest's hand has lost its power."

When the funeral was over, and the will read, the whole neighbourhood was astonished to hear that Gerard had left all his moneys, wordly goods and Ince Hall to Nathaniel Philipson, attorney, of Wigan in the County of Lancashire. The document was brief—a mere statement, with no embellishments—but its validity could not be disputed. There was the signature, shaky but recognizable, and those of two witnesses. It was curious, certainly, that Gerard should have called in for this purpose two completely illiterate menials, a girl of retarded mental development who helped in the kitchen and an old man who lived in a hut in the gardens and looked after Gerard's dogs. Neither could write, nor even reply intelligently to questions about the signing of the will; but there were their marks against their names, and that was legal enough for anybody.

Neither of Gerard's children was at the will-reading. Richard was away at Bath, where his young wife had been sent for her health, and Ellen was recovering from childbed, her son Robert having been born only a few days before her father's death. The bad news travelled to them with its customary speed. But even swifter had Philipson sped to take possession of his magnificent new home, in which he was already installed when a coach rattled up to its gates and a fury in green-striped satin descended from it. Sweeping past the servants, Ellen confronted the usurper in the drawing-room, where he sat at ease with his feet up on an elegant day-bed, drinking her father's best port.

In a tempest of words, including some rich Georgian oaths (for she was a young woman who rode to hounds and conversed with grooms as freely as with her equals), she told Philipson what she thought of his character and of the fraud he had perpetrated.

"Prove it!" he said lazily, when she ran out of breath.

"By God, I will!" She strode to a walnut secretaire, flung it open; pressed a spring revealing a "secret" drawer, and waved in Philipson's face the document it had contained.

"*There* is my father's true will, Master Lying Lawyer! Read it and laugh on the other side of your face!" Philipson unfolded and read, then gave her a slow, fat smile.

"Everything to you and your brother, except for some legacies to servants. Excellent, excellent; and very proper, of course. Unfortunately, ma'am, the will in my possession is of more recent date than this, which was drawn up two years ago. The older will is, of course, invalidated."

Ellen stormed until Philipson warned her mildly that she would do herself a mischief unless she abated her anger.

"I'll do you a mischief, more like," she returned. "There's been some villainy here that I'll find out. I'll have a watch set on you day and night—I'll question these dolts of servants myself, and that rascally sneaking clerk of yours. Don't take me for a fool, Master Philipson!"

He gazed thoughtfully at her, as she stood in the doorway, her handsome high-coloured face scarlet with rage, her feathered hat fallen a little askew on her auburn ringlets. With her closed fan she was beating an angry tattoo against a satin-skirted thigh.

"No, ma'am," said Philipson gently. "I don't take you for a fool."

She turned her back on him and marched out. Philipson followed her.

"Let me see you to your carriage." She ignored him, and swept out through the french door on to the terrace, round the side of the Hall where thick trees separated the front from the back. Her figure disappeared into their shadow in a flurry of green stripes, Philipson a few yards behind her.

She never reached her carriage, or her home. Philipson swore that he had last seen her crossing the front lawn, after which he turned and went back to the house. When she had not returned home by evening her frantic husband instituted a search of the neighbourhood—houses, barns, stables, woodlands. Then ponds and rivers were dragged, but no trace of the missing girl was found. It was surmised that the angry scene with Philipson, which had been overheard by the servants, had driven her into that temporary madness which sometimes enters into women after childbirth, and that in a fit of insanity she had wandered far away and destroyed herself.

Richard, her brother, had been much attached to her. Her disappearance, following the great wrong done to them both by the mysterious will, brought him to Ince Hall in a black rage. He met the lawyer strolling in the rose-garden, and without preamble ordered him to draw his sword. Philipson pointed out that he was not wearing one; on which the furious young man drew his own and fell on him with murderous intent. Such was Philipson's account of the affair, when he staggered back to the house bleeding from a deep wound in the left arm. He sent at once to a magistrate, and constables were bidden to find Richard Gerard and bring him to justice.

But he was not to be found; he had disappeared as completely as his sister. Fled the country, people said; half-crazed with temper, like her. His poor young wife never saw or heard from Richard again.

Philipson now gave up all his legal connections and retired to enjoy private life amid the luxuries of Ince Hall. His clerk had left him, gone no one knew where. It was the third strange disappearance, but little was thought of it since Roger's relations with his employer were known to have been bad. He had evidently sought employment elsewhere.

The years came and went, and the increasingly portly Philipson remained in his mansion. The trees round it grew thicker, the gardens flourished. It was on a damp spring morning that one of the gardeners decided to dig out a seedling lilac tree which had planted itself at the edge of the fine lawns at the back of the Hall. His spade, sinking into the soft earth, struck something that was not soft. Curious to see what he had disturbed, he dug round the object until it was loose enough to prise out. For a moment it baffled him, discoloured and caked with soil as it was. Then horrified recognition dawned. With a yell he dropped it and ran towards the house, shouting that he had dug up a human skull.

The bones they unearthed beneath the young lilac tree were readily identified, for the creatures that had consumed the victim's flesh had left what had clothed it; the rags of a green-striped dress, a few fragments of a velvet hat with pink plumes, a pearl ear-ring, an ivory fan from which the silk had rotted. Ellen was found.

No protests or denials by Philipson could avail against the storm of accusation which broke out against him. The legend of Ellen's suicide was now demolished. Suicides do not bury themselves four feet down, nor can they batter in the backs of their own skulls. It was a clear case of murder, and the motive not far to seek.

For a few days Philipson endured a running fire of abuse, threats, and broken windows. The servants left in a body. Alone in the great house, he began to see shadows in every corner. One particular shadow hovered night and day where the lilac tree had been; and another, a blood-stain on its shirt-breast, would peer out at him between the leaves of the shrubbery when he walked that way. A third shadow, in the rusty black suit of a clerk, would start up from the waters of the ornamental lake and point at him; or he would see its dead face grinning up from the calm surface, thick with lilies that grew more lushly here than anywhere else.

Within a week he had fled to lodgings in Wigan, where people knew little of him. There, a fat man grown thin, with whitened hair and haggard face, he dragged out his life until age and sickness brought him low. On his death-bed, to his landlady's surprise, he sent for a Roman Catholic priest. The priest came to him, though he was not a Papist, and listened gravely to the confession of the most terrified dying man he had ever seen. What passed between them was not for other ears; but the landlady, pressed against the door, heard Philipson babbling about a holy hand, a miracle, and a denial that had brought him to the doors of Hell. And she heard the priest reply solemnly: "God is not mocked, my son."

In time Bryn Hall was demolished. The hand of Father Arrowsmith was taken to Garswood Hall, the home of Sir Robert Gerard, and in the present century moved to the Roman Catholic church at Ashton-in-Makerfield. Here, in a shrine dedicated to the martyr priest, is his portrait, and scenes from his life in the jewel-colours of stained glass; while within a silver casket his hand lies, revered and at rest.

The Man Who Turned into a Cat

Cambridge creeps with ghosts. Since it is a city near as old as written English history, that is as one should expect it to be. This place of chiming bells, of soaring towers and rose-red battlements, of alleyways of legend and courts of splendour, is haunted not only by memories of great men and by the shades of donnish eccentrics who have vanished like grey moths into the dusk of time, but it has also here and there an inheritance of macabre horror.

Consider Jesus College. It began as the nunnery of St Radegund in the twelfth century. It sits behind a long sun-warmed, very old wall of red brick which marches along one side of Jesus Lane full of colour and warmth and old stories, full of reflected memories of men who passed this way, talking and laughing, and then died and perhaps linger on as amiable spirits. It is the sort of old wall which, like the faded gilt and smooth leather of an old book, promises flowers within. Scent of thyme and lavender and lilies, tall in the sun, and of roses, whose far wild roots sprang from the fields of Navarre.

All these sights and sounds and memories and people this old wall seems to promise. You feel it is the guardian of them all. And so indeed it is.

It is a sure and certain thing that Cromwell's Roundheads came here. They clattered down this stone path, stamped and rattled under that great doorway and kept their guard in what is now the Porter's

Lodge. They slept in the rooms of the Gate Tower. And it is in that tower that we shall find our first ghost of Jesus College.

The tale starts in 1643. Strafford had been beheaded two years earlier. Charles I, having lost his one strong man, was waging the Civil War with all the indecision of a weak and kindly man. Cromwell had occupied Cambridge with his Bible-banging, psalm-singing soldiers of the Eastern Counties Association.

Like all self-proclaimed "soldiers of the Lord", they were the biggest humbugs unhung. Vandalism and sacrilege were everyday affairs. Their violent behaviour and wilful damage were appalling. They gloried in destruction. With the zest of the ignorant, the fury of the envious, they smashed works of art, broke windows of old beauty and hammered lovely stone tracery to rubble.

Contemporary records in colleges tell the damning tale. They were men of mean souls, enemies of loveliness, haters of tradition, downcasters of beauty and sanctity.

Before that sad summer of 1643 had run its course of fear and trembling, fourteen of the sixteen Fellows of the College had been expelled. Two only remained in residence. With them were about half a score of scholars. The rest of the College was full of Cromwell's ranting, canting troops.

The two Fellows who remained were John Boyleston and Thomas Allen.

Allen committed suicide. That bald statement hides a lot. First, we must bear in mind that six months before Allen died, that ignorant fanatic, William Dowsing, the scourge of churches and chapels, descended on Cambridge like a plague. He was armed with Parliamentary powers to "reform" churches and, for that matter, college chapels. This ignorant oaf wrought monstrous damage in Cambridge. It is on record that on 28 December, 1642, in the presence of John Boyleston, he "digg'd up the steps" (i.e. the College chapel altar) "and brake down Superstitions and Angels, 120 at the least".

A certain Doctor John Sherman, a Fellow of Jesus, took careful note of these barbaric proceedings. He incorporated the whole disgraceful tale in his Latin History of the College, which was later published when Charles II ascended the throne and English air was once more fit to breathe. Sherman records that Boyleston was not the only witness of the desecration of the altar. Thomas Allen was there also. Dr Sherman remarks: "The one (i.e. Boyleston) stood behind a curtain to witness the evil work; the other, afflicted to behold the exequies of his Alma Mater, made his life a filial offering at her grave, and, to escape the hands of wicked rebels, laid violent hands on himself".

So far, so good. It was for long taken for granted, by those who did not know the darker side of the picture, that Allen had committed suicide. Sherman did not know—or perhaps did not remember a certain Adoniram Byfield. This man, Byfield, was a Roundhead chaplain, attached to Cromwell's troops in Cambridge. You can get some idea of the mean, cribbed character of the man, full of fanaticism and dark superstition, if you burrow about in the library of Jesus until you come on a pudgy leather-bound collection of old sermons of the Commonwealth times. Among the sermons is one dated 1643 and described as:

"A FAITHFUL ADMONICION of the Baalite sin of 'Enchanters & Stargazers', preacht to the Colonel Cromwell's Souldiers in Saint Pulcher's (i.e. Saint Sepulchre's) church, in Cambridge, by the fruit-full Minister Adoniram Byfield, late departed unto God, in the yeare 1643, touching that of Acts the seventh, verse 43, Ye took up the Tabernacle of Moloch, the Star of your god Rempham figures which ye made to worship them; & I will carrie you away beyond Babylon."

The title of this sermon, if it can be dignified as such, lays bare the mind and soul of Byfield. He stands revealed as one of those fanatical Bible-thumpers, who played remorselessly on the ignorance of the Roundhead troops and inflamed their superstitious prejudices against the "carnal learning" of the University scholars. Byfield was almost as ignorant as the men. He was quite as superstitious. He was one of those raving preachers whose like is still found in the eastern counties today, where the country people dismiss them, in one telling word, as "ranters".

This weasel of a man, with his dark mind, was given rooms on the first floor of the entrance tower of Jesus, immediately above the Great Gate. Below his bedchamber was the Porter's Lodge. The troops quartered in the College used it as their armoury. There they kept their swords, pistols and muskets. Above Byfield's rooms, on the third and last floor of the Gate Tower, "kept" Thomas Allen.

He was a man of mystery. Byfield saw him only half a dozen

times in the first three months of his sojourn in the Gate Tower. The truth is that Allen probably kept to his rooms as much as possible, at any rate by daylight, because the moment he appeared in the College he was hooted, whistled at and insulted by the soldiers. For when the Long Vacation of 1643 began, Allen was the only member of the College still in residence. Apart from his natural reluctance to expose himself to insults and possible showers of mud and stones, Allen was a mystic. His mind and enthusiasm were deep in the sciences of mathematics and astronomy. Both were regarded in those days as little less than black magic. Mathematicians were branded as necromancers. Thomas Hobbes says that, in his own days at Oxford, mathematics was held to be "smutched with the black art". Many a country squire and noble lord refused to send his son to Oxford University for fear that the youth's mind and soul should become poisoned by the "black art" of mathematics.

It is scarcely to be wondered at, therefore, that the small black pit of ignorance which represented the mind of Adoniram Byfield should be seething with prejudice and hatred against such "stargazers" and "enchanters" as Allen. Hence his sermon. There was a reason for his delivery of that sermon. First of all, a Cromwellian cornet, full of holy faith and little sense, fell down one of the steep, dark staircases of the College one night and broke his neck, just after he had left a prayer-meeting in an upper chamber. Then two or three soldiers were stricken down with dysentery. These occurrences started a great deal of gossip. The soldiers were convinced that the last scholar in the College, the mysterious Allen, was cursing them with his "black art", bewitching them with his spells. All this sank into the little mind of Byfield. There it gathered force until he was convinced that Allen was a magician.

We cannot altogether blame Byfield, for, night after night, he heard the voice of his mysterious neighbour in the room above, mumbling on in a ceaseless rise and fall of conversation. It went on hour after hour. No other voice gave answer. None of the words made any intelligible sense to the listening ears of Byfield.

More than once he caught sight of Allen standing before a blackboard, mounted on an easel. It was chalked with white figures and symbols, probably the most elementary mathematical calculations. To Byfield's mind they were the visible signs of "black magic", the alphabet of the Devil.

On more than one night of stars Byfield stood in the courtyard below and watched Allen's lighted window. More than once he saw Allen come to the window, put his spy-glass to his eye and turn it towards the stars. What else could this be but a ghastly telegraphy with the black spirits of the night?

Once, he swore, he heard the ceaseless mumble and muttering above him change to a sudden, shrill, high cry. He heard three words, charged with evil and terror:

"Avaunt, Sathanas; Avaunt!"

What else could that be but the magician, the necromancer, the dabbler in devilries, shrinking in terror from his dark master, Satan himself, who had just paid him a visit in the oak-pannelled chamber above Byfield's head?

A few nights later something happened which gave the Roundhead parson fresh grounds for fear. He heard Allen's door open cautiously above him. He heard Allen creep quietly down the steep, unlit, oaken staircase, past his own door, a flickering candle in his hand.

Byfield saw the thin line of pale yellow light under his own door.

Cautiously he lifted the latch of his door, opened it, crept down the stairs and saw Allen pass into the armoury beneath, the room which is the Porter's Lodge today. Byfield slipped down the stairs and into the court below. Through the lighted window, Byfield saw Allen walk up to a rack of pistols hanging on the wall. He took one down, cocked it, raised it to his eye as though taking aim, then lowered it, tried the weight of it in his hand and finally put it back again. Then he crept quietly out of the armoury and trod silently up the staircase, by the light of his flickering candle, to his own mysterious room high in the top of the tower. Next day one of the sick soldiers died. Byfield put two and two together. They added up to all that he had ever suspected, and worse.

Then began a new source of terror. Night after night, as Byfield lay quaking in his bed, muttering psalms to keep his spirits up and the evil spirits at bay, he heard Allen's door open. Immediately afterwards soft quick footsteps pattered down the narrow oaken staircase. They fled past his door to the bottom of the stairs and vanished, noiseless, into the night.

Two or three hours later, the same quick, soft steps returned, pattering at unnatural speed up the oaken stairs—pitch-dark, be it remembered—and into the room above. Then he heard Allen's door close.

Each night Cromwell's parson lay cold with fear in his bed, listening, praying, clutching his Bible, calling on his God to save him, racking his brains to know what those ghastly steps might mean.

He decided that they were the footsteps of the Evil One himself. But in what form did Satan visit his slave and servant in that room of mystery and cabalistic symbols overhead?

Finally, Byfield screwed up his courage.

He waited, candle in hand, prayers on his lips, until one night the soft swift feet fled by his door. Then he opened the door, holding the candle high aloft, and peered down the dark stairs. He saw nothing.

The following night, pale with fright and grim with resolve, he flung the door open again as the feet fled downstairs. Luckily, a lantern in the armoury threw a pale, yellow shaft of light across the foot of the stairs. By its light Byfield saw a cat, huge and black, whisk down the stairs and vanish into the dark night. He knew that two hours later it would return.

Faintly, up the stairs, above his head, Byfield heard papers rustling in the wind in Allen's room. The door stood half-open. A flickering candle shed yellow quavering light down the stairs. Not a sound came from the room. The muttering undertones of the necromancer's voice were stilled. Only the wind and the night silences possessed the room of magic.

Quietly Byfield crept upstairs. He peered through the half-open door of the top-floor room. The room was empty. He entered softly. There was the blackboard with its magic figures and numerals. There were the open books writ in Latin—that ungodly tongue. And papers and quill pens and endless pages of close writing—the visible signs of the Devil's work that went on night after night. There, on a small table by the window, stood the spy-glass, the prisms and other Devil's instruments, at whose foul use he could only guess. There was no Thomas Allen. Yet no human footsteps had descended the staircase since dusk had gloomed into darkness.

What, then, was the cat, huge, black, swift and foul, that had whisked down the stairs on feet soft and quick as the wind? Was it the Devil in the form of his own favourite animal? Or was it Thomas

Allen, translated by his own magic into the body of a great cat and now launched into the starlit night on another errand of death? Who would be the next victim among the soldiery by dawn? What Christian spirit was even now being caught up in the foul web of the muttering enchanter? Adoniram Byfield asked himself these questions. There could be only one answer. He pursed his thin lips and crept quietly down to the armoury.

The horn lanthorn still hung from a chain in the ceiling. Its fat, tall candle shed yellow light out of the open door into the entrance arch, flooding the bottom steps of the stairs. Whatever returned to Allen's chamber—man, cat or Devil, or all three in one form—must pass through that broad belt of yellow light.

Adoniram turned his eyes to the rack of six horse-pistols hanging on the wall. There were only five! He took one down, primed it carefully from a tiny flask of fine priming powder. Then he took up a larger powder horn, full of pistol powder of a coarser grain, tipped a full charge down the barrel, rammed down a bullet as thick as his little finger, cocked the pistol, taking note that the lock clicked sweetly, and made sure that the priming powder lay well and truly in the pan beneath the flint. Then he shrank into the shadows of the wall, his eyes fixed on the lighted space without the door.

An hour passed. He heard the bells of Cambridge ring out to the wheeling stars their carillon of midnight. They boomed and chimed.

So midnight came and went. Well Adoniram knew that from now till two or three of the clock was the time when ghosts rose whitely from the graves, tombs opened, spectral choirs sang in softly-lit chapels of abomination, and dark spirits were abroad on creaking wings.

Still he stood there, stiff against the wall, pale and grim, too intent to feel the cold, too fanatic to allow his ghostly fears to let his trigger-finger tremble.

Any minute now, within the next hour, the Thing—cat or man or Devil—would return. What if it flashed past him before he could fire? What if it fled up the stairs ahead of him, entered his own room and cast its black spell therein?

Suddenly be became aware of a presence. Unseen, unheard, it was out there in the darkness. Yet he felt it.

Then, without sound or movement, It was there—in the patch of light—not six feet away. A cat, black, malign, green-eyed with fury, fur on end.

Adoniram levelled the great horse-pistol. He cried, triumphant, hoarse:

"God shall shoot at them, suddenly shall they be wounded"— and fired.

The heavy report thundered and echoed in the stone archway, up the narrow oaken stairs and re-echoed with a crash of sound from the far walls of the inner grass-grown court.

A ghastly cry, not animal, not human, stabbed the night. It was the scream of a soul in torment. The cat, if it were a cat, whisked into the darkness with the speed of the Devil.

Adoniram put the smoking horse-pistol—it had jumped in his hand, with the heavy recoil, like a bucking horse—back into the rack. He felt exultant. A great glow warmed his heart and soul. The deed was done. The Evil Spirit had fled. He clambered the stairs to his chamber, not bothering to creep quietly, slammed his door and felt at peace. He slept soundly that night.

No pattering footsteps fled swift by his door. No streak of candle-light or shuffling foot of man told of the return of Thomas Allen to his room above. The door of his room stood open all night. The questing wind ruffled his papers, sent them fluttering like sprites down the stairs. His candle burnt low, guttered and died. Thomas Allen did not come home that night.

Next morning, when the troopers went with leathern buckets over to the King's Ditch to draw water for their horses, they found the body of Thomas Allen lying dead in the grove of trees which border that ditch to this day. A great horse-pistol bullet had torn a jagged hole through his chest. His mouth was open. His tongue would mutter its midnight spells no more. His eyes were wide—and full of horror. They had seen something in the stars at last to quiet their evil questing for ever.

There was a trail of blood, thick gouts of it, from the foot of the staircase by the Porter's Lodge, through the college and across the grass to the grove where the body lay. A pistol was missing from the rack in the armoury. One or two soldiers had heard the shot in the small hours. It was clear enough—the necromancer, haunted by his own evil, had shot himself outside the armoury door, and, by a superhuman effort, walked or dragged himself here to the grove, to die under the stars with whom he had communed for too long. Suicide. That was the general verdict. Byfield said nothing.

In his fanatic mind, he was convinced that he had shot Allen in the form of the cat. Already he saw himself facing his God on the dread Judgement Day, the curse of Cain heavy on his soul, Heaven denied him, Hell his remorseless end, because he had committed the unforgivable sin of murder. In his mind's eye he saw the Book opened, the Accuser confronting and the Judgement pronounced: "Now art thou cursed from the earth."

That night, he heard men with slow and lumbering steps and muttered words bring the dead body up the narrow stairway to the room above. They laid the dead man on his own bed, there in the empty room, with his books of magic, his prisms and evil instruments, his magic scrabblings on the blackboard. They closed the door and went away.

The silence was paralysing. It dropped like a pall on the Gate Tower. There was no man in the armoury below and a dead man in the room above.

Adoniram was utterly alone. The silent horror of the night gripped him. He fell on his knees and prayed in agony of mind that the dead might come alive again, that his sin might pass from him, that the curse of Cain be lifted from his soul, and all be as it was before he fired that pistol shot.

As he finished praying, he heard the door above open. Soft pattering steps crept down the stairs. They passed his door. They were gone before he could open it—had he dared. For a moment he felt a wave of relief. His prayer had been answered. He was not alone. The dead had come to life. No longer did the curse of murder lie on his soul.

Then fresh horror seized him. Allen was dead enough. He had seen that for himself. What then was this soft, pattering Thing which had gone out into the night?

He opened his door and listened. Not a sound. Allen's door above was open. So was his window. Adoniram Byfield heard again the soft rustle of the wind in the dead man's papers, felt the soft night breeze pass on his cheek. Somehow he must close that door, before the pattering, furry-footed Thing returned. He must shut off the mutilated body of Allen, with its staring eyes, pathetically open mouth, from his foul Spirit, which would assuredly return to possess it. Perhaps if he could do that, he, Adoniram Byfield, might earn pardon on the Judgement Day.

He steeled himself to creep up the stairs. At any moment the Thing might return. He reached Allen's door. It stood open. A new and guttering candle lit the room. The bed was empty. No dead man, shot-mangled, with staring eyes lay there. The coverlet was white and smooth.

A sharp breath of wind through the open window caught the candle flame. It wavered sideways, like a little yellow pennon. It flickered—went out.

Byfield stood there in the pregnant, listening dark. Then he heard it. Soft, furry footsteps were coming up the open stairs. Stealthily. Menacingly. There was no quick, cat-like scamper. They were stalking him.

Byfield shrank back, and yet back, into the darkened room—towards the bed. The furry feet were on the last stairs. They came softly over the threshold of the door.

Then, in the pitch-blackness, he saw it. In a lambent radiance he saw the cat—mangled, menacing, its chest and neck sagging in a bloody apron of tattered flesh. It crept towards him. Its eyes smoked with evil. It crouched to spring. Adoniram Byfield backed towards the bed. The cat followed, low as a tiger to the floor. The bed touched the back of his knees. He dropped down upon it, sitting. The crouching cat, bloody and torn, sprang through the air. . . .

"Oh, my God, make haste for my help!" babbled Adoniram Byfield in a last surge of words. He fell upon the bed, his hands scrabbling at the coverlet. They closed on the dead, stiff hands of the body of Thomas Allen.

When dawn came a few minutes later, greening in the east and palely lighting the chamber, there was no cat. The stiff body of Thomas Allen asked only for burial. Adoniram Byfield was on his knees gabbling for forgiveness.

And, as you will remember from the preface to his sermon, now in the College library, he died that same year.

The Dead Killed Him in His Own Grave

A man seeking treasure in an empty grave at midnight in the chapel of a famous Cambridge college. Suddenly, in the cold quiet of the dark chapel, the soft shuffling footsteps of a procession of dead men, newly risen from their graves. The low, haunting singing of an unseen choir of long-buried priests, dons and students. Then—a rending of timbers, a clanging crash which shook the college. And the midnight seeker of gold and silver lay dead, blood-spattered in the open grave.

Today, if you go to Jesus College in Cambridge and enter the chapel, you will find a worn gravestone near the south-west pier of the chapel tower where the transepts cross. You can pick out the pier from the others because it is the only one to have a dog-tooth moulding. Go down on hands and knees and, provided you have the right light and sharp sight, you may be able to pick out this curious inscription:

nkfull

mas

followed by the figures 652. The latter clearly means the year 1652.

Ten years earlier, just before the Civil War spread fear and blood-shed throughout England, a certain Mr John Poley, son of a Suffolk squire, whose descendants still live on the same estates today, set off in a coach, taking a pair of pistols and with two armed guards, to pay his loyal duty to His Majesty, King Charles the First, who was then at Nottingham gathering his armies about him. The coach carried a heavy load of gold and silver plate, the property of Jesus College. The College authorities, being loyal subjects and having no use for the upstart Cromwell (whose proper name was Williams, although historians are apt to overlook that fact), had decided that since the King needed men and money to defend his throne against the rebels, they, not being fighting men, would send him their plate in order that it might be melted down to help finance the King's armies.

Every member of the College from the Master downwards knew that at any moment they were likely to be expelled by order of Cromwell, the self-styled "King of the Fens" whose word was law in the Eastern Counties. So they got rid of the plate before Cromwell could lay his coarse hands upon it.

Not all the plate, however, was sent to the King. Some was buried within the College grounds. More was hidden in the buildings themselves. The chapel organ, a charming piece of work, which had been put into the chapel in 1634 by Richard Sterne, the Master, who was Archbishop Laud's chaplain, was also hidden. That was not difficult since it was quite small.

The Earl of Manchester, Cromwell's deputy, marched into the College at the head of a body of his troops in January, 1643, evicted the Master and Fellows, and installed new men in their places. He noted in the Treasury Book, in the course of an inventory of the College furnishings, that there were only three pieces of plate. The Earl, no fool, realized, if indeed he did not already know, that most of the plate had been sent to the King. It is possible that he heard the rumour that the rest of it had been hidden, but I can find no record of him ordering a search to be made for it. War was rather more important at that moment.

We might not know much more about this affair, had not *The Diary of George Evans 1649/1658* come to light in an edited form in the first quarter of this century. Evans, like Cromwell, was a Welshman. He was given a Fellowship of Jesus in 1650 by the Committee for Reforming the Universities. He came from Radnor, was an Independent and became Vicar or Rector of Marston Monceux in Shropshire in 1654. When Charles the Second came to the throne, Parson Evans, true to form, declared himself a Royalist and hung on to his living until he died in 1672. The only reason why we need take any heed of this Welsh opportunist is that, under the date of 11 June, 1652, he records this:

"June 11 (1652). Present ye Master, Mr Woodcocke and Mr Machin, fellows, with Mr Thomas Buck, Thankfull Thomas and Robert Hitchcock digging, we digged up ye treasury plate hidd in ye Masters orchard. In all were seventeen peeces (then follows a list). Searched till prayers. But Quaerendm whether there be not yit other peeces and ye treasure hidd by ye former societie. Thomas saith Mr Germyn cld avouch for more."

You will note the name of Thankfull Thomas. He is undoubtedly the man whose skeleton lies beneath the gravestone with that part-worn inscription upon it near to the south-west pier of the tower chapel.

Gervase Germyn was a middle-aged bachelor, a Master of Arts, who had been the College organist and choirmaster in the time of Richard Sterne, the expelled Master. He was a dry, sardonic little man, desperately poor, since he lost his job as organist when the organ was removed and hidden. He lived in lodgings in Cambridge and appeared to own only one suit of clothes, patched, worn and of semi-clerical cut. He looked like a hard-up parson. He had an odd, pedantic way of speech which made some people believe that he was a little queer in the head. If we regard him as an eccentric, by no means mad, whose ruling passion in life was church music and whose spiritual home was the College chapel, we have a fair picture of the man.

Thankfull Thomas was sexton of the chapel. The College Order Book records in the year 1650, "Thomas constitutus est Custos Templi". In fine, he was both chapel clerk and sexton. As such Thankfull Thomas considered that he was the boss of the chapel—when the Master or priests were not in sight.

Gervase Germyn had a key to the chapel. He had kept it from the day, ten years previously, when he had lost his job as organist. Nothing and nobody could keep him out of the chapel. Neither the new Master nor the new Fellows wanted to bar him from the place, since he was a harmless little man and pitiful.

Thankfull Thomas loathed the sight of him. He found Germyn roaming about the place early in the morning and late at night. He would appear like a ghost, from a dark corner, noiselessly, and give Thomas the shock of his life. Germyn had a sharp tongue, a supercilious manner and the habit of addressing Thomas as though the latter was not only his servant but his inferior, particularly in intellect. Thomas was a dour, pig-headed, greedy fellow, not well-educated but very jealous of what he considered to be his rights and duties. He boiled with rage inwardly when, perhaps in the course of dusting the choir stalls or polishing church vessels on a sunny afternoon of utter peace, with motes of dust dancing in the coloured light which filtered through stained-glass window, he would suddenly sense that he was being watched. Looking upward he would see the sardonic parchment face of Germyn peering down at him from the tower arcade or from the Nuns Gallery.

Thomas had heard the rumours of buried treasure. He jumped to the conclusion that Germyn had more than a clue to its whereabouts. That, he argued, was why the ex-organist was always prowling about the chapel and exploring every nook and cranny, high and low. He came to the conclusion that the treasure must be hidden near the chapel tower. In the top of that tower was the belfry. And in the belfry hung a huge old bell engraved with the lion of St Mark and an inscription in Latin. That bell, called Mark, had not been rung for years. It had been cast in pre-Reformation days and had belonged to the Nunnery of St Radegund, the original occupants of the College buildings before the College was formed. The reason why the heavy booming note of Mark was never heard was simple. The belfry timbers were so rotten that they were unsafe.

A dark winding staircase in the north-east angle wall of the north transept leads up to the arcaded Norman Gallery which you can still see. The old belfry was above it.

Thankfull Thomas had seen Germyn prowling about in the gallery more than once. One day he plucked up his courage, went up the dark staircase, and crept along the Norman Gallery which had no protecting railing. He had to clutch each pillar as he passed since the slightest slip would send him hurtling down to the stone floor below. There was a worm-eaten ladder on the roof of the transept which led up to the belfry window. Thomas was certain that he had seen Germyn climb this ladder. When, however, he himself reached the ladder and realized its shakiness, he dared not face it. He was much heavier than Germyn. He had a superstitious terror of the silent belfry and left it severely alone.

Thomas was far more at home on the floor of the chapel. He gave it the most loving attention. Not a stone was left untapped. He spent hours stamping on each one in turn and listening for the hollow note which would tell him that there was a secret chamber beneath it. A line of crosses cut into the flagstones on one part of the floor excited him tremendously. You can see a similar line of crosses cut in some of the paving stones in one of the inner courtyards in St James's Palace in London. They mark the burial place of "sixteen leprous maidens" who died there when the old palace was a hospital and not a palace. The crosses on the nave floor of Jesus College Chapel had, however, nothing to do with leprosy or buried bodies. They merely marked the old processional path of the nuns. Thomas hammered each one of them. Not the slightest note of hollowness rewarded him.

Then he arrived at a large plain stone not far from the south-west pier of the tower. The moment he banged on it he got the hollow sound he had been waiting for. There was a vault beneath. In that vault, Thomas decided, lay the missing treasure. He determined to get it. He noticed that immediately above the stone hung the old bellrope belonging to the dumb bell of St Mark.

The evening sunlight shone through the chapel windows on to the stone on a midsummer day in 1652. Thankfull Thomas was kneeling on the stone, examining it, running his fingers round the edges, tapping it and listening, when suddenly a shadow of a man fell across the stone. Thomas leapt to his feet. He thought it was the Master. It was Gervase Germyn.

"I bid you good evening, Goodman Thomas," said Germyn dryly. "I, like you, work late in this place. I have been visiting old friends, all, alas, dead, who lie under these stones. A word with one here and there, a jest with another, even a snatch of songs we sang long ago with yet another of the dead. We often commune here. I see that you do the same. Who, pray, is your friend who lies beneath that stone?" Gervase Germyn eyed the flushed, defiant Thomas with sardonic ridicule.

"I am no fool or idle fellow to talk to the dead," Thomas said surlily. "A Chapel Clerk has more important matters to do. I have no time for your wild fancies and let not your nose pry into my affairs further."

"Very true, Master Thomas," Germyn replied. "Very true. You are indeed right. This stone on which you are kneeling, and to which

I thought you were whispering or tapping a message, is not the grave of a man—yet. Has our Chapel Clerk made up his mind who *is* to be the tenant? One of our new Fellows, perhaps? Maybe my unworthy self. It would please me greatly to sleep my last sleep under the floor of this chapel which I served for so many years. But no doubt, Master Sexton, you have reserved the grave for yourself. That thought crossed my mind when I saw you lying on the stone. Measuring yourself for it as it were. But there, you are no man of education as you would admit, so I would not bother you with that riddle of the Prince of Denmark: 'What is he that builds stronger than either the mason, the shipwright, or the carpenter?' "

"I have no time for riddles and I am digging no grave," said Thomas. "Begone, Master Germyn."

"Tush, Goodman Thomas," Germyn answered suavely. "Are you so short of work as not to dig for death as for hid treasure? Some indeed may dig for treasure and find only death." He watched Thomas's face narrowly.

Thomas flushed, hesitated. Obviously Germyn knew what he had been looking for. Equally obviously, Germyn knew that the treasure lay under that stone. Better perhaps to compromise than to make an enemy of him.

"Hidden treasure, Master Germyn? There may be more sense in what you say than I thought of. Maybe we could look for it together. And if you take your fair share you may not be as poor as you look now. And no other man but we two need know of it."

"Nonsense, Thomas," Germyn said sharply. "I know nothing of this hidden treasure. It belongs to my friends the dead and with them it shall remain. I shall be no part of it to break trust with them. Let them hold it until the Resurrection, when their other friends who owned it may claim it from them.

"I have a great awe for the dead, Thomas. They can do so much and neither you nor I can do aught to harm *them*. But they—they have dreadful power. You are a brave man, Thomas, to stay in this chapel so often and so late. Do you not know that it is full of dead voices and the presence of dead men? This is their house in which they walk when night falls. Surely you know how the last Chapel Clerk, Goodman Deane, who held office before you, died?"

"Deane—they tell me he died raving mad. But why should that

trouble me? I knew not the man nor how weak his head may have been."

"Goodman Deane died only two years ago in August," Germyn replied evenly. "He was wandering in his head. A harmless man, but with no light of life or reason in his eyes. Always he would mutter to himself: 'I should have rung, I should have rung'. And so muttering, he died."

"What should he have rung?" asked Thomas.

"Do you not know the old belief that when the dead rise up out of their graves at night, and walk in the quiet of the sleeping world, the ringing of a church bell shall disperse them? They flee back to their graves and leave the night to the living.

"Old Mark could not speak for Goodman Deane on that night when the dead came alive in this chapel, for Mark has not spoken for twenty years or more. It was on the night of August 7th, which is the Festival of the Name of Jesus, the greatest night of the whole year for the poor folk who are dead. Here in this chapel they assemble—both men and women I am told—at midnight, for Lauds. They say you will hear them coming down a staircase which leads from outside and others entering by a door in the church wall which has long been blocked up. They line up on these crosses which you see here in the stone in a double line of men and women—for the old nuns are of the company—and then they go in procession round the church, dark though it may be. *They* need no light. Many here in this town of Cambridge say they have heard the singing, soft and low, of the dead but I have met no man who has set eyes on them, unless of course it was poor Deane. And he was in no state to tell us what he had seen."

Thomas looked at him with dull obstinacy. He had made up his mind to have no more truck and share no more secrets with this drivelling old man, who spoke such fancies. He determined to pass it off as of no account.

"An odd fancy, Master Germyn. Little credit to it since none can verify it. Why should it worry me, true or not, since I never enter this chapel after midnight? I do not believe your tale, Master Germyn, and I believe still less that you know nothing of the treasure. That in any case is none of my business. It is no doubt as unsubstantial as your ghosts. I bid you goodnight." He stumped off.

He left treasure-seeking strictly alone for a few weeks in order to raise no more suspicions in Germyn's mind. Then he decided to enter the church on a certain night, lock the door, display no light, take a crowbar and iron jemmies wherewith to lever up the long, flat stone and dispose of the matter once and for all. Either find the treasure where he thought it lay or accept defeat.

At a quarter past eleven on the night of 7 August, 1652—a date whose significance had gone clean out of his head—Thankfull Thomas, crowbar over shoulder, jemmies in hand, stole softly up to the chapel door, unlocked it quietly, slipped in and locked the door behind him. He was in the chapel alone—alone with the dead.

The distilled, yellow light of a near-harvest moon shone dimly through the windows. There was just enough light for Thomas to see his way to the stone. He knelt down, chipped at the edge of the stone, made an aperture big enough to take the end of the crowbar, inserted it and heaved hard on it. The stone, bedded in the floor for centuries, groaned, moved slightly. Thomas threw his weight once more on the crowbar. The stone moved gently upward. He slipped the jemmy into the crack to prevent that end of the stone slipping back in place. Then he went to work on the other end with the crowbar. Gradually he prised up the other end of the long slab. Another jemmy was slipped into the crack. Then Thomas thrust the crowbar between the middle of the stone and the lip of the vault and heaved mightily. Up came the stone. A second later it fell back against the foot of the tower with a hollow crash. A long dark vault, a grave was exposed. Thomas probed it gently with a crowbar. It was about five feet deep.

With his heart in his mouth he sat on the edge, felt for the bottom and dropped. The grave came up to his shoulders. Thomas bent down and on hands and knees groped from one end of the vault to the other, his hands exploring every inch of space. The vault was empty. All this had taken time, about three-quarters of an hour had passed.

Overhead the College clock boomed out the strokes of midnight. Thomas paid no heed. He was groping with his fingers on the floor of the vault to see if yet another stone slab was there, hiding the entrance to a lower vault.

Suddenly he stiffened. Cold fear gripped him.

Overhead in the locked, empty chapel he heard the soft, shuffling footsteps of quiet presences. They were converging from two sides of the chapel. They met. By the sound of their feet it was plain that they were arranging themselves in two orderly lines.

Thankfull Thomas crouched in his dark grave—paralysed.

Came the sound of soft music. A sweetly haunting melody. It rose, wavered, died away and rose again. There seemed to be no musical arrangement, but the cadences, the nuances of tone, were enchanting. Thomas almost lost his fear in wonder.

Then the music resolved itself into a continuous melody. A voice clear and haunting sang. The words of the psalm were plain to hear: "When the Lord turned again, the captivity of Sion then were we like unto them that grieved." The psalm went on to the end. Thomas listened, petrified. Then came the shuffle of feet. Somewhere in the darkness a door was opened softly.

In a mad moment of terror, Thankfull Thomas remembered Gervase Germyn's tale of the procession of dead men and women round the chapel. The feet above were moving. Soon they would reach the edge of his grave. The dead—men and women from centuries before—would look down upon his crouching form from eyeless sockets.

Thomas remembered that the ringing of a church bell was the only power on earth which could disperse this dread procession. He sprang from the grave. He leapt to the bellrope and swung on it. Up in the belfry of owls and bats, Great Mark boomed into sudden life. One resounding clang. The crash of falling timber. The shattering clang as the great bell hit the chancel floor, scattered the brains of Thankfull Thomas, rammed his crushed body into the grave he had dug and splintered itself in flying metal. Thankfull Thomas had opened his own grave. You may see the stone to this day.

When the Master and Fellows forced an entry into the chapel at dawn and men climbed up to the shattered belfry, they found, securely perched in a corner on the only unbroken piece of flooring, the exquisite little chamber organ which had been put there in 1642 to save it from Cromwell's godless troopers.

After the Restoration, Gervase Germyn returned as organist to the chapel he loved. It had been redecorated, refurbished and brought back to its full glory about 1663. A choral service was held to mark the return of the King and the return to the Anglican church. Germyn sat in his old place at the organ. The sweet voices of the boy choristers were singing the last verse of the 126th Psalm: "He that now goeth on his way weeping and beareth forth good seed; shall doubtless come again with joy and bring his sheaves with him." The organ notes suddenly faltered. The choir went on singing the Gloria without music.

Then the Master saw, with horror, that the thin, pitiful form of Gervase Germyn, who loved his chapel better than life itself, was slumped forward. The grey head was on the organ keys. Gervase Germyn had gone to join his friends, the Dead.

The Devil in the Flesh

Cranbrook, in Kent, is today a sleepy little market town, which to the casual observer is quite unenlivened by the boys' public school that has given it tone, if nothing else. Three hundred years ago it was sleepier still and only half its present size, yet it sheltered five old women who, at a time when witchcraft in Kent was officially a thing of the past, were destined to provide a day's honest diversion for the sophisticates of Maidstone by their trial and hanging there as witches. Incidentally, they were also to provide for themselves a permanent niche in the annals of English sorcery.

The discovery of the witchcraft activities of the five old dames sprang from the taunting of the aged Mother Ashby, described in the contemporary accounts as "the principal actress", by some soldiers of Colonel Humfrey's regiment. Meeting her in a Cranbrook street and having nothing to do the louts began to tease her.

"Where is your imp?" asked one.

"When did the Devil last lie with you?" demanded another.

"Let us see you naked, sitting astride . . ."

"God forbid!" laughed another. "Do you want to be made permanently incapable?"

". . . sitting astride your goat riding to kiss Old Nick's behind?"

And various other taunts of like kind.

Put out by their gibes, the old woman suddenly turned on them and cursed them. The nature of her curse pulled them up short, and their teasing changed instanter into a solemnity born of superstition and fear.

"The old bitch is truly a witch!" the one who had begun it all exclaimed.

"You're right!" agreed a companion. "No one but a witch could curse so."

And one of them, advancing on her, in his anger put out his hand to seize her, demanding, "Hey, old beldame, have you hexed us?"

When Mother Ashby ignored the question and shambled on her way, the young man's fear made him angry and he took her by the arm. The next instant he was standing looking first at his hand and then about him, for his hand was empty and Mother Ashby was nowhere in sight.

"Where did she go?" he asked. "Did you see her go?"

"One minute she was there, and as soon as you touched her she vanished."

"Let this be a lesson to you, you jackanapes," commented a veteran who had watched the encounter. "Show more respect for age, especially in a woman. She was doing you no harm. Now what spell she may put you under, God knows."

"Do you believe in witchcraft, then?" asked a young groom.

"What I believe is no matter," replied the veteran. "What I have heard, yes, and seen, with my own eyes, happened as a result of something very like what you have just done, only that can I bear witness to."

"Don't listen to him!" the groom laughed. "He's trying to scare you. What power can an ancient crone such as that old dame have?"

"But one moment she was here, and the next she was gone!" protested one of the group who was little more than a boy. "How do you explain that?"

The groom shrugged irritably, for he had seen the old woman vanish, and while all his reason told him that it could not in reality be so, it gave him no explanation for the disappearing trick.

"There are many things on the earth, in the sky and in the sea which are mysteries to me," he said, and turned away.

The groom's scepticism only served to disturb the young men more.

"He is challenging the Devil by not believing in him," said one.

"I wish to heaven we had let the old woman be. What possessed you to pick on her, Jim Kither?"

"It was just for fun," Kither tried to assure him. "If I'd known..."

Mother Ashby's four friends were as ancient and as confident in their witchcraft as herself. They were Mother Anne Martyn, Mother Mary Brown, Mother Mildred Wright and Mother Anne Wilson, and all of them lived in Cranbrook, in hovels of such dismal condition that many a man would have rejected them as shelters for his animals.

Mother Ashby, it was later revealed, had been the instigator of it all. The Devil had appeared to her in the night some thirty years before, not long after the death of her husband. He had been in the shape of a dark handsome man, and had persuaded her to lie with him, to which she had submitted with only the minimum of reluctance, and that more feigned than real, chiefly designed to bolster her *amour propre*.

The experience had not been unpleasant. She was to tell Sir Peter Warburton, the Judge of Assize, who sent her to the gallows, that never at any time "had she had any hurt of her carnal relations with the Devil".

The Devil had obviously found the encounter to his liking, too, for when he came again he suggested that if she would do this for him, and would keep herself for him, he would in return give her power over all her neighbours so that she could avenge herself of any injury or slight done to her. The suggestion had appealed to her, and she promised to be his servant in all things.

Not long after they had sealed their pact the Devil asked her whether she might not have any friends in similar circumstances to herself who would find the companionship of a virile male comforting. With singular unselfishness she had named four middle-aged widows and agreed to put her master's proposal to them, and, to be brief, they had all consented to become the Devil's mistresses.

For his part, the Devil had kept his promise, and from that time, two or three times a week the five women had met together in secret, and had cast their spells and concocted their charms and potions in corporate acts of witchcraft.

They must have been particularly beloved of the Devil, for besides disclosing the secrets of the witch's craft, and providing them with familiars to carry out their commands, he gave them one other gift unique in the world history of witchcraft, as I shall presently describe.

When Mother Ashby had encountered Colonel Humfrey's soldiers she had been on her way to a meeting with her cronies. They were waiting for her when she arrived at their rendezvous, and noted that she was out of countenance.

"What is it, Anne Ashby, that has upset you so?" Mildred Wright asked.

She told them what had happened.

"They must be punished," Mary Brown exclaimed, and her friends agreed with her.

"No, we will frighten them by punishing just one of them—the boy, James Kither, who began it all," Mother Ashby decided.

"How shall we punish him?" Anne Martyn asked.

"We will bewitch him so that he cannot pass water until he thinks he will burst," she replied, chuckling. "Anne Wilson, bring Majesty!"

Mother Wilson painfully pulled herself to her feet and, going a little way off, knelt down by a bush. Under the bush was a stone which she lifted, disclosing a small hole lined with moss. From the hole she took a small bundle, wrapped in a fine lawn cloth, and having replaced the stone, she scrambled to her feet, and with all the dignity her arthritic old body would allow, bore the bundle back to where her friends were squatting in a circle on the ground. She placed the bundle before Mother Ashby and took her place with her companions.

Mother Ashby, muttering under her breath, leaned forward and began to unwrap the cloth. As she revealed the contents of the bundle the old women drew in their breaths with sharp hisses of adoration.

An onlooker would have been puzzled by their obvious veneration for an object which looked like and in fact was, as a spectator was later to describe it, "a piece of dried-up flesh, a sinewy substance and scorched".

Placing the grisly talisman in the middle of the circle, she said, "Reach out your hands."

The five old women stretched out their hands and laid their fingertips on the dehydrated flesh. Mother Ashby recited an invocation and, in utter silence, motionless, their eyes unblinking, the five old women gazed at the flesh.

Presently Mother Ashby sighed deeply. None of the others stirred.

Under their fingers the dried strip of flesh began to move. It swelled and changed colour from the brown of dryness to the bluish-red of living flesh, until presently it was throbbing and pulsating and squirming, a shapeless monster sans teeth, sans eyes, sans nose, sans mouth, sans everything but living, moving flesh.

It began slowly at first, but gradually became more alive and more violent in its movements, until it started to slither noiselessly about the ground. The old women gazed at it fascinated, the whole of their concentration centred upon it, their eyes unblinking, their entire bodies absolutely motionless except for the rise and fall of their age-flat bosoms as they breathed.

Mother Ashby presently set up a crooning, meaningless sounds burbling from her lips. In harmony with the movements of the flesh upon the ground, the five old women swayed and rolled on their haunches, caught up in cataleptic ecstasy.

Then suddenly Mother Ashby cried, "Are you there, Majesty?" Immediately the flesh rose up on end and seemed to bow before her.

"You are welcome, Majesty," the old woman went on. "Majesty, I will harm James Kither in his bladder. Let him not void his water until he is in fear that he will burst from the pressure of it. Go and do my bidding."

Once more the swaying hunk of flesh bowed, and then by degrees it ceased its motion. In minutes it no longer lived, but was once again a dried, motionless strip of dehydrated "sinewy substance".

Mother Ashby stooped and picked it up, and reverentially wrapped the fine lawn square about it.

"Return Majesty to his secret abode, Mildred Wright," she said, handing the bundle to the old woman on her right, who pulled herself to her feet, took the package and shuffled off to the moss lined hole beneath the bush.

Towards dawn James Kither was rolling in agony on his palliasse, moaning and groaning and holding himself about his middle.

"What's amiss?" his neighbour asked.

Between gasps as spasms of pain seized him, Kither explained what was wrong with him. His friend could not advise him what to do.

"I shall burst! My God, I shall burst!" the sick man groaned.

Sweat poured down his face in rivulets and his whole body was wet as though he were immersed in a bath. He gritted his teeth as the pain in his belly increased beyond the point of tolerance.

"I am bursting!" he shouted.

But at that very moment the dam within him gave way.

When he was completely relieved, he lay listening to the speculations of his friends.

"I'll wager he was bewitched," one of them said, "and I'll wager I know who bewitched him—that old dame we teased in Cranbrook this morning."

After some argument, the majority of those in the party agreed.

"If you are right," James Kither said, "and I believe you are, if ever I lay eyes on that old witch again I'll carry her before the magistrate."

He laid eyes on Mother Ashby two days later, this time in the main street of Cranbrook. Going quietly up behind her, he seized her in both arms.

"So it is you, James Kither," the old woman said.

"How did you know my name?" he demanded.

"You believed you would burst," she chuckled. "That will teach you . . ."

"You confess you bewitched me?" he exclaimed. "Well, that does it."

And he hauled her before the magistrate and charged her with witchcraft. To her examiners she confessed everything, and named her associates. She even revealed the hiding-place of "the Devil in the flesh".

The magistrate ordered a search to be made for it, and when it was found and brought to him he handed her the bundle and bade her undo it. With fumbling fingers she uncovered the strip of dried flesh. Stretching out her hand, she touched it as though to caress it.

And immediately, to the astonishment and fear of all who saw it, it began to swell and to throb, to change colour and to become alive.

"Now we must part, Majesty," the old woman crooned to it, and took away her hand.

At once the movement ceased, the throbbing died away and the colour faded. Within a minute it was once again a strip of brown dried flesh.

Some weeks later, Mother Ashby and her four old friends faced the judge of assize in the Maidstone courthouse. After a trial lasting some hours, the jury returned a verdict of guilty against all five, and Sir Peter Warburton sentenced them to death.

On the following day Mother Ashby, Anne Martyn, Mary Brown and Mildred Wright were taken to the common place of execution and there hanged. What happened to Anne Wilson is not recorded.

As for "the Devil in the flesh", for several weeks it was placed on public display at The Swan Inn, in Maidstone, where there were constant crowds inspecting it. But never again did it come to life.

The Bo'sun's Body

It began to snow again as the tall young man's trudging feet dragged him thankfully under the lee of the dark, dilapidated mass of Sandown Castle. Whipping out of the black night on a south-easterly gale, the small, stinging flakes and sharp sea spray had made it a miserable plod across the exposed marshland road from Sandwich towards Deal. Now at last he could fumble his way behind a ruined Tudor wall. He staggered slightly as he did so, groped at nothing in the darkness, and went down on to shell-strewn stone, content to lie where he had fallen.

As he rested in the merciful shelter of the castle, Ambrose Gwinett came finally to a decision which had been eluding him. He would go no farther that night. An apprentice to a sailmaker in London, he had promised his widowed mother that want of funds should not keep him from spending that Christmas of 1723 with her at her little cottage between Deal and Dover. He had walked the eighty-odd miles from his place of work in the Old Kent Road, by way of Blackheath, Rochester, Chatham, Sittingbourne, Faversham, Canterbury and Sandwich, until now he was no more than a few hundred paces from the first houses of Deal, with his mother's cottage but three or four miles farther still.

With the instinct of a man who had never owned a watch, he judged the time to be between nine and ten o'clock. His thighs and calves ached and blisters burned his feet. Worse still, his stomach also burned and groaned, not merely because he had not eaten since noon, but because of what he had eaten then. It had been a meat pie, and too cheap to have been fresh. Several times since he had been forced to turn aside into the hedgerows, and much weakened it had left him. No, rather than go on he would seek rest in Deal for the night and let his mother see him in better shape and spirits in the morning.

Pulling his coat tightly to him, young Ambrose Gwinett rose stiffly to his feet and struck off along the shingle beach, lashed by wind, snow and spume, towards the pin-points of yellow light which marked the alternate houses and inns of the little smuggling town. His mother's friend, Mrs Minchins, kept the New Inn, and would certainly let him have a lodging which he could pay for later. His heart warmed at the prospect. His long walk was over.

Although it was such a night, the tap-room of the New Inn proved to be full of smoke, bustle and people. Hastily shutting the door before the gale could blow out every candle in the place, Ambrose Gwinett gazed round upon a host of faces dark with whiskers of a cut more associated with countrymen than seafarers.

As he crossed the room he met Mrs Minchins waddling fatly out from the back with a great piece of pie on a plate.

"Why, it's young Ambrose! And taller than ever, I declare! Come down for Christmas with your ma? Well, that is nice for her. But you've been poorly, have you?" She peered up into his face. "Not looking your old self at all. Outgrowing your strength, that's what it is."

Trying not to notice the pie, he told her his position and requested a night's lodging. She clucked agitatedly.

"Every bed in the house full," she exclaimed. "The town's chock-full for the Christmas market—them and their hens and their pigs and their turkeys. You never heard such a gobbling and grunting in your life. But listen, Ambrose! I know the very thing. You see that gentleman in the sailor coat on the end of the settle there?"

She pointed with the pie. Ambrose saw through the tobacco haze a bulky man, perhaps in his middle forties, who sat with his legs outstretched, sipping moderately from a small tankard.

"My uncle Collins," Mrs Minchins explained. "Just come ashore from the Indiaman that's berthed near the Naval Yard. Bo'sun, he is, and a more respectable, decent soul you'd never meet. Well, he's to spend his Christmas here instead of aboard, which is very nice for me and him, I'm sure, and I kept him a nice little room off the first landing. Now, Ambrose, if he won't mind, and you won't mind, I'll let you share his bed free, just for tonight, and more than welcome from a friend of your dear ma."

At that moment the bo'sun turned his head. As he caught the gaze of his elderly niece and her young companion, he smiled across at them, and his expression struck Ambrose Gwinett as altogether kindly and welcoming.

When the proposition was put to him the bo'sun assented without hesitation, made room for Ambrose beside him on the settle and called for some mulled ale to thaw his bones, waving aside the young man's protest that he could not pay for a return. The hot, spiced drink and the heat of the room soon had Ambrose removing his coat, and within an hour he was eased, warmed through and sleepy. Seeing his yawns, the bo'sun, who had been talking lightly of his sea travels, declared that he, too, was ready for his bed; so they rose together and made for the stairs.

The tap-room was much less crowded by now, so that several of its occupants were able to swear subsequently that they had distinctly heard a brief passage between the bo'sun and Mrs Minchins as she encountered the pair at the foot of the stairs. Bidding her goodnight, her uncle asked that his young friend's refreshment should be put down to his score: at which the landlady replied firmly that the house would bear the charge. At this, the bo'sun rummaged in his jacket pocket and brought out a silver coin. Saying that it was a souvenir of the Spanish Indies, he pressed it into the hand of his niece, who immediately popped it back into his pocket, retorting with mock indignation that she did not take presents from sailormen, a sally which sent the bo'sun off laughing up the stairs, followed by a very weary-looking young man.

Their room was large and the bed ample for the two of them, despite Ambrose's long frame. The wind outside, which had now diminished from a shriek to a moan as the gale died as rapidly as Channel gales often will, added to the sense of comfort within. Ambrose Gwinett, in his shirt and breeches, was asleep before the bo'sun had begun to snore.

It was no sound of the elements that woke them both soon after midnight, nor any noise within the sleeping inn: it was a spasm of pain in Ambrose Gwinett's unhappy stomach which pierced him so suddenly and violently that his whole body jerked and he cried out. Another, lesser pain followed. Snug though the bed was, he knew that a cold excursion to the back yard could not be postponed. The bo'sun, sympathizing sleepily, had the forethought to warn him that the back-door latch wanted some tricky handling. The best thing would be for Ambrose to feel in the bo'sun's jacket, hanging on the bedroom door, take out the knife he would find there, and use it to prise up the latch.

Ambrose Gwinett did as suggested, and within ten minutes was back in the room again, feeling much better. The bo'sun did not greet him from the darkness. Closing the door softly, so as not to wake him, Ambrose fumbled for the jacket to replace the knife. It was no longer hanging from its peg. Thinking he must have knocked it to the floor in his previous haste, he stooped and felt about for it. It was not there. Surprised, but too sleepy to be curious, Ambrose put down the knife on the wash-stand and got back into bed. He knew at once that he was alone.

Well, then, it was clear: the bo'sun had got up, put on his jacket and gone downstairs on some errand of his own. After all, he was the landlady's relative. Perhaps he had felt suddenly thirsty . . . or hungry . . . or . . . Ambrose Gwinett fell fast asleep, and did not wake again for several hours.

It was still quite dark. The wind moaned only fitfully, and there was no rattle of snow against the window. He felt rested and eager to be on his way. But for the lingering storm-clouds, he reckoned, it would be dawn light. He would put on his jacket and coat and go quietly, so as to waste no hours of his short visit home.

To his surprise his companion had not returned to the bed. Ambrose would have liked to bid him goodbye. Still, there could be another opportunity for that. He would need to take the bo'sun's knife with him to manipulate the back-door latch again, and could scarcely then leave it lying about for anyone to pick up and pocket. He would keep the knife and stroll back into Deal at his leisure to return it and buy his kind friend a Christmas glass.

Holding the knife, he went quietly through the dark inn to the back door, let himself out, placed the knife in his pocket and stepped off in excellent spirits towards his mother's home.

It was there, at the little cottage on a cliff-top, that two burly officers arrested Ambrose Gwinett that afternoon. The charge, they brusquely told his horror-stricken mother, was the murder of Richard Collins, bo'sun of the East Indiaman *Pole Star*.

Nearly speechless with astonishment and shock, Ambrose Gwinett managed to gasp out a denial. Ignoring it, they proceeded to search him roughly. In his jacket pocket they found a knife and a silver coin of curious type. On his trousers they detected the unmistakable marks of dried blood: and in the outhouse, lying beside the widow's washtub, they found a shirt with a large blood-stain down the outside of one of its sleeves.

Desperately seeking to remove the look which had come into his mother's eyes when she witnessed these discoveries, Ambrose Gwinett blurted out an account of his night at the inn. He admitted that the knife had belonged to the bo'sun, and explained the circumstances of its being in his possession. He volunteered the information that the coin, too, had been the bo'sun's. It was from the Spanish Indies, and he had seen Richard Collins try to press it upon his niece the evening before: though how it came to be in his, Ambrose Gwinett's, pocket now he could not begin to suggest. Nor could he offer any explanation for the bloodstains on his clothes, except to say that by the time he had reached his mother's cottage by the light of day he had become aware of the blood on his trousers; and on taking off his jacket for his wash had been amazed and horrified to find the marks on his shirt, which he had at once stripped off for his mother to wash later.

His mother eagerly confirmed this last detail. As to the rest, Ambrose could tell, she could not help but doubt. The thought tormented him far more than the officers' obvious disbelief of his whole story and his denial of all knowledge of Richard Collins's death.

As they dragged Ambrose Gwinett back along the road to Deal which he had recently trodden in such high spirits, the officers, sure that anything they told him would be no news to him, condescended to enlighten their prisoner about the murder.

Mrs Minchins, anticipating that her young guest would be eager to reach home without delay, had not been surprised to find him already gone when she had been about to prepare breakfast that morning. What had surprised her was that her uncle, who had not appeared downstairs, was not in his room. Only after glancing round and noticing that his coat was not to be seen either, had she chanced to approach the bed. To her horror she had seen that the sheets were heavily stained with blood. Running down into the street, she had raised an alarm which within minutes had been transmitted from end to end of the deceptively sleepy-looking little town whose history had been chequered with events of sensation and violence. In no time at all the landlady's tale had been told, repeated, amplified and transformed, and men were running about Deal's streets and narrow alleys, searching for a gigantic young fiend with a dripping knife and a pocket full of dead man's silver.

Blood had, indeed, been found in the streets. More level-headed investigators had found traces of it on the landing outside the bedroom, on the stairs, just inside and just outside the inn's front door, and, leading in a distinct trail from there, across the street and down to the water's edge at the public quay. (Here Ambrose Gwinett interrupted his informants to tell them that he had used only the back door of the inn. They laughed heartily, as if this were some joke, and said he would have to do better than that when it came to the Assizes.)

The blood trail to the water's edge had spelled its meaning plain to all Deal. The murderer, having dealt with his victim in the secrecy of the bedroom, had dragged him downstairs, across the dark and deserted road, and had pitched him off the quay into the steeply shelving Channel. Unless it had been weighted, the body would not be long in returning to shore, knowledgeable boatmen had proclaimed. Meanwhile, although some slight efforts had been made to discover it bobbing in the sheltered Downs between the shore and the Goodwin Sands, thoughts had been more upon murderer than murdered. A warrant had been issued without hesitation, and, directed by Mrs Minchins, the officers had duly made their arrest.

Ambrose Gwinett protested in vain all the way into Deal. It brought only a tightening of the grip on his arms and renewed assurances that it was lucky for him that he had been reached by responsible officers of the law before the townsfolk of Deal could find him. The truth of this Ambrose was able to judge for himself when they had passed Deal Castle and entered the town. News of his arrest seemed to spread ahead of them like running fire, bringing men, women and children tumbling out of their cottages to threaten and jeer. Among them, Ambrose saw Mrs Minchins, and made as if to step towards her: but his escort pulled him savagely back. He saw, in the look of loathing she gave as he passed on, that no appeal to her could help.

This was proved when he appeared before the magistrate, sitting in a crowded Town Hall. Mrs Minchins was the chief giver of evidence, and she spared no detail of what had occurred and been said in her inn the night before. She was able to identify the knife as the bo'sun's: the blade sat somewhat loosely in the handle, and he had remarked to her only a few hours before his death that he must see about getting it made firm again. She would have recognized the silver coin anywhere. Some men who had overheard the final conversation between niece and uncle in the tap-room bore out her evidence.

Ghastly pale, his mouth almost too dry with fear to articulate, Ambrose Gwinett could not offer one fact that might be proved in his favour. Besides the circumstance of his having been the last person to be seen with the bo'sun, there were the tangible facts of the blood, the knife and the coin to ascribe the crime to him alone, with his poverty as a clear motive. Rousing himself, he denied his guilt with a vehemence which, together with his known character, caused some of his more level-headed hearers to murmur to one another and listen with anxiety for the magistrate's words. But there could be no doubt what those words would be: Ambrose Gwinett was committed for trial at the Assizes.

The next few weeks were a nightmare for him. Rack his brains as he would, hour upon hour in his freezing cell, he could find no single fact or argument upon which to build hopefully for his coming trial. Knowing himself to be innocent, he was yet so hemmed in by circumstances suggesting guilt that there seemed to be no possible road for him to tread other than that to the gallows. At night, as he slept fitfully, his tormented mind would relive the scenes in the inn. At first, it continued to show him everything as he knew it to have been: but as days went by and his physical condition declined, and fear and hopelessness grew, his dreaming became delirium. He saw himself now returning to that bedroom, knife in hand. Plainly, he heard the slight click of the door behind him, then his own breathing as he stood waiting for a sound from his room-mate. None came, and the ancient floorboards creaked under his cautious tread as he crossed to the bed. Just then, the storm clouds outside split and parted, to reveal the moon, whose rays outlined the humped form under the bedclothes. The blade glinted as the knife rose in Ambrose Gwinett's hand, to plunge flashing downward into yielding cloth and flesh. Several times more it rose and fell, until a dark stain began to spread over the bedclothes. Clouds raced across the moon again, extinguishing its light as with a shutter.

Then Ambrose Gwinett was in panic: thrusting his hand into the pocket of the hanging jacket, pulling out the coin he knew to be there, then seizing the jacket itself, stripping back the bedclothes and quickly dressing the inert figure. Soon he was dragging the figure from the bed, pleased with his own strength and cunning, and heaving it silently, step by step, down the dark staircase and into the street. A cautious look round: no one was stirring. It took him no more than another minute to drag the body across to the deserted quay and, with an effortless push, send it flopping into water deep enough to carry it well away on the outgoing morning tide. Then Ambrose Gwinett was suddenly frightened once more; and there was the knife still in his hand, and blood on his clothes, and the silver coin burning like a cinder in his pocket; and he was running.

It was always during this running that Ambrose Gwinett awoke from his increasingly vivid dream: but whereas he had at first wakened with relief, reassured that his overwrought imagination had been in control of his mind and that the truth of the matter was that he was a wholly innocent victim of inexplicable circumstances, now he came to a point where waking no longer brought comfort. It brought first doubt. Perhaps his dream was truth, and his waking memories lies. Perhaps, in some moment of fever caused by his poisoned stomach, he had unknowingly committed the horrible crime. Perhaps, as he had heard it said to be possible, he had never wakened at all that night, but had carried out the whole matter in his sleep.

Then doubt turned into near-certainty: if he had had much more time to wait before his trial, perhaps Ambrose Gwinett would have given way to certainty itself. Friends who had visited him had already begun to go away shaking their heads at his growing disinclination to feel that his innocence must bear him safely through.

The trial saved him from becoming utterly convinced that he was an unwitting murderer. Once more he was able to summon all his strength and sincerity in telling what he knew to be the truth. By now, too, he had learned that public feeling towards him had undergone no little change. Although several weeks had passed since the night of tragedy, no trace had been found of the bo'sun's body. Whenever a ship had been wrecked on the Goodwins the shrewd Deal people had seldom had far to look for the washed-up remains of crew or cargo. They could be predicted to come ashore at one or another of several points, but Bo'sun Collins had not. While this did not prove that he had not been thrown into the water, weighted or unweighted, it did mean that there was no corpse in the case; and there was spreading revulsion of feeling that a man should be accused of murder, however palpable his guilt, where murder had not been shown to have been done.

The point was strongly made at the trial: but it did not save Ambrose Gwinett. In the face of his inability to rebut the many damning features of the evidence against him, producing only denials in return, he was found guilty by the jury and sentenced to death without hesitation by the judge. His execution fixed for three days after the trial, he was led more gently back to his cell, his head bowed in final hopelessness.

Three days later he stood on the makeshift scaffold, his thinness and pallor making him appear taller than ever. A dense crowd milled around, sympathetic on the whole but eager for the spectacle of a hanging. Having applauded with feeling his speech protesting his innocence for the last time, they craned forward to miss no detail of the final act.

The executioner was a local man of no great experience or skill. He heaved mightily on the free end of the rope whose noose lay round Ambrose Gwinett's neck, pulling his victim into the air to a cry of approval from the crowd. Deftly, the executioner lashed the free end to one of the uprights, grinned and waved to the crowd, then stepped jauntily down to be carried off to a waiting pot of ale.

That should have been the end of the tragic tale of Ambrose Gwinett: but it is not. Executions were less formal affairs in those days than subsequently, and after a curious glance or two at the suspended body the crowd dispersed rapidly. Several young men, however, remained, to clamber swiftly on to the scaffold. While one seized hold of the body and took its weight, another slashed at the rope. In a few seconds Ambrose Gwinett was being borne away to the cart in which his waiting coffin lay. Gently, the long form was placed within and, assuming grave expressions, the young men climbed into the cart and urged the horse into a reverent gait.

As soon as they were clear of the town they began to work feverishly to resuscitate Ambrose Gwinett.

His great height had saved him. When the rope suspending him had been tied and left it had given sufficiently to bring his toes down into contact with the scaffold floor. Although the initial jerk, together with the anticipation that his last moment had come, had made him unconscious, his friends' swift action had enabled him to get away with half a throttling. Within two hours he was snugly in bed in his mother's cottage, sore and shocked, but otherwise quite himself.

As soon as he was fully recovered, Ambrose Gwinett needed no urging by his friends to quit the country, never to return. He hastened to Portsmouth, found a man-o'-war about to sail, gave a false name and, in those days of the press-gang, was only too readily accepted as a volunteer.

Regretting only that he could never hope to see his mother again, Ambrose Gwinett found naval service entirely to his liking. His intelligence took him swiftly through the lower grades and, within five years, out of the forecastle and on to the quarterdeck as master's mate. In this capacity he chanced to sail one day into a port in the West Indies. His ship was to be paid off there and Ambrose Gwinett and several other members of the crew were to join another warship that had recently arrived short of hands.

One of the first persons he met as he stepped aboard his new ship was the man for whose murder he had been hanged five years before.

Ambrose Gwinett's amazement was nothing to the astonishment of Richard Collins when he heard of the near-tragedy his sudden disappearance from Deal that winter's night had precipitated. By way of explanation he himself had a remarkable tale to tell.

A few hours before his fateful meeting with Ambrose Gwinett he had been bled by a Deal surgeon for a pain in his side. It had eased him considerably and he had not troubled to say anything about it to his niece or anyone else. In the middle of the night, when awakened by Ambrose's bout of stomach pain, the bo'sun had discovered that the bandage had slipped off his arm while he had slept and that the vein had been bleeding freely into the bed. Thanking his lucky stars for the unexpected awakening, he had got up quickly in Ambrose's absence, flung on his jacket and hurried down and out of the front door, making for the surgeon's house nearby. He had never got there. Just as he had closed the inn door the press-gang pounced on him. Against all his protests, and a request that they allow him at least to tell his niece what had occurred, he was hustled down to the quay, bleeding all the way, and into a boat which took him to a frigate already under way for the East Indies.

There were no niceties about being pressed into the Royal Navy. No word was sent to relatives of impressed men, and once aboard ship they were lost to all who knew them until they might chance to return some day to that same port, for there was no opportunity for any but the highest officers to write home. So it was that Richard Collins had vanished as if from life itself: and so it was also that he had heard no word of his supposed murder and the trial and hanging of the man whom circumstance had condemned so unanswerably. When Ambrose Gwinett told him that even this explanation did not account for the silver coin having been found in his pocket, the bo'sun exclaimed that nothing could be simpler. The knife blade had been loose in its handle, and several times he had been forced to prise out the coin when it had got wedged in the gap. When Ambrose Gwinett had borrowed the knife, he had unwittingly borrowed the coin as well.

So "murderer" and "victim" became shipmates and firm friends. And when they got back to England at last they made their joint story known to the authorities, by whom it was passed on to the judge and jury (to their considerable remorse) who had tried and convicted Ambrose Gwinett on purely circumstantial evidence. It has often been asserted that, even in the absence of a body, the evidence against an accused person has left no room for doubt of his guilt. The case of Ambrose Gwinett is a reminder from nearly two hundred and fifty years ago as to how dangerous, and horrible in its implications, such a finding could be.

A Warning to Sceptics

Two young men strolled down one of the graceful streets of Dublin. It was a fair city in fact as well as by repute. Molly Malone had not yet pushed her apochryphal barrow over its cobbles; grime had not stained its buildings, nor age and neglect brought them down in the world. The bricks of the tall, beautiful Georgian houses were still fresh and pink, for George III had been king for only just over twenty years. The year was 1783.

Dermot O'Brien and John Sullivan had come simultaneously to the end of their university careers. Since late boyhood they had studied together at Trinity College, sharing bench and book, their friendship a matter of wonder to their fellow-collegians. This was admirable, but not in itself an exceptional or remarkable thing. What made it so was the fact that Dermot was a Protestant and John a Roman Catholic.

Throughout the eighteenth century Ireland had seethed with religious unrest. The old Penal Laws brought in to crush the Irish Jacobites of the previous century were still partially in force: Catholics were banned from many social privileges, denied the common rights of citizens, often forced into emigration or surface conformity. The Patriot Movement had improved the situation slightly, the Relief Bill of '82 had restored Catholics to the status of landowners and allowed them independent schools. But the shadow of intolerance still darkened the land.

It had begun long before, when the hated Cromwell had brought death and destruction to Ireland. The struggle between Orange and Green, and the defeat of Papist King James by Protestant King Billy, in 1688, caused such bitter feeling that it is still, even in this twentieth century, possible to get into considerable trouble by singing *The Battle of the Boyne Wather* in the streets of Belfast or Dublin on a Saturday night. When the nineteenth century had come in, and the atmosphere had been cleared somewhat after the emotional storms of the previous twenty years, the poet, humorist Tom Moore was still conscious enough of the thunder muttering in his native mountains to write *Intolerance: a Satire*, a poem full of barbs:

> *Oh! turn awhile, and, though the shamrock wreathes*
> *My homely harp, yet shall the song it breathes*
> *Of Ireland's slavery, and of Ireland's woes,*
> *Live, when the memory of her tyrant foes*
> *Shall but exist, all future knaves to warn,*
> *Embalm'd in hate, and canonised by scorn.*

He tells the friend to whom his Satire is addressed that could he see fair Ireland in Springtime, his heart

> *Would burn, to think that such a blooming part*
> *Of the world's garden, rich in nature's charms,*
> *And fill'd with social souls and vigorous arms,*
> *Should be the victim of that canting crew,*
> *So smooth, so godly—yet so devilish too;*
> *Who, armed at once with prayer-books and with whips,*
> *Blood on their hands and Scripture on their lips,*
> *Tyrants by creed, and torturers by text,*
> *Make this life hell, in honour of the next!*

Rather, said liberal Tom, would he be a Pagan,

> *And take my chance with Socrates for bliss,*
> *Than be the Christian of a faith like this,*
> *Which builds on heavenly cant its earthly sway,*
> *And in a convert mourns to lose a prey . . .*

FIFTY GREAT HORROR STORIES

Which, while it dooms dissenting souls to know
Nor bliss above nor liberty below,
Adds the slave's suffering to the sinner's fear,
And, lest he 'scape hereafter, racks him here!

But this was in the future, when English politicians were actually working for Catholic emancipation. The story so curiously echoed in Moore's words happened a bare century after the Battle of the Boyne, the last stand of Catholic Ireland in arms, and the emigration to France of the flower of its nobility, who refused to take the oath of allegiance to William III of England. Old people still alive could remember the early days of the Penal Laws that followed: religion and politics were inextricably woven in a web of hate.

In such bitterness had John Sullivan been reared: the son of a family looked down on by their neighbours as "dirty Papists", himself designed for the priesthood. His father, instead of sending him to the English College at Douai to begin his training, had wisely taken the temperature of the times and given his son the advantage of a wider education for the world, at Trinity. Here he met some contempt, some indifference, plenty of open condemnation, whenever the subject of religion was raised among the students. There was an unwritten law governing social gatherings that it should not be discussed, for the combination of hot Irish tempers, strong liquor, and passionate feelings invariably led to the spilling of blood and subsequent trouble with the authorities.

From Dermot O'Brien, however, John Sullivan never heard a word of criticism or covert proselytism. Said one who knew him:

"Though frequently they entered into a debate concerning different subjects, and, at times, made religion the matter of dispute; yet everything tended to increase their friendship, which was continually improving, and raised to the highest pitch, during the term of years they lived together as fellow-collegians. Nothing could break off their intimacy, or dissolve the band of union which was so strongly cemented between them."

So they strolled, this summer day, unaware of the pleas of beggars in the gutter, the provocative flutter of fans from sedan-chairs, the cries of street-vendors. For this was the last day they would spend together in Dublin. Dermot, having received the education of a gentleman, as befitted the son of a wealthy lace-merchant, was about to enter his father's business. John was to travel in Europe, in furtherance of his father's determination that he should learn all that was possible before entering the restrictive world of the cloister.

They paused at the corner of St Stephen's Green, where their ways parted, and stood silent, as men do who have so much to say that nothing can be said. Both faces were grave: John's the pale, long countenance of the dark Celt, Dermot's round, ruddy, normally cheerful.

"We part then, John," he said at last. "Let's not drag out the moment. 'Tis not the end, after all. Though the world takes us different ways, let's make a pact to write our thoughts and our experiences to each other, never failing, and to meet when we can."

"A bargain. It needs but a small flame to keep friendship's fire alight," replied John. "And should we at any time be within twenty miles of each other, let's compact to meet."

"Within twenty? Fifty! A hundred!" Dermot cried. "While I've a horse to carry me I'll find you and crack a bottle with you, John, and we'll talk down the sun and the moon, be you priest or abbot or Cardinal or the Pope himself!"

They shook hands solemnly. It was John who first turned on his heel and walked swiftly away, not once looking back.

In the nine years that followed they kept up a regular correspondence, as they had promised. Dermot's letters told of the increasing prosperity of his business, the success of his partnership with his father, the modest pleasures of the society in which they moved, the newest political developments. There had been bitter strife when the Society of United Irishmen had turned revolutionary and opened negotiations with France for an Irish republic. The Protestant reply to this was the foundation of the Orange Society. Fresh hatred was engendered between the two religious parties, "and gun-peal and slogan-cry waked many a glen serene". Long-silent poets revived the glories of Ireland personified, Kathleen ni Houlihan, Dark Rosaleen.

The Ulster Presbyterians of the north then rose up on their own account and made a national rebellion seem inevitable. Catholic hopes were high, Dermot reported with admirable impartiality. Then came the peasants' rising in Wexford, and its failure. Wolfe Tone was a martyr-suicide in prison. And among those who died in fighting for his cause was John Sullivan's own brother, Patrick.

Dermot called on the Sullivan family to offer his commiserations, but was coldly received, he wrote regretfully to his friend.

The letters he received from John (now Father Sullivan) were far shorter and scantier than his own. There was little time for writing in the rigorous curriculum of a priest; little to say that would interest a member of the laity, especially the Protestant laity. The fire of their friendship remained alight, but the flame was very low, and burnt palely now.

Dermot, after the death of his father in 1792, decided to enhance his foreign business by a tour of the Continent. His journey would take him to Holland, within easy reach of Brussels, where John Sullivan was now established in a small monastery. When Dermot wrote to tell him of his impending arrival, asking him to arrange a meeting, he replied that it would be perfectly easy, as he did not belong to an enclosed order and was allowed to mix in the world as freely as he wished, within reason.

Dermot's first action after arriving at his Brussels inn, the Lion d'Or, was to send a servant to beg for Father Sullivan's presence at supper that night. Having seen his baggage disposed of, he went down to the public room to enjoy a much-needed drink. Two or three travellers were already there. Dermot, a gregarious soul who had suffered much in the past months from the limitations of language, surveyed them in the hope of finding among them someone with whom he could talk without the necessity for translating his thoughts into painful French. What a pity, he reflected, that Trinity had given him such a good grounding in Latin and none at all in the languages actually spoken!

His eye rested on the back view of a man sitting alone at a small table, a bottle of wine before him. He wore the uniform of an English officer. There was something about the set of his slim shoulders and neatly queued hair which seemed vaguely familiar. When he turned, revealing a handsome swarthy face very reminiscent of a youthful Charles James Fox, recognition and delight blazed in Dermot's eyes.

"Michael! Michael Byrne, as I live!"

The soldier started, looked round, and leapt to his feet, his face alight with welcome.

"If it's not yourself, Dermot O'Brien, 'tis your fetch! Why, man, how come you here?"

In the half-hour of excited conversation that followed the two exiled Irishmen exchanged complete dossiers. Byrne, after leaving college, had entered military service, later joining a crack English regiment. Now a captain, he was in charge of a force garrisoned in Brussels, on its way to meet the invading Dumouriez, whose Revolutionary army was threatening Belgium with the Terror that raged in France.

Over another bottle of the excellent wine the pair happily discoursed of college memories and mutual friends, including Father Sullivan. Dermot told Byrne of the meeting they were to have at supper, and invited him to join the party.

"Sure, I won't spoil the fun!" said Byrne good-naturedly. "You'll be wanting to talk the hind leg off a donkey, as you two always did."

"No, no, you must join us! Nothing could be happier than that you should be staying here. Providence must have designed it so."

Byrne agreed, but pointed out delicately that, as he now served the forces of the country Sullivan had always referred to as Bloody England, there might be a certain tenseness in the social atmosphere. A Catholic himself, Byrne belonged to that liberal Horatian species which (politically speaking) is not passion's slave. Not himself of a religious nature, he was inclined to consider the whole thing nonsensical.

Seven o'clock struck from the massive Dutch clock in the hall of the Lion d'Or. With it entered a tall figure, black-cassocked and broad-hatted. Dermot had been prepared for his old friend's costume but not for the change in the man himself. The long face, always pallid, now had the look of old parchment, giving him the appearance of a Spaniard rather than a Celt. The dark blue eyes had sunk deeper, the mobile mouth had become a straight, thin line. If, as he said, Father Sullivan was allowed to partake of worldly pleasures at will, he showed little sign of it. His gaunt figure and sunken cheeks gave evidence of a life of asceticism. The youth who had relished a meal of steak and porter in Dublin was gone for ever, lost in this seemingly middle-aged man whose actual years did not number thirty.

The two friends met, as they had parted, in momentary silence, each taking in the change in the other. Then Dermot stepped forward, hands outstretched.

"My dear old John! It does my heart good to see you!"

The priest received impassively the embrace of his old comrade, now so prosperous and portly, brilliant in high-collared snuff-brown coat, embroidered waistcoat and tight blue pantaloons: a bird of paradise in contrast with his own black plumage. He smiled.

"God be with you, my son."

Dermot started back. "Don't call me that, for pity's sake, John, alanna! Won't you leave the reverend father outside now, and be the boy you used to be? Sure, formalities are for strangers, not for dear old friends."

"Very well, Dermot, then. For you I will break a rule of my Order. But I shall have to do penance for it, you know!" Dermot laughed, leading him into the supper-room. Here Captain Byrne was waiting, as was a laden table of the best fare the Lion could offer. A polite greeting was exchanged between priest and soldier. The three sat down to a pleasant evening of food, drink and talk. Dermot beamed like morning sun on the Wicklow mountains, chattering like their streams. Byrne told story after story, exciting or humorous, about his campaigns, while Father Sullivan demonstrated that he had developed from a silent youth into a sophisticated conversationalist with a knowledge of world affairs outdoing that of either of his companions. Laughter rose high, only ebbing when the persecution of the faithful in France was mentioned. Then the priest's affable expression changed to one of stern condemnation. He spoke of Buonaparte as Antichrist, of the Revolutionary leaders as minions of hell. "And in hell shall they burn for ever, in torment unspeakable!"

Byrne tactfully changed the subject to a more festive one. Brandy was called for, and drunk freely. Through the rosy haze of wine-fumes and smoke Dermot contemplated happily the presence of his two old friends at his table. The talk turned to women. Byrne told some racy anecdotes of his amorous education in six or seven countries, heavily censored out of respect for the priest, who listened smilingly and suggested that the gallant captain should appear before him and make an official confession at the earliest possible opportunity. "Ah, but I'm a reformed character, Father!" said Byrne, producing a case containing charming miniatures of his wife and their two small children. Dermot admitted himself still a bachelor, but gave his friends a detailed description of the charms, physical and pecuniary, of Miss Maria O'Grady, the Dublin heiress for whose hand he was thinking of proposing. And then, too soon, it was midnight. Before Dermot was assisted to bed by a sympathetic waiter, an arrangement had been made for another supper the following evening, at which only Dermot and Father Sullivan would be present, as Byrne had a regimental engagement.

Another pleasant meal followed. The two men settled down to bridge the gap of years. Almost could Dermot believe that Time had ticked backwards: the supper-room of the Lion d'Or merged into the little panelled room in his Dublin lodgings, where two boys had thrashed out the affairs of the world between them. The slight constraint which had separated Dermot and the priest the night before, despite their mirth, vanished utterly. Said Father Sullivan, pushing back his chair and smiling at Dermot over the rim of a well-filled glass:

"Ah, Dermot, 'tis a miracle I see before me! A man with the soul of a little child. If you were only of the Faith I could make a saint of you."

"But as I'm a heretic, I'll roast in hell—isn't that it, now?" said Dermot, laughing.

"Alas, true enough," Father Sullivan sighed.

"Ah, come now, John! Never tell me you truly believe such things, and you a grown man with a head as full of sense as an egg's full of meat. No, no, 'tis but a form of words. You'll be telling me next the Real Presence is in the bread and wine." As he spoke the words, he noticed that the wine before them at that moment appeared to be having an effect on his friend, whose pale face had suddenly darkened with a flush from brow to lips. When the priest answered him, he realized with a mild shock that it was a flush of anger.

"Do you presume to doubt that?" asked Father Sullivan in a clipped voice. Dermot laughed.

"Why, sure we had all this out in our young days. Didn't I reply to you then what poor Jane Grey answered to her Papist questioners —'After all, the baker made Him.'"

"That is rank heresy. I cannot listen to it." The flush had receded, leaving the priest's face paler than ever. "You were always a Protestant: I see you have become a blasphemer." He half-rose from the table. Dermot pulled him down again.

"John, John, be easy! We used to debate these things freely

enough. Maybe I've grown more liberal these days—call me a sceptic if you like—and you more hidebound. I half-believed you once, when you used to tell me so earnestly of your miracles, and your devils, and your Virgin Births. Now we're both men of the world, living in changing times. There is freedom in the air, revolution; what have we to do with ancient superstitions?" In this vein he continued, the wine speaking through him: demolishing with a breath all doctrinal stumbling-blocks from the foundation of the Roman Church over the bones of Peter to the newest Papal bull.

The priest sat motionless as a figure in stone, but a nerve twitched by his mouth. Dermot saw that he had gone too far, and stretched out a placatory hand.

"I've offended you, John. I'll say no more of it. Let's drink a toast, and talk of matters less debatable." He refilled their glasses. "To Old Friends!"

Father Sullivan's tight lips relaxed into a faint smile. He drank, and the awkward incident was over. It was two hours before the friends parted, their subsequent conversation having been as cheerful and amicable as it had been before Dermot had raised the vexed question of religion. As he was leaving the inn, the priest shook Dermot's hand warmly, saying:

"You have given me two excellent evenings of entertainment, my old friend. I wish I could repay your hospitality; but, as you know, we poor priests have no means to do so. If, however, you would care to take a simple meal with me tomorrow evening in the monastery, and see how we live there, I shall be only too happy." Dermot readily accepted, and went to bed as merry, if less overflown with wine, than on the previous night.

He slept quickly; a sleep that should have held only pleasant dreams. But the refreshing deep slumber of the first hour gave way to a vision so vivid that there was no room in it for the half-consciousness that reassures the sleeper: it is only a dream, it will pass. He was in a small room—a cell, he thought, from its window-less walls and bareness. He lay flat on the ground, with no pillow or coverings. An uneasy sense of constriction made him try his limbs: they were all tightly bound, so that he could stir neither hand nor foot, nor even lift his head to see what bonds held him, for some kind of yoke or bar lay heavily across his throat. His senses were unnaturally acute, sharpened by fear. There was some kind of soft hissing sound in the room, as of whispering, or escaping air. He turned his head this way and that, trying to locate it; then, in the way of dreams, the constriction at his throat disappeared and he was able to raise his head and see what lay about him. As he did so he felt himself screaming—the terrible soundless scream of nightmare.

Around him crouched a circle of loathsome creatures. In the semi-darkness he could make out the forms of great rats, giant spiders; rope-like coils ending in small flat heads that he knew, without having seen them before, were deadly cobras, rattlesnakes, vipers. And he knew that the faint sound of hissing came from them and was their warning of attack.

Suddenly, as if at an unheard signal, they began to move towards him, creeping and slithering. Rigid, paralysed with a terror beyond his experience, he lay and felt them advancing over his legs; felt the dry cold of scales slide over the skin of his hands, and the patter of rat-feet on his body. Again and again he tried to shriek, but the muscles of his throat would not obey him. Then the first bite came, and another, and another, and he began to heave and struggle in his bonds. There was a weight on his chest, a heavy form that shifted and changed shape and elongated itself until the spotted body was reared on end, and the spade-head of a serpent was poised above his own, its tongue flickering in and out. It struck, and blackness rushed upon him.

He was lying on a bed; the blackness was the friendly dark of the inn bedroom. The wetness on his face was not blood, but mingled sweat and tears. For some minutes he was unable to move, so great was the fear that still possessed him. Then he managed to grope on the table beside him, find his tinder-box, and light a candle. He watched the shaking of his hands as he did so, and caught sight in a mirror of his ghastly face. "Lazarus," he said aloud. "Like Lazarus, back from the dead."

There was neither brandy nor wine in the room. When he was sufficiently in control of himself to stand, he pulled on slippers and his great-coat and set off downstairs, where he knew he would find some restorative. The house was quiet and dark. As he began to descend the lower staircase he saw a candle-glimmer advancing towards him. Its bearer was Michael Byrne, still dressed for out-doors. On the narrow landing they met, and the captain's eyes widened in astonishment.

"Holy Mary, man! What ails you? You look as if you were dying!"

"Wh-what time is it?" Dermot managed to ask.

"Time? Why, it wants a quarter to one. I've only just now come in."

"So early," said Dermot slowly. "So early. I thought it had been hours—centuries."

Byrne, who had seen badly frightened men before, took his arm and steered him towards his own room. There he lit several candles, sat Dermot in a chair, and made him drink a stiff glass of brandy.

"Now," he said, "tell me what's troubling you."

Dermot, hesitating a little at first, related his nightmare. Byrne did not smile. "When I was a boy in Donegal," he said, "there was an old wife used to interpret dreams. To dream of snakes, she'd tell you, meant a treacherous friend."

"That can't be the case with me," said Dermot confidently. "I trust my friends as I would myself."

"Good, good. Then it may be you were talking of snakes this evening with Father Sullivan, and so dreamed of them?"

"Of snakes? Not at all. The nearest we got to them was when one of us mentioned St Patrick, for we were speaking of religion." He outlined the conversation, adding that he was ashamed of his attempts to argue with a man so obviously dedicated to his faith as John Sullivan. "It was mere presumption on my part, and might well have caused a breach between us."

Byrne poured another drink and sat toying with it, the fingers of his other hand beating a thoughtful tattoo. Then he said:

"Will you take a piece of advice? Don't go to the monastery to supper."

Dermot's mouth fell open. "Not go? But I promised! And what harm can there be?"

"No harm at all, perhaps. But I feel in my heart that there is something—that the holy father means ill towards you."

"I would trust John with my life!" returned Dermot vigorously.

Byrne shook his head, smiling. "You are too trusting, my friend, an innocent abroad. Go if you must: but *if* you go—why, then, *I wish you well out of it again.*"

They said goodnight. Dermot returned to bed and slept well for the rest of the night, a candle burning by his side.

Dusk was falling on the following evening as he went to his rendezvous. Father Sullivan had appointed a meeting in the Grande Place, so that he might personally conduct his friend into the monastery, avoiding the formalities he would otherwise have had to go through. Prompt to his time he appeared, a tall, black figure walking slowly, reading his breviary as he came. They met and greeted each other warmly. "I hoped you would not be late," said the priest, "everything is prepared for you. As we are in good time, perhaps you would like to see some of our more curious and interesting monastic buildings before we sup?"

Dermot agreed, though he was hungry and had little zest for antiquities. He would not again willingly offend his friend. He followed the priest across the square to the fine old houses that flanked it on one side. Between two of these a small flight of steps led down to a heavy studded door.

"You would not expect, would you now, that the precincts of the monastery would extend so far? Yet the Church's arm is long, her domains are wide." He produced a large key and unlocked the door, ushered in his guest, and relocked it. They were in a bare, chilly room with roughcast walls: once, Dermot imagined, part of kitchen premises. He did not see anything particularly ecclesiastical about it, and was just about to inquire its history when the look on his friend's face arrested him. The benign smile had vanished with the shutting of the door. In its place was a pale mask of hatred.

"Heretic! Damned heretic!" the priest spat, and the forked tongues of the nightmare serpents flickered again in Dermot's brain. "What did you mean last night by affronting me—degrading our blessed religion—contradicting the tenets of our Mother Church? Now you are in my power I will make you pay dearly for it."

Dermot gasped, then laughed. "Come, come, John, you can make a better joke than that! 'Tis poor entertainment for friends."

"There can be no friendship between a son of the Church and such as you," retorted the priest. "You and your kind murdered my brother. How can we be friends?"

"Well, if it was not a joke—which I can't truly believe—I must have offended you worse than I knew, and I humbly apologize."

Father Sullivan raked him with a contemptuous look.

"Too late," he said, and pulled a bell-rope that hung by the wall. At the end of the room two folding doors opened. Through them

Dermot saw a larger room, obviously a disused kitchen, by the empty hooks planted in its ceiling-beams. But it was now in use again. In the huge open fireplace burnt a high leaping fire of logs. Before it stood two men, their appearance shockingly familiar, though (as with the serpents) Dermot had not seen them in the flesh before. They were stripped to the waist, wearing only rough breeches; their faces were covered by black masks. Even without the array of fearful instruments about them, he knew them for executioners.

"I don't understand, John," he said. "What does it mean?"

The priest smiled coldly. "It means the end of a heretic," he said. "This is the entertainment I promised you last night."

Dermot felt the sweat starting on his forehead, for he knew well enough now that no joke was intended.

"But *why*?" he pleaded. "I may have spoken foolishly last night but it was in all innocence. As to Patrick's death, I was most sorry for it. Why should you wish to—to kill me?"

"Can our religion flourish, while such as you live?" returned the other, and his face was now transfigured into the likeness of a devil. "So perish all Protestants!"

Dermot heard himself stammering out something about their boyhood days, their old friendship, the kindness with which they had met again. The priest listened impassively, then made a sign, at which the two executioners seized Dermot. One held him while the other bound him hand and foot.

"There are several alternatives," the priest mused. "The traditional end for heretics is by burning, that their black souls may be purified by fire. As you see," he nodded towards the flames, "the faggots are lit and the stake is ready." Dermot's eyes followed his to a trunk of wood, some seven feet high, on its side on the floor. Placed behind the grate, its end in the chimney, it would serve . . . He looked away from it, shuddering.

"Or," said Sullivan, "we have all the apparatus for the process of hanging, drawing, and quartering: so often inflicted by heretics upon our martyred priests." He described the operation lingeringly, displaying the various instruments used in it, and pointing out the convenient ceiling-hooks.

Dermot seemed to be standing outside his body, watching and hearing a white-faced figure trembling in the hands of the two executioners. He noted with detachment that some remnants of courage and resource remained to him even yet. Temporize! Temporize! said his brain insistently. Somehow he dragged out a question.

"The room—these men—you told me we would visit the monastery. Surely this is not . . ."

Sullivan laughed shortly. "Monastic premises? No. Nor are these —gentlemen—brothers of our order. The place and the men are hired. It is easy enough."

"But—but then," stammered Dermot, "your Father Superior does not know you are proposing to carry out—murder—in the name of your Church? He could not approve such a terrible thing!"

The priest shrugged. "He is a weak, complaisant man, not fit to rule. One day I shall stand in his place and restore to the church its Holy Office—as I do now. It is all for the good of your soul, you know." He rubbed his hands in anticipation, and surveyed Dermot with a dreadful smile. Meeting his eyes, Dermot saw that he was quite mad.

"Strip him," Sullivan commanded the men. They began to tear off Dermot's clothes, neckcloth, coat, shirt, while he struggled as he had struggled in his dream at the first bite of the reptiles.

"Stop!" he managed to say. "At least allow me a prayer! Even the Inquisition allowed that to a man about to die!"

Sullivan looked impatient. "For what a heretic's prayer is worth, you may make one. But be quick about it." At a gesture, the men released Dermot sufficiently to allow him to kneel. His mind was blank with terror; blankness shot with drifting irrelevant images: a scene of duck-shooting in boglands, Miss O'Grady's pretty hands on the pianoforte keyboard. Then suddenly a surge of strength came to him, and he prayed, for an instant, as he had never prayed before in his life. The conforming sceptic believed at last, and sent up a desperate plea to the One in Whose gentle name these things were done.

Sullivan looked at his watch. "Enough," he said. "Give him a taste of the fire. Brand him." One of the men jerked Dermot to his feet while the other thrust a sharp metal rod into the flames and held it until it glowed white. Then he approached Dermot and held the tip close to his bare flesh, scorching it.

"Now!" Sullivan ordered. As if on a word of command, a roar

of voices and a fusillade of hammering broke out beyond the folding doors. The figures in the ghastly tableau froze into immobility, listening. Then there came a crash as the studded door gave. The priest looked round like a trapped animal and rushed to a small door at the rear of the room. It was locked. He fumbled for the key, muttering frantically to himself. The executioners dropped their instruments and hovered uncertainly. Then the folding doors burst open, and Michael Byrne stood before them, brandishing a sword: an avenging angel in the uniform of His Majesty King George III.

Months afterwards, when Dermot had returned to Dublin, the man who had delivered him from the flames called to pay his respects and to drink a glass of wine. They talked of this, and of that: of Byrne's lady's expected third child, of Dermot's engagement to Miss O'Grady. And, last, of the evening neither would forget.

"Strangely enough," said Dermot, surveying the colour of the wine against the candle-light, "it has taught me understanding. When I talked with the Father Superior and John's brother priests, and knew their wisdom and kindness, I knew also how far from the flock my friend had wandered: back into the cruel past, the Dark Ages. My poor old friend: I hope his soul is quieter now."

"He was well enough, when I saw him last," said Byrne. "His frenzy seemed burnt out, but his memory is gone. They let him work in the monastery gardens and care for the hens. He is happy, in a childish way."

"I wish I had not provoked him. It was because I was his friend that the fanaticism came upon him," said Dermot. "My tattling tongue was his ruin, and almost my death."

"True," the soldier observed. "And even though you'd kissed the Blarney Stone before you harangued him, 'tis a very true saying:

> '*A man convinced against his will*
> *Is of the same opinion still.*'

"Slainte." He drank off his glass.

Double Damnation

Jessy Tamson laboriously polished the already shining panes of her master's first-floor drawing-room window. In fact, the room had three windows, extending from floor to ceiling, so that small Jessy had to stand on the top of a step-ladder to reach the top panes.

She liked cleaning the front windows because they overlooked the street, with its tall, sedate houses, its area railings behind which interesting dramas took place between servants and tradesmen, its coaches and sedan-chairs, with their glimpses of fine ladies and gentlemen. For this was a street of wealthy men's dwellings. Here lived the tobacco merchants, Glasgow's *nouveaux riches*, one of whom was Jessy's employer, Mr Blair. For over ten years now, since the early 1770s, Glasgow had been importing half the tobacco that came into Britain. Jessy wished that she could be lady's maid to Mrs Blair or one of the daughters, and handle fine silks and satins, and perhaps be given a cast-off gown now and then. Dressed like Miss Flora or Miss Eliza, with her hair powdered and a Parliamentary patch on her cheek, where was the lad that wouldn't run after her? As it was, there were plenty to look up and wink at the pretty brown-haired girl on the step-ladder, for all her rough red hands.

She tossed her head at the thought. Perhaps Duncan would be a wee bit less sure of himself if she had a few more followers at her petticoat-tails. He was getting very off-hand, inclined to be late for their meetings, not so eager to prolong their strolls on the banks of Clyde or through the romantic shades of Kelvin Grove on those evenings when Jessy was allowed out.

What was Duncan, after all? Only a surgeon's apprentice. Perhaps he saw himself taking examinations, becoming a doctor like his master, Dr Bute, too fine to marry a servant-girl. But he *had* promised marriage when they first began courting, and Jessy was too trusting a girl to take seriously the prospect of Duncan throwing her over—such a good young man as he was, three times at kirk every Sunday, and sober-minded as one of the elders themselves. Hadn't she given him proof enough of her trust, that summer night when they exchanged vows under the trees by the river—vows that by Scots law bound them in solemn betrothal? Jessy met the interested gaze of an errand-boy with a reproving stare, and slowly descended the ladder. Somehow, running up and down steps was not as easy as it had been. Perhaps she was getting fat; indeed, she had not felt altogether well for some weeks. There were other symptoms, too, which troubled her, and she wished her mother were alive to advise her about them. But Mammie had died with the last bairn, and most of Jessy's small wage went to help her father bring up the younger ones.

Some streets away, Dr Andrew Bute was conducting an operation. The screams and roars of the unfortunate patient did not discompose the doctor at all: he was used to them, and besides, these difficult cases were made so much easier by the skill and professional calm of his assistant. Whether it were a matter of blood-letting, applying leeches, making up a prescription, or cautery, Duncan Foulis could be relied on. Even now, with all this din going on (the patient's wife, locked out on the landing, was adding to it) Duncan's hand showed not a tremor as he supplied the doctor with scalpel, lancet or forceps. Some apprentices of Duncan's limited experience would be green-faced now, swigging the brandy which was the patient's only anaesthetic, or swooning outright. But not Duncan. His long, pale face was its usual colour. He would make a doctor, no question of it.

When the operation was over, the blood mopped up, the instruments casually wiped with a none-too-clean cloth, surgeon and apprentice returned to Dr Bute's home. As they left the patient's house the doctor patted Duncan briskly on the back.

"Weel done," he said. It was high praise indeed, but then Duncan deserved it. Not only was he an efficient assistant, but his general character was excellent. His attendance at kirk was unfailing. Certainly, such attendance was compulsory under the stern Presbyterian law, but many young men of Duncan's age were openly or covertly rebellious. One, Robert Burns by name, was making his name notorious throughout the Mauchline district by his scandalous verses in defiance of the kirk-session and its Calvanist rule; not to mention the additional scandal of his drinking and his amours. But Duncan Foulis neither smoked tobacco, swore, drank nor wrote lewd rhymes. Only on one count could godly eyebrows be raised at his name. He was seen too much in the company of Jessy Tamson.

It was the practice of the kirk elders to keep a close watch on the private activities of their flock, any shortcomings being punished with a severity in which religious zeal was frequently heightened by personal spite. A backslider would not be fined only, but would be submitted to public shame and obloquy. In that simple, devil-fearing society, the spiritual punishment was by far the more dreaded.

Duncan's evening walks with Jessy had not gone unnoticed by William Rae, leading elder of Duncan's parish. It was his pleasure, as well as his duty, to keep tracks on any courting couple in the hope of catching them *in flagrante delicto*. A great deal of entertainment could be had in the name of moral vigilance, Rae had discovered. So far his stealthy pursuit of Duncan and Jessy had revealed no evidence of actual sin. It was quite possible that their courtship was a straight path to matrimony. But Rae doubted a little. Jessy, though an honest enough girl, was of a lower station in life than Duncan, coming from a humble cottage on the outskirts of the town. Her father was a farm labourer, whose poor wage would not have kept his six young children but for the money Jessy gave him. And Jessy herself had gone barefoot until the Blairs had taken her into their household. No, she was not a likely wife for young Foulis, son of a decent clerk in a counting-house. They were worth watching.

Duncan Foulis was quite aware that Rae followed them. His pale, sharp eyes, glancing back over his shoulder, had often taken in the distant figure of the old man, walking fast when they hastened their steps, pausing to admire some imaginary detail of landscape when they paused, dodging out of sight when they turned. And Duncan was beginning to worry. For a time he had been infatuated with Jessy, ready to marry her. Then, because his nature was as essentially cold as hers was warm, his passion began to fade: her fondness became an irritant. And yet—the flesh was weak, and Jessy's body was plump and sweet. Plumper than it had been, he thought, glancing down at her as she trotted by his side through the summer meadow. They had taken to strolling on the Green, Glasgow's pleasant playground on the north side of the river, rather than in more retired paths, for it was more difficult for Rae to follow them in open country. Jessy was a little breathless, striving to keep up with her lover's long strides.

"Canna we sit doon a while?" she asked. "I'm wearit, Duncan."

"It's no' like you to weary so soon, Jess," he said, as they seated themselves on a fallen tree. "Are you no' weel?"

Jessy shrugged. "I'm no' ill, Duncan. I was gey sick a few weeks syne, ilka morn, and I had a wheen giddy turns. But I'm better noo." She laughed. "Faither says I eat like yin o' the pigs!"

Duncan moved to the end of the log, and surveyed her figure. The pink-flowered dress that was her best, and that she always wore on her walks with him, strained at its seams, and the muslin fichu round her shoulders seemed to have shrunk, so ample was her bosom. Why had he never noticed before? He began to ask her questions. When, surprised and bashful, she had answered them, his face was whiter than her fichu, the freckles on it standing out like halfpennies. With a sudden movement he got to his feet.

"It's time we went hame," he said shortly.

He did not sleep that night. Disgrace, ruin, stared him in the face. He could not marry her; she was no fit wife for a surgeon, too ignorant, even, to recognize her condition. Even if he did, and their secret handfasting were acknowledged as a legal betrothal, he would be arraigned before the kirk session for the crime of fornication, and together he and Jessy would have to stand up on a Sunday morning before all the congregation, on the dreaded "cutty stool" of repentance, and hear their sin proclaimed in a ranting hell-fire sermon, while the unco' guid licked their lips. At the mere thought of it he beat his head with his fists and groaned aloud. Never to be respected again, never to be the white lamb of the flock, a potential elder of the kirk: and all for a sin that would be no sin if he were to find a better-born girl than Jessy, and marry her.

When morning came he was red-eyed, exhausted with lack of sleep. Dr Bute looked at him curiously, hoping his assistant was not coming down with the prevalent cholera. But that evening Duncan Foulis was himself again; calm and sensible. Before leaving the surgery he put everything carefully to rights, paying particular attention to Dr Bute's case of instruments. Then he set out to meet Jessy. Again their way was across the Green, along the pleasant walk by the river, towards the Rutherglen road. This time Duncan did not suggest going home early. The sun had gone down from a sky of orange and amethyst and the last blackbird was twittering when they reached the stile where they usually paused to embrace. Never had Duncan been gentler, more lover-like, to his lass. Her brown eyes shone with a tender light as her arms met round his neck.

"Am I bonnie as ever, Duncan?"

"Aye, Jessy." He put his hand into the inner pocket of his coat. "I've a wee something for you, lassie."

Jessy's face lit with excitement. "It's no'—no' a *ring*? Duncan, dinna tease me so! Give me—give me!" She prised at his closed fist.

With his left arm he encircled her firmly, holding her a little away from him.

"Aye, I'll give it you," he said.

As he uncurled his fingers the rosy evening light struck on something that was not round and gold, but long, silvery and sharp. The hand that held it did not shake.

Jessy Tamson's disappearance caused no great stir. Mistress Blair was annoyed at the loss of her servant and at the deceitfulness of the girl, to have run off in the night with no warning. Jessy's father concluded that she had grown too grand for her family and had taken a place where she need not give him any of her wages. It was an unkind judgement, for Jessy had always been generous with her money and unstinting in her care for him and her brothers and sisters; but the constant hard labour served by an eighteenth-century farm-hand had an embittering effect upon the character. There were whispers, of course. Some said that she had got into trouble and run away from the inevitable scandal. Others openly named Duncan Foulis, who parried criticism by an air of wounded pride, allowing it to be understood that he was deeply hurt by the desertion of his sweetheart. William Rae smiled complacently.

"He's weel rid o' yon. She's gaun tae hide her shame. Better she take it to anither parish than oors."

The weeks came and went, and no word was heard of Jessy.

Another maid polished the Blairs' windows and kindled their fires. Rab Tamson took up with a comfortable widow who, to his surprise and relief, agreed to marry him and look after the bairns. Duncan Foulis exchanged glances in kirk with Arabella Caird, daughter of the town's most prosperous apothecary, receiving from her eyes encouraging messages. He spoke to her father, and was kindly received. It was as though Jessy had never been: as though Duncan had shut her in behind a great iron door within his mind, beyond which no memory of her could penetrate.

Only in the night-hours did she escape and clutch at him with her small reddened hands, and then he could see every detail of her appearance, from her neat cap to her worn slippers; the telltale shadows below the eyes, the apron-strings tight round the thickened waist. He thanked God, from whatever piety was in him, that he always saw her thus, and not as she must be now. On that terrible vision the iron door slammed shut.

There were bad moments, too, in the daytime, when Dr Bute became irritable because something he needed was not at hand; had not been at hand for some time. Duncan had not seen it, could not tell him what might have happened to it. Eventually the doctor rode over to Edinburgh and bought another.

At these times an almost irresistible compulsion would come over Duncan to leave the house and run through the streets to the Green, along the river-path, until he came to the stile, and there fall down and writhe like the worm that he was, calling on Jessy's name and begging her for God's love to be alive again. So clear was the picture of himself in this act of penance that he seemed to hear his own voice crying and wailing, seemed to see the sweat and tears on his face, the grass torn up by his scrabbling fingers. Then he would rally, saying to himself, "If that can be clear, which is but fancy, why not this?" and summon before his mind an image of Jessy by the stile, Jessy well and laughing, laughing to the babe in her arms. But the vision would not stay. There was nothing for him but to fall on his knees and pray, passionately, that the images might leave him.

He was to marry Arabella Caird two weeks before New Year.

"That's maybe why he's no' at kirk the day," said one of the inspectors appointed to round up those who dared to default from church attendance.

"Wha's that, then?" inquired his colleague, who had paused to take a wee nip from his pocket flask in the shelter of one of the trees that bounded the Green.

"Why, Duncan Foulis. Man! Yon's a queer place to lig, on a winter's morn!"

He pointed to a figure that lay, prostrate and face down, on the grass a few yards away. It writhed and curled like one in an epileptic fit, its fingers tearing up clods of earth and grass blades. Cautiously the two inspectors approached.

"The lad's ta'en sick, or else gaun wud (mad)," said the first. "Speak till him, Jamie."

"Duncan!" The man approached, and bent to touch the heaving figure on the shoulder. But before he could do so Duncan Foulis had leapt to his feet, turning on them a face of such mortal agony that they shrank back, and crying with the voice of a soul in hell:

"Miserable, miserable! I'm a miserable man! Look in the water."

Turning, he climbed across the stile in the nearby wall, and hurried off along the river path towards Rutherglen. As he went his voice floated back to them.

"Miserable, miserable! Look in the water."

They did not trouble to watch him out of sight, for both had hastened towards the river-bank. There had been little rain for weeks, and the river was running low. Together they looked down into the clear, slow-moving water. Then Jamie broke off a long dry branch from a tree that overhung the river, and, crouching at the edge, began to fish with it.

"Can ye see aught doon there?" anxiously inquired his friend.

"Aye. I think so. Gie's a haun'. I'm gaun in."

Stripping off boots and hose, he waded into the shallows, and in a few moments his improvised rod had tangled with something: a piece of cloth that detached itself and floated towards them. It was or had been a white material, printed with a pattern of pink flowers.

They did not recognize what had been Jessy Tamson, when they fished it out of the Clyde: indeed, her own father was unable to do so. But they remembered her best frock, and the little jet bracelet that was her only finery still encircling her arm-bone. The skirt of her frock had been weighted by large stones tied in its folds, which had kept her securely out of sight at the bottom of the river.

They carried her into the town on a hurdle improvised from branches, for what was left of her weighed but little. As the cortège passed the church on the edge of the Green its bell struck a solemn "One", like a knell for the dead girl. The congregation was streaming out, the firstcomers arriving at the gate in time to be stopped in their tracks by what they saw. The Sabbath decorum was broken by cries of horror, the bearers surrounded by eager morbid questioners, gathered like flies about the bier.

Suddenly Jamie paused in his explanations. His head jerked up, and he pointed to the church gate.

"Look yon!"

Emerging through the gate, with the tail-end of the congregation, was Duncan Foulis. Tall, pale, black-suited, composed as ever, he approached the knot of people.

"What's a' the steer?" he asked.

Suddenly silenced, the crowd parted to let him through. He looked down at the fish-gnawed, sodden remains in their shreds of finery, his face impassive.

"God rest her saul, whoever she was," he said, and turned to go.

Jamie snatched at his sleeve. "Ye ken fine wha she was! Did you no' tell us whaur she lay in the river?"

"Aye", broke in the other, "and a' but tell us ye kilt her?"

"I've no notion what you mean," replied Duncan.

Jamie bent and pulled out an object from the tangle of soaking rags. "What's *this*, then, villain?" he cried.

It was a surgeon's scalpel.

Neither questioning nor downright browbeating could produce any confession of guilt from Duncan Foulis. So clear seemed the case against him that he was arrested, imprisoned, and tried before a judge. Presumptive evidence of murder was so strong that the jury would have brought in a unanimous verdict of Guilty, but for one fact: the prisoner had an unshakeable alibi for the time of his alleged confession. He had been in full view of the congregation, the kirk elders, and the preacher, William Rae, throughout the service, which had lasted two and a half hours. By no possible chance could he have been on the Green at the time when the two inspectors vowed they had seen and spoken to him, and their sworn affidavits were set aside. A church full of witnesses was enough to offset their evidence and the silent testimony of Dr Bute's missing scalpel, buried in Jessy Tamson's rib-cage.

Yet, though no legal punishment overtook him, Duncan Foulis's life was ruined. Dr Bute refused to employ him any longer; Miss Caird broke off the betrothal. Neighbours shunned him. At last he was forced to leave Glasgow and live where he was unknown; if life it could be called, companioned as he was, day and night, by the terrible conscience which had projected his living image to the spot where he had murdered Jessy, and forced from it his own voice to make his confession.

The case of Duncan Foulis is a strange, almost incredible one; but it is completely authenticated, though the names of the personages have been changed. It is only one among many of a similar kind. Phantasms of the living are almost as common as phantasms of the dead, and have kinship with them in that they are almost invariably projected by feelings of frustration, desire or anxiety. Two classic examples are royal. When Elizabeth I of England was dying she refused to go to bed, telling her adviser, the Lord Admiral, that "there were spirits there that troubled her—if he were in the habit of seeing such things in his bed as she did in hers, he would not try to persuade her to go there". For three days she sat upon a stool, refusing to move, and, when pulled up, stood obstinately on her feet for fifteen hours, before collapsing on to cushions strewn upon the floor by her attendants. While she lay there, constantly watched, a lady-in-waiting was horrified to see the gaunt figure of the Queen stalking through her throne-room. Screaming, she ran back. There Elizabeth lay, still on the floor. Mental agony, extreme remorse, had driven her astral form out of her body, seeking, perhaps, the souls of those she had sent to their deaths—her cousin Mary, and the man who had plotted with her, the beloved Earl of Essex, her physician Rodrigo Lopez, and countless religious martyrs.

Similarly, the Empress Catherine of Russia, dying in fear after a scandalous life, appeared as a ghostly double seated upon her throne. Hearing of the apparition, she staggered from bed and, seeing it, ordered her guards to fire on it.

Many more instances are known—a mother anxious for her child, a doctor unable to attend his patients, a madman who, struggling in his strait-jacket, projected his image into the bedroom of his nephew so clearly that the young man wondered what the strange garment could be in which his uncle chose to pay this unexpected call. But of all motives, guilt and remorse seem to be the most powerful. In the case of Duncan Foulis and Jessy Tamson, it was sufficient to produce the most unusual effect of a collective hallucination; and that on two hard-headed Presbyterian Scotsmen, unimaginative to a degree, who were so convinced by what they had seen and (even more remarkably) heard that they were prepared to swear to it in a court of law.

And perjury was then, as now, a very serious offence.

The Tongueless Woman of Glamis Castle

Lord Strathmore remarked: "There are legends of every sort of ghost here. A tongueless woman running across the park, pointing to her bleeding mouth. Jock the Runner who races wildly up the drive. A Mad Earl who walks about on the roof. Then there is the poor little ghost of the Black Boy. He sits on a little stone seat by the door into the Queen Mother's sitting-room. He's supposed to be a negro servant or page boy whom they treated unkindly two hundred years ago or more. Oh, we've lots of 'em."

The Earl of Strathmore said this quietly, a mere matter-of-fact statement. We were at lunch in the small dining-room at Glamis Castle. Glamis is said to be the most haunted house in Scotland, indeed, in the whole of Britain. Some of the legends are rubbish, fostered and elaborated by Victorian writers and others since. Some legends, however, hover on the brink of credibility. A few are utterly true.

Two tales of horror stand out. One is true, the other so macabre that you can believe it or not. I have the word of Lord Strathmore, and of his aunt, the late Dowager Lady Granville, sister of the Queen Mother, and others for the truth of some of these things.

Glamis, at first sight, is unforgettable. I came on a sharp day of champagne sunlight and saw suddenly the soaring pile of keep and tower, pepper-pot turrets and battlements, rise, splendidly unreal, pinky-grey against a winter sunset of orange and green. Far off the snowy line of the Grampians was a backcloth of unearthly beauty. The flag of the Lyons flew stiffly in the wind.

It was a castle not of this world, but of the world of Hans Andersen. A castle of ghosts and queens, reaching to the stars. The air of ethereal unreality impresses one instantly. It does not awe. Glamis has not that overmastering sense of brutish power and dark cruelty which so many Norman castles, even in ruin, emanate. Too often the dungeon and the rack, the thumbscrew and the press, have left their foreign mark of Latin cruelty.

Glamis has, rather, the sense of a family stronghold, a place of succour and security for its lord and his people. And so, indeed, it was when rings of fortified walls with successive embattled gateways surrounded it. Yet it has more dark secrets than perhaps any castle in Britain. Not least, that macabre fresco of violent death outlined on the wooden floor of an upper room. There, not many years ago, the Queen Mother's great-aunt remembered seeing, stained in the floorboards, the outline of a dead body where, as Lady Elphinstone says, "a man had lain outstretched and blood had run practically all round him".

I think of a prettier little cameo of memory—an evening of frosty light when, by the corner of the kitchen-garden wall, where the trees in Bents Wood were magical with snow, a couple of woodcock, chasing each other with the speed of snipe, nearly flew smack into my bottom waistcoat button. That, somehow, does not happen to one on ordinary days in humdrum places.

The gentlest ghost, and that most often seen, is the "Grey Lady". She appears in the chapel. No one quite knows who she is—this gentle, forgotten Lyon who says her prayers in the sunlight.

Few families are older then the Lyon family, for centuries Thanes of Glamis. They had their own army more than six hundred years ago, their private hangman more recently than that. The Hangman's Chamber at Glamis, white-walled, bare of furniture, is not a room one would choose to sleep in.

They kept a hangman, not because they were tyrants, but because the Scottish kings gave them, as Thanes of Glamis, the responsibility of maintaining justice, law and order throughout the wide lands of Angus. That power was never abused.

"There was never yet an arrogant Lyon," said a local farmer to me. "Always guid men an' gentle leddies." Pomposity has never been their middle name. How many great families can claim the same?

A woman brought the first royal blood into the family in 1372 when Sir John Lyon, tall and fair, nicknamed "The White Lyon", married Princess Joanna, daughter of King Robert II of Scotland. She brought him the castle and lands of Glamis and the title and powers of Thane of Glamis, a king with power of life and death.

That was the beginning of the family at Glamis. Today the castle stands a grey-pink soaring pile of towers, battlements and chimneys in a great park between the Grampian Mountains and the heathery skyline of the Sidlaw Hills.

King Malcolm II of Scotland was murdered there. His ghost may open your bedroom door. Shakespeare placed the murder of Duncan, by Macbeth, in the stone-floored, vaulted Duncan's Hall of the castle, and when the Queen Mother was a child this was the one room through which she and her sisters always scuttled at top speed.

No family has had more fantastic ups and downs. A Lady Glamis was burnt as a witch by James V, yet a few years later Mary, Queen of Scots, dined with the family and stayed the night.

"The Glamis family are the first to fight in war. The last to quarrel in peace. The first to help anyone in trouble." That is how Wullie Savage, taxi-driver of Kirriemuir, summed up the Bowes-Lyons as he drove me on my first visit. And he added: "One of the best presents that Buckingham Palace ever had came from Glamis."

Today, the Commonwealth echoes that proud, local boast. And Wullie Savage, be it noted, is not a tenant on the Glamis Estate; he is just a typical, local Scot who takes an immense pride in the local family, which has more than made good on the greatest stage in history.

It is men such as Wullie Savage and George Fairweather, the retired head keeper, who remember the old tales and legends which you will not find always in the family archives. Such tales are handed down from father to son, from grandfather to grandson, round the peat fire at night when the wind hammers in the chimney and the Scots pines above the burn sing their harp-song of the North.

Every great Scots family, particularly in the Highlands, had its own "Seneachie", or family chronicler. He was the immemorial story-teller, the man whose task, usually hereditary, was to pass on from generation to generation, by word of mouth, old tales of family feuds and clan battles, of births, marriages and deaths, of good lairds and bad lairds, of fairies, ghosts and hauntings of the kelpie or water-horse, who, in Caithness particularly, haunts the deep lochs and, when he comes to the surface, gallops the water under the moon with hooves of fire. They told me of such a kelpie who haunts Loch Calder in the heart of a flat, wet moorland in mid-Caithness. He terrified the district to such an extent that the Laird defied superstition and declared that he would have the kelpie out of it once and for all. He ringed the Loch with his clansmen and retainers and by incantation and thrashing the water with poles drove the kelpie to the surface. The great beast, flashing fire from its nostrils and striking fire from the water with its hooves, galloped straight at the ring of terror-stricken men and, with a snort of blue flame, leapt clean over them and disappeared with a hiss of scalding spray into the next loch half a mile down the glen. And there it still is.

There is no water-horse to haunt the Dean Water at Glamis where the Queen Mother learnt to catch her first trout, but there is, bricked up somewhere in the sixteen-feet-thick walls, the Room of Skulls. No one, indeed, seems to doubt its truth. Long ago, when the neighbouring Lindsays and Ogilvies were constantly at each other's throats, raiding and counter-raiding, burning and murdering, a party of Ogilvies, on the run from the Lindsays, arrived panting and wounded at the outer gateway in the ring of fortified walls which then surrounded Glamis. They begged the Lord of Glamis for sanctuary. He had little love for either family. However, he promised to put them in a secret room where no one would disturb them.

No one did disturb them. The door to the secret room remained locked for a century or more until a later Lord of Glamis opened it, shone a light into the black recesses of the room—and collapsed in a dead faint. The floor was littered with the grinning skulls and contorted skeletons of the Ogilvies who had starved to death. Some had eaten flesh off their own arms.

The room was bricked up and its location is now lost. Lord Strathmore, who does not doubt the truth of this story, told me: "There are probably half a dozen rooms bricked up in this place." Searching through the papers in the Charter Room, I came across Sir Walter Scott's account of the strange sense of other-worldly fascination with which Glamis impressed him when he first stayed there as a young man of twenty-two in 1793. He described his first visit thus:

"The night I spent at Glamis was one of the two periods distant from each other at which I could recollect experiencing that degree of superstitious awe which my countrymen call eerie... The heavy pile contains much in its appearance, and in the tradition connected with it, impressive to the imagination. It was the scene of the murder of a Scottish king of great antiquity, not indeed the gracious Duncan, with whom the name naturally associates itself, but Malcolm II.

"The extreme antiquity of the building is vouched by the thickness of the walls and the wild straggling arrangement of the accommodation within doors. As the late Earl seldom resided at Glamis, it was, when I was there, but half furnished, and that with moveables of great antiquity, which, with the pieces of chivalric armour hanging on the walls, greatly contributed to the general effect of the whole.

"Peter Proctor, seneschal of the Castle, conducted me to my apartments in a distant part of the building. I must own that when I heard door after door shut, after my conductor had retired, I began to consider myself as too far from the living, and somewhat too near the dead. We had passed through what is called the King's Room, a vaulted apartment garnished with stags' antlers and other trophies of the chase, and said by tradition to be the spot of Malcolm's murder, and I had an idea of the vicinity of the Castle Chapel.

"In spite of the truth of history, the whole night scene in Macbeth's Castle rushed at once upon me and struck my mind more forcibly than even when I have seen its terrors represented by John Kemble and his inimitable sister. In a word I experienced sensations which, though not remarkable for timidity or superstition, did not fail to affect me to the point of being disagreeable, while they were mingled at the same time with a strange and indescribable sort of pleasure, the recollection of which affords me gratification at this moment."

Whilst at Glamis, Scott drank a pint of wine to the health of the absent Earl from the famous "Lion of Glammis". This is a splendid silver-gilt beaker nine inches high. It was made at Augsburg early in the seventeenth century and is stamped with the letter "E".

There is no doubt that Scott had this beaker in mind as the prototype of the "Pocolum Potatorium" of the Baron of Bradwardine in *Waverley*, the Blessed Bear. He said himself that he "ought perhaps to be ashamed of ʟccording" that he had the honour of swallowing the contents of the Lion; and the recollection of the feat served to suggest the story of the "Bear of Bradwardine".

Scott swallowed his pint of port, but there was, according to legend, a maidservant at Glamis who nightly sucked her pint of blood or more from the living as they slept. She was a vampire. Finally she was caught in the act, bundled into a secret room and left to die. Since vampires do not die it is a pretty thought that in her secret tomb she still lies, her eyes closed, but her flesh alive, her teeth sharp, her menace still potent.

I have often wondered whether by any stretch of coincidence this story of the vampire could tie up with the most appalling legend of all, that of the Tongueless Woman. Many people, over the years, claim to have seen her pale, pleading face staring out of an iron-barred window in one of the turrets. One man, in particular, learned more of the macabre tale than just the face at the window. According to the late Sir David Bowes-Lyon, the Queen Mother's brother, who may have picked up the tale when he was a boy, the man was a guest who was taking a late stroll after dinner on a lawn, close under the castle walls, when he saw the girl gripping the window bars and staring into the night with a distracted look on her face. He was about to speak to her when she disappeared abruptly as though someone had pulled her away from the window. There came one appalling scream—then utter silence. It was one minute to midnight.

About five minutes later as he stood undecided on the lawn he heard soft thuds down the winding staircase of the tower and the sound of heavy breathing. A moment later the tower door opened and a hideous old woman "with a fiendish face" staggered out with a large sack on her back. When she saw him she ran like a stag, in spite of the heavy sack, straight for the woods in the park. Her long black cloak flapped in the night wind and her black hair trailed behind her in the most approved witch fashion. She looked the incarnation of evil. The guest felt certain that the girl, or her body, was bundled up in the sack, but he failed to explain why he did not chase the old woman.

The sequel came years later high in a lonely mountain pass in northern Italy. Snow was falling. It had been drifting down in soft flakes for most of the afternoon. Then a great wind came out of a dark cleft in the high mountains which made a wall of gloom against the sky. Within minutes it was blowing a blizzard. The solitary figure plodding up the valley was white from head to foot. The snow froze on him and it stuck to his clothes. It froze on his eyebrows and eyelashes. Half blinded, almost numbed with cold, he staggered on. The thought passed through his mind that he might stick it for another hour, but not for the night. No human being could live out such a night in such a temperature. Fatalistically, he plodded on.

Suddenly out of the swirling snow-mist came the form of a St Bernard dog. It nuzzled him, licked his hand and gave a deep bark. Men's voices came out of the snow-gloom. A moment later a party of monks surrounded him. They took him up the valley to their monastery, a squat, stone fortress of a place, clinging to a terrace in the side of a mountain. A peasant had warned them that the English traveller from the holiday village far down at the foot of the valley was out walking alone and likely to be lost.

The Abbot spoke fair English. "It was fortunate, *signor*, that our woodman told us word of your walk. Otherwise I fear that you would have been lost tonight."

"And probably dead," the Englishman added. "I am sure I owe you my life. Once before I was caught in a snow blizzard and rescued by a shepherd whose dog found me when I had almost given up hope. That was in the high mountains of Scotland."

"Scotland!" said the Abbot. "You know Scotland. It is strange but there is a woman with no tongue—and no hands—who has lived for many years in a nunnery in the next valley. We know nothing of her except that she is English, or should I say Scottish. It is all a mystery. We do not speak of her."

The Englishman begged for more details. Finally, he persuaded the monks since he told them that he felt he had the answer to the mystery. That, as he confessed later, was pure instinct; nothing more than a wayward guess.

Next morning the monks took him, in bright sunlight, over smooth-hard snow, to the nunnery in the next valley. There they spoke with the Mother Superior. She spoke then with the Englishman who, inexplicably, seemed to know something of the woman in her charge.

Finally, almost reluctantly, she led him down a bare, pave-stoned passage, and flung open a door of a room. A woman, who had been sitting at a table, rose at their entrance. She had the face which he had last seen imploring help at the window at Glamis. She had no hands. And she could not speak.

Was she the vampire who had been punished barbarously, but not murdered?

Trapped in a Flooded Tunnel

As soon as his head began to clear after the first devastating shock of sudden disaster, the young engineer began struggling to free himself. Stabbing pain forced him to modify his efforts. His right leg was trapped as if in a vice and was obviously damaged; he realized that he must have sustained serious internal injuries. Then the lights went out, leaving him in darkness, with rising river water and slime already surging round him at waist level.

"Collins! Ball! Where are you?" he yelled, naming two tunnellers with whom he had been working at the moment of disaster. His voice echoed through the entrance gallery, but there was no reply. Could his companions be pinned down under water? If so, their chances of escape would be negligible. And there had been at least four other men who had just joined the shift. He shouted again, but still there was nothing but the echo of his own voice and the roar of water, mud and debris.

He stopped shouting and concentrated his strength on renewed struggles to free his trapped limb. Everything, he recalled, had happened with relentless swiftness. There had been nothing to presage impending horror; then sudden disaster, overwhelming in its violence, had left seven men battling for their lives.

All had been engaged in the early stage of boring a tunnel under the bed of the River Thames to link St Mary's, Rotherhithe, with a point near the junction of Wapping Lane and Wapping High Street.

At one moment they were working with calm precision inside the protection of a great cast-iron shield; the next, a sudden influx of river water, mud, slime and miscellaneous refuse had swept all the men from their lofty perches like so many matchsticks.

So great was the impact that they were washed back on to a wooden platform which served as a working base for labourers removing excavated soil and for bricklayers who were lining the new tunnel as the shield was pushed slowly forward. Under the weight of the inrushing flood this platform had collapsed with a splintering, rending crash.

All the hapless tunnellers had been borne down in the wreckage to find themselves floundering in a mounting sea of foul slime. The stench that now filled the tunnel was appalling, for the Thames at that time was little better than an open sewer.

The water level seemed to be rising a little less rapidly now, and the young engineer renewed his struggles, gritting his teeth against the agonizing pain. He suspected that debris of some kind had momentarily jammed the breach in the tunnel head, but the crown was barely fourteen feet below the river bed at its deepest point and pressures were enormous. Whatever it was that was acting as a temporary dam could not be expected to hold for long and the flood would be all the more vehement once the obstruction gave way.

The trapped man reflected with grim irony that his plight had been brought about by his own zeal. There had been no call for him to work with the professional diggers inside the shield. It had been his immense interest in every aspect of the project that had prompted him to lend a hand.

He had no illusions about the peril that engulfed him. It was not his first experience of flooding. In an earlier flood he had rushed from his office above ground on hearing that an elderly engine-man, named Tillert, was missing down below. He had grabbed a coil of rope and had gone down into the flooded tunnel and had found the old man groping helplessly in the dark with water nearly breast-high. He had managed to lead Tillert to the shaft and had helped to haul him to the surface.

No such eleventh-hour rescue now seemed possible for him or his six silent companions. He shouted again in a forlorn hope, but there was no answering call.

Little by little his eyes became a trifle more used to the surrounding gloom, and he thought he could just detect some dark shapes floating past him in the swirling flood. He guessed that these were empty cement kegs or odd scraps of wood from the wrecked staging, as well as odd flotsam sucked in through the breach in the river bed. After the previous flooding they had found pieces of bone china, an old shoe buckle, wood blocks and a shovel they recognized as one they had lost during diving-bell operations in the river above.

He now paused in his struggles for a moment to plunge one hand below the water to find precisely how he was trapped. His groping fingers came upon a great baulk of timber that was pressing upon his knee, pinning it against another part of the collapsed platform, thus making him a prisoner. It dawned upon him that he probably owed his survival so far to the fact that he had been pinned in this way, with his head above the flood level instead of in the depths. But it was also clear that unless he could extricate himself the noisome water must engulf him in the end. He faced a ghastly death by delayed action.

Not that it could be long delayed now. The stream from the river bed was gushing in with renewed force and the level was rising fast.

Still groping round in the region of his trapped limb he became aware of a horrible coating of slime that seemed to be settling everywhere, and the very discovery suddenly kindled a spark of fresh hope in his alert mind. Wasn't it just possible that the foul slime might serve as a sort of lubricant? He scooped up a handful and began to plaster more and more round the point where his leg was most firmly held. Though he lacked sufficient strength to thrust the heavy baulk of timber to one side, there was at least the slender possibility that he might slither out of his trap.

He started to experiment at once and thought he could detect some very slight movement. But he was far from strong. Work in the tunnel had taken its toll. The casualty rate from tunnel sickness had been high. Men had been driven blind, some permanently; others had been laid up for varying periods. The engineer owed his own early promotion to the fact that his predecessor had been forced to resign through illness. Then three assistants had all been struck down in turn. One had died, a second had become blind in one eye. The trapped man had been smitten, too, and off duty for a long time. Only his keen interest in the project had brought him back to the job, his physical strength sadly undermined.

But his iron will remained, even though the odds against his escaping from his present plight were wellnigh incalculable. The strange thing was that while, in a detached sort of way, he accepted his journey's end as a matter of course and something almost inevitable once he and his companions had been flushed out of the shield, he could not banish his private dream of seeing the completion of this great tunnel.

Since the sinking of the first shaft, every moment had been fraught with challenge. Early on it had become apparent that the geologists had blundered in reporting that the Thames bed was lined with strong, blue clay, impervious to water. The tunnellers had soon come upon vertical seams of sand and silt which had clogged the pumps used for keeping the workings drained. The trapped man's father, whose project it was, had recommended the construction of a special drift-way to cope with flooding, but the company had ruled this out for reasons of economy. A grim mistake, as the present disaster showed.

As these and other thoughts raced through his brain he recalled, also, how at the ceremony marking the start of this great undertaking his father had laid the initial brick, while he himself had been permitted to lay the second. He had taken great pride in this privilege, but now he asked himself if he had, in fact, started to build his own tomb that day.

This thought he now rejected vigorously as he redoubled his efforts to wriggle free. Again he became aware of a curiously detached sensation, as if he were a spectator, looking on at all that was taking place; and the darkness seemed to accentuate this feeling. Past, present and future seemed to merge into one, for mingled with his thoughts was a vision of the celebration he was confident must come. In fancy he witnessed the laying of the final brick to mark the completion of the great tunnel, designed to replace the existing ferry which daily carried 3,700 people between Rotherhithe and Wapping.

And all the time he kept up his struggles, though every exertion caused him excruciating pain. He knew that if he could only lever his trapped limb upward the pressure must ease as his leg narrowed. But all the time the noxious water was rising, and the dank, sour stench was almost overpowering.

He had no means of knowing the extent of his injuries, but the risk of contamination from the foul mud and water was just one more horror that did not bear dwelling upon.

His sole consideration now was to escape from this tunnel of death, and at last, with one desperate wrench, he succeeded in getting his injured leg free. The feeling of triumph was great, but the effort left him momentarily exhausted and in such agonizing pain that even in that dank, chill, tomb-like atmosphere he found himself suddenly drenched in sweat.

Somehow he summoned up sufficient strength to disentangle himself from the loose wreckage which now surrounded him. Then, standing erect, he began to lurch in what, from the flow of the swirling water, he guessed must be the direction of the shaft. But he knew it to be fully three hundred feet away, a formidable distance to cover in his present weakened state.

He was still pain-racked and in a semi-fainting condition, and with the flood water now nearly breast high he found it increasingly difficult to make progress without being swept off his feet.

But he continued to limp doggedly on through the sinister gloom, again half aware that indistinguishable objects were swirling around him.

Every now and then he found himself floundering helplessly into great mounds of glutinous mud and the task of lifting his aching limbs clear of these obstructions seemed to demand impossible effort. Yet he ploughed on, hoping desperately with every painful, dragging step that his scanty measure of remaining strength and flagging will-power would not entirely desert him.

By some odd chance he stumbled presently into what he identified from memory as a small, elevated recess, and his groping hand closed instinctively upon a rope rail attached to the wall at that point. He grasped it fiercely to support himself for a few moments while he rested from his exertions.

While he waited, panting, he called out in one forlorn cry to his companions, Collins and Ball, only to be shocked to hear how much his voice had weakened. There was no answer, and the grim fear reasserted itself that both men must have met the dreadful fate of being ground into the mud beneath the collapsed staging.

Then, perhaps through some freak of acoustics, the noise of the rush and roar of water in the confined space of the tunnel seemed to increase until it conjured up an impression of cannon in battle. In the same instant the mounting flood poured into the raised alcove where he was resting. He found it hard to relinquish the comforting grasp of that rope rail, but he knew that he must get on quickly if he were to make a final bid to reach the shaft before the waters rose too high.

He was now much too obsessed with the idea of getting out of the death trap to pay any heed to his aching knee or the bruises and blows he sustained from jagged chunks of timber hurled about in the seething waters. Time was running out.

Still floundering desperately in the darkness, he was suddenly astounded to find himself on the fringe of a group of struggling men, now up to their necks in water, and apparently battling in near panic to force a way through mounds of miscellaneous wreckage which blocked their way to the shaft steps. Then, in a sudden flash, he remembered that there was an alternative outlet. There was, indeed, a second set of stairs, a little to one side of the others, which had been put in specially for the benefit of visitors who, at certain times, were admitted to view a limited section of the tunnel workings at one shilling a time.

Instantly he called to the struggling men, now silhouetted in a faint aura of light which filtered down the shaft, a prefabricated structure fifty feet across and forty-two feet deep. But even before the echo of his shout died away there came a roar and he felt himself caught up in an immense, gushing wave which came surging down the tunnel, indicating that the breach in the river bed must have widened. Such was the overwhelming force of this sudden upsurge that the helpless man found himself being swept up the shaft like a bobbing cork. And the volume of water was so great that it momentarily lapped the rim of the shaft, where he had sufficient presence of mind to hang on grimly till someone grabbed hold of him and dragged him to safety—an escape that came near to a miracle.

There was no such miracle for those clustered round the old stairs. Though barely seconds behind the engineer in making for the other exit, they were caught in a freak downwash of that same mighty wave and sucked back relentlessly into the slime and darkness. These luckless men were six in number—Ball, Collins and four miners. All perished in the fearful slime.

The young engineer was laid up for fourteen weeks while his internal injuries and damaged leg healed under skilled treatment and he recovered slowly from the effects of his ordeal to make the sad discovery that he was the sole survivor.

While convalescing at Brighton he made an attempt to fill in his diary for that grim day of 12 January 1828. He could find few words, but the few he penned contained the laconic confession: "I never expected to get out."

NOTE: The survivor not only went back to work in the tunnel; he saw the job through.

But there were three further floodings, and for one seven-year period work had to be abandoned.

Yet his vision at death's door was fulfilled, for he saw the tunnel's completion in 1843. He also lived on to achieve great fame as a builder of bridges, railways and steamships.

He was Isambard Kingdom Brunel, famous son of a famous father, Sir Mark Isambard Brunel, the French engineer who conceived the tunnel, and an English mother whose maiden name was Kingdom.

The Girl in the Flame-red Dress

It was 1960 that Sue Wilson rented the house outside Buckingham. She'd been widowed six months—Martin was killed in Malaya—and fortunately old Colonel Bartlett, who'd known them both for years, was able and anxious to help. He was abroad, would be for three years or more, and was happy to let Sue have Wheldon House for a peppercorn rent—far better than letting the tax man take his cut.

Sue and the three children soon settled in. She managed to get work helping at the primary school, where she was soon loved and respected by her tiny pupils, and this, as much as anything, ensured that John, Helen and Dick, aged eight, six and three, had plenty of friends to play with. Children came back from school to have tea with them in the large, dark house at the top of the hill, to look with mingled interest and suspicion at the countless portraits of Colonel Bartlett's ancestors which festooned the hall and drawing-room, to tap the huge barometer, or to search for ghosts.

John, Helen and Dick for their part preferred going out with their small friends, to their smaller houses, where were few family portraits and barometers, but where the colours were bright and clean and gay. As they had an endless stream of invitations, the time came when Sue decided she must throw a mammoth children's party in repayment for at least some of the kindness her own had received. Up to now she had not had more than two or three at a time, for fear of the damage a larger group of excited children might do in a house as old as Wheldon.

Invitations were carefully constructed from thick card by the two older ones, who wrote out laboriously, "John, Helen and Dick invite you to come to a Party. Saturday, April 17th, at half past three. We do hope you can come. RSVP". Some forty of these were cut out, written and posted: exactly the same number were accepted.

Seldom can Wheldon House have had such a shaking. The children behaved themselves, but the thunder of eighty feet down the creaking, protesting passages, the shrieks of little children lost in unexplored parts of the house, must have woken every ghost that ever hid there. Not that Wheldon seemed to have a history of ghosts—a fact that disappointed John, Helen and Dick very much indeed: it was soppy, living in a huge and uncomfortable house, if you didn't have a ghost.

"C'mon, John—where's ya ghost? Gotta have a ghost in a house like this——" There were squeals of laughter, and a little boy, waving his arms about under a table-cloth (how on earth had he got hold of it?), chased a dozen others from the hall, through the billiard room, to the echoing, uncarpeted, drawing room.

Half past six, and parents came to collect them. Sue, who had saved the housekeeping money for weeks, was able to produce glasses of sherry for all. The parents seemed reluctant to break up the party, and soon there were two functions going on in the same house—forty children milling about, shouting at the tops of their lungs; rather less than that number of adults, sitting about the hall and billiard room, glass in hand.

By half past seven, when overtired children had started to cry, the move began. "Bye-bye, say thank you, Willy, to Mrs Wilson for the lovely party", "Bye-bye Mrs Wilson thank you for the lovely party", "Bye-bye, Willy, thank *you* for coming". By eight o'clock she was able to contemplate the shambles of her rented home, to wonder how many days of hard work it would take to put it in shape again. Just as well Colonel Bartlett wasn't expected back from abroad. What *would* he think?

"John——"

"Yes, Mum?"

"Get the other two off to bed, will you? Then maybe you can

give me a hand for a minute or two, down here, clearing up. Though I suppose we *could* do it tomorrow."

"Yes, Mum. Tomorrow. *Ohhh!*"

She looked up to the half-landing on which her three children had stood, so happy, so dishevelled, and saw them turned in horror, faces in profile to her. They were staring up the dark passage which led to the east wing.

The two smaller ones suddenly broke and ran down the stair to her, arms out in terror. "Oh Mummy, Mummy—it's dreadful!"

"What is, darlings? What's wrong?"

They flung themselves at her at the foot of the stairway, buried themselves in her skirt. She looked up at her elder son. "John—*John!* For goodness sake—what is it?"

"Don't know, Mum. Maybe we were—were seeing things." John was going to be the staunch older brother.

"What did you *think* you saw?"

"Lady in a red dress. Running away up the passage. And Mummy——"

"Yes, yes?"

"She was on fire, Mummy. And she was crying, even though we couldn't hear anything. I know she was crying. Sort of screaming, waving her arms. Only not making a sound."

"Oh Johnnie—I think you *must* have been seeing things——"

But suddenly there was a scream from the little girl, who had disentangled herself from her mother's skirt, seen something, and now rushed round behind for safety. "Oh Mummy—*Mummy!* It's awful, it's back. LOOK!"

Then Sue saw it. Indeed, she could hardly fail to see the girl in the flame-red dress, for the apparition suddenly came out from the east wing, burst on the half-landing where Johnnie was standing, then ran, or stumbled, down the staircase. And—heaven above, it was true!—she was in flames. The whole dress, from the high lace-and-satin collar to the ankle-length skirt, was a mass of flame.

Sue Wilson was a woman of resource and she picked up a travel rug from the floor, a thing two of the children had dressed up in, and hurled herself at the girl as she came down the staircase; flung her arms, with the rug in them, right round the poor, silently screaming, creature, and fell with her to the stair, rolling over and over to the bottom.

There was nothing there. Gasping, she got to her feet, rug in hand, stared about her. "Where—where did she go?"

"Oh Mummy—you sort of missed her. She went right on. Out the door, Mummy——"

"But, Dick—*the door is closed*——"

So there *was* a ghost, after all. But what a horrifying one. And in front of the children, too. Though now she thought of it, none of her own three looked shaken by the experience.

"It *was* a ghost, Mummy—wasn't it?"

"I suppose so, Helen. A ghost. I didn't think I believed in them——"

"*We* knew about it! Didn't we, Dick? We knew about the burning lady. They know *all* about it at school, Mummy. Oh—it's *terribly* exciting!"

They calmed down. "It's all right, Mummy, you see, she's been on fire for years and years and years. So she can't mind, really. Can she?"

"I just don't know, Johnnie. But tell me what they say at school."

The next day the vicar called. He had heard what happened, he wished to explain the whole matter. As a minister of the Church, he of course denied the possibility of ghosts "—ghosts and other psychic phenomena, Mrs Wilson". Tricks could be played, though, on the imagination, particularly when such a story—such a ghastly and true story—was common knowledge. The horror of 1819. It was fully documented, and all three principals in the tragedy were listed in parish records.

And the girl herself—poor, poor creature—was buried in the churchyard. If Mrs Wilson cared to come along, the vicar would be only too happy to show the grave to her. Perhaps she might come to matins on Sunday. And bring the children. That would be killing two birds with one stone, would it not?

Sue listened to the story, went to church on Sunday and was shown the grave. "Teresa—beloved wife of Giles Bartlett. 10 May 1801—1 June 1819."

So she had been a Bartlett—and the poor creature had died a few weeks after her eighteenth birthday.

Some of the details from the vicar seemed improbable and she wrote a careful letter to Colonel Bartlett in Nice. No, of course she wasn't in the slightest alarmed: the children had thought it a lark, a tremendous lark. She was just interested, that was all. Just interested.

Colonel Bartlett wrote back by return. "My dear Susan. I hardly know whether to apologize or congratulate. Yes, indeed, we have a family ghost. No doubt the vicar—old gasbag—has described her. I never volunteered the information because frankly I never thought for a moment Teresa would put in an appearance. *I've* never seen her. Nor did my father. Though my grandmother always maintained *she* had. Teresa died at the height of a monster party, thrown especially for her. They always say she'll only come back when another as big (and as noisy!) takes place. I congratulate you!"

Sue looked about her. Today the house was back in order. But it was no difficult feat to picture it all as it had been four days ago, after the children's party.

"This is the story, then. And I hope you've a strong stomach."

She looked at the clock. Half past three. Children on the way back from school. Should she leave it till later, when they were in bed? After dinner?

She would read it now. All fifteen closely written pages. She dumped herself firmly in the armchair by the billiard-room fire.

"My ancestor, a Lady Bartlett of the early 19th century, had a much beloved only son. His name was Giles, and from all accounts he was a fine, upstanding fellow, with a mind of his own. Sadly, he disappears from history at the end of this story. Giles was twenty when he met Teresa, the daughter, not of our local vicar, which in Lady B's eyes might have been just acceptable, but of a Methodist— of all things—from Towcester. Teresa Wrightson was beautiful, gentle and highly intelligent, and the fact that she was not well-born might seem unimportant today. But not in the eyes of Lady B. Giles, of course, fell madly in love with Teresa—he was lucky, I suppose, that she responded, because half the neighbourhood, from Aylesbury to Towcester, was madly in love with Teresa Wrightson. Heirs to great estates, farmers' sons, students out from Oxford, every male was hooked on Teresa.

"But it was to Giles—heaven knows why--that she gave her heart. One wonders whether he deserved it. For his mother, Lady Bartlett—who was thirty-nine and a famous beauty, at the time— was able to get him to refuse to marry Teresa. She would be quite, quite unsuitable—a deplorable *mésalliance*—and for *both* their sakes (that was Lady B's punch line: for *both* their sakes) Giles must not marry her.

"Giles agreed. Agreed to go abroad for six months, to Sweden where distant members of my family have always been involved in business in Gothenburg. He went to Gothenburg in the middle of 1818, and there he was fêted, shown the sights—whatever they are—of Gothenburg, and the pretty Swedish girls. And did very little work.

"On 4th February, 1819, Giles returned. This was as it had been planned between his mother and the family lawyers. He then went —also as planned—to digs in London, from which he became articled to solicitors in Lincoln's Inn. And from London he wrote a letter to Teresa, asking her to come immediately and marry him.

"She did. Giles and Teresa were married, surrounded by friends, in Chelsea Parish Church. There are reports of the ceremony, and it went well. A handsome young couple—terribly young and terribly in love—with a churchful of young and eager friends wishing them luck. And, far more important, an uncle of hers, who offered Giles a job at several times his old salary. Which of course he accepted. Hardly surprising that they should feel confident of the future. Confident enough even to write Lady Bartlett.

"Giles wrote, told her of the marriage, apologized for not asking her. He hinted at the truth which was that she wouldn't have come in any case. He rhapsodized on—I've got the letter—saying he hoped some day he might present his wife to his mother—the most important women in his life. The *only* women in his life. He tactfully, carefully, mentioned the marvellous job, which Teresa's uncle——

"So perhaps he almost expected his mother's reply. And of course —she was *delighted* he'd married that *charming* girl. From the moment Lady B had clapped eyes on Teresa Wrightson, she'd known this was a girl in a million. And so on. The only reason why she, Giles's mama, had objected to betrothal in the first place, was that they were both so *young*.

"Sadly, Giles was young enough to believe this. (But as you know, Susan, when a woman takes a hate on another, because of what she thinks the other plans to do with her husband or son or lover or whatever, that hatred goes on, right to the grave. Giles didn't know this.) They accepted, with delight, an invitation to spend a fortnight at Wheldon. Lady B would be absolutely thrilled to have them both under her roof, her long-lost son and his delightful new bride. It would be the proudest moment of her life. And of course, some day, he—and she—would inherit the place.

"They came. The stage-coach in those days, the main coach to the north, passed through East Claydon and on, via Padbury, to Buckingham, Towcester and the rest of it. They travelled on it, were set down at the age-old Verney Arms in East Claydon, were lifted from there by Lady B's coachman.

"Lady B couldn't have been kinder. She kissed her new daughter-in-law with affection, even fervour. Teresa was taken below stairs to see the cook, the scullery maids, the butler, the footmen, the lot (all the things which you, dear Susan, must miss—just as I do). This was the new young mistress: some day when she, Lady Bartlett, had passed on, her son and his lovely bride would reign in her stead.

"And naturally, young Teresa—just eighteen—was thrilled. Not for her own sake, but for Giles's. She knew how he'd felt about being sent abroad. It was Giles coming back into his own.

"And on June the first, there was the ball. A ruddy great ball, with an orchestra playing in what is now the billiard room (and where you're probably reading this) and the whole ground floor lit up like a fairy palace. As was the custom in those days (may still be, I don't know much about these things now) various county bigwigs were persuaded to throw dinners for twenty, to bring their guests to the ball afterwards. It began at nine-thirty. My great-great-great-great-great (I *think* that's right) grandmother threw a dinner party for forty, in the house, and the servants cheerfully cleared the whole damn thing up at the end, to make room for whatever the dining room was supposed to be that night. I believe that night, and with forty place settings, it took less than ten minutes to clear.

"No matter. At nine-thirty, as predicted, the first party arrived. Ten minutes later, another. By quarter past ten, the ball was assembled. The best part of two hundred people, some coming from as far as London. The orchestra—also from London, and spending the night at Wheldon—had got stuck into the first waltz. *Their* morale, in particular, was soaring, with no problem about getting back, a prospect of unlimited food and drink and warm beds. The party, within seconds of kick-off, was an assured success.

"At exactly ten-thirty, Lady B sought out Teresa. She was looking particularly lovely, and in fact startling—for the year 1819 —in that she was wearing a red dress. *You've seen it, Susan.* So I'll just remind you that, apart from being red, dark red, it had a square of lace across the bosom which ran up to the neck and joined the red satin, with ribbon, to make a collar, like a choirboy's. There was a red flower at the bottom of the lace, and the skirt flared out, with a pleat at each side, to a wide thing touching the ground. She was wearing—at this stage—no jewellery of any sort."

"Oh, my God," said Susan. She sat there alone in the great room with its billiard table dwarfed in the corner, the cues like fire-arms against the wall. Then she got up. She went out into the hall, looked up the wide staircase where only four days before the girl—Teresa Wrightson—had rushed down.

With a dreadful hollowness at the pit of the stomach, she went back to the armchair in the billiard room, started to read.

"Old Lady B—but one must beware of thinking of her in these terms because she was far from old, and exceedingly glamorous— took Teresa aside, away from the pounding and scraping of the orchestra, the shuffling of four hundred feet, and said, 'My dear, I've long wanted to do something for you. I felt you must wonder why I didn't at first welcome you with open arms. Well—that's all over now. You are my one and only, dearest daughter-in-law. And for you, there is only one gift I can give. Apart, of course, from my son. That is my diamond necklace.'

"And no doubt Teresa gasped at this—because old Lady B's necklace (which is still with us, in a safe) was an extraordinary piece of jewellery. Hundreds and hundreds of diamonds, some of them enormous, set into a thing like—well, you know the thing I mean. Only one doesn't see it in diamonds.

" 'So come with me, dear—we'll go up to my room and put it on. Yes, dear, it will be your very own. All your own, from tonight. And you can make an entrance with it, down the stairs.'

"The band was playing like mad, and only a few people noticed the two leave, go up the stair (just as it is today, Susan, and no doubt as unsafe and as creaky) with the old girl carrying a candle. They got to the half-landing—where you saw all this happening—turned right into the passage towards the east wing. They walked along chatting and then somehow Lady B's candle blew out. This was the only one they had between them, and she asked Teresa to go back to the party, find Giles, get him to bring another. They needed a second candle, silly of her to start off with only one, and they could re-light the first from the one he brought.

"And—this was important—*Giles* had to bring it. She wanted, she said, Giles to see how lovely his bride looked in the necklace, before anyone else.

"Flushed with excitement and gratitude, Teresa walked quickly back to the half-landing and down into the hall—and the ball. There was no difficulty in finding Giles, for he came up to her, complete with partner, to ask what she wanted. She told him, he managed to jettison a girl gracefully in the midst of an old-fashioned waltz, and took a silver candle-stick off a table. Together they went up the stair.

"They went up the steps at the end of the east wing, the short flight, and back along the floor above till they got to Lady B's room. (A huge place, full of lumber now, junk of all sorts, which you probably haven't visited, but may want to, now. A sagging floor and a view out over the pond. And just to make sure you've got the right place, the initials 'T.B.' carved high up on the right-hand window frame. Not poor Teresa's. Just mine.)

"Lady B opened the drawer of her dressing table, took out her red-leather jewel-box. (That's in the safe too—big enough to store a few dozen eggs or a brace of pheasants.) Slowly, lovingly, she opened it—and Teresa gasped as she drew out the necklace, like a fisherman pulling in a net full of glittering fish.

"The older woman carefully clasped it around her neck.

" 'Stand there, dear—that's the best place, you can see the whole of yourself in the mirror. Goodness, how lovely you look! Giles dear—doesn't your bride look lovely?'

"Teresa was wedged into a corner of the room, looking at herself in the long mirror.

" '*Isn't* she lovely?' said Lady B to her son. 'Oh how thrilled I am that at last there's someone to carry them off, show them to advantage.' (You can imagine, Susan, what a mother-in-law means, when she says this.) And she got Giles up close, very close, to his glittering, embarrassed bride, candle in hand. 'Just *look* at the diamonds round her throat, in that light——'

"And then she pushed him.

"She pushed Giles with all her might, so that the candle set fire, instantly, to the lace round Teresa's neck, and a second later, to the rest of it. Within five seconds, the girl was ablaze.

" 'Oh, oh, goodness!' cried Lady B. 'We must put it out——' Or words to that effect, one assumes. And if the poor girl had stayed put for a moment, perhaps Giles might have succeeded.

"But she looked at him, suddenly, with a look of hatred. As if she knew this was part of a plan. While he turned, absolutely frantic, for a jug of water to throw—it was just there, a yard or two off, in those pre-plumbing days—she turned and ran down the steps to the big corridor, along that corridor you know so well, on to the landing and down the main stairs, while the orchestra stopped playing and everyone rushed, in a moment of hideous panic, to help her.

"Through all this—the reports all agree—she uttered not a sound. Just like your ghost.

"They knocked her to the ground, wrapped her in rugs, poured water, absurdly, on top of these—but it was far too late. The dress had been burnt by the time she reached the ballroom, and when the flames were gone and they unrolled the rug, it was to find her body, terribly burnt—and naked. Only the necklace, untouched, survived.

"There were three doctors among the guests, but it was too late. She made no sound: she was dying fast. When poor Giles caught up with her, lay weeping beside her, she just turned her face away. And died.

"It turned out that the chambermaid had been putting those old stone hot-water bottles (hundreds of them in the pantry cupboard) into the family beds, and she was standing, terrified, in the shadows. She gave evidence at the trial, and Lady B was sentenced and ultimately hanged.

"Oh *yes*, Susan—I have an ancestress who was, very deservedly, hanged. So perhaps I may be forgiven for not rushing at you with the story——"

"Mum—we're *back*!"

"As for Giles, he went to Australia right after. And no one has since heard a sound from him or his putative descendants. Which is why my branch of the family owns Wheldon today——"

"*Mum!*"

"Yes, dears?"

"You know, the others say—if we can make a *real din*, a really smashing one, Mum, then we can get that silly old ghost out. That's what they say, Mum. How about it, eh, Mum?—let's make a *real* din. Make the lady come out, down the stairs, again. And this time, maybe we can catch her——"

With This Ring

Between the increasingly fashionable health resort of Bournemouth and the ancient town of Christchurch there stood, in the 1870s, a tiny village now covered by the suburban sprawl of Boscombe. Perched on a pine-clad cliff, it enjoyed exhilarating air and an unrivalled view across the Channel to the Isle of Wight. Now that the railway had come to Bournemouth, more and more visitors were becoming drawn to this pleasant place and building for themselves fine modern houses, elaborately gabled and ornamented.

In one of these, small but elegant, lived Mrs Elizabeth Grey. Her stockbroker husband had died, leaving her a young widow with two small daughters, Mary and Ellen. Mary, the younger, having shown signs of delicate lungs, Mrs Grey decided to move her household from London to this healthier neighbourhood. Her decision had been justified; Mary recovered entirely from her early weakness, and the sisters grew up to be robust young women, with a fondness for open air and exercise far from typical of their generation. Whatever the weather, they were to be seen every day walking in the lanes, exploring old smugglers' haunts, climbing venturesomely down the chines in skirts far shorter than their mother thought proper, or gathering the wild flowers that grew in profusion. Sometimes, when the sun was too strong for these pursuits, they played croquet on the lawn, or played on the swing that had been suspended for them between two tall trees, laughing merrily and pushing each other higher and higher. But their favourite pastime was to take a picnic luncheon to Ayscliffe Fall, a celebrated waterfall about a quarter of a mile from their own garden. Here they would lie in the dappled shadows, a basket of sandwiches, cakes and lemonade beside them, sketching or talking of those things that fill the minds of young girls: above all, talking of lovers.

Even in that sparsely-populated district there were young men in plenty. Families were large, and there had been no youth-devouring war since the Crimea. As the girls grew up, few evenings passed without a tributary visit to Ayscliffe House from one or other of the eligible bachelors of Hampshire. Ellen Grey was comely, but Mary was outstandingly pretty, and of a livelier disposition than her sister. The fame of her charms had spread into Bournemouth itself, which, flirt as she was, delighted her. She would bestow a favour with one hand, and take it away with the other; graciously accept an invitation, and change her mind at the last moment; all with a grace and good humour that disarmed exasperated young men who might have been angry with another girl. Pressed for an answer to the most important of questions, she would say nothing but turn to her piano and sing lightly one of her favourite Scots songs.

> I'm ower young, I'm ower young,
> I'm ower young to marry yet;
> I'm ower young—'twould be a sin
> To take me frae my Mammy yet!

Among Mary's suitors was one who would not take "no" for an answer. John Bodneys rode daily from the inland village where he lived, eight miles away, to court her. He was twenty-three, six years older than Mary, and was employed in the office of his father, a solicitor. Friends said they would make a handsome couple: John, big, dark-haired, of a Byronic cast of features; Mary, slight, blonde and blue-eyed. He had, he told her, prospects: he could give her everything she wanted.

"But I want no more than I have now," replied Mary.

"I can give you love, Mary! A love you will never receive from any man but me."

"They all say that," said Mary composedly, fingering the piano.

"But they don't mean it as I do! Put that damned music away

and listen. Mary, I love you, I adore you, your face comes between me and everything else in the world. How can you treat me so lightly, so cruelly?"

"Perhaps I wouldn't if you weren't so very serious about it, John. You know I don't like serious people or things. I think I'm too young for them."

"I can wait for you!" he cried eagerly. "You'll change—you'll learn how much a love like mine can mean."

"Perhaps I will . . . I don't know. Look, the sun's out and there's Ellen back from her walk. Let's go and play croquet."

"I don't want to play croquet! Mary, you must give me an answer. I'll wait a year, if you like—until you're eighteen, old enough to know your own mind."

"Oh, very well," she answered indifferently. "I suppose you may ask me again then. But don't shout so, or look so black, or you'll frighten me and I won't answer you at all."

He watched her move lightly away through the french doors out into the sunlit garden, and his look was that of one who sees a treasure-chest crammed with gold beyond his reach.

In the year that followed it seemed that Mary was indeed changing, as he had hoped. She became quieter, less of a romp, more willing to help her mother with domestic and social duties. Sometimes, sitting by the waterfall, she would gaze at the tumbling diamond drops with an air of intense concentration, pencil to her lips, then scribble busily. The watchful, loving Ellen saw that her sister had taken to writing verse; and she smiled to herself.

John Bodneys was delighted at the change in his beloved, who had begun to be kinder to him. That she was also kinder to her other suitors he did not know, for it aroused his jealousy too sharply to see her in their company, and he arranged his visits to avoid this, even though it might mean the sacrifice of a precious hour with her. In September she was to have her eighteenth birthday, and when he reminded her of this, and of her promise, she did not answer pertly as once she would have done, but smiled with a new, charming shyness.

"She is mine," he thought triumphantly.

What John Bodneys did not know was that among the young men who came to Ayscliffe House was one Basil Osborne. He had never set eyes on Osborne, who had recently come to live in

Bournemouth with his parents in one of the handsome new villas near the town centre. There, at an evening party, Mary and he had met and had at once fallen in love.

Basil Osborne was physically and temperamentally a direct contrast to John Bodneys. Fair, ruddy-complexioned and athletic, he was of as sunny a disposition as Mary, and Mrs Grey sometimes thought they could easily be mistaken for brother and sister, and wished she had had such a son. At least he would be her son-in-law: she wholly approved of the match, as did Basil's parents. There seemed no reason why the engagement should not be announced, but the young couple wished to defer it until Basil's coming of age, which occurred a week before Mary's birthday.

"At least, my dear," said Mrs Grey, "I think you should tell John before the engagement is made public. He will be disappointed and humiliated if he hears of it only when everybody else does."

"I don't *want* to tell him," replied Mary. "I want nobody to know until Basil's party, because it's my secret, and I shall never have such a lovely secret again, Mama!"

On Basil's birthday night a splendid celebration was held at his father's house. Amid champagne, kisses and congratulations, the happy news was broken, and the date of the wedding fixed for six weeks to the day.

Next morning Mary sat down at her bureau and wrote a letter to John Bodneys. A year ago, she wrote, he had asked her to give him an answer to his proposal of marriage on the day she became eighteen. That would be very soon—in less than a week—but she would give him his answer now. It was No, and she was very sorry to disappoint him, but she had fallen in love with someone else and they were to be married, and John was to be happy in her happiness, and come to the wedding.

"There!" she said, sealing the envelope. "That settles everything."

"Oh, my dear!" Ellen shook her head. "I'm afraid it doesn't. He will be down here directly, and we shall have goodness knows what storms and tempers."

But no answer came to the letter, and not a sign of John Bodneys did they see for the next six weeks. The evening before Mary's wedding Ellen was gathering ferns in the wood near Ayscliffe House when a rustling sound behind her made her turn sharply round. The figure that hurried swiftly away among the trees might have been Bodneys—it had his height and style of dress—but it might not have been. She told Mary about the incident as they were laying out the bridal clothes.

"Oh, poor John!" said Mary, but without much feeling. "I expect he'd come for a last glimpse of me and didn't want to talk to you."

The next morning, a golden October sun shone on a happy, radiant bride, as she left the parish church on her husband's arm. "There's a good omen for her!" remarked the spectators. Children threw flowers at her feet, the purple of Michaelmas daisy and the red and white of late roses. She picked up a white rose, kissed it, and put it in her bosom, and the happy villagers cheered and blessed her.

By Mary's wish the simple reception was held in the drawing-room of Ayscliffe House, the guests being friends from the neighbourhood and neighbours of Basil's parents in Bournemouth. Toasts were proposed, healths drunk, both mothers wept. In the late afternoon, guests began to talk of leaving: it was time for the married couple to depart for their honeymoon. Mary went upstairs to change into street clothes, accompanied by Ellen.

In the bedroom they had shared for so many years the sisters embraced fondly, and Ellen could not keep back her tears.

"I shall miss you so, Mary! How can I bear it?"

"Dearest Nell, I shan't be far away, you know that—only at Ringwood. We shall see almost as much of each other . . . no, we shan't. And I can't help feeling very sad too, to be going away from you and this dear home." She looked round at the pleasant room, the big comfortable bed they had shared, the friendly light windows leading to a pretty balcony with a flight of steps down to the little enclosed garden that had always been "the girls' garden".

"Nell, will you leave me alone, just for a few minutes, to say goodbye to it?"

"But I haven't unhooked you yet—you can never manage all those hooks!"

"I'll call you when I'm ready," said Mary. "I shan't be long."

Ellen, at the door, looked back and saw her sister, still in her bridal white, standing pensively by the window. She stroked the pink striped curtain, and gently laid her cheek against it in farewell. Ellen went slowly downstairs and rejoined the party in the drawing-room, who were now drinking tea.

Fifteen minutes passed, and half an hour, and still Mary had not come down.

"I think you'd better fetch her, Ellen," said Mrs Grey. "Chapman says the horses are getting very restless, and Basil thinks they ought to be on their way soon."

Ellen returned upstairs and tapped at the door. "Mary, dear!"

There was no reply. Ellen called again, and knocked, more loudly, answered only by silence. She shook the handle, and found that the door was locked. Alarmed, she rushed downstairs and returned accompanied by her mother and Basil. They called in concert, without result. Basil's usually ruddy face was pale.

"We must break the door in," he said.

The door was strong, but the shoulders of the young men in the party were stronger, and at last it burst open.

The room was empty. Mary's going-away dress lay on the bed, with its matching bonnet and gloves; of her there was no sign. The party ran out on to the balcony, and into the enclosed garden. But she was not there. Only, on the path from the balcony steps lay something small and white. It was the rose Mary had worn as she walked from her wedding.

Basil picked it up, held it in his hands, then put it in his buttonhole, with the mechanical action of a sleepwalker.

It was his last link with his bride.

For days afterwards the countryside was searched for her. The police circulated a description throughout the country; advertisements appeared in newspapers, checks were made at railway stations and ports. But nobody had seen the missing girl. *The Mystery of Edwin Drood* was still fresh in the public mind, with its great unsolved question, and the disappearance of Mary Osborne appeared to be a real-life parallel. Mary was called "the Mistletoe Bough bride", from the gruesome popular song which related how a fair young lady disappeared during a game of hide-and-seek on her wedding night:

> *They sought her that night, they sought her next day,*
> *They sought her in vain till a week passed away,*
> *In the highest, the lowest, the loneliest spot,*
> *Young Lovel sought wildly but found her not.*
> *And years flew by, and their grief at last*
> *Was told as a sorrowful tale long past.*

So it was with the mystery of Mary. It was thought that she had either had some form of brainstorm and made away with herself, perhaps by drowning, or that she had eloped with a lover. If so, it was not with John Bodneys, for he was still at home, a silent, unapproachable man. Some months later he went abroad, and was not seen again in the district.

Basil Osborne did not re-marry, even when Mary had been missing long enough for her death to be presumed. He died comparatively young, in the house that was to have been theirs, for he had kept it on in the pathetic hope that one day she might come home. Mrs Grey had died only a few years after the darkened wedding day. Of the joyful bridal party only Ellen remained; changed from the cheerful girl she had been to a prematurely ageing woman, withdrawn in manner—a little mad, some said, from the shock. It was as though she and Mary had been identical twins rather than mere sisters. She remained in Ayscliffe House, with only one servant for company, Maggie Williams, who had grown up with the sisters and had been devoted to Mary.

Eighteen years passed. One November night, a great gale rose, and wrought havoc on the coast of Hampshire. Chimney-pots came down, fishing-boats were swamped, trees fell and outbuildings collapsed. When morning came, it was seen that the great oak that grew by the waterfall had been one of the victims. The wind, sweeping round the corner of the cliff, had brought it crashing down on neighbouring trees, completely blocking the path that led past the fall. Workmen were sent to clear it away and remove the rocks and boulders it had brought down with it. Suddenly one of them paused, and peered into a cleft between two large rocks.

"Looks like somebody's dropped the family jools down 'ere," he said.

His mate looked over his shoulder.

"Where? Can't see nothing."

The man pointed. "Bit of red shiny stuff—look, the sun's right on it now. There, by that bunch of dry twigs."

The other had keener eyes. He stooped closer and uttered an oath
"Them's no twigs, George. Them's the bones of a 'uman hand."

They called their companions, rolled away the smaller rock, and stood looking down at what lay there. It was a natural tomb they had uncovered. In the narrow rocky bed lay the scattered bones of a complete skeleton. The skull had rolled some distance away; one of the men picked it up.

"Young, whoever it was. Most of the teeth there."

A wisp of hair adhered to the dry brown dome; it was impossible to tell what the colour had been, or what clothes had once covered the body, for only scattered rags remained. The only identification left was the red-stoned ring on the finger-bone, with a wedding-ring below it.

They collected the bones, carried them to their cart, and drove off to the village. The news spread like wildfire, and speculation flourished. Had it been an accident or a murder? The doctor arrived, and pronounced the remains to be those of a young woman. Then one of the older inhabitants remembered.

"Could it be Mary Osborne?"

They sent for Ellen, and she came to the room at the police station which was used as an occasional mortuary. Dressed in the black she had worn for eighteen years, she stood by the table on which lay something covered by a sheet. When they pulled the sheet aside she did not shudder, but looked steadily at the bones, as if clothing them with flesh. Her gaze paused at the hand.

"That is the garnet engagement ring she wore on her wedding-day."

"Then the . . . body, ma'am?"

"It is my sister."

And with a calmness that horrified the watchers, she stooped and kissed the bony brow. Then she turned and went out of the room, looking neither to right nor to left; and none dared to go after and comfort her.

They buried Mary in the churchyard that she had last entered as a bride. Before the coffin was closed, Ellen made a request that appalled the undertaker.

"Give me her hand."

They dared not refuse a woman who seemed, in her quiet way, to be half-mad. The frail carpals, metacarpals and phalanges were detached and given to her. She carried home all of Mary that would ever revisit Ayscliffe House.

Soon afterwards Ellen fell ill. It was said that the shock had been too much for her; that her heart had broken at last, now that she knew Mary was dead. The Rector's wife, calling to inquire after her, was startled and somewhat revolted to see, on a table in the drawing-room, a small glass box in which was displayed on black velvet the skeleton hand, the rings on the third finger polished and shining.

"*Very* bad taste. Quite blasphemous, indeed. I shall ask my husband to protest."

"He won't do no good, ma'am," said Maggie Williams. "She's set on keeping it there, and I'm to have it when she's gone."

"You, Maggie? But surely you would not wish to keep such a gruesome thing! You will have it decently reburied, of course."

"Never, ma'am. She says she'll *walk* if I do. And I don't want no haunting."

On her deathbed, Ellen again made Maggie swear never to part with the hand. Maggie ventured to question her dying mistress as to the reason behind this stern command. "For I can't see what good it'll do, ma'am, to her that's gone."

The sunken eyelids lifted.

"One day it will avenge her, Maggie. I cannot tell you how, but I know this to be true."

Within a few hours, Ellen Grey was dead. When the will was read, Maggie found to her delighted astonishment that she was the principal legatee. Sums had been left to the Church and to a few of Ellen's favourite charities: the rest, with the house, was to be Maggie's.

With such an unexpected fortune, Maggie could hardly consider continuing in service. She was an active woman, still on the right side of fifty. She decided that the best course would be to buy a public house and run it herself. Within a few weeks of the sale of Ayscliffe House, a small inn called the Seven Stars, on the Christchurch Road, became available. It had a good reputation and an excellent carriage trade. Maggie bought it and threw herself with housewifely zeal into the work of modernization and improvement. Old cupboards and settles were ripped out, bright wallpaper and chocolate paint adorned the walls, anaglypta covered the old smoke-blackened ceilings; behind the bar erupted dazzling mirrors in ornate settings. On the bar itself, prominently displayed, was the skeleton hand in its casket: for Maggie was faithful to her vow, and had, besides, a shrewd idea that the grisly relic might attract customers.

She was perfectly right. Never an evening passed but someone would make a gruesome joke about it or retell the old story to a stranger. Such was the case one wild winter night, when the wind roared about the inn and the signboard creaked and groaned—just as the old gallows used to do, remarked a customer who remembered the days of public gibbets.

"It was such another night as this when the great oak came down," he added.

"Ah. Twenty years ago, and more," said another.

"Maybe they'd never have found the skeleton, but for that."

"What skeleton?" A tall man in a cloak and cap—not one of the regulars—spoke from the fireside where he had been drinking his ale, one foot on the fender.

"Why, *that*," answered Maggie from behind the bar, pointing to the hand. The stranger moved nearer, his eyes fixed on the glass box. "Terrible grim, he looked," they remembered afterwards.

"Don't you know the story of it?" Maggie asked. "Sim here'll tell you it, for the price of a pint—won't you, Sim?"

But the stranger did not respond. He was leaning on the bar, half-swooning, his cheeks paper-white, staring down at the bones. "Blood, blood," he muttered. "Blood, blood." With his own right hand he touched the box. Those who were there swore to each other that they saw blood drip from his finger-tips. He seemed about to collapse, and two of the men led him to a bench, took off his cap and loosened his collar. An awful suspicion had seized Maggie. When she saw his face, she knew that her guess had been right. She had been a young girl last time she had seen that face, but it was not one to be forgotten.

"Mr Bodneys!"

He stirred, and groaned.

"Yes, I am John Bodneys. I had to come back—I meant to stay away, never to see the place again. But it drew me like a magnet."

"You killed her—our Miss Mary!"

"Yes, I killed her. I was mad with jealousy when she married that man. I stayed in the woods all the day of the wedding; I could not bear to come nearer. Then it was too much for me, and I hid in the garden below her balcony. When I saw her at the window, alone, I rushed in and begged her to come away with me—yes, even then, with his rings on her finger!"

The company listened in horror as the tale poured out, as fluently as if he had told it over and over again.

"When she refused, I said I would take her by force—make her mine, so that her fine puppy of a bridegroom would never want her. I dragged her out and down the steps—she tried to scream but I stopped her mouth. Somehow I got her down the path as far as the waterfall. Then I pulled her up over the rocks, towards the wood at the top. She struggled like a wild cat—she tore my face. I think I half-choked her. Then she fell—down between the rocks, into a deep cleft. I couldn't see her, or tell whether she was alive or dead. I waited a little, but she made no sound; and I was afraid, and ran away from that dreadful place, and went home."

"How could you! How could you!" cried Maggie.

"Do you think I haven't paid for it in hell these many years? But not enough, I know that. Take me to a magistrate, and let them hang me as I deserve."

But before they could hang John Bodneys he died; of no disease the prison authorities could identify. Maggie took the skeleton hand to the Rector of Ayscliffe, and it was buried with Mary's remains. As her sister had prophesied, it had done its avenging work, and now could rest.

The Vampire of Croglin

The district that surrounds Penrith, in Cumberland, is not only wildly beautiful but much haunted. Edenhall, with its magic Cup that held the luck of the house; the Weird Hill of Wallow Crag, where the spirit of the terrible Sir Jamie Lowther used to walk; the ghosts of King Arthur and his knights by the road to Lowther Castle, known as the King's Round Table. At Little Salkeld is a circle of stones called Long Meg and her Daughters, thought to have been a Druidical temple; and here, when one of the stones was lifted, there took place what a native of those parts guardedly called "manifestations of an unpleasant nature".

It is old country, where Man has not yet got the upper hand in spite of the spread of communications. Nature spirits dwell on riverside and lonely crag, old Romans and Britons fight out their battles still, castles hold within their massive walls more than their flesh-and-blood inhabitants.

Croglin Hall, in the village of Croglin, north-east of Penrith, had stood for centuries; a lonely, low-built house owned by a family called Fisher. In 1874 the Fishers departed and a Mr Edward Cranswell, from Australia, bought it and moved in with his young sister and brother, Amelia and Michael. Coming from that great continent, they thought nothing of the isolated situation of their new home, or of the wild landscape surrounding it. Compared with the outback, the district was populous: the Hall was neighboured by the little churchyard, whose ancient memorials dating from Norman days charmed the young people who had grown up in a young country.

Edward Cranswell, however, did not assume foolishly that a peaceful rustic spot was automatically danger-free. There were wandering marauders in the bush: they might well exist in Cumberland. Because of the curious architecture of the house, all the windows were on ground level and extremely vulnerable. Cranswell gave orders that they should be made to fasten securely, and that every night bedroom doors should be locked and each window kept shut. No outcry was made by his Victorian household: night air was still thought to be bad for one.

It was a summer night in 1875, when the Cranswells had been in the house about a year, that Amelia Cranswell sat up in bed and wished that her brother could be persuaded to relax his rule. The day had been hot with a sultry heat not often felt in the far north of England. The burning rays of the sun had given way at dusk to a brilliant full moon, and the young Cranswells had stayed up until nearly midnight, strolling in the garden. Michael quoted Romeo. Amelia retaliated with several verses "To the Moon" from the *Poetical Album* which was her favourite reading, for she was a romantic young lady. Then, as the night began to chill, Michael led his sister back to the house. Their brother and the servants were already in bed.

It was fortunate that Amelia's bedroom windows overlooked the wide lawn of the Hall, now a sheet of palest silver, like a calm sea. Behind it a row of tall trees marked the end of the grounds, beyond which lay the churchyard. Amelia was quite unable to sleep for the heat and stuffiness of her room. She sat up in bed, suffering in the high-necked, bishop-sleeved nightdress of the period, but consoling herself with the beauty of the scene outside. She began to grow a little sleepy. Her mind strayed to other, even brighter, moons in the far-off Antipodes: to a calm bay of the Pacific, the water motionless as grass, just as the grass outside was. Her eyes were closing, her head began to sink towards the pillow. Suddenly a movement outside roused her. She sat up with a jerk.

There was somebody crossing the lawn. Edward's fears about night wanderers were justified, after all. The moonlight could not be as bright as she had thought, for she could not make out any details of the figure which—oh, horrors!—was approaching her window with a sort of motion between hopping and skimming.

In barely a moment, the terrified girl saw a face appear at her window. What kind of a face she could never afterwards say, except that it was dreadful. A scratching noise on the glass told her that the person outside was attempting to break in: it was trying to force a diamond pane out of the leads that held it.

Amelia fell, rather than jumped, out of bed, and ran to the locked door. Fumbling with the key, she knocked it on to the floor. She knelt and scrabbled for it, the noises at the window growing louder and louder. In her panic, she failed to find the key; the moonlight did not reach into that corner of the room, and her carpet was thickly patterned. She began to shriek, and went on shrieking.

The window-pane fell inwards. As it did so, Amelia heard the pounding footsteps of Edward approaching her door, followed by those of Michael. She could hear them outside, shouting her name.

"Amelia! What is it? What's the matter! Let us in, for heaven's sake!"

The door-handle rattled and turned in vain. A new sound at the window brought her to her feet, and her screams broke out afresh, chilling the blood of the listening men. A thin arm—was it of bone? —came through the hole where the pane had been, and the window-hasp was lifted. Amelia opened her mouth to shriek again, but no sound came. Her clenched fists flew to her mouth, and she watched, her back to the door, as Something opened the window and climbed in.

Five minutes later the frantic brothers managed to burst open the door. The window was swinging open. On the floor lay Amelia, her white lawn nightdress covered with great patches of fresh blood, which was still running from cruel wounds on her shoulders and bosom, from which the nightdress had been torn. Her face and throat were lacerated by savage scratches or bites. She was mercifully unconscious.

Out of the corner of his eye Michael caught sight of Something running—hopping?—across the lawn. He rushed out of the house and gave chase, but whatever it had been had vanished completely. The lawn was empty and quiet. An owl hooted, and far off a fox barked.

Had it been a fox, the brothers asked themselves, which had savaged their sister—or some other creature of the wild? The doctor who treated Amelia's injuries confirmed that they were mainly bites.

"Some kind of dingo?" Michael suggested. His brother pointed out that wild dogs are not a common feature of the English landscape, and that in any case dogs do not remove panes from windows in order to open them. Amelia was at first too ill to be questioned about what she had seen, but when she was able to talk described it as semi-human and terribly emaciated.

"A half-starved maniac, living wild," Edward Cranswell concluded. "Better get a band of local men together and flush him out."

He found willing co-operation, for, the Cranswells now heard for the first time, other attacks of the same kind had been made in the neighbourhood, always with a woman or girl as the victim. Most had been lucky, with their menfolk at hand when the attacker struck. But one child had been marked for life. In the reticent way of country-dwellers, nobody had thought to warn the Cranswells of the peril that lurked near them.

The most sensible thing, obviously, was for Edward Cranswell to sell Croglin Hall: but it would not be easy to sell after such an alarming occurrence. The next best thing would be for Amelia to leave it, as she was the only one threatened. This she refused to do. In spite of the shock she had received, she insisted on returning to it after a recuperative holiday in Switzerland, and occupying her old room. The brothers could do nothing to persuade her otherwise. But Edward said that in future all bedroom doors were to be left unlocked, so that if she saw or heard anything suspicious she could escape quickly.

His precaution was wise. One night the silence of Croglin Hall was again broken by Amelia's terrified screams. She had heard the dreadful scratching at the window, and seen the face that was not a face peering at her through the panes. But this time help was at hand. The brothers now slept in bedrooms opposite their sister's, and Edward kept a pistol under his pillow. At the first shriek, he was out of bed and into Amelia's room, joined in a moment by Michael. They were in time. The window was unbroken. Edward pointed towards the lawn.

"There he goes! I'm after him. You stay here with Amelia."

He tore along the passage, out of the front door, across the lawns, the fleeing figure still in sight. When he judged himself near enough he fired. He fancied that the thing wavered in its course, but he had evidently not wounded it seriously, for it fled on, to the end of the Hall gardens, through the trees and over the churchyard wall.

Edward Cranswell was not as young as he had been, and excitement and running had almost knocked the breath out of his body. But he plodded gamely on, reached the wall (fortunately a low one) and scrambled over it.

When he landed on the soft earth on the other side his quarry was still in sight, moving more slowly now, sometimes lost among the tombstones, then reappearing, a crouching feral shape. He fired again. The thing put on a spurt of speed, and suddenly was gone.

It had only been a few yards in front of him. There was nowhere conceivable for it to hide, except behind a gravestone. He dashed from one to another, peering among the mounds, the thrill of the chase driving out a certain creeping of the flesh that was beginning to assail him. At last he stopped and surveyed the territory.

"Only one place he could have gone. In there," he decided. Facing him was a small temple-like building, which had been pointed out to him as the family vault of the Fishers, the former owners of Croglin Hall. He contemplated the grim-looking doors. The night was dark; he was alone. Edward Cranswell chose the better part of valour, and went back to the house.

Next morning he and Michael, together with four neighbours, entered the Fisher vault. What they saw halted them at the entrance. The two Australians had never before seen the interior of an English burial-place. They expected decorous gloom: instead, they found chaos. The vault held some sixteen coffins, ranged on stone shelves, and of varying dates, judging by their condition. Some were little more than blackened boxes, others modern caskets with tarnished silver handles and legible inscriptions. Every one had been broken into with savage force. Smashed lids and hacked sides gave them the appearance of strong-boxes rifled by a hasty thief: and rifled, indeed, they had been. The damp earth floor of the vault was strewn with their contents. Yellowed ancient bones, whiter ones, skulls which had become detached and rolled away from their owners, bodies still only half-decomposed—all lay in battlefield riot at the feet of the appalled men.

The Cranswells stood stupefied: they had been prepared for confrontation with a vicious fugitive, but not for this gruesome sight. And where, in any case, was their quarry?

It was one of their farmer neighbours who found him. Stepping forward, picking his way among the remains, he held his lantern high over a coffin on the floor at the far end of the vault.

"Here's yin been let alone," he said. The others crowded forward and peered down at what lay within. It was the shrivelled body of a tall man, emaciated almost to a skeleton: it might have served as a model for one of the grisly *memento mori* figures often found below the effigies of pious Tudor churchmen. A few rags clung to the prominent rib-cage and stick-like limbs. Suddenly Edward Cranswell gave a cry, and pointed.

"There! That's where my bullet got him!"

The left leg of the body, bent up towards them and stiffened in death, was barely fleshed: but in the stringy calf-muscles was a wound that had recently bled.

By common consent, within a few days of its discovery the corpse was solemnly burned. From that day forward neither Amelia Cranswell nor any other inhabitant of the Croglin district was troubled again by the "vampire".

But *was* it, in fact, a vampire? The bodies of the long-dead do not bleed: nor would a genuine vampire be likely to be interested in the sustenance to be obtained from other ancient corpses. His wrecking of the Fisher coffins is, therefore, apparently motiveless if he belonged to the realm of the supernormal. The behaviour of one of the very few vampires on record in England, a man of thirteenth-century Berwick-on-Tweed, resembles that of the Thing of Croglin in that he wandered the countryside, biting and worrying people to death: but there are no stories of attacks by him on dead bodies. It seems far more likely that the Croglin terrorist was, as the Cranswells had concluded before the discovery in the vault, a wandering lunatic, with necrophiliac tendencies and a homicidal mania directed towards women.

But it was long ago, and in a lonely place, and nobody cared to ask too many questions.

Donovan's Drop

Not many miles from Dublin is a spot called Donovan's Drop. There are other places with similar names, but the way in which this ruin—set among flat, open fields—got its title is odder than most.

The story, alas, is only too true. There are villagers galore who, for the price of a Guinness, will tell it with relish and detail.

The Donovan concerned was an extremely beautiful young woman. Though when our story begins, she was neither a Donovan nor in Ireland: she was living in London with her widowed mother, in a large house in Belgrave Square, with a flock of servants devoted to their mistress and her lovely nineteen-year-old daughter. There are few private houses left in Belgrave Square today: but this was 1874, when large town houses and servants were a commonplace. The affection her servants held for Mrs Darcy and her daughter was heightened by sympathy: not long past, Rosemary had been knocked down by a runaway horse-and-dray, and the heavy vehicle, passing over her leg just above the knee, had severed it.

In these days of technology, "wooden legs" are works of engineering and the wearer can pass in the street as a whole person. In mid-nineteenth century, this was not so. The operation itself was painful and dangerous: the wooden leg which took the place of Rosemary's was hideous, heavy and inflexible. Even under the long skirts of the day, no girl with such a disability could disguise it.

At first Rosemary was accompanied on her convalescent walks

about Belgrave Square by servants, but she grew tired of this and persuaded them to leave her. And though her walk was not quite natural, the people who stole glances at her—or stared openly—did so not because of her gait but because of her beauty. She was tall, with red-gold hair and the face of a laughing angel. Many wanted to get in conversation with her, but she was shy, embarrassed by her disability, and as they passed she turned her head away. She was always accompanied by her small terrier, and while she turned to look at a flower-bed, or consider the position of the sun, he would snarl.

Despite careful rejection of contact with the rest of the human race—at least in Belgrave Square—she became aware of a young man who took a walk each afternoon at the same time as she. They would pass each other several times, while the terrier snapped and snarled and the young man slowed down and seemed about to stop or raise his hat. Then, rebuffed, he would walk on. Although Rosemary tried not to look, it wasn't long before she had seen that he was a remarkably handsome fellow of no more than thirty. He was rich, too, for his clothes, though plain, were well cut, and obviously expensive. He had a dark, Celtic quality about the skin and eyes.

But in 1874 no well-brought-up young lady would dream of speaking with a stranger, however handsome. She changed the time of her walk—only to find to her annoyance that he too had chosen to alter his schedule. He was still in evidence, each day, slowing down as she approached, then, rejected, walking on. And to make matters worse, the terrier, by virtue of having encountered the same gentleman half a dozen times each day, no longer snarled but jumped with affection to lick the stranger's hand.

It was too much. Furiously, she abandoned walks in Belgrave Square. For the rest of that week she stayed indoors. At least, at the end of it, there would be opportunity for fresh air and walks: for on Thursday night she and her mother were travelling south to Brighton, to spend the weekend with friends.

Imagine, then, her confusion on finding the man from Belgrave Square as fellow-guest. They were introduced by their hostess, and his name was revealed as Marcus Donovan, from Dublin. He was —though he made light of the fact—a member of the Irish landed gentry. His family home, Ballykatrin, was being completely redecorated: this had made him decide to spend the summer in London.

On being introduced Mr Donovan said, with the most charming of smiles, "I have had the pleasure of seeing this lady on my walks in London. Hers is a beauty I could never forget." He made a little bow and Rosemary felt herself blushing to the roots of her hair. Fortunately the conversation now became general, and she was able to agree that the ride in the train had been agreeable, that the sea air did good the moment one sensed it.

"And so," said Mr Donovan, "you live the year round in London, Miss Darcy?"

"Yes—er, that is——"

"I quite understand. You are fortunate in having civilization at your doorstep, an oyster waiting to be opened. And at the same time, friends like our host and hostess, with whom you may enter into rustic pursuits."

"Yes——" said Rosemary. She wasn't clear what he meant, but there was no denying that he spoke beautifully. And he was very handsome.

During a rapturous weekend in which he danced attendance on Rosemary and yet managed to delight the other guests as well, he asked if he might call on her mother and herself when they got back to town. Blushing again, Rosemary agreed.

Three weeks later, after a whirlwind courtship, she found herself engaged—and almost fainting with delight at the thought. Her accident, six months back, had seemed to remove all chance of marriage. Perhaps there might be the odd fortune hunter, prepared to share his bed, at least for a while, with a one-legged heiress—and whom she could only rebuff—but Marcus Donovan was a very rich man in his own right, to whom her tiny fortune was obviously laughable. Indeed, he showered to many gifts upon her mother that the old lady was in a state of speechless gratitude.

And the huge diamond-and-sapphire ring he gave Rosemary as mark of their engagement was the most superb piece of jewellery she had ever seen.

He had shown her miniatures and a silver-mounted photo of Ballykatrin; told her of the staff who ran it. When, early in August, they were married at St-Martin-in-the-Fields and took the steamer that night for Ireland, she felt she was going home. And the next afternoon, when they reached it, she was sure. Nothing was too much trouble, her every whim was satisfied almost before she divulged it. And Ballykatrin, if sombre, was huge and awe-inspiring.

That night there was a ball to which came gentry from dozens of miles around. An orchestra came from Dublin, and a chef to supplement the more homely food which Marcus Donovan preferred and which was normally prepared for him by the old cook, Mrs Riley. There were over two-hundred guests, with dancing and champagne till dawn, and the last tired guest departing as the sun crept up the sky.

"Poor darling," said Marcus. He put an arm gently on her shoulder as the last carriage drove off. "Poor darling Rosemary—you're exhausted. What a selfish fool I am, exhibiting you like this, all night."

"Dear, dear, Marcus—I'm not tired. I love you, Marcus. And I could dance forever."

And though the orchestra had long departed, the two danced silently round the empty ballroom, as brightening sunlight drowned the gleam of candelabra.

Hours later, when she woke with a sigh of pleasure to find him by her side in the big four-poster, she remembered something. He opened his eyes, kissed her.

"Darling Marcus. How long have you lived here, at Ballykatrin?"

"Why do you ask?"

"Because—because no one seems to have known you very long."

"I see." He sat up on his elbow and looked down at her, with an expression she hadn't noticed before. "No one has known me long?"

"That was only an impression, Marcus. But, oh, the party was so wonderful, and I danced so much, and——"

"They're right. I *haven't* lived here long. Not very long. But this is Donovan country—and Ballykatrin is Donovan land."

"Of course, Marcus——"

"I was brought up abroad, Rosemary. In America. Does that surprise you?"

"Perhaps."

"My father was a younger son, and he left—for the New World —many years ago. Ballykatrin was his father's and *his* father's before that, Rosemary. But the Donovans here fell on hard times and the place was sold. My father's intention had always been to buy it back—but he died. So I took over his business—and came back to do what he'd wanted to do himself."

"Of course, Marcus. You must be terribly proud, having your family home back. And I—I'm proud, with you——"

It was only during the next week that she realized how little she had known of Marcus. Not that it mattered: he was most of the things a girl could want.

Not till the autumn did she learn that her husband still had interests in the States and these necessitated his travelling there. A letter arrived and after reading it at breakfast he announced casually, "I shall have to go to America."

"*America*, Marcus? But why?"

"Business, my dear."

"Oh. May I come with you, Marcus?"

"No, my dear. But I won't be long. A fortnight going, a fortnight at my business in New York, another fortnight back to my beloved. *That* won't be long, will it, dearest?"

"Oh, Marcus, it *will* be."

But he was adamant: she would stay behind.

That evening she accompanied him to the attic to choose a case. It ran the whole length of a wing of the house, a cob-webbed cavern with awkwardly placed beams. She disliked it and she was glad when a leather trunk was selected and they prepared to go down the small winding stair to the bedroom floor.

Then she saw another, much bigger, case, a wooden thing with iron bands. "What's in that chest, Marcus? The one with the padlock?"

It had been almost completely hidden. Only a chance ray had caught the metal of the enormous padlock.

"Nothing."

"But, goodness me—if there's nothing in it—why such a huge lock?"

"I tell you, there's *nothing in it*. Nothing at all. And as for why there should be such a lock, I have no idea at all."

"Yes, Marcus."

He held the candle up so it almost blinded her, close to her face. "And I would warn you, Rosemary, not to go—snooping—about in the attic. There are unpleasant insects: spiders and the rest, living under those slates. A bite could be serious. Go ahead, and I'll follow with this case——"

Three days later he was gone. He would be back in the third week of December, would stay a few days in England doing business and get back early on the morning of Christmas Eve.

She heard from him, a short, very affectionate letter written in Liverpool before he embarked. "Be cheerful, dearest. Our separation upsets me as much as it does you—no, far, far more. But I will be back Christmas Eve, and there, by our own fireside my darling, I will tell you of my adventures!"

A second letter, written on board ship and sent back with the vessel on its return, told again how he missed her, how he was counting the days till their reunion. Their reunion on Christmas Eve.

A fortnight later, when it seemed she could hardly wait longer for her husband's return, she was seized by a sudden and irrational desire to go up into the attic and open the padlocked chest.

There was a big jar of keys in Marcus's dressing room, keys of all sizes: it seemed reasonable that one of these might unlock the big padlock.

At first, the chest was itself hard to find; she began to wonder whether she had seen it. Then suddenly she fell over it in the dark.

Methodically, she set to work with the keys. It was difficult, in the flickering, draught-torn light of a single candle, but she worked through the collection, one by one. Some refused to budge inside the lock, others spun impotent within. Many, though appearing the right size, were too large for the keyhole.

And suddenly, three things happened at once: the key turned, the candle went out, and there was a crash of ironmongery as the aged padlock disintegrated. With madly trembling fingers she struck a match, got the candle going and looked with horror at what she had done. For though now she had achieved her object of opening the chest, she had left unmistakable evidence behind. Dear God—what would Marcus say?

There was no point in trying to purchase another padlock; there could not be two such devices in all Ireland.

She was shaking with fright as she lifted the heavy wooden lid, held the flickering candle high over the opened chest.

It was empty.

But no—it was not. It was deep and at the bottom, among crumpled sheets of tissue-paper, were two sizeable parcels wrapped in brown paper. Something about their appearance—though she had no conscious idea of what they contained—seemed to sicken her, and for a moment she almost collapsed.

Then she leant inside the box and gingerly felt one.

It was heavy. She couldn't move it without using both hands, and in trying to put the candle down she let it out. She relit it, placed it carefully on the upturned lid, reached for the first parcel.

She got it out, heart pounding, and tried to read the label. It was dirty and written, very small, in a familiar hand. "In loving memory", it said, "of Elizabeth. Died 24th December, 1870."

With hands that shook so she could hardly use them, she undid the brown paper.

Inside was a single wooden leg.

Oh God—what did it *mean*? She reached for the second, lifted it, read the dirty, almost illegible label. "In loving memory of Mary-Jane. Died——"

There was scarce need to open it, but she did. Faint with fright, she wrapped both legs again, lowered them to the bottom of the chest.

As she did so, her hand knocked the candle. It fell to the bottom of the chest, and instantly the tissue paper caught fire, then the brown wrapping. Flames spat up like serpents' tongues to light the whole of the attic. Panic-stricken, almost in tears, she beat at the flames with bare hands. Then, realizing that closing the chest might extinguish them, she dragged the heavy lid to. As it thumped shut, foul smoke oozed from the sides, choking her.

The smoke stopped: she lifted the lid a fraction. The fire had gone and she lifted it completely. Lighting a match, she retrieved the remains of the candle, relit it.

The lining of the case, a quilted silk, was ruined: at first her thoughts were entirely of this. Then, as the significance of what she had found began to dawn on her, she reached into the charred contents of the box.

The paper had burnt away and the two legs—how macabre; one had never considered the idea of a pair—lay naked and charred. She stared at them in the oily light of the candle and for a moment it seemed incredible that they should have got so burnt, so charred, in so few moments. The labels were gone.

There was nothing to do but close it, tuck the broken padlock out of sight. Then with a heave she pushed the whole affair six inches farther into the darkness. With luck, when and if Marcus came up, it wouldn't catch his eye.

That night in bed, the things she had seen refused to leave her mind, and sleep refused to come. To whom had the two limbs belonged? To whom had Marcus—for the handwriting was unmistakable—held them in "Loving Memory"? Had he been married before?

She had never asked him: it seemed hardly the question a girl would feel the need to put. She lay awake, staring horror-struck at the bedroom ceiling, trying not to see through it in her imagination to the hateful things above.

The next day panic set in. He was due in forty-eight hours, a letter had arrived, posted in London. "My dearest," it said. "I cannot bear to wait till Christmas Eve, when you and I will be united—by our own fireside——"

The blood drained from her face. *Christmas Eve.* Surely that had been the date on the parcels? In loving memory of Elizabeth, Christmas Eve—— In loving memory of Mary-Jane, Christmas Eve—— In loving memory of Rosemary, Christmas Eve——

And the fire. The enormous, yawning fireplace.

When Mrs Riley came in, Rosemary Donovan was unconscious on the floor. She woke to find she had been carried and put on her bed under a coverlet. The stump of her leg ached terribly. "There now, me dear—you and your poor leg. Faith, and it must have been your empty stomach, me dear, you didn't eat hardly none of your breakfast. I came in to see about meals for the master's return. Madam——"

And it was to Mrs Riley that she told the story of her discoveries in the attic.

"There, there, me dear—madam. You've had a bad dream, that's all. Only a bad dream."

Throughout the day she found herself too weak to get up: the urge to flee the house which surged over her became an impossibility. Once she sat on the edge of the bed, head in hands, praying for strength to stand, to run. When she got to her feet, the room swam, and she collapsed.

And it was thus, a day later, the morning of Christmas Eve, that her husband found her. The servants explained she had been taken ill—it had been dreadfully cold—but that she was mending well. He kissed her with obvious solicitude, she responded with the love she had held for him all along, and immediately felt better. The whole thing had been a dream, a ghastly dream.

During the afternoon, Mrs Riley volunteered information to the master that his wife had had a crazy dream about wooden legs in a box. He listened with interest, then nodded and went off.

That afternoon, Rosemary Donovan took herself for a walk in the grounds. It was a soft, Irish, December day, with a little cloud and a lot of blue sky. When she came in, refreshed—it could never have happened; what a fool she had been—she changed immediately for dinner and went down to the drawing-room. The servants had got the fire going in its huge fireplace, and the flames cast great shadows on the ceiling.

And it was when he, too, came down, more handsome than ever, with half a dozen parcels for her to unwrap—"On this Christmas Eve, my darling——" that he saw her pale.

She stood absolutely still, in the centre of the room, staring at him as if he were a total stranger.

"Is something wrong, my darling?"

She opened her lips and said nothing.

"Come sit by the fire, darling. *What* a wonderful fire——" He put an arm on her shoulder.

And it happened.

With a scream that seemed to come from outside herself, a huge and dreadful sound that swamped all others—swamped the angry crackling of the monster fire, her husband's voice, the ponderous ticking of the grandfather clock—she seized the ten-inch silver paper-knife from a coffee table and with all her strength plunged it into his breast.

He fell with his mouth wide open, a look of shocked surprise on his face. The blood spurted in a frightening torrent over the floor.

Rosemary Donovan was found guilty and sentenced to death. She made no effort to plead innocence—or insanity. When Mrs Riley the cook volunteered the tale of her "dream" and the charred legs in the attic chest, she shook her head: she had no memory of anything—before doing this wicked deed.

At Mrs Riley's insistence the attic was inspected: no chest was there, no sign of conflagration. Obviously the English girl was a witch, and possessed of the devil. Sentence was confirmed.

A week later it was carried out.

And though that was miles away, for Rosemary Donovan's drop to death was in Dublin jail, the site of Ballykatrin is to this day "Donovan's Drop"—the place where the English witch died. The Witch With the Wooden Leg. The house itself burnt down long ago—it was the English witch's spell, people still maintain—and now only the wind from the Irish Sea winds its way through the ruins.

Though the locals maintain that if the wind is right, on Christmas Eve, you can hear the tap-tap-tap of a wooden leg, making its way through the open, ruined rooms of Ballykatrin.

The Beaked Horror Which Sank a Ship

The ship, riding light, lurched hideously in the long Atlantic swell. A beam sea, which came from nowhere, hit her suddenly on the port quarter. The deck slid away from under our feet like a wall. By luck and the grace of God I snatched at a rope and hung on. The mate slid feet first into the scuppers. A mill-race of frothing water a few yards below seemed to reach up and take him. Miraculously he did not shoot feet first overboard.

"That was a near go," he grinned as he scrambled up. The ship righted herself. I breathed again.

"I thought you'd gone for good," I said. "Fat lot of use I'd have been to you. I can't even swim."

"Oh, they'd have put the ship about and like enough picked me up," he said brightly. "I've had a nearer touch than that. But if you go to sea for a living you should learn to stand on your legs—not lose 'em as I did. My own dam' fault."

We were off the Grand Banks of Newfoundland where the Labrador Current sweeps south. It is the path of the iceberg. That is not the only hazard. Sea fogs, in that part of the North Atlantic, shut down suddenly like blankets of doom. Then, when the foghorns bellow like bull seals, or wail tremulously as though shuddering with fear, is the time of cold fear. Fear of the iceberg, drifting noiseless through grey mist. Only the tip may show above water. Even if that tip is a glittering pinnacle of ice a hundred feet or more high, there will be at least four-fifths of the berg under water. So if the look-out in the crow's-nest shouts suddenly "Ice on the starboard bow" when the berg lies well away to starboard, there is no guarantee that in the next minute the ship may not rip up her bottom on submerged ice. That is why the deep-sea sailor who earns his bread in small ships makes one feel very humble. The hazards of the urban rat-race are nothing compared with the cold horrors of the deep sea. I said as much to the mate.

"I could almost see that run of water reaching up to snatch you overboard," I said.

He laughed. "It ud be a dam' sight worse if a stinking great tentacle fifteen foot long with suckers on it like saucers came inboard and clapped itself round you and you saw a filthy great thing with eyes like motor-bike headlights and a dam' great parrot beak big enough to bite your head off reaching for you out of the water." He looked quizzically sideways for the shock effect. And added: "We might even be sailing over one of the bastards right now".

"What on earth are you talking about?" I asked.

"Giant squids—bloody great octopuses," he said. "The Banks fishermen'll tell you that they come here after the cod. Greatest cod fishing grounds in the world right under our keel this minute. Every sort of predator fish is after 'em as well as the fishing boats from Portugal, Newfoundland, and the Maritimes. They reckon there are squids down below that could turn a boat over and kill a man as easy as wink.

"I'd sooner be 'man overboard' any day and chance my arm at swimming until they picked me up than face one of those rotten things. Just think of 'em."

I thought. A sudden vision of nightmare horror. A hideous round-topped disembodied Thing with huge glaring eyes, a hard, bony, beak-like mouth and enormous tentacles floating through the green aisles of the undersea world seeking its prey. A Thing whose trailing hideous arms could crush a boat, enwrap a man, draw him relentlessly towards that snapping beak and then cut, slash and mutilate his face and body—and devour him.

The giant squid was the nightmare of sailor-men a thousand years ago. It is the nightmare of men who go to sea in small boats to certain parts of the world to this day. When the Vikings set sail in their dragon-headed long-ships from Norwegian fjords, their gunwales shield-hung, their banked oars dipping and glittering, the raven pennant flickering at the mast-head and the blood-curdling war-cry "Yuch! Hey! Saa-saa!" going before them down the long wind, they feared neither Saxon chieftain, fighting desperately for his stockaded thorpe, nor the massed ranks of the swordsmen of Egbert or Alfred the Great who would meet them knee-deep in the surges of English beaches and hack and hew until the tide-edge ran red. Their trade was blood and the sword.

When Eric the Red and his Norsemen sailed south by Greenland and hit the North American coast long before Columbus steered west, the men of the long-ships took the risks of ice and fog and the steep mountains of Atlantic seas as part of their trade. They feared one thing only with an overmastering dread, a superstitious awe— the Kraken. The hideous sea monster, tentacled and glaring, whose clammy, writhing arm could scatter their long sweeps like matches, entwine itself about the raven-headed ship, overturn it and, in a black, inky cloud of its own creation, drown and devour the crew. Neither wind, wave, storm, sleet, floating berg nor grinding floe was like this terror of the sea. The legend of the Kraken is probably the oldest of all myths of the deep-sea's horrors. But is it a myth?

Consider the cuttlefish—that nasty little horror which swarms, in certain phases of the weather, on the British coast. The giant squid, the horrifying octopus, is no more than a cuttlefish. This is what *The Boy's Own Natural History** has to say about it.

"The Mollusca have neither spine nor bones, the nervous system consisting of a number of nervous knobs called 'ganglia', which give off filamentous nerves in different directions.

"Few Molluscs possess eyes, but in one or two, as the snails and slugs, those organs are to be found, and in the higher Molluscs, such as the cuttlefish, we see not only large and brilliant eyes, but also organs of hearing.

"The Cephalopoda, so called from the organs of movement surrounding the head, are divided into 'naked' and 'testaceous', or covered with a shell.

"The Common Cuttlefish is an example of a naked cephalopodous mollusc. This repulsive-looking creature is common on our shores, and is, in spite of its unpleasant appearance, often used for food. Its eight long and flexible arms are covered with suckers of various

* Published last century.

sizes, enabling their owner not only to fix itself firmly to the rocks on which it dwells, but to seize and retain with the greatest tenacity any unfortunate fish or shell that may happen to come within its reach. Its powerful parrot-like beak enables it not only to devour fishes, but even to crush the shells and crustacea that are entangled in its deadly embraces. In this country the Cuttle does not grow to any great size, but in the Indian Seas it is absolutely dangerous, and the crews of boats are forced to be armed with a hatchet, to cut off the arms of the cuttlefish.

"There are few who have not heard of the colour called 'sepia'. This is, or ought to be, prepared from a black pigment, secreted by the cuttlefish, and used in order to escape its foes, by blackening the water with the ink, and hurrying off under shelter of the dense cloud of its own creating. Dr Buckland actually drew a portrait of a fossil cuttlefish with some of its own ink that still remained in its body.

"The substance sold in the shops as cuttlefish bone is a chalky substance secreted from the mouth of the fish, and composed of an infinite number of plates, joined by myriads of little pillars.

"The entire body is soft, and encased in a coarse, leather-like skin, unprotected by any shell."

Legends of giant, many-armed sea monsters which would attack boats and kill their crews are common amongst the folk-lore of all seafaring nations. You will find them etched on Mycenean urns and pictured in Japanese coloured prints and woodcuts and even in stained-glass windows. All sailors of all nations fear this lurking horror of the deep sea.

Not until comparatively recent years have the legends been proved by fact. Gradually scientists have pieced the evidence together, mainly from dead and damaged carcasses cast ashore. One was stranded on the coast of Zeeland in about 1847. Another came ashore at the Skaw in 1854, and then in 1861 Shetland fishermen, ranging the beach for kelp, came across a hideous tentacled creature stranded and dead among off-shore rocks. In that year the captain of the French corvette *Alecton* produced definite living proof. His ship was cruising about 120 miles north-east of Teneriffe in the Canary Islands when the look-out shouted excitedly. Through the glasses the captain could see a giant squid swimming on the surface. He immediately let fly at it with a light naval gun. The shell killed the creature and the crew tried hard to haul it aboard. They had no lifting tackle and had to give it up as a bad job. That is not to be wondered at since they estimated the length of its body at 15 feet *without the tentacles* and its weight at no less than two tons.

When the captain's report was sent to the *Academie des Sciences* the French zoologists, with the usual "scientific caution" of their kind, refused to believe it. Less than ten years later carcasses of giant squid were washed ashore on the coast of Newfoundland. The Reverend M. Harvey and Professor A. E. Verrill of Yale University collected accounts and specimens and Verrill gives the account of his findings in the *Transactions* of the Connecticut Academy of Arts and Sciences.

Then came the final conclusive horror. When next you feed your canary on sixpenn'orth of cuttlefish bones from the pet shop— think of what happened to the crew of the 150-ton wooden schooner *Pearl* in the Bay of Bengal on 4 July, 1874. Somebody aboard the schooner saw a gigantic horror with eyes like motor-car headlamps and a huge horny beak basking on the hot surface of the sea. Its waving tentacles, 30 feet long or more, spread round it like a nightmare net. Some fool ran for a rifle. He took careful aim and pulled the trigger. The bullet thudded into the body of the Thing.

Then, to the horror of the crew, the Thing, flailing its tentacles like a gigantic sea-going helicopter, swam straight for the schooner. It attacked the ship. Enormous tentacles curled over the decks, twisted snake-like round the funnel and upper works. Its huge horny beak snapped at the rigging. The nightmare eyes glared hellishly at the horror-stricken crew. The air was foetid with the appalling stench of the creature. The slimy tentacles gripped and heaved and, believe it or not, actually pulled the schooner over on her beam-ends and sank her! The crew were thrown into the sea, which was inky black with the creature's own discharge of fluid. The tentacles, clammy, irresistible, armed with huge suckers, dragged more than one wretched, screaming man to a hideous death in those snapping jaws.

Some of the crew got away in a boat. They lived to tell the tale. That is how and why even scientists now accept the truth of the most horrifying sea drama of all time.

The Dog-Man Horror of the Valley

Before we come to the telling of this tale, consider the background of the age-old fear of the werewolf.

Primitive man had four prime fears which dominated his skin-clad life. They made him tread warily by day and sleep fitfully by night. They were the Wolf, the Cat, the Horned-Beast and the Snake. Those fears dominate us, to lesser or greater degree, today. It depends on where we live. The Cat is the lion, the tiger, the jaguar or the leopard, still the first enemies of defenceless natives in Africa, India, Asia and South America.

The Horned-Beast, if you are an African, is the bush buffalo, the dreaded *Bos caffer*, deadlier and more cunning than the lion. Plenty of other Horned-Beasts, including bulls and domestic cows, put the wind up the average person. The Snake, sinuous, silent, sliding death, is the abiding fear of those who live in tropic countries. The South American dreads the death-grip of the mighty anaconda as much as the African fears the coils of the python or the death-in-seconds bite of the mamba.

In Europe the wolf is the beast of fear. Fenris, the Witches' Horse, the Grey Rider, is the epitome of four-footed horror. The Voice in the Night which stops the heart. When man turns into wolf, the horror is devilish.

In the whole range of psychic study there is no more fascinating subject than that of lycanthropy, the evil art by which human beings are supposed to be able to transform themselves or other people into the form of wolves.

Whether one believes in it or not—and disbelief is no hindrance to the enormous amount of interest which it affords—it is impossible to overlook the amazingly widespread belief in lycanthropy which exists in Europe today.

In Lithuania, Hungary, Poland, Czechoslovakia, Transylvania, Luxembourg and France, the belief in "men-wolf-fiends" is still deeply rooted.

French peasants in the remote parts of the Haute Savoie, the Vosges and the Ardennes are as fearful of the dreaded *loup garou* as the East Germans are of the *wahrwolf* or the Russians of the *volkadlak* of the gloomy forests.

Usually the werewolf is regarded as a grisly creature, murdering women and children on lonely forest roads in order to satisfy the insane craving for human flesh with which the victim is cursed, but actually there are a good many records of werewolves which have behaved in a most exemplary manner.

The story of Little Red Riding Hood is, of course, a folk tale of the werewolf, while the Three Bears probably derive from a similar belief. Bears were second favourites with the medieval sorcerers whose favourite form of fun was to turn themselves or other people into animals.

Hares came next, and in Scotland at the present day there are plenty of peasants in the Western Isles who believe in the Magic Hare . . . the hare which can only be killed with silver shot.

In England the belief in werewolves died out in the sixteenth century, but the words "turncoat" and "turnskin" perpetuate the old belief.

The business of turning oneself into a werewolf is not simple. The methods vary. A set formula of words, a sort of incantation to the Devil, is the essential theme. Without this formula the enchanter can accomplish nothing.

The simplest of accompanying methods is to put on a girdle of the skin of the animal into which one wishes to be transformed. This must be done at dead of night, by the light of a fire in the deepest part of the forest, and the aspirant werewolf must remove all other clothing.

In Transylvania a magic salve is rubbed on the naked body, while the Russian believes in drinking the rainwater which has collected in the footprints of a wolf.

Poland possesses certain magic streams whose water is said to turn one into a werewolf whether one wishes it or not. There is a legend of a Polish colonel who was so transformed about sixty years ago. He had drunk from the stream while out shooting in the forest.

To eat the brains of a wolf is another powerful "medicine", but the most interesting of all the necessary ingredients are the lycanthropous fungi which grow in certain parts of the enormous forest of Biealowicza in Poland.

This fungus, which is found in deep, damp pits, in old, wet quarries and sometimes on the banks of streams, is of definite interest, since the natives of Liberia and Sierra Leone in West Africa include a very similar fungus in the decoctions employed by the secret societies of Leopard Men.

The most recent case of a suspected werewolf in Britain is the Merioneth example, which was seen by an Oxford professor, his wife and guest in the 'eighties.

The professor, who was a keen fisherman, took a cottage for a month or two on the shores of one of the many little mountain lakes of that wild Welsh county. It was a hot summer and the waters of the lake dropped many feet below their usual level. The shores were rimmed by a broad belt of stones and shingle, usually covered by water.

One day, while wading a few yards out from the shore, throwing an ineffectual fly for trout which refused to rise, the professor stubbed an academic toe on a skull. He fished it up and examined it. It was quite the most peculiar skull he had ever seen—shaped like that of a dog, but much broader in the head than any dog ever pupped. He took it back to the cottage and placed it in the kitchen.

That evening he and his guest went for a walk, leaving his wife to prepare supper. She was laying the table in the small front living-room when she thought she heard something scratching at the kitchen door at the back of the tiny cottage.

She went into the kitchen. The door and windows were shut. A lamp stood on the table. Outside it was dark. Something was scratching at the door, snuffling and breathing heavily. She stood a moment, irresolute. Evidently a sheep-dog wanted a night's rest.

The next moment two great paws reared against the window

and a hideous face, half-dog, half-human, glared in. She saw in the lamplight the slavering jaws and red-rimmed eyes of a creature larger than a wolf, with the eyes and forehead of a man.

Then the vision vanished. She heard the pattering of footsteps, running round the cottage. The creature was going to the front door. In a wild panic she rushed through the cottage to the front door and slammed and bolted it.

A moment later came the same scratching and snuffling, the same heavy, menacing breathing. The beast was trying a new entry to the house.

For half an hour the woman waited in a state of acute fear. The creature did not show itself again, but its footsteps padded ceaselessly round and round the cottage. The professor's wife, the prisoner of a Something to which she dared not attempt to put a name, waited in terror for the returning footsteps of her husband and his friend.

At last she heard them returning. Their voices and laughter came up the path. She wondered if the Beast would attack them, screamed an hysterical warning into the night, flung open the door and rushed down the path to meet them in a sudden reckless frenzy of relief.

The professor met her with mild amazement. "My dear, what on earth is the matter? You seem quite distraught."

She explained.

"Ah! I did see something running down the path towards the lake as you ran out of the door," he said.

Then he calmed her and sent her to bed. He and his companion waited far into the small hours.

At two in the morning, a light rain falling, the hills silent, the cottage quiet as the grave, the night black without, the listeners heard the stealthy footsteps of an animal circling the cottage. They hid, one on either side of the kitchen window. On the table lay the skull.

The footsteps drew nearer, passed under the window, halted. Then the soft thud of two wet paws on glass, the scratching of slipping claws on the window-panes; and a hideous wolf-like head with the eyes of a man glared into their faces at a range of only a few inches.

They could see every detail, the eyeballs, the short tongue, human and not canine in structure, the short, bristly greyish hairs on the jaws and the remarkable breadth of the skull. Then the nightmare vanished into the darkness.

Footsteps sounded on the path, retreating. They flung open the door, armed with pokers and a shotgun, and rushed in pursuit. In the dim light of the stars they saw a huge dog-like form galloping ahead. It reached the lake shore, ran down the shingle and vanished into the water.

Not a ripple marked the place of its disappearance.

Next morning the professor measured the skull, took it to the water's edge and flung it far into the lake whence it came. The werewolf of Merioneth was never seen again.

But the measurements of the skull coincided with the average measurements of the human skull in one notable detail. The width of the cranium was infinitely greater than that of a dog's and approximately the same as that of a human being.

This example (and there are definite records of it) points to the possibility of the werewolf spirit having reappeared solely owing to the loss of its skull.

Old Merioneth folk-tales certainly speak of a "man-wolf" which terrorized the shepherds on the sheep-walks of the lonely hills a century and a half ago. There is also a story, so vague as to be unreliable even in these records of the fantastic, of a woman who was followed down a mountain-side by "a great grey dog with the eyes of a man" about 1830.

I came across an extraordinary variation of the Fear of the Wolf in Arctic Labrador only a few years ago when, at the suggestion of Lord Beaverbrook, and on the invitation of the Prime Minister of Newfoundland, I went far north into virtually untrodden country to write a book on the past, present and economic future of Labrador, "the world's last virgin treasure-house".

There, in that grey-green wilderness of rocky hills, stunted fir and spruce, endless lakes and green muskegs or quivering swamps, one found an enduring belief in ghosts and supernatural happenings, some of which I have told in *50 Great Ghost Stories*.*

Up beyond the stupendous Hamilton Falls, higher than Niagara, at a remote Indian camp known as Mile 274, my Red-Indian guide, Ashuanipi Joe, told me of a pack of wolves which haunt the forest on whose edge lies the pathetic camp of log cabins and tin shacks,

* Odhams, 1966.

patched with flattened petrol cans, roofed with corrugated-iron, utterly lonely, without shop, church or any civilized amenity other than the railroad telephone.

A husky dog, one of that hardy, savage, half-wild race of stiff-coated, muscular dogs which pull the trappers' sledges over endless miles of frozen snow, had mated with a wolf. The result was a hunting pack of hybrid dog-wolves. The Indians said that they had "double cunning". They were a worse menace to life and limb than the wild-bred, grey timber wolves, those gaunt, great beasts which can pull down a man single-handed and tear out his throat. The dog-cross meant that the hunting pack had not only the ferocity of the wild wolf, but that, from their husky mother, bred and trained by man, they knew all the ways—and the weaknesses—of man.

"Night come," said Ashuanipi Joe, "and their wolf eyes shine in the forest like fire-light. They come close to camp. They know us. We frightened of dem husky-wolves. Bad spirits. Always one man sit up at night with gun. This bad—but worse when dem husky-wolves breed many more. No man or woman safe from them."

Who knows but that, from such beginnings, a new fear of a different sort of werewolf and an up-to-date mythology of a new sort of lycanthropy may not spring up among the wretched half-breeds, Indians and Esquimaux, who inhabit "the land that God forgot"?

Here in Britain the legend of the wolf lingers faintly. The last wolf in northern Scotland was killed at Loth in Sutherland by the hunter, Polson. I had the veritable story itself from Polson's great-great-great-grandson, now gamekeeper to a friend, the Earl of Cromartie. The legend of the wolf and the fear of the wolf are still told over the peat fire in lonely crofts up the misty glens.

In England, the wolf lives on in place-names—Wolferton on the Queen's estate in Norfolk; Woolverston in Suffolk; Wolvercote in Oxfordshire; Wolverton in Buckinghamshire and again in Hampshire; Wolvey in Warwickshire; Wolviston in Durham; Wolfeton in Dorset and, don't forget it, Wolverhampton itself.

The wolf in England vanished when the great mediaeval forests were cleared. It lingered until long after in Scotland, Ireland and Wales. And the last werewolf was seen, so they say, in that lonely cottage on a night of paralysing fear when old men alive today were young boys.

They Ate their Young Shipmate

"Look out!"

The warning shout came from Edwin Stephens, the mate, stationed in the bows of the yawl-rigged yacht *Mignonette*, as she ploughed her way southward on her long voyage to Sydney. It was 3 July, 1884, a day of fate for everyone on board. Troubles had multiplied since they had crossed the Equator, sixteen days previously, to run into one storm after another.

The mate's warning cry had been prompted by the sight of a tremendous sea bearing down upon them. His shipmates, three in number, clung desperately to the boom till the menacing wave passed. Just one great wave, but its force was terrifying. It swept the lee bulwarks clean away.

"My God!" yelled Stephens in a frenzy. "Her side's knocked in!"

It was only too true. The butt ends were open, and the captain, thirty-eight-year-old Thomas Dudley, saw all too plainly that his vessel must founder.

He rapped out his orders to the crew with lightning presence of mind, and no crew ever acted with greater alacrity. Their thirteen-foot-long dinghy was launched without mishap. The ship's boy, nineteen-year-old Richard Parker, ordered to get the fresh-water breaker, did so and flung it overboard as ordered so that it could be picked up at leisure once they were clear of the yacht.

Meanwhile, Captain Dudley wrenched the binnacle compass from the deck by sheer brute force and passed it into the dinghy as it dropped astern. He then rushed to the cabin for his chronometer and sextant. Finding himself waist deep in water, he flung these precious items on to the deck. Before he could follow he heard his shipmates yelling to him that the yacht was sinking; yet, cool-headed still, he lingered to grab up some tins of provisions before clambering up on deck.

He dropped some in his haste but managed to cling on to two of the tins while he grabbed up chronometer and sextant. Then, and only then, in the tradition of the sea, did he leave his ship to join the others in the tossing dinghy.

They had barely rowed a boat's length astern when the yacht sank before their eyes. She was gone within five minutes of that murderous wave's first onslaught.

When they recovered their breath they realized that their plight was desperate indeed. Their first concern was to recover the fresh-water breaker, but though they rowed around over a large area they were unable to find it.

All they were able to retrieve was its wooden stand, the captain pointing out that, with one of the bottom boards of the dinghy, it might serve as a makeshift sea-anchor.

The loss of the fresh water was a crushing blow; and another came when they examined the two tins for which the captain had risked his life. They did not contain meat, as he had imagined, but turnips—a pound in each tin.

But they could not linger to dwell upon their bad luck. All had to set to and bale, for they were shipping water fast.

The able seaman of the party was Edward Brooks, from Bright-lingsea, and he was just a year younger than the captain and mate. None could guess what terrible ordeals lay ahead of them.

That night they were startled by the sudden appearance of a big shark which came nosing round their craft. Once it knocked against the side of the dinghy with such force as to set it rocking, but, to the occupants' intense relief, it then made off and did not return.

For the next four days they contrived to sustain themselves on a ration of one ounce of turnip a day per man. But they were grateful even for that, for the moisture helped in some small measure to ease their increasing thirst, if only for a brief moment. They were

in tropic waters, sea all around them, somewhere westward of
Africa, about 27 degrees South and 10 degrees West.

Then, on the fourth day, they suddenly spotted a turtle floating
on the surface close to their boat. They managed to grapple it and
haul it aboard and, elated by their catch, they recklessly opened their
second tin of turnips and consumed the lot.

They killed the turtle and drank some of its blood to help slake
their fearful thirst, draining the rest into the chronometer case for
future use. The flesh they cut into strips, eating some raw and
festooning other strips all round their boat. They reckoned that this
would keep them going for a time; but that same day seawater
washed into the chronometer case and their precious turtle's blood
had to be thrown away.

Days dragged by without respite save for occasional showers of
rain. By spreading oilskins over their arms they contrived to save
a few drops, but not enough to satisfy their increasing thirst or to
ease their burning throats. When they looked at each other they
saw that their eyes were bloodshot and their skins already blackened
by the sun.

The temptation to drink seawater was great, but Captain Dudley
sternly warned against it. Better, he counselled, to drink their own
urine, and from the eighth day onward, when their frantic prayers
for rain were unanswered, that revolting practice had to be resorted
to.

There were about fifteen days when nothing occurred to break
the terrible monotony or to ease their increasing torments. Each
sunrise found them drifting in open sea; each evening the sun went
down on the same featureless expanse of water which mocked their
raging thirst.

No one spoke much, and when they did their voices emerged in
hoarse, unnatural croakings, and the effort was such that they soon
lapsed into silence again. Each became a prey to his own thoughts.
Captain Dudley, a gaunt travesty of his former resolute, clear-
headed self, cursed the day when he had made the bargain to sail
the *Mignonette* from Southampton to Sydney for a fee of £200—
half down and the balance to be collected on safe delivery to the
new owner down under.

No doubt he thought frequently of his wife and children in
England and resigned himself to the probability that he would never

see them again. It was patent that they could not survive much longer under these cruel conditions.

Similar thoughts pervaded the mind of Edwin Stephens, the mate, a family man from Southampton, with a wife and five children, against Dudley's three.

Edward Brooks, being single, lacked such home ties, but, an earnest, God-fearing man, he prayed a lot and scanned the horizon continuously.

Dick Parker, also from Southampton, had youth on his side until, ignoring his captain's grim warning, he had taken furtive sips of seawater, with the result that he was now suffering added torments for his folly.

All were now too weak to row except for absurdly short periods. So, rigging up one of the oars as a makeshift mast, with a strand of painter for shrouds and stays, and tying their shirts together to form a sail, they sought desperately to keep going. At least it was better than aimless drifting, and it gave them something to take their minds off their own sufferings.

Not that it was very successful in that respect, for their sufferings rapidly increased. On the eighteenth day, when they had had no water for five consecutive days, they were near breaking point. It was at this stage, when all were frantic with the gnawing torture of combined hunger and thirst; their tongues shrivelled; their throats on fire, that Captain Dudley voiced a terrible suggestion.

Why not cast lots, he asked, to decide which of their number should be killed for food that would at least sustain the other three and thus give them an added chance of survival?

Edward Brooks spoke up firmly on this. He refused to entertain such a ghastly proposal. Far, far better, he protested, that they should all take their chance together and, if God so willed it, all perish together.

Young Dick Parker, lying in torment in the bottom of their frail dinghy, though only half conscious, must have overheard some portions of the grim conversation going on among the others, for he presently began to stir restlessly and seemed to echo the sentiment Brooks had just uttered.

"We shall all die," he moaned feebly. "We shall all die."

The others looked down upon him guiltily, but he ceased to toss and turn and lapsed into silence again.

Edwin Stephens, who had so far contributed little to the discussion, clearly had little stomach for the outrageous proposition his captain had put forward, and he now sought to bring the dismal discussion to an end by urging deferment.

"Suppose we wait," he said earnestly. "Suppose we wait and see what daylight brings forth?"

No doubt the others were willing enough to shelve the dreadful debate for the time being; but it was Captain Dudley who spoke.

"So let it be," he said grimly. "But it is hard for four to die when one might save the rest."

What passed through each man's mind during the ensuing hours of darkness cannot be guessed. All were at the peak of their sufferings as they waited for the dawn; but when the sun rose next day the scene around their drifting boat was unchanged.

Their own condition, on the other hand, had greatly worsened and the physical and mental horrors they were suffering had become well nigh unendurable. Listlessly, and in stony silence, they watched the empty horizon. If only a sail would appear . . . It was a vain wish. The unbroken line remained. They were quite alone in what seemed like a limitless ocean.

It is probable that no one among them was at all anxious to resume the dreadful discussion they had broken off at Stephens's suggestion on the previous night. But after a long, oppressive silence, Captain Dudley cleared his parched throat and returned to his theme.

After all, he told them, the suggestion he had made, repulsive though it was, seemed to him to be the only rational solution to the dreadful plight in which they found themselves. To his mind it really presented their only remaining hope of securing the survival of some of them. They had got to face the reality of their situation. Their sufferings would grow worse. They had to do something or all must perish, perhaps in a very short time.

But now he discarded all suggestion that they should draw lots to decide who should make the necessary sacrifice in order to keep the others alive. He said outright that, after due reflection, he thought that young Dick Parker should logically be the one to lay down his life.

It was painfully evident that Captain Dudley must have been brooding deeply over the matter throughout the long night hours, for, strained and haggard, he now proceeded to list a string of pretexts to justify his specific choice for the benefit of his hearers.

In the first place, he pointed out, truthfully enough, the suffering lad was almost dead anyway and could not possibly be expected to last for very much longer. It must be clear to them all that Parker was suffering even greater torments than they themselves were—perhaps because of his own foolishness in disregarding the advice of his seniors and drinking seawater on the sly, thus aggravating the already unspeakable tortures of a raging thirst.

And was the notion he had proposed really so terrible?

"Human flesh has been eaten before," he told them, but his words, though uttered with feeling and conviction, were received by the others in a deathly, chilling silence. Seeing their squeamishness, the captain proceeded to enlarge on his arguments. After all, he went on, Parker was only a young lad and an orphan without responsibilities who would not be missed or mourned by anyone, whereas both he and Stephens were married men with large families to support.

Brooks, who had been listening attentively to this harangue, now looked his captain squarely in the eye and proceeded to repeat the views he had expressed with such sincerity on the previous day. He said outright that he, for one, could never be a party to such a terrible act as that now being advocated by the captain. But even as he said this he could guess from the signs that were being exchanged between captain and mate that he would almost certainly be outvoted when it came to a final decision. All he could do was to lodge his firm conviction that the deed would be murder on the high seas and something in which he could never bring himself to participate.

While all this was going on poor young Dick Parker was lying in the bottom of the boat, his face pillowed in the crook of an arm. He was utterly and completely exhausted, suffering intensely, and, not surprisingly, oblivious of the fatal argument going on over his head.

Captain Dudley and the mate were again exchanging glances that could mean only one thing. Brooks, sickened and revolted, and paralysed with a feeling of utter helplessness, turned away and crept dejectedly up into the very bows of the boat to bury his head beneath a tarpaulin. He could not bear to be a witness of the terrible scene he knew must inevitably be enacted. Perhaps, cowering beneath the sheltering tarpaulin, he tried to pray silently for some miracle to intervene.

A prayer, spoken aloud, was on the captain's arid lips at any rate —not for a miracle to save them all but for Divine forgiveness for the evil act that he and the mate were about to perform. This done, he bent low over the ship's boy and said in a slow and solemn tone: "Now, Dick, your time has come."

The lad, recognizing his captain's voice, began to stir feebly and murmured: "What? Me, sir?"

"Yes, my boy," replied Captain Dudley hoarsely and, ordering the mate to grasp the lad's feet, he opened his penknife. A flickering moment of hesitation, perhaps, then he thrust the sharp point of the blade deeply into the youngster's jugular vein.

There was not the slightest attempt at remonstrance or resistance on the victim's part. Perhaps he was only dimly aware of what was happening. Perhaps he was too miserable and pain-racked to care. In any case it was over in a flash. For young Richard Parker the adventurous voyage was ended. He died in a few moments.

Not so the agonies of hunger and thirst of those who lived on. Such was the frenzy of their craving for something to assuage their terrible thirsts that the others rushed forward with unrestrained eagerness in order to catch the gushing blood in the empty turnip tins and to divide it between them. Even Brooks, shaken and horror-stricken, scrambled out from beneath his tarpaulin to make sure of his ration. Gone were religious scruples; gone all moral niceties; gone all trace of squeamishness in the urgency of his ravening need.

They took great gulps of the soothing, warm, sweet blood of their dead comrade; and when they had all drunk their fill, they stripped the unfortunate youth and laid him naked under the glaring, tropic sun. Captain Dudley now took up his bloodstained penknife and resolutely proceeded to slit open the defenceless corpse. Hurriedly he now cut out both heart and liver and proceeded to divide them fairly, cutting each palpitating organ into three pieces.

The half-demented men greedily grabbed their portions in their fingers and crammed the bloody morsels into their parched mouths with an uncontrollable haste. Avidly they chewed the still warm organs, blood oozing from the corners of their lips and trickling down their jowls in scarlet rivulets. Their dreadful, unspeakable sufferings had reduced them all to the level of savage jungle beasts. Jammed closely together in that small boat, they must have presented a macabre spectacle.

While this ghastly orgy was enacted the naked remains of the luckless Richard Parker were left lying exposed in the bottom of the dinghy. But at last someone covered them with a tarpaulin sheet and the nightmare voyage through silent, relentless seas continued as before. Out of the sudden death of one the lives of three had been preserved. But for how long? As long as the flesh of their dead shipmate lasted? And then? There can have been little ease for those bloodstained three that night.

When daylight came again they looked upon the same bleak waste of sea and sky; but rain clouds were blowing up and later a brief shower gave them a few drops of rainwater; too few.

The three survivors were glumly silent now; dazed and stunned and perhaps deeply conscience-smitten as each recalled the macabre events of the preceding day. At intervals, when a sudden gust of wind half lifted a corner of the tarpaulin in the bottom of the boat, an icy chill would set them all shuddering and, in such moments, it seemed impossible to dispel a haunting illusion that young Dick Parker had come back from the dead and was stirring restively underneath that rough shroud, still tormented by acute hunger and raging thirst.

It was a long time before they could bring themselves to turn back the tarpaulin and bring their eyes to bear upon the bloody and mutilated body of their erstwhile comrade.

Though refortified in some small measure, their sufferings were still intense and their spirits were sinking fast. Day followed day, night followed night, with no respite; nothing to kindle hope. For four dreadful days and four hideous nights there were recurrent reminders that their young shipmate would stir no more. For at intervals the captain would take up the gory penknife to slice off fresh strips of flesh from the fast-decaying corpse.

Badly though they all felt the need for sustenance, each new desecration of the hapless corpse filled them with increasing nausea. They could not bear to look upon it now, so mutilated and revolting had it become. Yet the tainted flesh meant continuing life for them, a life that had become perpetual horror.

Then, on their twenty-eighth day at sea, when they had actually drifted some 1,050 miles all told, deliverance came. It came while they were engaged in one of their horrible raids upon the ribboned corpse, and with a shout even more dramatic than that cry of "Look out!" that had presaged their ghastly ordeal. Brooks, pausing in the act of conveying a strip of putrid flesh to his mouth, chanced to look across the horizon he had scanned so frequently in vain; and, this time, something caught his eye. It appeared as a small speck upon the far horizon; but at once he shouted frenziedly: "Sail, oh!"

They covered up the corpse and made a wild scramble for the oars. But they were much too feeble to row with any noticeable effect, and the sail seemed far away in another world. As they tried to pull on their oars they prayed fervently that someone on that ship would spot them.

Horrible anxiety consumed them. They had a feeling of being suspended in time and space, for the distance between them seemed to narrow with agonizing slowness, and all strength drained from their weakened bodies. But at last they were able to identify the approaching vessel as a brigantine. Somehow they forced their aching bodies to keep the oars moving, though it had now become apparent that they had been sighted and that the vessel had changed course towards them.

Yet all of one and a half hours elapsed before they found themselves alongside and, as in a hazy dream, became suddenly aware that human hands were stretching downward to help them aboard.

The brigantine was a German vessel, the *Montezuma*, and her master, Captain Simmonsen, made haste to succour the rescued men. It is to Captain Dudley's everlasting credit that he confessed at once that the putrid and disfigured remains under the tarpaulin were those of his ship's boy, Richard Parker, whom he had slain with his own hand.

Captain Simmonsen ventured no strictures. He had the evidence of his own eyes to tell him what the three survivors must have suffered. They were mere skeletons, gaunt and wild eyed; weak, delirious and stumbling. He saw that they were cared for, ordered the remnants of the dead man to be sewn into sailcloth and committed to the deep.

Present at these last rites was a sad-faced youngster whose appearance sent a shudder through the rescued men. For an instant it seemed that the spectre of the dead man had returned to haunt them in their moment of rescue. In a way it had. For, by an astonishing coincidence, the sad-faced youngster, an ordinary seaman on the German vessel, was the dead man's only brother!

On their return to England (they were landed at Falmouth) all three survivors made voluntary statements on the tragedy. Dudley and Stephens were later tried and sentenced to death for murder on the high seas; but the Home Secretary intervened with a respite, awaiting Her Majesty's pleasure, and the sentence was subsequently commuted to six months' imprisonment.

The Mate of the *Squando*

As the Norwegian barque *Squando* lay alongside the quay at Oslo
that day in 1886 her crew moved briskly about the final preparations
for her sailing down Oslo Fjord, out into the North Sea, thence into
the Atlantic and across to San Francisco. Under the mate's critical
eye they worked with neither enthusiasm nor resentment, but with
the resignation born of life at sea, where work could only be expected to be hard, living poor and pay poorer still. If they and
thousands of sailormen like them ever stopped to wonder why they
stuck to the hardest and least rewarded of all occupations, few stayed
long for an answer. All they asked—but rarely got—was a good
passage, a dry berth, and enough pay at the end of it to enjoy a
few days ashore before returning, with parched tongue, throbbing
head and empty pockets, to the same vessel or another, to a mate
as tough or tougher, and to a master more or less iron-hearted than
the last one.

The *Squando*'s passage promised nothing that might break this
pattern—until one of the working sailors, raising his head at the
sound of horse's hooves and wheels approaching along the quay
and halting alongside the vessel, swore with sufficient originality to
cause his shipmates to glance at him and then in the direction in
which he was staring. They saw, getting down from a cab, the
familiar figure of their master—and a woman: and the cabby was
already heaving down pieces of luggage from a pile recognizably

in excess of the seagoing requirements of the captain of a barque.

"He's bringing her aboard!"

"She's going to sail."

"Never!"

"Hey, you!" The mate's voice cracked like a whip amongst them. "Get down there and fetch those things. And watch your tongues in front of the Old Man's missis."

"His missis!"

"Was you imaginin' something else?"

"She . . . ain't sailing . . ."

"She's sailing all right. Now, get on down!"

Had there been a hint of bitterness, or something else, in the mate's tone, or in his eye as he watched the woman pick her way up the narrow gangplank? The sailors would not have detected it. Subtle divination was not the strongest point of those inarticulate men, to whom a crojick was a crojick, a rope's end a rope's end— and a woman aboard ship a cause of restlessness and resentment at best, and, at worst, a harbinger of certain ill luck.

But there could be no protest. It was a case of put up with it, or find another ship: and it was too late for that. Articles had been signed, advance notes for a month's pay already in the lodging-house keepers' hands: and the mate was by now conversing with the master, with the words "tide" and "cast off" floating between them. Indeed, barely had the lady been escorted to the after cabin and her luggage placed on the long table than the Old Man was gruffly telling her he'd be down to see her directly, and was stumping off to supervise the vessel's sailing. The *Squando's* crew could only apply themselves to their duties, though there now hung at the back of the minds of the more superstitious an uncertainty, even a fear, which they would in time see amply justified.

For a time, though, all seemed to be well, and the barque's passage westward proceeded normally. The mates and bosun drove the men as hard as ever; the "doctor" cooked as ineptly as most of his kind; the biscuit delivered up to its eaters its inevitably generous bonus of living content. Then word began to reach the fo'c'sle of uneasy happenings in the after cabin. Whenever the captain's "tiger" came forward for a yarn with the seamen after serving the officers' meal he could be sure, for a change, of a respectfully attentive

audience for the latest instalment of a developing saga of growing
hostility between the Old Man, his missis and the mate: especially
the two latter.

"Sweet as pie, they was, at first," he would repeat for the ump-
teenth time. "Matter of fact, I got to reckoning she was up to
something with 'im when 'er Old Man was out of the way."

"What d'yer see, tiger?" The inevitable, hopeful question.

"Nothin'. But I never heard the like of a cross word between
'er and the —— mate until jest these last few days. But, by Jiminy,
you should 'ear 'er now! Soon as 'e speaks 'is mind about a thing
she's down 'is throat like a fish 'ook. Tears 'im to pieces every time."

"Serve the —— right! What about the Old Man, though?"

"Didn't seem to reckon much to it at first. Just sat there, lookin'
at 'is plate while she tore the —— mate in strips. But now, 'e's
changin', too. Joins in with 'er. Two of 'em on to 'im! And now
the —— mate's started answerin' of 'em back, like 'e couldn't
stomach it no longer. By Jiminy, you should jest 'ear the three of
'em at it!"

And soon the crew did hear them at it, as the hostility between
the couple and the mate erupted occasionally into an outdoor
shouting match which none of them troubled to conceal. At first
the crew reacted with delight, gratified to see their natural enemy,
the mate, being tongue-lashed by a woman, even though he did
subsequently vent his ill humour on them. Then, gradually, pleasure
gave way to unease. More than once, master and mate had been
heard to disagree sharply over some detail of the ship's working,
and once the mate was seen to turn his back while the Old Man was
addressing him and stamp away. Old seamen shook their heads and
hoped there'd be none of that if ever the *Squando* should run into
bad conditions and cool seamanship be needed. And one night the
"tiger" came hurrying forward, bursting to deliver himself of a
tale of how he'd seen the —— mate and the Old Man's missis nearly
collide as he went to enter the after cabin just as she was coming
out, and how they'd just stood and glared at one another for a full
half-minute before she'd elbowed him aside and swept on: and how
"that look she gave 'im, shipmates, would of brought out every
weevil from every biscuit aboard and sent 'em fightin' to be first
over the side, afore she could give 'em a look like it and shrivel 'em
to dust."

It was a relieved crew who eventually worked the *Squando* into San Francisco Bay and let the anchor go. It would be a day or two before unloading could begin, and more before it was finished and the men free to make up their minds about their next passage: but several were already declaring, as they had done often enough in the last weeks, that they wouldn't be seen dead aboard the *Squando* when she sailed again while that woman remained aboard her and the squabbling in the after cabin continued. More phlegmatic hands declared that, for certain, the mate must have been handed his marching orders by now. They would soon see him going ashore, not to return.

One wonders whether the mate himself had this same possibility in mind soon afterwards when he was told that he was wanted in the after cabin. At any rate, he went readily enough and found the Old Man and his wife both there. They were clearly awaiting him —she with an iron bar in her hand, the master with a knife.

Before the mate could turn back from the doorway they were both on him. The mate was a powerful man, but the suddenness of the attack took him at a disadvantage. He went down on the cabin floor, lashing out with his legs, trying to shield his face and head with his arms, while the woman beat at him with all her force and the captain darted in thrust after thrust with the knife. Desperation lent the mate strength, but horror benumbed his mind. His attackers seemed berserk, the woman as vicious as, if not more so than, the man. Afraid now for his life, the mate cried out at the top of his voice. An instant later the woman's iron bar eluded his feebly protecting arm and smashed down across his head. Blood-drops splashed ceiling and walls and a trickle of it spread rapidly across the floor as he lapsed into near-unconsciousness.

Another blow landed on him, and another: and then the woman straightened up, to lean back panting against the panelling. Her face was ghastly: a combination of blood-lust, triumph and horror. Her husband's expression resembled hers as he stared across the little cabin at her.

There was blood everywhere: on their hands, their clothes, on the walls, the ceiling; and more of it oozed steadily from the mate's shattered head and from several more places in his body.

The two fiends listened, panting: no footfalls approached: no one was calling to ask if anything was amiss. The woman threw down her weapon and gestured to her husband, and together they heaved the mate's unconscious form on to the cabin table. Quickly, they stripped off his bloodstained clothes and threw them into a bundle.

Then they hacked off his head.

But the mate's screams had been heard. They were heard by men who, for several weeks, had been half expecting some kind of drama to take place aboard their uneasy ship. Now that it had occurred, it had clearly come in some terrible form that was far beyond ordinary sailormen's capacities. They sent for the police.

The delay before they were confronted gave the master and his wife some time to try to conceal what they had done. It was not enough. Though they managed to weight both the headless body and the bundle of clothes and slip them into the dark water of the bay, together with the iron bar, it would have taken days of work and gallons of hot water and soap to remove all the grisly traces of blood from their skin, their hair, their clothes, and from the walls, ceiling and furnishings of that cabin, small though it was. When the police did at length arrive they needed no more than a glance to tell that their summons had been justified. After only a brief search one of the policemen had the unenviable distinction of finding the piece of evidence which would leave no doubt as to what had occurred: under the captain's bunk, in a bucket, he discovered the mate's head.

It has not been recorded why the couple struck down the mate with such diabolical fury, or even why the quarrelling had begun soon after the voyage's start, to mount eventually to so terrible a crescendo. There were plenty who were ready to say that the captain's wife had made overtures to the mate, who had rejected them. In her scorned fury she had worked to turn her husband against the officer with whom on previous passages he had been on friendly enough terms. There seems no doubt that it was her efforts that gave the tragedy its impetus: but, whether reluctantly or voluntarily, her husband had undoubtedly acted with her in the end, and would, if discovery had not overtaken them, have put to sea soon enough to get rid of the tell-tale head in deep water, from which there could be no chance of its returning to identify the rest of the body, if it were found.

The body, the clothes and the iron bar were found. The master and his wife were tried and hanged. And wise old seamen shook their heads and asserted that it didn't matter what kind of woman she'd been: the fact that she'd been a woman, and aboard ship, had been enough to make certain something awful would happen—and it had.

But not even the most pessimistic of these seagoing Cassandras could have predicted what else was in store for the *Squando*. After her baptism of disaster she would never know peace again.

When at length she sailed from San Francisco she carried none of her previous crew. They had departed thankfully to less fated berths. The *Squando*'s terrible story had been for a time the talk of sailor-town, and her agents had found it no easy matter to sign on new officers and crew: but at length they had succeeded, and the barque sailed southward for the Horn and home.

Before she was many days out the grumbling began. News of it soon reached the new master's ears, and he promptly gave orders for the men to lay aft and speak their minds. Most kept silent, but a vociferous group of four, who seemed from their attitude to have gained some measure of dominance over the rest, told the skipper squarely that the food was unfit for pigs, and demanded to know what he intended to do about it. The master was a reasonable man: he also knew the type of men who made up the only crew that had been found in San Francisco willing to sail the ill-starred *Squando*. There could be trouble. Instead of demanding, as some skippers would not have hesitated to do in the circumstances, whether the men thought they were on a pleasure cruise for the good of their health, and roaring them back to work and out of his sight, he took the mild line that the grub was all that was available, and asked what they thought he could do to change it. It was the wrong tack. He was dealing with men who had no sympathy to offer, and who could only recognize mildness in an officer as a clear sign of weakness.

From that day on, as the *Squando* sailed down the coast of Mexico, incident after incident of rebellious behaviour occurred, as if the crew wished to test the breaking point of discipline. The truculent four had now emerged as ringleaders and were swaggering about in open insubordination, triumphant in the knowledge that the rest of the hands feared them and that the master, by evading their first challenge, had placed himself in a position of weakness which it would take a far stronger man than he to retrieve.

Some way after the Horn, the four suddenly made their move.

One of the mates was in his cabin at the time. They slammed the door on him and locked it. Next, they seized the other mate, pinioned his arms, and dragged him, roaring with fury, to join his brother officer. Then they went looking for the Old Man.

They found him ready for them, marlin-spike in hand, his face determined. The weakness they had taken for granted seemed suddenly to have left him, and they hesitated. But, with the rest of the crew hanging back neutrally, they were four to one and knew they must prevail. They moved in. Raising the marlin-spike, the captain ordered them back. They rushed him.

The master fought back bravely and effectively, but the odds were too great. Sooner or later a blow had to land on an undefended part—and one did. He went down with a groan. The mutineers paused for a moment, looking at one another and examining the still man briefly. Then the watching crew at last protested at what they saw was to happen. The four attackers were lifting the inert form and were carrying it towards the ship's side. The protest came too late. There was a heave and a splash, and another master of the *Squando* went to an untimely grave.

It is not known whether this one had been dead when they threw him over, or merely unconscious—or whether they cared which he was. All that was of importance to the mutineers was that they were now in command. The rest of the crew were ordered, with threats, to get about their duties and give no trouble. The two mates were released from their cabin and assured that if they did not sail the barque coastwards without trying any trickery they would share the captain's fate.

So the *Squando* turned towards South America. When land was close in sight the four mutineers had a boat lowered and rowed quickly away. There was nothing the mates and crew of the barque could do but put back to sea and continue their passage home to Norway, carrying a fearful tale with them.

The earlier incident had already been well reported in Norway and discussed and embellished around all the seaports. The addition of such a second narrative rendered the *Squando*, in sailormen's minds, something to be avoided like the sea serpent. Her owners could not attract crews, and it seemed for a time that she might even be broken up. Eventually a less susceptible master agreed to take her to sea and somehow found a crew. He never returned from the voyage. Cutting his hand severely, he contracted blood poisoning and died at sea.

The man who replaced him was no luckier. One night, during rough weather, he missed his footing at the top of the poop stair, failed to hold himself by the handrail, and was flung violently on to the deck below. He died soon after, and yet again the *Squando* completed a passage under her mate's command. He took her into Bathurst, New Brunswick, about thirty miles south of New York, where officers and crew thankfully left her to rot for all they cared. *Squando* was a name already known in all the seaports of the Americas: and by now a supernatural element had crept into the stories sailormen were telling about her. They were saying—even those who had never so much as set eyes on her—that no natural cause could account for the violent deaths of four officers in a row, two of them attributable to murder. There was something unexplained aboard the *Squando*: some presence which sailed with her whenever she left port and proceeded to wreak its next ghastly crime. Not surprisingly, this "something" was credited with an identity. It was, said the narrators, leaning forward and lowering their tone, the murdered mate, relentlessly lingering to take revenge on all captains.

The fact that only captains had suffered in this apparent vendetta did nothing to convince humble seamen that they themselves might expect to remain immune. During the next few months many men were approached to sign articles in the *Squando*, and all refused. In Norway, her owners grew desperate. While their ship lay at her moorings in the American port she was accumulating debt and losing trade. Only one solution remained: to change her name, persuade at whatever cost a skeleton crew to sail her, and get her away to some port where she might be taken for anything but herself.

Preparations were made for this to be done. Meanwhile, the owners instructed their agent to employ a watchman aboard the empty ship. A man was duly found—he must have had a landsman's lack of superstition, or been desperate for a job—and went aboard one evening to begin his duties. Naturally, he made straight for the most comfortable apartment in the ship, the after cabin, and sat down with his lantern and his pipe to listen to the ship sounds of creaking rigging, lapping water and scurrying rats, with frequent unidentifiable noises which would make a man on his own suddenly listen intently and even open the door and peer out into the darkness, and listen again, and then return to the comforting circle of his lamp's rays.

So the watchman sat: until, after a while, he began to feel uneasily aware that he was no longer alone in the little cabin. Having looked all round, and seen nothing unusual, and having ascertained that it was only his pipe's smoke that was making that strange wreathing shape which seemed to sit across the table from him, he still could not get rid of a feeling that there was another being close to him. When he listened intently now he seemed to hear it breathing, slowly and heavily. When he moved he half expected to see . . . No, by God, he *saw*!

It stood near to the door—a slowly materializing form of a human male, naked and seemingly mottled with great blotches of some sort. But one part of it was failing to appear like the rest—and that was the head.

The watchman was on his feet, yet unable to move, both from sheer petrification and because the *thing* was between him and the only place worth running to, the cabin door. He could only stare as the spectre assumed more and more solid form, enabling him to recognize the blotches which covered it all over as patches of blood.

The headless figure began to move, a grotesque motion which brought it along the far side of the table, round the end, and now on to the watchman's side, approaching him slowly. It was only a few feet away: two more strides would bring it to him, and then . . .

But it never got there. With a wild and successful grab for his lamp, the watchman bolted across to the door, flung it open and stumbled up on to the deck and safety.

That was the end of the *Squando* as such. What they renamed her we do not know. Neither, for sure, did any of the men who subsequently sailed in her—or they would never have done so.

Ripe Stilton

Whenever I drive back to London from the north of England I visit the village of Stilton, in Huntingdonshire. I do not go there from necessity, but from choice. If I were to use the motorway, it would be well off my route: but I prefer the A1, the historic Great North Road, both in its own right and because it enables me, by making only a slight detour near Norman Cross, to pass through Stilton.

It is a prettily unpretentious little village, set principally in a straight line along the road. Its stone buildings look solid and sleepy, and its pubs honestly unsophisticated. What draws me to Stilton, though, is the handwritten sign displayed in many a window, STILTON CHEESE SOLD HERE.

Stilton cheese, I love you! Oh, yes, there is a time for your Double Gloucester, your Wensleydale, Cheddar, Leicestershire, Telaggio, Bel Paese, Brie, Camembert, Limburg, Emmenthaler and all the rest of them. But when there's a decanter of port and a fine, ripe Stilton on the table, that's the moment when you can say to yourself, "Why go abroad, when I can stay at home and have *this*!"

Some say you should mellow the cheese itself with port, like giving a new pipe a dose of whisky before the first smoke. I've tried both, and I can't say I believe there's much in them. Stilton is Stilton: one fixed point in a changing world—and so, when I drive back from the north I never fail to call and buy some of it, even if it's as little as half a pound.

One wet September evening, after a tense, uncomfortable drive from Leeds on the busy road, I let myself into my flat in Kensington with relief to be home without at least a dent or two in my car, let alone in myself. It had been one of those journeys when overtaking, through the fine spray of wet mud flung up by fast-moving vehicles, had been a constant risk. Yet I had had to push on, because I was expecting Mark Eaton for dinner, and I'd set off later than I had intended. As I neared Stilton I hesitated whether to turn off and use up ten minutes or so of precious time: but I decided I would. It would be a brief respite from the frenzy of the road before the last eighty-odd miles; and a piece of Stilton would add the only touch of distinction to what would be a knocked-together meal.

I am glad I made the detour that day: otherwise, I shouldn't have this story to tell now.

Mark is a junior director of one of my publishers. We don't see much of one another outside his office, but I'd given him dinner once before and we'd got on so famously, talking into the small hours—which one seldom seems to do these days—that I'd been looking forward to an opportunity to ask him again. Now, by cutting things so fine, I had probably spoiled the evening, and I was annoyed. I need not have worried. A wash and change of clothes and a couple of stiff drinks relaxed me in nice time for his arrival. He waved aside my apologies and lent a hand with the can-opener. All in all, it was a jolly good meal, with one of my dwindling stock of a modest '53 Bordeaux to give it savour. As I'd hoped, the appearance of a great wedge of Stilton, straight from the village, drew an appreciative exclamation and a dismissal of my mumblings about the non-vintage, off-licence port which was all there'd been time to organize to go with it.

We munched and sipped contentedly, with the curtains drawn to shut out the dank evening and the gas-fire burning for the first time since late spring. Yes, I was glad I'd made that detour.

"Stilton," said Mark, helping himself to another piece, "always reminds me of something very strange that happened to my grandfather."

"At Stilton?"

"No, no. I don't suppose he went near there in his life. He was a Staffordshire man—from the Potteries—and he seldom went far away, he told me, apart from his honeymoon in the Isle of Man. He was in the first war in Flanders for a while, and I think that cured him of ever wanting to leave his village again.

"However, about three years ago my parents persuaded him down to Gloucester for a week. I was home on vacation at the time and took him about in the car quite a bit. He wasn't exactly one for showing what he felt, but I think he rather enjoyed it and knew he'd been missing something. I never saw him again before he died."

I pushed the plate across to Mark.

"Last piece."

"No—you."

"Go on!"

He grinned, took the last greeny-yellow fragment, popped it into his mouth, savoured it on his tongue for a moment, then ate it slowly, nodding final appreciation. He sipped his port and I refilled our glasses. The gas fire buzzed. We were warm, cosy and content.

"One morning," Mark went on, "he told us this story. He'd been away from his village on one of those rare trips—a little holiday, or something—and arrived back by bus one afternoon. His cottage was up on a little hillside behind the church, and as he walked to it he was surprised to see an empty hearse and a couple of big black cars standing in the roadway in front of the churchyard. As you'll imagine, this dismayed him quite a bit. He'd lived in that village for more than half a century, and there wasn't a soul in it he didn't know. It hadn't a wealthy 'end': it was just a little community of people of Grandad's own kind, craftsmen and artisans who went in a mile or two to the potteries every morning by bicycle or bus, and came home every evening, and shut their doors behind them, and minded their own business. But they had some sort of relationship with one another over the years, and the fact that there was a funeral going on in the church meant to Grandad that some familiar figure wouldn't be seen about any more, which is always a bit sad, isn't it? So he went over to one of the chauffeurs waiting there and asked whose funeral it was.

"The cars were from Stafford and the chap didn't know any names, but his mate in the other car said he thought it was someone called Monckton: an old man.

"Now, this staggered Grandad completely. His one really close friend in that village—in the world, in fact—was a man a year or two older than himself, called Jack Monckton. They'd known one another all their lives: been to school, in the army, in the same pottery—everything. Next to Grandma, Jack Monckton was the one person in the world who had been really mutual with Grandad, because my father had left home quite young and moved on to a different plane entirely. Since Grandma's death a few years before these two old chaps had meant everything to each other, though I'm jolly sure neither of them would have admitted it. They were both retired, and both widowers, and just by going walks together, and playing a bit of bowls, and sitting in the pub, even if they'd nothing to say, they kept each other happy.

"And now, here was poor old Grandad just back off the bus in time for his friend's funeral. He told us he thought he was going to have a heart attack himself with the shock of it. There wasn't another Monckton in the village, and it was unlikely that it was some stranger from elsewhere who had asked to be buried there. In his unaccustomed absence, his one great friend of a lifetime had been taken away from him for ever. You can imagine how he felt.

"Grandad wondered what to do. He thought of hurrying on home to get rid of his suitcase and put on a black coat he had: but the chauffeurs told him they reckoned it would be over within a few more minutes. He was wearing his best suit and coat, as people do when they make a special journey, and he decided that, rather than miss his friend's last moments above ground, he would go into the church as he was, leaving his suitcase in the porch.

"So he did, hoping against hope that it wouldn't be Jack Monckton they were going to bury after all. But from the people he saw there, and the sympathetic glances and nods he got as he walked in, he knew that the worst had happened. He sank down into a pew and listened to the last of the service in utter misery.

"When the ceremony ended and they were preparing to lift the coffin, the verger, who of course knew how close Grandad and Monckton had been, came up and whispered to him that, as there were no relatives, he might lead the mourners if he wished. Grandad was much moved, and said he would be proud to. So, as the coffin came past, he left his pew and took his place immediately behind it.

"They came out into the daylight and moved slowly along a path between old gravestones. Grandad was too shocked by the whole business to feel any surprise at the direction they were taking. The new part of the graveyard lay round the other side of the church: they were going into a rather unkempt corner occupied by those grim-looking box-shaped tombs with iron railings and a lot of old ivy. The pall-bearers halted in front of one of these, and this really did surprise Grandad, for he saw that one end of it had been removed, to reveal the dark interior of a vault, reached by crumbling stone steps. This was very strange. He had never heard his friend speak of a family vault: he wasn't in that class ... And yet, come to think of it, the matter of burial was one which, by unspoken consent, had never been raised between them. Perhaps this was indeed an old Monckton vault dating from a time when there had been more of a family of them. Grandad tried to see an inscription on the stone which had been removed to give access to the interior, but there was none. He told himself he must look round the other sides of the tomb afterwards.

"The coffin was now disappearing down the steps. Grandad hesitated and looked round at the other mourners. He found that they were standing in a semi-circle, a few paces removed, as though deferentially giving him precedence. He glanced at the verger who stood beside him. With a gesture, the man invited him to enter the vault, moving forward himself and producing a small electric torch from his pocket.

"With the torchlight bobbing about his feet, Grandad descended the broken stairs. An unwelcoming smell rose about him: a compound of damp, and decaying stone and wood, and one or two other, indefinable elements. It was chill and horrible. Grandad wished he had stayed with the other mourners.

"The pall-bearers were respectfully setting the coffin upon a stone shelf. By the light of the verger's torch, Grandad saw other shelves about the walls, all burdened with the dark shapes of coffins, with here and there a dried-up wreath that would surely flake to pieces if he were to touch it. Despite his distaste, Grandad was impressed by the antiquity of it all, and a little awed that his plain old friend should finish up in such surroundings: but he had seen enough and felt glad that he had decided to be cremated when his time came.

"He turned to follow the pall-bearers up the steps—and suddenly froze with alarm. He was alone. The torch, which he had thought to be still in the verger's hand, he now saw was lying on one of the steps, its beam playing steadily into the vault. Of the verger himself and the others there was no sign: and the little square of daylight at the head of the steps had disappeared.

"For some moments he just stood there 'gawping'. He couldn't take it in. Then he picked up the torch and turned it round to shine up the steps to the entrance. The beam fell on a flat stone: someone had replaced the end of the tomb.

"Once again the poor old man thought he was going to have a stroke. He reeled, and dropped the torch; but luckily it didn't go out, and perhaps bending down for it brought the blood back into his head and saved him from collapsing. At any rate, it restored his presence of mind. He shone his way carefully up the steps and listened at the entrance. He could hear nothing. He called. There came no answer. He pushed the stone: but it did not budge.

"Well, I know what I would have done, and Grandad did it—he yelled blue murder. He got his shoulder to that stone, and heaved, and shouted, and heaved, but neither had the least effect. When he stopped, gasping for breath and feeling his heart trying to burst out of his chest, he heard nothing except the buzzing in his ears of his own racing circulation.

"And then, suddenly, he did hear something else. He listened hard. Yes, there it was! They'd realized their ghastly mistake—for it *must* have been a mistake—and were coming back for him. By gow, he'd have a thing or two to say to them! But . . . no. The sounds weren't coming from the other side of the stone at all. They were with him in the tomb!

"Slowly, Grandad shone the torch round the vault. There were more coffins than he'd realized, and one or two he hadn't noticed before had crumbled with decay, so that the grey-white of bones was clearly visible within. Then, when the beam had traversed all the walls, it came finally to rest on the gleaming varnish and shining brass fittings of the newest coffin, old Jack Monckton's. And as Grandad stared at it, its lid quivered as though struck hard from inside; and then again; and then it burst open with a great rending noise. There were more splintering sounds as fragments of wood flew out and fell to the floor. Then, slowly, the head, shoulders and trunk of Jack Monckton rose up into a sitting position.

"No longer knowing whether he was mad, or dead, or delirious,

or what, Grandad could only stare as his old friend heaved himself
out of his coffin and lowered a leg to the stone floor, to stand erect.
The thought flashed through Grandad's mind that this was one of
those seeming miracles one reads about occasionally when death has
been presumed prematurely and the 'corpse' revives in time to give
everyone a very nasty shock: in which case, what a blessing it was
that he happened to have got shut in with his friend by merest
chance, so that in a few moments they would be saved together.
He descended the steps, peering across the vault. Jack Monckton,
dressed in his best suit, was by this time moving slowly towards
him, and Grandad considerately lowered the torch, so that it
shouldn't shine in his friend's eyes. He turned the beam to shine on
his own face, and said huskily, 'Jack, old friend: look, it's me.'

"Monckton did not answer. Grandad could feel him coming
closer. Worried again, he flashed the light on the advancing figure
—and recoiled on seeing that the flesh of his friend's face was already
a mass of decomposition.

"Now, Grandad admitted to us, he screamed, and it was the first
time in his life he'd ever done so. He screamed, at the same time
backing away, stumbling with his heels against the bottom step.
He threw out an arm to save himself, but fell down awkwardly
on the steps. The torch, falling at his side, shone upwards into the
misshapen features as two suppurating hands reached out to claw
at my grandfather's face.

"That was the last thing he knew."

The gas fire buzzed. Mark tossed off the last of his neglected port
and held out his glass with a grin. I spilt some as I poured.

"That," I protested, "was one of the most disgusting stories I've
ever heard. Its only redeeming feature is that it's completely untrue."

"No, no," he retorted, with a shake of his head and a frown. "It's
just as Grandad told it to us. You could ask my people, if you ever
meet them." He grinned suddenly. "Perhaps I have missed out one
little detail, though."

"Little! You've missed out *the* detail."

He interrupted: "I should have told you this first, but I think
you'll agree it would have spoilt the story. You see, the evening
before Grandad told us all this we'd all gone out to a restaurant
together. The old man hadn't been keen at all. He wasn't used to
posh places, he said, and he'd be too uneasy to eat a bite in one.

All the same, my people insisted, and so he came with us. Well, it wasn't a success. He didn't know what to order, and when the food did come he didn't like the unfamiliar way his plain choice looked. He ate very little, which, of course, affected us all, and none of us enjoyed ours. There was just one thing that saved the meal, and that was a fine Stilton cheese they offered us afterwards. Grandad perked up as soon as he saw it coming. 'Stilton!' he exclaimed. 'Now that's something they can't muck about with!' And he ate a large portion and called for some more."

"Just a minute," I halted him. "Are you going to say this whole thing was a cheese-dream?"

Mark merely grinned.

"Well!" I exclaimed. "They call you the new progressive publishing type, and you trot out a revolting yarn that hangs on one of the oldest devices in the game."

He said mildly, "There's one more thing you haven't heard yet."

"If you'll give me a moment to run through all the clichés of that kind of situation, I'll tell you what it is."

He nodded. "I'm sure you will, so I might as well tell you. You see, Grandad described this awful dream at breakfast on the day he was leaving. The dinner the night before had been intended as a sort of special send-off, though it hadn't really worked. Well, he finished telling us this, and then got up to go and pack his case, saying as he did so that after a nightmare like that he'd be glad to get back to familiar surroundings and to see his friend Jack Monckton in the flesh again. He'd felt guilty enough about leaving the poor old chap alone for a week, as it was.

"While he was upstairs the telephone went. Mother answered it. It was a bad connection, and there was a lot of shouting to identify the caller. It turned out to be the rector at Grandad's village. He was sorry to trouble us, but Grandad had left our number with his next-door neighbour, in case of any emergency arising, and as they weren't sure just when he'd be coming home they'd thought they'd better ring up. It was nothing to alarm Grandad about, but just to say that his old friend Jack Monckton had passed away in the night: and they all thought that, in the absence of any relatives, it was owed to Grandad to lead the mourners, if he felt like coming back for the funeral."

I gave Mark my special hard look.

"And you're saying all this is true?"

"Absolutely."

It was my turn to grin. "Your Grandad," I said, measuring my tones like the Lord Chief Justice, "was Professor of Byzantine History in the University of Tokyo. I heard his name once, and wondered if there was any connection with you, and someone told me there was."

Mark threw himself back in his chair, threshing his legs as he shook with delighted laughter, in which I joined.

"Well, yes," he groaned at length. "You win. Only . . ."

"Now what?"

"It still happens to be true. It happened in Shropshire about 1890 to a man named Reginald Easton. I've always thought it had the elements of a good after-dinner yarn; and it has, hasn't it?"

Hasn't it?

The Princess of Thebes

The Director of the Department of Oriental Antiquities, Herr
Wieser (as we shall call him), pushed his spectacles up on his forehead, a habit of his when puzzled. His assistant swung round from
his desk in pleasurable anticipation. Something interesting had
evidently turned up in the post.

"Extraordinary thing, this, Bruch," said his chief. He threw a
letter across, and Bruch caught it deftly. After reading it, he glanced
up at Herr Wieser and began to read it again.

"Well, what d'you think of it?" Wieser enquired.

"All nonsense, of course. The old chap must be raving. The
mummy of Princess Nitokris here in Dresden! In a back street, at
that; and nobody knows about it except this Doktor—can't read it—
Schulze, it looks like."

"I've heard of him before, as it happens," said Wieser. "We
bought a papyrus from him not long after we opened—that would
be before your time, wouldn't it?"

"Yes, I only came in '91. All right, was it?"

"Very nice. You know it, of course—Case 44—musician-
priestess of Amen-Re."

"Oh, that. Yes. Charming. But this mummy: *if* it's true (and I
don't believe it for a second) it would be priceless. Nitokris—a
royal princess—Divine Adoratrice of Amen-Re at Thebes—daughter

of the first king of the twenty-sixth dynasty! Where on earth could he have got her from?"

Wieser took back the letter. "Came into his possession from a source he cannot reveal," he says. " 'A lifelong Egyptologist, I recognized its immense value and beauty at once. The sarcophagus is in perfect condition, the colours brilliant, finely inscribed with texts from the Book of the Dead, and bearing representations of Nitokris and the godesses Nut and Hathor, the latter slightly defaced. The mummy itself is in excellent condition. Remarkable, when you consider the process had been deteriorating steadily . . .' "

"Exactly," put in Bruch.

" '. . . and a heart scarab remains suspended from the neck.' "

"I suppose he's got the canopic jars as well, but doesn't care to mention them in case we think he's boasting," Bruch observed with sarcasm.

" 'Nitokris was, as of course you know, Herr Direktor, a royal princess, daughter of Psammetichus, who obtained her adoption by Shepenwepet II, Divine Adoratrice of Thebes as her successor in the god's temple . . .' Yes, well, we know all that. The point is, Bruch, is the man mad, or has he really got something priceless? I never heard of an *Egyptologist* called Schulze."

"Probably a private collector who likes to keep things to himself —or a maniac, as you suggest, Herr Wieser."

Wieser gazed through the window of his austere, handsome office, across the Theater-Platz to the wide-flowing Elbe. The Albertinum Museum, which housed Dresden's collection of Oriental and classical antiquities, had only been completed five years previously, in 1889, a fine new building on the old arsenal site. Wieser was proud of it, and of the collection over which he presided. Dresden called itself the Florence of Germany, from the treasures of the ancient world which were housed in its noble buildings—the Kunstakademie, the Japanese Palace, the Zwinger, the Georgentor. In time the Albertinum might rival the British Museum in London. Its Direktor could not afford to ignore any possible acquisition, however unlikely. He rose briskly, pushing back his chair.

"There's only one thing for it—we must go and see, Bruch. If we make fools of ourselves it can't be helped."

A short walk through the streets in the crisp wintry air brought them to their destination. Dresden's picturesque Altstadt was rapidly losing its medieval charms, as one old building after another fell beneath the demolisher's hammer, and tall-storeyed German Renaissance wedding-cakes rose in their place. But the Wenceslausstrasse lay in a quarter as yet unfashionable, and its old houses, huddled together as if for mutual protection, preserved their black timbering and lowering gables, from beneath which strange little goblin faces, carved centuries ago, peered down at the passer-by. Bruch snorted.

"Not a very promising district!"

"You can't tell," said Wieser. Having pulled vainly at the old bell for some two minutes he decided that it was not working, and performed a sharp rat-tat on the door-panel with the snuff-box he always carried.

"Dr Schulze isn't up yet, and his keeper's gone out for the day," suggested Bruch. At that moment the door opened. An elderly man, tall, stooping and shabbily dressed, stood before them.

"Dr Schulze?" enquired Wieser. The old man bowed his head courteously.

"The same. And you must be the Herr Direktor of the Museum, and——?"

"Herr Bruch, my assistant."

"Come in, gentlemen."

Schulze led them upstairs (the banisters were dangerously rickety, Wieser noticed) to a first-floor parlour. The room, like its furniture, was old and dark. The worn armchair, the fly-blown paper that covered the panelling, the cheap cloth on the table, did not suggest affluence: nor did the black basalt clock look like the possession of a connoisseur. Like the hall and staircase, the room was heavy with the musty odour of an old uncherished house: a blend of damp, dirt, and dry rot, with overtones of mouse.

"Sit down, gentlemen. I am sorry I cannot offer you more comfortable chairs. I spend most of my time in my study, and entertain few visitors."

An awkward silence fell, broken by Wieser.

"I received your letter this morning, Herr Doktor, and was naturally interested."

Schulze appeared to withdraw himself from a dream engendered by the small flickering fire in the rusty grate.

"My letter. Yes."

"Frankly, I found it difficult to believe that so rare and valuable a thing as the mummy of Princess Nitokris could exist, even in a private collection, without the knowledge of museum authorities. My first reaction was to regard your story as a fairy tale."

"It is strange, I agree. But there are many strange things, even outside the *Märchen* of Grimm. I am honoured that you took the trouble to investigate the circumstances."

For one who had written in a reasonably business-like manner Doktor Schulze seemed uncommonly vague. Wieser was getting impatient, and Bruch's smile, with its implication of "I told you so!" was broadening. Wieser shifted to the edge of his chair, which had badly broken springs.

"Perhaps we could see this mummy, Dr Schulze? Our time is limited."

"Certainly. I shall be very happy to show her to you."

He led them from the room, through a small low doorway, down an unlit flight of steps. Bruch stumbled and clutched at the wall. Beneath their feet the floorboards creaked ominously. Outside the winter sun shone, but in this house it might have been evening. "*Mehr Licht!*" quoted Bruch facetiously.

They were standing before a door, low-arched and worm-pitted. Schulze produced a key. Before inserting it he turned and fixed on them an enigmatic look in which were blended fear, questioning and pride. A mother showing off her child, an impoverished trades-man his wares, might look so. The assumed vagueness had been all salesmanship.

Schulze turned the key and entered the room before them. Both men blinked at the change of light. The window was shuttered, the only illumination that of two candelabra, in the centre of the room, some seven feet apart. Schulze beckoned them on.

They were standing beside a long wooden chest, painted in bright colours that sprang out at them in the yellow light of the candles. The lid bore the figure of a woman in half-relief, life-size. She was young and pretty, even by the standard of 1894. The straight bands of a dark wig framed a delicate oval face, the open eyes kohl-ringed, up-slanted, a deer's eyes; the straight nose almost Greek, the mouth small and sensitive. Beneath the long falls of hair the breasts were half revealed, the arms folded under them. The robe that outlined her figure was brilliant with designs. Set in vertical bands were the forms of serpents, birds, scarab-beetles, animal-headed gods, scenes from Nitokris's life and of her soul's presentation to Amen-Re, Neith, Hathor and Anubis. Vivid, enigmatic, death-defying, the image stared up half smiling at her visitors.

"It is a rich time, the Saite Period, a time of revived splendour," Schulze said.

Wieser did not reply. He had produced an eyeglass, and was busy studying the detail of the paintings. Then he straightened.

"May we see the mummy?"

Schulze lifted off the lid of the coffer, loose-fitting and unhinged, and laid it tenderly on the floor. Within lay a figure tightly wrapped from head to foot in brown-stained linen, cross-strapped with narrow bands of the same. Nitokris had been small, not much above five feet. The figure was well defined, slim and rounded. On the breast lay a small greenish stone, the heart-scarab which had been buried with the body as an amulet. Wieser picked it up and read the hieroglyphic inscription.

"Do not stand up against me as witness, O heart, thou art weighed when in the judgment hall of Osiris."

Schulze, who had formerly seemed abstracted, was now tense with excitement. He looked eagerly from one man to the other.

"She is beautiful? You admire her? You have nothing like her in your collection? She is a matchless piece of burial art?"

Wieser carefully kept his voice unenthusiastic. "The coffer is certainly decorative, and appears to belong to the Saite Period. As to the mummy, it seems well preserved. I should like to have a closer look at it, at the Albertinum."

"You may! You may! You will find nothing wrong, all perfect."

Wieser and Bruch exchanged glances, and the younger man said:

"We think, however, that you should give us some information as to how the mummy came to be in your possession, Dr Schulze. For the reputation of the Museum, we cannot take chances."

"I cannot tell you," Schulze replied. "I have sworn it. But you may believe me when I say I have full rights. She is mine to sell, to give away, to keep if I wish."

"You will not object, however, if we check with the police?" Wieser asked.

Schulze shrugged and smiled. "You may do as you please."

Next day the fragile coffer was carried down the steep stairs of the house in Wenceslausstrasse. By noon it was in place on a trestle in a workro m at the Albertinum, under a blaze of gaslight, subjected to the searching eyes of Dresden's experts. They peered, they tested, they lifted the light body and examined the image of the cow-headed goddess Hathor on the coffer's underside.

"The coffin-paintings are remarkably fresh, probably retouched; the decoration and symbolism correct in every particular," reported Professor Bahn, the Museum's chief authority on the Late Dynastic Period. "The nomens and prenomens in the cartouches indicate that the subject was Nitokris, daughter of Psammetichus I, and sister of his successor, Necho II. The effigy represents a woman younger than Nitokris is known to have been at her death, and the features do not bear any resemblance to the somewhat negroid Psammetichus, but are probably conventionalized."

Police investigations and overseas inquiries revealed no mummy-theft from museum or private collection. After much debate, the Albertinum authorities decided to buy the mummy. When they heard Dr Schulze's price they recoiled in horror. It was more than had ever been paid for a single acquisition.

"It's fortunate," said Bruch dryly, "that the lady is so slender, for Schulze is demanding no less than her weight in gold." But Wieser's enthusiasm overcame all objections, and the mummy formally passed into the possession of the Albertinum. As Schulze received his payment, he remarked wistfully, "I am sorry to part with Nitokris. But she is in her proper place."

No glass case large enough to contain the coffer was available; so, to protect the precious exhibit from too-curious sightseers, the dais on which it stood was roped off, and an attendant always kept it in sight. Alone, in the centre of the gallery, Nitokris lay in state, a faint smile on her painted lips, the stone beetle no longer resting over the cavity where her heart had been, but displayed in a case beside her.

Wieser was a man of organized thought, not given to absence of mind. It was all the more surprising to his wife when, one cold and unpleasant evening, as he doffed his hat and cape in the hall, he clapped his hand to one capacious pocket with a cry of irritation.

"Confound it! I've left the thing on my desk."

Frau Wieser pointed out that the meal was almost ready and the new cook's temper uncertain. Her husband replied that the document

in question was indispensable to his work that evening, for next
morning a meeting was to be held at which he had to give his
considered opinion on a highly debatable papyrus of the Ptolemaic
Period. There was nothing for it, he must return to the Albertinum.

He arrived at the private entrance cold, wet and in no mood for
nonsense, and was the more annoyed to be intercepted at the top of
the staircase by one of the cleaning women, the elderly Frau Schmidt,
in an obvious state of alarm.

"Oh, sir! Oh, sir!" she gasped, her bucket slopping its contents
on the linoleum, her knot of hair descending on to her shoulders.

"Well, what is it, Frau Schmidt? I'm in a great hurry."

"Something dreadful, sir. I can't tell you . . ."

Visions flashed through Wieser's mind of manuscripts set on fire,
canopic jars broken, priceless statues smashed by a maniac. His mind
was greatly relieved when the cleaner went on, "Sir, I've seen a
ghost." Wieser stopped and patted her arm reassuringly.

"Come, come now, you mean you *think* you've seen a ghost.
Why, I've seen some very odd things up there after dark myself.
Mostly reflections in the glass cases."

"No, no, it wasn't nothing like that!" she whimpered. "It was a
woman, and she passed me, just by the Egyptian Gallery door, and
she didn't make no noise: only flitted past, and when I got into the
Assyrian Room there wasn't nobody there."

"Another cleaner, perhaps," suggested Wieser.

"No, 'cause they'd all gone except me and Frau Wuttke, and it
wasn't her—more like a young woman."

"Then," said Wieser briskly, "it was somebody who concealed
herself before the Museum shut, hoping to steal something valuable.
Naturally, the intruder would be quietly shod. Let us go and search
Frau Schmidt."

Together they searched every corner of the long, silent galleries.
Nobody was hiding behind the mummy-cases or under table or
desk. Painted eyes stared out at nothing: the proud, prick-eared cats
of Bast kept eternal guard on mummified mice and falcons. There
was, as Frau Schmidt had said, nothing living in the whole place,
beyond themselves. Wieser persuaded her without much difficulty
that she had been the victim of illusion. He spoke with authority,
and she was glad to agree with him. Calmer, and slightly ashamed
of herself, she put on her shawl and departed. Wieser collected

his document, had a word with the nightwatchman, and went home once again.

Albrecht, the night-watchman, was an old soldier of phlegmatic disposition, quite the last person to make up foolish tales: yet, two nights later, he imagined that he saw a figure similar to that seen by Frau Schmidt. He must have had a word with the cleaner before she went off duty, Wieser and Bruch agreed. These peasant types were notably superstitious and infected each other with fears. If Albrecht developed ridiculous fancies, he would have to go—though he might not be easy to replace, once the rumour got around that the Albertinum was haunted. When a couple of nights had passed without incident, they congratulated each other.

It was almost four o'clock, two days before Christmas. Against a red winter sky the tower of the Hofkirche stood tall and black; homing birds wheeled round the city's cupolas and spires. Bruch, alone in his office, found his eyes straining at small print, and moved to light the lamp. Match in hand, he bent over the wick; then, as something beyond him moved, paused in his task.

"*Who in God's name are you?*"

Against the wall, by the door, a woman was standing. The light was so poor that he had only an impression of her appearance: she was short, wearing a long cloak and some kind of head-covering, and he thought afterwards that she had looked young. Then she was gone, and Bruch was rushing headlong down the corridor and banging at Wieser's door.

Unless Frau Schmidt, Albrecht and Bruch were all ready for the madhouse, there was no doubt that something uncanny was going on in the Albertinum. The spectral lady was seen by others. A visitor, inspecting a mummy-case, met her round the corner of it, and when he had been revived by brandy reported that her face had been pretty, but its expression wild and pleading. A small boy who had strayed away from his mother to explore the Egyptian Gallery told of a "poor lady" who had held out her hands to him. Then a student from Strehlen, a youth of strong nerves with an eye for detail sharpened on archaeological research, furnished the authorities with a fuller description of the visitant. She was about twenty, he said, dark-eyed and attractive, but looked very pale and ill; she wore a cloak of grey tweed with a riding-collar, which she held tightly at the neck. He could not see the colour of her hair, which was concealed by a white scarf. Objects in the room had been visible through her body.

Wieser laid this and the other descriptions before his wife.

"One hesitates to believe in such things, but it's all happened since we got the mummy of Nitokris. Surely the Redemption . . .? I mean, as a Christian, one knows that the souls of the dead are in good care. And if it were Nitokris herself, her spirit would have been walking since—good heavens, since about 630 B.C."

"A long time," said Frau Wieser, who was embroidering a wool-work flower on a cushion. "And if it were Nitokris, she would be unlikely to be wearing a nineteenth-century cloak."

Her husband stared at her open-mouthed. "So she was, according to this boy! What do you make of that, Maria?"

"Either that your dead princess sensibly prefers modern costume —or that she is not Nitokris at all. And in either case I should get Pastor Schilling to come and exorcize the place."

"You are always right, *Weibchen*. I will ask him to do it on Sunday."

It was many years since Pastor Schilling had been invited to perform the service of exorcism. A good Lutheran, he considered it a rite somewhat Papistical in its implications. If, however, a lost or strayed human soul were wandering in his parish it was his clear duty to send it back to its proper place. The service was duly held on a bleak Sunday afternoon of early January. The windows were shuttered, as always at weekends, and gaslight lent the Egyptian Gallery an unnatural foggy appearance, depressing to the spirits of the small company. The last prayer said, and the pastor again in his outdoor coat and heavy scarf, Wieser asked him:

"Do you think it has been successful?"

The pastor, folding his cassock, shrugged. "I am not experienced in these things. Ask Father Johann at the Altkirche. But I can tell you, Herr Wieser, there is something bad in this room, something which disturbs me. I don't like it and I shall be glad to leave."

Bruch essayed a mild joke. "Too many graven images, Pastor? Paganism rampant?"

"No, my son," replied Schilling gravely. "The people of old Egypt were in their way highly spiritual, and worshipped sincerely according to their lights. No, it is something else. It is—almost—a smell of corruption."

"That's odd," said Bruch. "One of the cleaning women has been complaining that we have a dead rat somewhere."

The pastor looked round and sniffed. "There is something—yes,, a sort of sickliness. Perhaps it is a rat, and not an evil emanation. Do you not perceive it, Herr Wieser?"

"Unfortunately I have a cold," returned Wieser, "and a poor sense of smell at the best of times. But, now you mention . . ."

"It's stronger here," said Bruch, who had moved into the middle of the gallery. "Could there be something wrong with our Nitokris?"

Wieser laughed. "Very little *can* go wrong with a mummy embalmed for thousands of years. The body is barely more than skeletal, the vital organs removed and replaced by spices. No, I think we won't disturb Nitokris."

They left the gallery, first extinguishing the lights. The gas globes faded into dullness, wall-hangings and sarcophagus paintings lost colour. They walked down the stairs towards the entrance. As they were about to leave Wieser gave an exclamation of annoyance.

"My memory is getting worse and worse. I have left the keys on my desk, and I must lock the place up. You two go on—I'll catch you up."

He went back up the dusty stairs, past the seated stone figure of a Pharaoh, beneath a tomb-scene inscribed with a hymn to Osiris. He opened his office door. There were the keys, where he had put them down. He stretched out his hand to touch them; and saw that he was not alone in the room. At the other side of the desk, in the visitor's chair, sat the shadowy form of a woman. In the fading light he could see that her face was very pale, her head shrouded. Some sort of garment covered the rest of her from head to foot. Wieser stared at her, panic-frozen, for he knew, now, only too well, that the exorcism had not been successful.

Silently she rose from the chair, and with a dreadful, anguished smile drew off the covering from her head and let the cloak drop from her shoulders. Beneath it she was naked: but Wieser's emotions were not those of aroused desire. Her slender body was spectral thin, wasted by the hand of death, marked by the stains of decomposition. But that was not the worst. Over the heart and below the rib-cage were great gaping wounds, dark with dried blood; another wound divided the scalp. For a moment—to Wieser an eternity—

she stood before him, a dumb pleading in her face, as though begging him to avenge the cruelty that had been done. Then there was nothing, but the room as it had been.

Wieser never knew how he got out of his office and down to the entrance. But somehow he was in the street running and shouting after the distant, strolling figures of Bruch and Pastor Schilling.

"Come back! Come back! Come back!"

The mummy-coffer was opened next day, and the grave-wrappings removed from what it contained: not, they saw with horror, the dried frame of a long-dead princess, but the decomposing corpse of a young woman whose death had taken place not more than two months previously. A clumsy attempt at embalming had been made.

When they went to the house in the Wenceslausstrasse, Dr Schulze had gone: it seemed that he, too, had visited the Egyptian Gallery and noticed something unusual about the air. Evidence in his "study" showed that he had been a superb artist in the manufacture of objects designed to deceive archaeologists. Not content with producing false papyri and such harmless fakes, he had decided to achieve a *chef d'oeuvre*—a mummy in its sarcophagus. The remains of several animals indicated that he had learned something of the technique of embalming; and this had emboldened him to try his hand on a human subject. Unfortunately for him, his funerary skill did not equal his artistic powers. The identity of his victim was never discovered. She was thought to have been a young prostitute he had lured to his rooms. When they caught him in Prague, still practising his art, he did not deny the murder but would disclose no details of its subject. Just before his execution they questioned him for the last time.

"What does it matter?" he said. "She was nothing. I made a royal princess of Egypt out of nothing. I could have made kings, emperors. I am a god."

But they hanged him at dawn next day, and he died like a mortal.

Death Takes Vengeance

Even the least impressionable of us are sometimes conscious of an apprehension about things unseen, particularly in certain places and at certain times when unknown influences surround us.

Are the dead really gone from us for ever, or do they still haunt our earthly life? We cannot explain the connecting link, but the ghosts of the departed have the power to lurk at our side, and may suddenly reveal themselves, leaving us helplessly exposed. They often return for a specific purpose—to scare us and to frighten us.

Just such an unquiet spirit was that of the obsessionally jealous wife of Arthur Noakes, who returned to haunt her husband. She was permitted to disturb his peace in a most terrifying way and avenge the wrong which she had endured at his hands during her lifetime. For he had a weakness for the opposite sex, and the very jealous Edith had suffered much bitterness and heartache.

On her death-bed Edith vowed that if Arthur continued to chase other women and make love to them, she would haunt him so that he would be afraid even to look at a member of the opposite sex. What she had never been able to achieve in her lifetime she hoped to do from the grave.

Arthur Noakes took not the slightest notice of his wife's dying threat, and as soon as was decently possible he started looking around for an attractive woman. Secretly Arthur thought that now he was a free man at last he would enjoy his freedom to his heart's content. Perhaps he would marry again one day. Wives did have their uses, but there was plenty of time for that.

Being the owner of the only drapery and haberdashery in the small Sussex town of Newhurst in the last century, Arthur had always enjoyed a fairly wide choice from amongst his clientele, but often the most desirable would disdain to go out with a married man. Now, as a passably good-looking widower, he expected to have an even wider choice.

His roving eye soon alighted upon a comely young widow who often went into his shop for ribbons and lace, and whose widowhood had not in any way dampened her naturally gay disposition and love of life. However, when Arthur first approached Mabel she appeared to be a little reluctant, despite the come-hither expression in her pretty blue eyes.

"After all, Mr Noakes, isn't it rather early for you to be seeking the companionship of another lady, with your poor wife scarcely cold in her grave?"

Arthur shuddered involuntarily at the mention of Edith, but his eagerness to possess this bundle of apparently demure charms quickly overcame his temporary foreboding. He realized that Mabel, born of typically strait-laced parents, was simply being wary of her precious reputation.

"My dear young lady, it seems as though I have been in love with you for ever, and I could no longer withhold my feelings for you without informing you of them. If you are reluctant to walk out with me openly—and I can appreciate your reticence—could we not arrange a rendezvous outside the town where no one would see us?"

Mabel's eyes were now contemplating her dainty, buttoned shoe as with her right foot she brushed the floor lightly to and fro in a coquettish manner. Arthur's hopes ran high as he feasted his eyes on her slim ankles, and noted the wavering flush on her cheeks and the coyness of her smile.

She raised her eyes once more to his. "Where could we meet without being seen?" she asked, pretending to be shy about asking such a forward question.

Arthur knew just the place, for he had been there before. Living in a small community, secrecy was sometimes essential to conduct affairs with success. He told Mabel about the place in glowingly romantic terms, and she agreed to meet him there the following evening.

It was a charmingly romantic spot close by a bridge which spanned a quiet stream and was an ideal place for lovers. Arthur got there first, and his new love did not keep him waiting long. His joy was complete when he saw her coming across the bridge. No one else ever seemed to pass that way, even in those warm summer nights, and they met there several times to kiss and make love without fear of being disturbed.

Then one night Mabel was late, and Arthur was getting more and more disturbed, watching the bridge for her as the light slowly faded. What had happened? Perhaps she was keeping him waiting on purpose to make him keener. Maybe she was not coming at all. He had almost decided to go when he saw her hurrying across the bridge.

Thinking he would teach her a lesson, he hid behind a tree and waited until she had reached their usual trysting place, then he crept up beind her and suddenly put his arms around her slender waist.

Arthur got the shock of his life. She seemed to disintegrate coldly into nothingness, at the same moment turning her face towards him. It was horrible—horrible beyond description. Instead of Mabel's pretty smiling face with her dancing eyes and rosy cheeks, the face he saw was that of his dead wife—chalk-white, with glazed, dead eyes, but grinning at him in a way which filled him with horror and fear. He sprang away from her with a cry of revulsion and terror.

The phantom pointed a warning finger at him, then vanished before his eyes. He was reminded of his wife's death-bed vow and fled from the spot as fast as his shaking legs could carry him.

Over the bridge and half-way up the road he saw Mabel coming towards him. But was it really his pretty little widow, or that same dreadful phantom wearing Mabel's clothes? He waited in fear and trembling, panting after his unaccustomed exertions, for he had never run so fast in all his life, and in the half-light of dusk he could not be certain until she was close to him.

"Were you getting impatient, love?" she asked, laughing lightly as she put her arms around his neck and kissed him.

His relief was great, for she was warm and smelled of lily-of-the-valley, a perfume Mabel always used. But Arthur disengaged himself from those clinging arms with trembling hands, remembering that other smell of the grave and the ghostly warning of his dead wife.

"What's the matter, Arthur? You're shaking. Are you angry with me for being late? Or did someone jump out at you from behind a bush?"

Arthur tried to pull himself together and took refuge in showing annoyance at her lateness. He asked her what had kept her.

"Sorry I'm so late, Arthur. My mother-in-law arrived and I couldn't get rid of her. But never mind, I'm here now. Let's walk to our nice little spot by the bridge and I'll make it up to you."

She spoke in her most seductive mood, cuddling up to him in a way which normally would have made his blood run hot in his veins. But tonight he shivered at the thought of going back to where he had seen that grinning apparition of his dead wife. He suggested that instead they should go to the music hall. He fancied lively company, and entertainment, with a drop of Scotch inside him to help him forget the fearsome apparition.

But Mabel refused to be seen with him in such a place, and when he declined to change his mind she told him that he didn't love her any more. "And if you go there you might as well find yourself one of those fancy women who frequent such places, Arthur Noakes."

Arthur remonstrated with her, declaring that he still loved her, but Mabel was proud and obstinate and declared that if he left her now to go to "that place", she would never meet him again, for it was obvious that her love and companionship were no longer desirable or necessary to him, and they might as well part company.

But Arthur was still shaken, and Mabel's attitude seemed petty and small-minded and he did not believe that she would refuse to see him the next time he asked her. But of one thing he was certain —he would never again use that romantic little spot on the banks of the river as a trysting place.

Arthur enjoyed himself at the music hall, and after a few drinks and a jolly time joining in the songs with a buxom songstress who singled him out for her attentions, he began to feel that the whole ghastly happening had been a figment of his imagination. How could a dead woman appear like that?

He expected Mabel to turn up at the shop within the next day or so, but when she did she was with a friend and ignored him.

With her nose in the air, she chose to be served by his assistant. Well, if that's your attitude, young madam, he thought, I can soon find someone else, preferably someone not so fussy about being seen around with me.

Arthur's next choice was a married woman whose husband was in the navy and conveniently away on his ship most of the time. After he had been going round with her quite a lot in mixed company, Alice eventually invited him to her home. Alice was not exactly pretty, but passably good looking, with a warm heart and a voluptuous body. Arthur arrived at her house in a fever of anticipation, for he had no doubt that he would be offered all the home comforts.

Alice had cooked a nice meal for him and there were beer and gin to drink. She even produced a very good cigar, possibly her husband's, thought Arthur, grinning to himself as she lit it for him with loving care. He sank back into the soft cushions of the settee with a feeling of well-being. Alice sat beside him. He caressed and cuddled her and they exchanged kisses. Then she got up.

"Finish your cigar while I get undressed, Arthur," she said, her eyes shining with invitation. "And come upstairs when I call you."

"You bet I will, sweetheart," he said eagerly. "And don't be too long."

It seemed only a minute or two, however, before Alice returned, still dressed, but different, bringing a draft of cold air with her. He stood up, dropping his cigar on the carpet, uncaring that it was burning a hole.

He was petrified with fear, for it was not Alice who stood before him, but Edith's ghost, her white dead face grinning at him in the most horrible way. He just stood there in that room where only a short time ago he had been feeling so happy and full of desire. Now he was rooted to the spot in terror, for Edith's ice-cold, skinny arms were around his neck, her dead eyes mocking him, and from her bloodless lips came the odour of rotting flesh.

At that moment a soft voice called from above: "You can come up now, Arthur darling." The frightful apparition then disappeared. But Arthur could still feel those bony arms around his neck, and the dank cold smell of the grave and the sickening odour of corruption were not concealed even by the still smouldering cigar.

Suddenly he was galvanized into action. Into the hallway he went, oblivious of the inviting figure in the diaphanous negligee waiting for him at the top of the stairs. Alice watched in amazement as he struggled to open the door without bothering to close it again and rushed out, down the path and into the street as though he was being chased by all the demons of hell.

That was the end of that little romance, and Arthur stayed at home every evening for the next week consoling himself with Scotch. He was becoming a bundle of nerves and his employees as well as his customers noticed the change in him. He was short-tempered, even rude, and many of his regulars remarked that if there had been another haberdasher in Newhurst they would certainly not patronize Mr Noakes.

When his chief assistant gave in his notice, telling his employer why in no uncertain terms, Arthur realized that he could not go on like this. Something drastic must be done. He decided to sell up his business and go to London. In the big city teeming with life Edith's ghost would no longer haunt him and he could make a fresh start. He set the wheels in motion and by Christmas his business was sold and he was installed in a small hotel near Charing Cross Station. He spent a quiet Christmas in the hotel, where there were no women under the age of forty, therefore no temptations in that direction, his only lapse being a drink which he took in his room.

After the holiday he started to look for a business similar to the one he had left in Newhurst, and eventually found one in Greenwich. It took every penny of his capital to buy it, but the turnover was good and he had living accommodation as well as the shop and storerooms. He was feeling much happier and in better spirits.

He had two women assistants, one of whom immediately attracted Arthur. Her name was Mary Thompson and she lived with her parents, working to help with the household expenses as her father was an invalid as a result of wounds sustained during his army service.

Mary's chief interest was Penny Readings—the Victorian name for amateur dramatics—and Arthur was soon invited to join her small circle of friends with the same interests. Arthur helped with the readings and as prompter, and he also gave clothing and materials for stage drapes. Mary was very grateful to her employer and they were soon on more than friendly terms, a development to which

Mary was by no means averse. Arthur cut down on his drinking and began to enjoy life once more.

One night the company were having a dress rehearsal of *The Murder in the Red Barn* which they were performing for a charitable organization. The lights were dimmed for the scene between Maria and her lover in the barn just before he murdered her. Whether it was the eeriness of the scene and the creepy atmosphere of the empty hall, Arthur did not know, but as he was prompting in the darkness of the wings he glanced up from the printed page for a second and in the dimness beyond the stage he thought he saw once more the ghostly features of his dead wife. His hands started shaking so much that he was unable to hold the book which fell to the ground. Mary, standing beside him, immediately took over.

Fearfully he turned towards her. Was it really Mary? Or had Edith once again taken the place of his present amour?

"Whatever is the matter with you, Arthur? You look ghastly," Mary whispered with concern. "I hope you haven't caught a chill."

Arthur clung tightly to her proffered hand, warm and comforting, telling himself that he must have imagined that brief glimpse of death. He tried to control his fit of trembling and assured Mary that he was all right, perhaps a little cold and tired, but he could not rid himself of the certainty that the hateful apparition of his dead wife had followed him to London.

When the rehearsal was over, Mary insisted on returning with him to his rooms above the shop and buying a bottle of whisky on the way.

"You need a good hot drink of whisky and milk," she told him, "and I am going to see that you have it before you go to bed."

In the ordinary way Arthur would have welcomed the suggestion with glee, but tonight he was afraid and tried to dissuade her.

"I promise you I'll have my hot milk and whisky. There is no need for you to trouble, though it's very sweet of you, Mary dear."

But Mary was not to be dissuaded, and as Arthur opened the door for her to go inside he could not resist a quick and fearful look behind him. They climbed the stairs, lit dimly by a single gas bracket on the half-landing, and entered his living room. Quickly he lit the lamp on the table and also the two brackets on either side of the mantelpiece before he put a match to the gas-fire and the gas-ring on which to heat the milk. He grabbed a pan from a shelf and poured some milk into it which he soon had warming.

Mary laughed as he bustled around with competence and speed, though she thought that it was not very complimentary to herself. He hadn't even attempted to kiss her since they had come in, which was most unusual for Arthur, who did not usually let an opportunity go by when they were alone together.

"I'm not afraid of catching your germs, you know," she told him provocatively as she took his hands and placed his arms around her waist, holding her face up to be kissed. Arthur could not resist that, and the milk boiled over before he released her. As Mary rescued what was left of it, he went to get a cloth to clean up the mess on the hearth, when he heard the distinct sound of a door banging downstairs.

Mary heard it too and told him he must have left the outer door open when they had come in.

"You'd better go down and fasten it properly, dear," she told him, as he stood there reluctant to leave the cosy room.

He felt all icy inside. He knew very well that the door had been securely locked when they came in, but he could not tell Mary that he was afraid of the dark and terrified of what he might find down there.

Quickly he ran downstairs, anxious to get it over. The door was closed, so he pushed home the bolt as fast as his trembling fingers could.

Suddenly he became aware of that awful odour of death, and he turned around in terror, knowing what he would see. There she was, standing in his path, obstructing his way up the stairs. There was a greenish look about her face, the cheeks falling in with decay. Her mouth was half eaten away, making her grinning jaws more macabre than ever. And when she clasped her bony arms around his neck and forced him to look into her eyeless sockets, which nevertheless seemed to be fixed upon him accusingly, his terror was more than he could stand.

Then Mary called his name from above, and the phantom vanished, leaving him chilled to the marrow, sickened with fear, and nauseated by that evil, all-pervading smell from the grave. Overwhelmed by the horror of it, he slowly went up the stairs. When Mary saw him she was appalled: he was white as a sheet and shaking with fear.

Of only one thing he was certain. He must get rid of her. But Mary was intent on looking after him, making him sit in front of the fire, giving him sweetened hot milk and whisky. He downed it in one gulp, thinking that it was surprisingly hot considering what had taken place since the milk had boiled over. But then he realized that it must have been only a few moments between his bolting the door and his return, yet it seemed as though he had been hours clasped to that bundle of bones and decaying flesh which had once been his wife.

Mary was busy filling his stone hot-water bottle. "You've got a thorough chill, dear, and I think you should stay in bed tomorrow. We can manage in the shop, and I will come up and look after you when we're not busy."

Arthur was alarmed at such an idea. Edith would never permit it! That horrible apparition would return. Rather than that, Mary must go, but he felt too exhausted to tell her then.

Eventually, when she had finally left him, he went to bed and sank into a restless sleep which was instantly filled with appalling nightmare. His dead wife was in bed with him, bringing that macabre chill and vile smell. Her bony arms were surprisingly heavy across his chest and he felt as though he was unable to breathe. He tried to wake up but he could not. From the depths he fought to regain consciousness in order to move and get away from that terrifying weight which was preventing him from breathing. He fought and fought to get free, groaning in agony, and at last he woke up.

The next day he said to Mary: "I'm fed up with your Penny Readings. I want more gaiety, more freedom. You're far too possessive, Mary, and I want no more of it. I want men friends to have a drink and a joke with. Life's too short and I want to go out and enjoy myself. Stay on at the shop if you wish, but our relationship will be business only from now on."

Arthur felt a cad when he saw Mary's tearful face, but what else could he do? Edith was winning. Her dying threat was coming true. He could not escape.

Mary's sorrowful expression every time he happened to look her way drove him to the pub at the corner and he took to going there often, arriving back at the shop half drunk and incapable of being civil to his customers. Then Mary left and he got a young man named Gilbert to help him, but Gilbert was not averse to swindling his employer, who was often in no fit state to deal with business.

Arthur did not seem to care. Edith's ghost no longer bothered him, but his health was failing through not taking proper meals, and drinking too much

One Sunday he had a longing to see Newhurst once more. It was dusk when he arrived there, thin and emaciated. No one recognized him. Disconsolately he wandered around, eventually finding himself at the church.

A light drizzle was falling. The service had long finished, and there was no one about. Except Edith. But a young Edith, just as she had been when they had first met. She was beckoning him into the churchyard. Eagerly he went, his footsteps unsteady as he followed her to her grave.

Beside her wet gravestone she opened her arms to him, and he went to her like a trusting child. As the dead arms closed around him she began to change, slowly becoming the ghastly sight which he had encountered that last appalling time he had seen her—the same decaying cheeks, eyeless sockets, grinning jaws. His heart was thumping painfully. His throat felt constricted, and he was unable to breathe. It was like his nightmare again, those awful asphyxiating arms around him. But this was no dream. He could feel the gentle rain on his face. He was suffocating in that terrible embrace. She was taking him with her to the grave. Utter victory was hers.

Next morning Arthur's body was found lying across his wife's grave. They would not have recognized him, but he had his wallet in his pocket with his name inside.

He was buried in the same grave as his wife, for all his old friends thought that he must have been fonder of her than he had professed to be, or he would never have returned to be with her in the next world.

His friends only learned what had happened when one of them went to a séance and Arthur's voice came through the medium and told the story of what Edith had done to him.

A Date with a Spider

Pedro crept silently up the dark, rickety stairway, one hand gripping the decaying wooden slats with each step upwards, the other tightly grasping a round tin which was just too large for him to hold properly in his small, grubby hand.

When he reached the top he crouched there for a few moments, listening. He looked downwards to see if anyone was about, and, seeing no one, gave a sigh of relief. He knew that he wasn't allowed up these rickety old stairs to the loft above. But he had to feed his animal friends no matter where they chose to live.

He stood up and pushed open what was left of the door. It squeaked as though in pain, and Pedro knew that his friend the spider would recognize the sound and come to see what succulent morsel he had brought today.

Just enough light came through the broken shutters which half covered the windowless opening near the thatched eaves to enable Pedro to step carefully over the half-rotted wooden joists which smelt of worms and beetles—though none lived there any more, as this splendid and magnificent spider ate every living thing which strayed within its reach.

Pedro was always fascinated at the sight of his huge spider friend. Its round black body was almost as big as a plate. Its long hairy legs, like those of a land-crab, seemed hardly to touch the floor as it moved silently and swiftly along.

The spider came confidently and unhurriedly across the floor towards him, its beady eyes, shining and unblinking, fixed inexorably on the little boy with the tin.

"Hello, Mr Spider, look what I've got for you today," whispered Pedro in a conspiratorial voice. He opened the tin and set a meal of live ants before the spider. "You like these, don't you," he said as he watched the monster's sickle-shaped jaws demolish the contents of the tin in seconds.

Pedro sighed. "You're so greedy," he scolded softly. "And what's more, you eat too quickly. It's taken me ages to catch all those ants." Ah well, never mind. He had lots of time to get more.

"Where's that boy got to?" grumbled Maria, wiping her hands on her apron before she opened the door leading into the bar.

Maria, dark and pretty, was still in her twenties. She had huge eyes and her black hair was coiled in the nape of her graceful neck. As she went in she saw Josef busy cleaning the counter which did duty as bar and reception desk.

She stood for a few moments watching her husband's bare, brown back and the way his muscles moved as he worked. The sight of his bare back still gave her pleasure, although they had been married for some years. They were laughed at in the village, because Josef didn't go after the Indian girls, and Maria would not have the slightest familiarity from the soldiers.

But Maria was determined that they were not going to spend their lives rotting in this river backwoods. One day they would leave it for ever and go to civilization. The surest way of staying in this place for ever was to slip into the same kind of life as everybody else. Nearly all the younger married women in the place were sluts. Maria was determined not to be one. Besides, she was still in love with her husband.

"Is Pedro with you?" she asked.

"No, *carissima*."

"This place," she said, "is falling to pieces. Everything in it is rotten. It's impossible to try to keep it decent. And heaven knows what places Pedro gets into."

Josef grinned and then made a grab for her as she passed him. "I know. One day we will leave." He caught her neatly by her slim waist and pulled her to him.

"One kiss, my love," he demanded.

"Let us go soon, Josef," she pleaded. "If you keep putting it off we shall be here for the rest of our lives." She struggled with him. He was only interested in kissing her. "Josef, you must think of the boy as well. This is not a good place for him to grow up in."

Josef looked serious for a moment. "I know, *carissima*. But it costs money to move. One day we will have saved enough."

"One day! One day! It is always one day. That day never comes."

"Oh, give me a kiss."

"You have all the kisses you want from me, Josef," she said, struggling half-heartedly with him. "Some people are never satisfied. Where's that son of yours? That's more important."

"Oh, he's all right. He's got a good brain, like his father. Going to be handsome too. All the girls will be after him."

"Well, let's make sure they're nice clean city girls, and not these back-river savages."

"By heaven, I'll have that kiss."

She put her arms around his neck and gave it to him. "There! How long has this love affair with you been going on? Years and years. We're an old married couple by now. It's a wonder you aren't tired of me."

He rubbed his nose against hers. "You've got no competition in this place. That's the trouble. Now in the city, it would be different. So don't you be in too great a hurry to go."

"What makes you think I'm afraid of competition?"

Maria broke away suddenly as she saw a stranger standing in the doorway. He had just come in from the merciless sun outside and was standing watching them, fanning himself with his hat.

Maria gave a little curtsy. "Good day, *señor*. Pardon us."

"Don't make excuses for being young, *señora*. They told me I could get a room here for the night. I'm on my way down-river in the morning."

He was middle-aged and looked as though he might be a trader of some sort. He told them his name was Hartmann.

"I'm afraid our best rooms are taken, *señor*," said Maria. "But we have one other room."

"Any room will do. I've learnt not to be too fussy in this country."

Maria went upstairs to prepare the room. It was one they did not often use. It was at the back, underneath the loft, and was closed in by the overhanging trees which grew on the steaming banks of the river.

As Maria reached the landing she bumped into her son, a tin clutched to his chest.

"So there you are, Pedro. I've been looking for you. I hope you haven't been up in that loft. I've told you it's dangerous up there."

Pedro said nothing, but looked at her with his great eyes which were an exact replica of her own. She continued on her way up the stairs, and Pedro felt relieved that she seemed too preoccupied to wait for an answer to her question. He knew well enough that if he betrayed the great spider in the loft, the poor creature would be summarily dispatched by his father who had no time for such things.

Grown-ups just didn't understand spiders.

Maria went into the back room which still had that stale smell they didn't seem to be able to get rid of. She opened the shutters, but there was not a movement outside to disturb the lush forest where the trees were a glory of colour and full of parrots and macaws. The temperature was that of a hot-house and down by the river the flies and mosquitoes hovered in clouds.

She sighed. Anyway, the room was a great deal better than would be found in the filthy posadas farther up the trail. At least the bed was clean.

She went about making the place as comfortable as possible.

That night Hartmann lay sweating in the darkness. A nameless fear had suddenly awakened him from a heavy sleep.

He felt the hairy legs of some hideous thing on his bare chest. With a startled movement of his hand he brushed the thing away, and as he did so he received a vicious, numbing bite.

The creature brushed by his face with a faint hissing noise. He shrank back in terror as it disappeared into the darkness above.

Hartmann did not realize that he had been bitten by a dreaded apazauca until it was too late. He was suddenly stricken with a paralysing agony and before he could struggle out of bed he lost consciousness.

Josef found Hartmann dead in the morning. His body was black. He locked the door before going downstairs to tell Maria.

"Mother of God," she whispered, crossing herself. "He must have had the plague."

"There's been no plague on the river for years," said Josef. "I don't like this, Maria. It will be bad for business."

Maria nodded. The brightness had gone from her eyes. This was a terrible thing to happen. You could never tell what would be the result.

The red-trousered Brazilian soldiers who came to take Hartmann's body gave Josef some queer looks and he got some even queerer looks from the customers in the saloon.

"How's the letting business, Josef? Prosperous?"

"Not when your guests die," grunted Josef.

"I understand he was poisoned."

"Well, I certainly didn't poison him."

Pedro had been kept in the kitchen, and he was getting very impatient, standing first on one foot and then on the other, wondering what Mr Spider would think about his being so late with his breakfast. Every now and then he peeped into his tin to make sure that none of his little captives had escaped.

His mother had been working at the store, but as soon as the soldiers left she went to find her husband, and Pedro, watching for this very opportunity, slipped out with her, hidden behind her long skirts.

They were busy talking and did not notice him. He slid through the door and was up the stairs as quickly as anything.

He negotiated the stairs to the loft a little more carefully than usual, but wasted no time. Poor Mr Spider must be very hungry, he thought, as he pushed open the creaky old door.

He stood for a few moments in the doorway, screwing up his eyes till they got used to the light. He was surprised that the spider had not come to meet him as usual. Instead it was high up in the corner and seemed to be fast asleep.

Pedro took a few steps nearer and softly called: "Here I am, Mr Spider. I'm sorry I'm late."

The creature did not move and Pedro began to be afraid that it was dead, so he called again, a little louder this time.

"Here I am, spider. I've brought your breakfast."

At last the spider moved and ran down one of the blackened wooden uprights to the floor. As Pedro made a move towards it, the creature turned, seemed to go back on its haunches, and sat there, its inhuman eyes fixed on the child with deadly malevolence. Its sickle jaws were working and it was making a faint, hissing noise.

But Pedro was not in the least afraid. The spider was just hungry and impatient. You couldn't really blame it, and it was really impossible to explain why he had kept it waiting.

The boy moved closer to the deadly creature, opened his tin and held out his offering.

"I'm sorry I'm late this morning, Mr Spider," he pleaded. "But a man died in his bed and the soldiers came to take him away."

The spider moved forward quickly and fell voraciously on the tin of insects. Pedro watched with fascinated satisfaction as the creature consumed its meal.

"My Mamma would not let me leave her," Pedro whispered to the huge creature. "But I did manage to get away, didn't I?"

He picked up the now empty tin and stood up. The spider crouched there, its cold, beady eyes fixed on the child, its jaws still working.

"I must go now," said Pedro. "Mamma will be looking for me. Good-bye, Mr Spider."

He made his way slowly down the stairs, keeping a watchful eye ahead of him in case Mamma should suddenly appear. He didn't want to be caught up there, or it would spoil everything.

He reached the landing safely. Now, if he could only slip back through the door, as he did when he went up, and then through the kitchen, no one would know that he had been up into the loft.

As he paused by the door he heard a loud, gruff voice.

"Take my word for it, he was poisoned. I've seen them like that before. Black as sin."

"He ate the same food as we did," said his Mamma in a strange, tense voice.

"He was robbed too. He was flashing a bag of money in here last night, and it wasn't there when we buried him."

"All the man's belongings were intact when I locked his door, Sergeant." That was his Papa speaking and Pedro thought his voice sounded different somehow. "The soldier's pay is very poor. You can hardly blame them," continued Josef.

"Here—are you accusing us?" exclaimed the Sergeant angrily.

"I'm not accusing anyone, so long as no one's accusing me."

"You'd better watch your step, Josef Morello. Everyone here knows you are trying to raise the money to get out of the place. And you're finding it's not so easy once you're stuck in a hole like this."

Pedro stood still outside the door. He dared not go in while the Sergeant was there. He had always been afraid of the Sergeant.

After he heard the Sergeant go, there was silence for a while. Then Pedro heard the sound of weeping. That was Mamma. He must go to her now.

He opened the door slowly. Mamma was weeping in Papa's arms, and he was stroking her black hair and trying to console her. Pedro ran over to them, the tears starting in his own eyes as he reached his Mamma's skirts at last and buried his face in them.

A few days later a half-caste Indian trader slept in the room. He was found dead in the morning, his body as black as the other had been.

Maria clung to her husband as the soldiers came for the body.

"What will happen to us?" she moaned. "There is a curse on us."

Josef pushed her gently away from him. "I'm going to search every nook and cranny in that room. Perhaps there's a snake there."

As he picked up a stick to take with him, the door opened to admit the Sergeant. There was a grim look on his thick, coarse, face.

"Josef Morello, I'm arresting you for murder."

Josef stood rooted to the spot, too stunned to speak.

Maria cried out: "No! No! You can't arrest him. He would not harm anyone. It was a snake. It must have been."

The Sergeant laughed harshly. "It was a snake all right," he said, grabbing Josef by the arm. "This one. Come along."

Maria cried out in despair and anguish, and Josef came to life at last, protesting strongly.

"Before the Holy Mother of God, I am innocent. Why should I kill my customers?"

"Why? Because they were both carrying money, and it's missing. We all know you want money badly to get out of here."

"They were robbed by the soldiers who came for the bodies," declared Josef.

The Sergeant glared at him belligerently. "And how are you going to prove that?"

"I am innocent, I tell you. By the Holy Virgin, I am innocent."
Josef was desperate.

"The Colonel will decide that."

"The Colonel?"

"Colonel Branza. The Comisario."

Josef went white. The Comisario in those days had power of summary trial and execution. There were no courts of law in the Amazon at the turn of the century. Murder was a pastime. Justice was rough, and Colonel Branza had an evil reputation. He enjoyed hangings.

When Josef was brought handcuffed in front of Branza, he knew from the look on the Colonel's face that he did not stand a chance.

The trial was perfunctory and Josef was not allowed to question the witnesses.

"Well," barked Branza, when such evidence as there was had been presented, "what have you to say?"

"I am innocent," protested Josef. "Before God I am innocent. Because these men were found dead in my house it doesn't mean I killed them."

"Can you suggest any other way in which they died?"

"They must have caught some plague."

"What—both of them? They came from different districts. They were poisoned in your house. The case is open and shut. You will be hanged at eight in the morning. Take him away, Sergeant."

The Sergeant pushed Josef violently out of the room and across the dirty mud compound to the cramped, filthy lockup.

Pedro was feeling very unhappy. Ever since Papa had gone away Mamma would not let him out of her sight. He had tried to slip away to feed his friend the spider several times, but Mamma had caught him half-way up the stairs and had slapped him. He had cried and Mamma had cried too, and he wished with all his heart that Papa would soon come back to them and they would be happy again as they had been before that horrible Sergeant took Papa away.

His grandfather had come unexpectedly to visit them and was talking to and comforting his Mamma, so perhaps he would be able to feed his spider tonight or tomorrow.

"I can't find anything in that room," old Morello was saying to

Maria. "Do you know what I'm going to do? I'm going to sleep there tonight."

"Oh, Papa——" exclaimed Maria in alarm.

"It's the only way I can see of saving my son."

"But if you die like the other two?"

"Then at least I won't have died in vain," said old Morello grimly. "The Comisario will know that my son can't be responsible for my death—so neither can he be responsible for the other two."

"Oh, Papa Morello, I can't let you do it."

"You must let me sleep in that room, Maria. It's the only way of proving Josef's innocence."

Maria burst into tears and threw herself into her father-in-law's arms.

"I have lived my life, child," he said, patting her. "You and Josef are just starting."

Pedro could not sleep that night for worrying about his friend the spider. How hungry he must be! And supposing he couldn't feed him tomorrow either. Grandpa would be watching him as well as Mamma, because Mamma had told him how Pedro was always going up those old stairs and they weren't safe.

Pedro tossed and turned in his little bed. The moon was shining so brightly that he could see clearly across the room. He could see Mamma lying in the big bed on the other side of the room, but she wasn't asleep either. She seemed to be staring up at the ceiling and listening for something. If only Mamma would go to sleep perhaps he would be able to go and see his spider tonight. He brightened at the idea. He had the ants all ready in the tin which was under his bed. He imagined himself creeping out of the room, tiptoeing carefully past Grandpa's room, slowly up the stairs, step by step, at last reaching the top and there would be Mr Spider waiting patiently for his supper.

He sat up in bed. Mamma seemed to be asleep now. At least she had turned her back to him. He did not know that she was crying silently to herself.

He felt quite excited as he got out of bed carefully and picked up his precious tin. Walking like a ghost on the boards, he left the room. Everything went just as he had imagined until, when he opened the creaky old door and looked inside he could not see

Mr Spider anywhere, though the moonlight made it brighter than day.

He waited for a few minutes, but there was no sign of the spider. He walked carefully across the rotting floorboards to see if he might be asleep in the corner. Stepping gingerly over an extra-wide hole where part of the floor was missing, he saw the spider down below on one of the beams of the room where his grandfather was sleeping.

Bending down, Pedro called softly: "Mr Spider—Mr Spider, come back. I've got your supper now."

But the spider took no notice of him. It was moving down the slanting beam to a point just over his grandfather's bed.

Pedro did not know what to do. Should he wait, or should he take his friend's supper into his grandfather's room? He considered for a while, but was afraid to wait too long in case Mamma woke up and found him missing.

He made his way carefully down the rickety stairs. He stood outside his grandfather's room for a few moments, then he opened the door very softly to see if the spider was still there.

Pedro turned the handle slowly, hoping it would not make a noise. The door was open at last. He peeped inside.

There was Mr Spider sitting on the bed. His grandfather was fast asleep, so he took his tin over to the bed and opened it to offer the juicy morsels to the creature which was already posing itself to strike its death blow at his grandfather's bare chest.

"I couldn't help being late, Mr Spider," whispered Pedro, hoping desperately that the creature would somehow understand. "But I'll bring you more tomorrow to make up for it."

For a second the spider wriggled as though disturbed from its purpose by the child's presence. The next instant there was a scream from the doorway. Pedro spun round to see his mother standing there, hand to mouth in terror, her eyes fixed on the monstrous spider on her father-in-law's bed.

Morello woke instantly. He saw the creature coming for him, its sickle-shaped jaws moving. With a quick movement he tossed the blanket into the air.

The spider fell on the floor and ran towards Pedro, who was bewildered by his grandfather's antics. Suddenly Maria pulled him away. Morello's knife flashed in the air and the next moment the spider was impaled on the floor, squirming to death, its powerful poison drooling on the boards.

Maria let out a long breath.

"An apazauca," said Morello tensely. "Haven't seen one that size for years. And that was hundreds of miles up-river near the mountains."

When Pedro saw that the spider was dead he began to cry.

"He killed my spider," he wept. "And I only just gave him his supper. Mamma, why did he kill my spider?"

Maria looked at her son aghast. "You fed it?"

"Yes, every day."

With a thrill of horror, Maria picked up the child.

"Mother of God! Come away, son."

But Pedro soon forgot the loss of his friend the spider when Papa came home and they were all happy together once more. He promised that he would never go up those rickety old stairs again. And anyway, Papa said that they would soon all be going to a big town called Pernambuco, which Pedro had never heard of before.

Ole Rockin' Chair

A snipe's sharp alarm-cry rang out across the rice swamps. With
a whirr of wings the bird shot upward, as though propelled by
some erratic rocket, into a twisting, turning course from which it
instantly recovered to sweep away in fast, straight flight.

"Goddamn it!" raged the man who, too late, had fumbled the
second cartridge into the breech, snapped the gun together and flung
it to his shoulder. He lowered it again, and as he did so met the
questioning eye of a keyed-up dog. He shook his head.

"You and me both," he told it. "But at least those guys don't
have it over me. No, sir!"

"Those guys" were his two fellow-shooters, now making their
disconsolate way across the spongy ground to rejoin him, their
guns, broken, under their arms, their game bags hanging limply
from their shoulders, empty as his own. The other dog trailed back
with them, exchanged a meaningful glance with his brother and
lay down to wait for the homeward trudge. For the dog knew that
a trudge it would be. He knew the way men walked, and the tone
of voice they used after a fruitless day's shooting. And of all the
days' sport he had ever participated in, this had been just about the
most fruitless.

"O.K.," one of the men said. "Let's go."

No one answered him. With the two dogs trotting before them,
the little party began their tramp along the line of a dike under

a sky already beginning to shade at the edges into evening gloom. Soon the stars would begin to twinkle through.

They were in the flat prairie region of south-western Louisiana with its wide reclaimed tracts for the growing of sugar, cotton and rice, watered by dikes fed by streams which flowed sluggishly into the Bay of Mexico. The waters of the bay were a few miles from the place where the party had been shooting, but the men had not seen them. Like all that country, this was a district of featureless prairie with few points more than twenty or thirty feet above sea-level and nowhere to climb for a long view.

Not that the three New Yorkers would have troubled themselves with distant prospects. What had brought them to Louisiana for the first time was not its scenery, but the reported abundance of snipe. In that, they had not been misled. They had seen plenty of the birds that afternoon. But it takes quickness of hand and eye to hit a snipe, with its swift, dodging rise, and the men had not a single one to show for their efforts. They knew this was attributable as much to their clumsiness from lack of practice as to the birds' evasive skill, and that they could look forward to better results with each succeeding day of the week they had at their disposal. Still, they could not help giving vent to disappointment.

They gave vent to something else when, after nearly an hour of threading their way along dikes and then amongst a tangle of evergreen vegetation, they realized they were lost. Though each in turn exercised his hunch as to the direction to take, none of them could find the small house they had rented for their holiday. The dogs, equally strange to the neighbourhood, were no help, merely running confusedly about, sniffing unfamiliar trails and looking questioningly to their master for guidance which was not forthcoming. It was getting quite dark.

For the best part of another hour the men and dogs wandered this way and that amongst the lush, drooping greenery without finding a single familiar feature. Although they knew there was nothing to harm them in that region, and the evening was mild and fine, they were tired and hungry after so much unaccustomed exercise. So it was with relief that they suddenly found themselves confronted by a pair of dilapidated wooden gateposts, rotten and barely managing to stand up, from which drooped the few remaining sticks of what had been a wide and no doubt handsome gate.

Beyond the gateway, the almost indistinguishable line of a broad carriage drive disappeared into a tangle of creepers and fallen trees.

Well, they agreed, where there had been a gateway and a drive, there must be, or have been, a house: and there was at least a chance that if they followed that way they would find some inhabitant who could direct them to their own place. They set off up the ruined drive.

Progress was difficult. The wide gravelled track was almost obliterated by foliage, which they had to shoulder aside, stepping high over the snares of coiled creeper stems. But they soon came to the end of the tangle, to find themselves staring through the dusk across ruined lawns towards weed-clad stone terraces and steps leading up to the still graceful shape of a long, white colonial house.

With a pleased bark the dogs dashed towards it, followed more tentatively by the men, who, knowing more about such things, could see that every window was shuttered and that all the other indications pointed to there being no one in residence. Their hammering on the porticoed door confirmed that view. Though they banged together, hard, they got no response. Without much hope, they decided to try the back.

To their surprise and delight as they rounded the building, they saw, in what looked like a servant's small lodging some distance from the house, the yellow gleam of lamplight. The dogs barked again. The light moved, and a door opened to reveal the tall figure of a man holding a lamp and peering out.

At the sight of three men with guns approaching he moved as if to shut the door again. But Ben, the owner of the dogs and arranger of the shooting holiday, called out a cheerful greeting which made him pause and wait for them to come up.

He was a negro. His hair was white and his face lined with age. He was very lean, and his shoulders were bent, but, even so, he stood a head higher than any of the three sportsmen: in his prime he must have been all of seven feet tall.

He stared at them suspiciously as Walt told him their predicament. The negro nodded.

"Yessuh. I sure know that place, and I can sure direct you. But it's gonna take you one hour walkin' there, even in the daylight. You never gonna make it this night. No, suh!"

They looked at one another, and their shoulders went slack with helplessness. They had taken entirely the wrong direction. As the old man said, they couldn't hope to pick their way through this confused terrain by night, even if they'd had a torch, which they hadn't. Walt gestured towards the long, low shape of the house.

"Anyone home?"

Something strange flashed across the negro's eyes, and he replied, too quickly, "Ain't nobody lives there no more. All locked up."

"Do you have the keys?"

The answer came hesitatingly.

"I . . . has them, suh."

"Well, then . . ."

The odd look was back in the old man's expression, and he did not speak. But Ed, the oldest of the three and a travelling representative who knew from everyday experience that persuasion is often better achieved by other means than words, was already stretching out a hand holding two ten-dollar bills. The old man's eyes widened momentarily. He glanced from one to another of the strangers, then took the bills and thrust them into the pocket of his trousers.

"Well, gen'lemen, I guess you gotta sleep somewheres. But . . ."

He broke off, shaking his head, and disappeared into his shack to fetch a large bunch of keys. Then he led them across to the house, the yellow light from his oil lamp breaking the darkness into grotesquely dancing shadows as they went. They followed him round to the front door and waited without speaking as he fumbled a key into the lock. It turned with difficulty and the tall door squeaked stiffly as he pushed it open. The two dogs surged forward —then stopped, blocking the men's way.

"C'mon!" ordered Ben, their owner, and nudged one of them with his foot. The dog moved, but not forward. It ran to one side, then to the other, then stood still again, quivering and growling. Its brother did the same.

"For Pete's sake!" Ben exclaimed, and brushed the dogs aside to step into the hall. The other men followed him, and then, reluctantly, as if not wishing to be left alone, the dogs.

Walt, who dealt in real estate, whistled aloud at what the beams of the negro's lamp showed him. What a figure a place like this would fetch in New York State! It was a superb specimen of colonial graciousness. From the spacious panelled hall the generous sweep of a staircase disappeared into the darkness, with a hint of a circular galleried landing at its head. Heavy oaken doors led off the hall on all sides. Yes, sir, here was some house! Ah, but Walt's trained nose could smell the rot in those handsome panelled walls, the decay crumbling away that dust-deep oaken floor. What had been a fine southern mansion was now a rotting shell, which would eventually disintegrate and collapse.

His companions, too, could sense the corruption in the air, and they shivered simultaneously. The negro saw them, and asked, "Well, gen'lemen?"

"Well, hell!" grinned Ed, the extrovert. "Any place we can light up a fire, without burning the whole heap down?"

The negro nodded and led on, opening one of the doors and ushering them into a large room. To their surprise it was completely furnished, though dust and cobwebs covered everything the lamp-light showed them.

"Say, this is the Ritz!" Ed exclaimed. "Anyone seen the head waiter?"

For the first time the negro grinned.

"I guess you'se lookin' at him right now, suh. You want somet'n to eat, I 'spect I can rustle up maybe some eggs and coffee."

Another ten-dollar bill was in Ed's hand before the negro had finished.

"Boy, you're on," he assured the old fellow.

Within half an hour the benighted trio were congratulating themselves on an experience to make the boys back in New York envious. In the capacious Adam-style fireplace a heap of logs burnt fiercely, multiplying the light of two lamps the negro had produced in addition to his own. The three men lounged luxuriously in arm-chairs, having beaten what dust they could out of the upholstery, sipping from mugs of good coffee laced with their own supply of brandy. Only the dogs seemed to be less than contented. Although the fire attracted them, they would not rest in front of it, but kept roaming to the edge of the shadows to stand and stare for a moment into the farther recesses of the room, occasionally whimpering as they returned to try to settle at the feet of Ben, their master.

The old negro—they had elicited that his name was Jake— drained the mug into which they had poured a generous measure of brandy and nodded his thanks.

"No, suh," he repeated, answering Walt's question. "Ain't nobody lived here since forty years. Never will now, neither."

Walt nodded agreement.

"Sure, the place is a wreck. But why didn't anyone want it in the first place?"

Jake shook his head gravely.

"Them dawgs knows why, suh."

He got to his feet abruptly.

"Sleep soun', gen'lemen, and there'll be fried bacon and eggs and coffee, soon as it's light enough to see. Guess you'll want to be away real early."

He took up one of the lamps and moved off. Ben began to ask him what his remark about the dogs signified, but he either did not hear or pretended he did not. He went out of the room, closing the door quietly behind him, and they heard the muffled thud of the front door.

Desultorily, the three sportsmen discussed the house, and Jake, and his parting remark: but, materialists all, their talk was of a bantering kind and drew them into no serious speculation about a fully furnished home of charm and quality which had stood un-tenanted for forty years. Then Ed, who had been yawning with increasing frequency, thrust out his legs, stretched his arms beyond his head, and said, "Well, it's the sack for me." Without waiting for the others' reaction he turned on to one side, snuggled deep into the armchair cushions, and, oblivious of the remaining dust, got his head down for sleep.

Ben wrinkled his nose at Walt, then turned to bang some more dust out of his own cushions. He regarded the result doubtfully, but said, "Guess it's this or the rug," and followed Ed's example. The dogs watched him uncomfortably, still unable to compose them-selves but sitting obediently near their master's feet.

Walt regarded his chair, then got to his feet. "Guess you fellas won't be wanting both these," he said, and took up one of the lamps.

Ben opened one eye. "Where you going?"

Walt grinned. "If there's chairs and all down here, then there's beds and all up there." He indicated the ceiling with his eyes. "You coming?"

Ben considered for a moment, then shut the eye again. "Hell, no. This is fine."

Walt shrugged and lit himself from the room. After the warmth of the fire the air in the shadowed hall was chill, and he half turned to go back into the room. But curiosity had now added to his motive for going aloft. He crossed to the broad staircase and, lighting his steps carefully for fear of rotten patches, ascended.

As he had guessed, the stairs led to a galleried landing, from which several bedroom doors opened. He chose one and looked in. Its decoration and furnishing showed it to have been a children's room, and Walt backed out again, promising himself something grander. He found it two doors away: a big, square bedroom, dominated by a looming four-poster bed. Like the rest of the house the room was fully furnished, the fine quality of the pieces apparent even under their festoons of dust-laden cobwebs. From the character of the furniture, Walt judged it to have been occupied by a man, doubtless the master of the house. A man would occupy it again this night for the first time in forty years. He prodded the bed. Dust rose. He pulled back the heavy tapestried counterpane, and found that the blanket beneath was quite clean, in spite of its musty smell. Jerking off his boots, Walt swung himself on to the bed. Yes, this would do fine. He reached for the lamp, which he had placed on a circular Georgian commode, one of a pair standing on either side of the bed.

As he leaned across, a movement caught the corner of his vision. He paused. The lamplight was close to his face, making the surrounding shadows closer and deeper than before, and he saw nothing in them. But then a sound reached his ear. *Creak, creak; creak, creak; creak, creak.* It had a rhythm. It was like . . . like the movement of a rocking chair.

Walt sat up and peered. He had already noticed a rocking chair standing beside the empty fireplace. He could see it now. And it was rocking.

Walt blinked and stared harder. *Creak, creak; creak, creak. . . .*

If he had only heard it, and seen nothing, he could have put it down to some freak of sound in an old house: if he had only seen it, and not heard, he could have blamed a New Yorker's unfamiliarity with the tricks of lamplight. But he could hear *and* see that chair rocking: and how could he account for that?

He got off the bed and carried the lamp across the room, his stockinged feet making no sound on the dust-filled carpet. It had occurred to him that one of Ben's dogs might have followed him upstairs and into the room, and was settling itself into the rocking chair for the night. It was unlikely, for he had seen no dog and he had shut the bedroom door behind him, so that it could not have entered since. As he came up to the chair he saw that he was right. No dog and nobody was in it. And still the chair continued to rock.

Walt put his hand on the Victorian bobbin-work chair-back. He felt the movement die under his touch. The chair stood still and silent. Walt contemplated it for some moments. He was a practical man, and he sought a practical explanation for what he had seen. But he found none, and, reminding himself that seemingly inexplicable things had a way of happening for reasons which might be found simple later, he turned and went back to bed. He had barely got his feet off the ground when he heard again the *creak, creak; creak, creak* from the fireside shadows.

This time, Walt thought, he had it. The floorboards were defective in places from age and decay, and the motion of his crossing the room had set up some disturbance in them which had transmitted itself to the chair and set it rocking.

Even as he thought this he knew it would not wash. No brief agitation would make any rocking chair in this world move steadily and continuously, as this one was doing: it could only be done deliberately, by someone pushing it rhythmically. Or sitting rocking in it.

Walt stayed where he was, watching and listening. For a moment he wished he had brought his gun upstairs with him: but he shook the thought away as unworthy of a true-blooded American. All the same, he toyed with the idea of slipping quietly off the bed, picking up his boots and tiptoeing from the room. If his companions noticed his return they would believe a story that he had not found the upstairs cosy. But, as he lay there, a sudden new sound reached him. It was the single, pronounced *creeeak!* that a rocking chair gives out when its occupant rises to his feet. It was followed by the smaller sounds of the chair settling back on its rockers . . . and then silence.

No—not silence. There was the sound now of something else; the quiet, slow creak of footsteps.

Sitting up rigid, Walt stared into the dark. He could see the motionless chair: but that was all. In all the shadows nothing moved.

Yet his ears told him plainly that footfalls were crossing the floor space between the chair and the window.

By now they had, in fact, reached the window and ceased. There came a gentle tapping, again a rhythmic sound, which Walt recognized as the contemplative drumming of the fingers which an unoccupied person will make unconsciously, rapping out the pattern of a tune. He almost expected to hear a low whistling or humming to accompany it, but did not. And still there was nothing to see.

The rhythm continued for a little while. Walt, as fascinated as he was perturbed, found himself trying to identify the tune, as if it might have told him something about the unseen drummer. Just as he thought he nearly had it, it stopped in mid-rhythm, and there was no mistaking the cause: something had made the *person* at the window switch from repose to alertness, as if a period of waiting had suddenly come to its end.

Then there came the final sound. It was unmistakable. It was the slow whetting of a knife.

Walt acknowledged now that what he had often been assured by over-imaginative or incurably romantic friends—although he had never accepted a word of it—was, in fact, true: that this materialistic, twentieth-century world still harboured forces and *beings* whose activities were on a plane of consciousness almost imperceptible to the human senses. He knew beyond doubt that he was witnessing what his fumbling mind told him was a haunting connected somehow with this long-deserted house and room: and reason reassured him that it could no more impinge on his physical actuality than he could interfere with its supernatural working out. Whatever was about to happen had no doubt taken place many times before, and would again after he had gone. This evening's performance would continue, whether he stayed to watch it or not. Therefore, he might as well hold tight, sit still, and watch it as he would watch a play.

This train of thought occupied no more than a few seconds of time. Meanwhile, the rasp of the knife continued, and Walt, who was by now growing almost fanciful, thought he heard concentrated in it all the hatred in this world, or another one. It stopped. Immediately, Walt's eyes caught a movement in the shadows near the window. Thrusting back the temptation to seize the lamp and hold it high, he lay still and watched. Gradually, the shadows wavered, merged, and seemed to solidify—until there stood beside the window the undeniable figure of a tall man.

Once more Walt's rational mind took over, and signalled to him that Jake, their negro host, had seen the lamplight in the window, waited, then climbed up the outside of the house and looked in. Satisfied that there was only one occupant of the room, and that the dogs were not with him, he had quietly entered by the window, with robbery in mind.

It was absurd, and Walt knew it: not only because this in no way accounted for the moving rocking chair and the other effects; but because the figure now moving slowly from the shadows towards him, though much the same height as old Jake's, and undoubtedly a negro, was neither stooped nor lean, but had the massive build of a professional wrestler.

Slowly the figure advanced: and though he reminded himself that he was watching something on another plane of being, which could not possibly step up, or down, to his, Walt felt a shiver of alarm as he realized that the staring, glaring eyes of the giant were riveted on his own—and that the something which now glinted in the lamplight as one of the muscled arms rose slowly was nothing else but a very real-looking knife.

At that moment the figure stopped moving. The head was cocked slightly to one side in an attitude of listening. It remained briefly motionless until, evidently satisfied, the massive figure moved again. Now it was at the foot of the bed, now moving to pass alongside next the window. Now the knife was raised above its head, the point aimed unwaveringly at Walt's chest or throat.

Pure, primitive instinct got the better of Walt at last. Flinging himself from the bed, on the doorward side, he seized the lamp and fled. Just as he was reaching for the door-knob, his eye caught the flashing arc of the descending knife-blade, and he heard a grunt of mingled effort and satisfaction. He did not stop for more. Wrenching the door open, he went down the stairs, with none of the caution he had shown in ascending and careless of what his friends might think of his haste. Watching a play was one thing, he told himself: audience participation was quite another.

With many a crack about the state of his mind, imagination and digestion, his awakened companions insisted on his leading them back to the bedroom to show them tangible evidence of a story so uncharacteristic of a down-to-earth real estate agent. Of course, they found nothing untoward. The chair did not rock for them. No footprints other than Walt's own marked the thick dust on the carpet. The blanket on which he had lain bore no rip from a plunging knife.

All the same, the dogs, which had accompanied them upstairs, refused flatly to enter that room, but hung about the landing, whimpering continuously until the men emerged and took them back to the firelit sitting-room for the remainder of a night in which neither Walt nor the dogs spent much time asleep.

With daylight a beaming Jake appeared, surrounded by a delicious aroma of bacon and coffee.

"Trust you all done slep' well, gen'lmen," he commented, setting out the breakfast in a rough and ready way.

"Are you kidding?" Walt replied, and something in his tone made the old man's eyes jerk up to meet his.

Ed broke off a yawn to guffaw. Walt said quietly, "Tell me, Jake, how come you live in that shack of yours, when you could have this whole place to yourself?"

The negro stared back at him, then asked, "You heard somet'n'?"

Walt nodded. "And seen."

Jake's eyes widened. He stood up straight.

"You was . . . up there?"

Ben was leaning forward now. "Say, what is this?"

Jake shook his head slowly and sat down on the arm of Ed's chair. "An' you askin' me why I don't live in here!"

Then he told them a story of forty years before: of how the old Colonel, who had inherited the house from his uncle—"as kind and sweet ole gen'leman as ever drew breath"—had turned out to be a harsh, miserly master who would, if he could, have restored the principles of slavery to his servants and plantation workers; how his negro valet, Pete, a gigantic young man and hot-headed, had been unable to bear any longer his master's constant criticism and sneering insults; how one night, when the Colonel had been unwell and had ordered Pete to sit up in the rocking chair in his bedroom, in case he should wake and require anything, Pete had bided his time until the old man had fallen asleep and had then knifed him to death at a single stroke.

Pete had come down and boasted of it to his fellow servants: but they, horrified in spite of what they had suffered from a tyrannical master, would not cover up for him, but offered him a chance to get clear of the district before giving news of the murder. Against their protests, Pete had run up to the bedroom again and seized what portable valuables he could before making off across the rice plantations. But he had gone scarcely any distance when Jake and the others had heard him scream out, and seen him turn to cry to them that the old Colonel was running alongside him. They could see nothing of this: only Pete, turning again and stumbling on a few more steps, then screaming again, then flinging up his arms as though to ward off some invisible assault; then, with a terrible cry for mercy, overbalancing and falling into the dike, where he had disappeared so rapidly that it almost seemed that he had been pulled down from below.

"You're kiddin'!" Ed broke the awed silence. Jake shook his head emphatically.

"No, *suh*! What cause I done got to kid you?"

He glared offendedly at Ed, who shifted uncomfortably.

"Well, hell, if he went down in the dike, why'd he want to be haunting the house and all?"

Jake nodded. "Coloured folks say the devil didn't want none of him: sent him back to go on hauntin' this here house so's he'll get real sick of it in time, and then mebbe they'll let him into Hell." He grinned suddenly. "Course, you white fellas won't believe none of that."

Ed and Ben laughed. But Walt said slowly, "I don't know. I don't know."

Then they finished their excellent breakfast, rewarded Jake with yet another couple of bills, and set off cheerfully in the direction he pointed. That day they filled their bags with snipe, and slept that night in their own, rented beds, while two exhausted dogs snored unstirring on the veranda in the mild Louisiana air.

The Frightened Corpse

Many years ago the countries of the Eastern Mediterranean were subject to epidemics of typhus and cholera of a frequency and severity unknown today. They were accepted as the way of life. Hygiene was imperfectly understood. There were no effective ways of combating the terrible diseases which killed people in their thousands. Contact with natives who cared little about hygiene was often dangerous for Europeans who had not the Arabs' resistance to the dangerous germs. Which made life difficult for those who came from northerly climes.

Many found alcohol a good antidote. Among these was a man named Winterton who had been cashiered from the British Army and had gone to Damascus in the early years of this century. He did not, however, give himself over wholly to alcohol. He earned his living by buying and selling anything from pins to precious stones. He had a cheap flat in the Arab quarter, and though he submerged himself in the Syrian life he never lost his identity or became slovenly. He was always immaculately turned out in clean white trousers and shirt, and always wore his row of medals on his jacket.

His best friend was Hassan, an Arab shopkeeper who sold curios, carpets, silks, decorated slippers, necklaces, baskets, and many other wares. He was short and fat and never looked clean. His coffee-coloured Roman features were encompassed by lank black hair and unkempt beard. He always wore shabby espadrilles and looked as though he slept in his clothes.

In fact, to look at them, the two friends were as different as could be imagined. But both were scholars in their way and were interested in psychical research. They spent hours discussing the mysteries of the occult. Hassan was much travelled and had seen many strange things in the East.

But the strangest event in his whole life was when his friend Winterton was struck down by cholera in an epidemic which swept through Damascus.

Hassan and Winterton had made a pact that which ever died first would endeavour to appear to the other, either at the point of death or soon after. They had discussed this many times and had come to the conclusion that it should be possible for someone who possessed strong powers of concentration.

When he heard that Winterton was a cholera victim, Hassan knew that it would be madness to try to see him, and that the harassed authorities at the overworked hospital, where Winterton had been taken, would deny him entrance. They had enough problems on their hands.

The matter seemed solved when Hassan got a message that Winterton had died. But Hassan, despite his great interest in his occult theories, felt not the slightest elation at the prospect of one of them being put to the test. He was genuinely upset at Winterton's death, which was too great a price to pay for the testing of theories.

All the same, he was not surprised when that evening, after he had closed his shop and was alone with his melancholy thoughts in his little room above it, Winterton came to him. After all, this was their pact. Naturally Winterton would honour it, as they both had solemnly sworn that they would, and Hassan had thought of little else since he had heard of Winterton's death.

Winterton was just the same, calm, upright and amazingly alert, despite his intemperate habits. Yet Hassan saw instantly that his friend was different. He experienced a thrill of fear and uncertain pleasure as he seemed to discern a strange unearthly glow which surrounded Winterton now, and Hassan realized that he was appearing to him, not as he had last seen him, but in his astral body. He was still wearing his medals, but his drill suit was crumpled and dirty and covered with disinfectant powder which he tried to get rid of by flicking at it with his handkerchief. The smell of it filled the room.

Hassan spoke to him, expressing his deep sorrow at his friend's fatal misfortune.

"When I heard the terrible news that you had died from the cholera," he said, pulling at his beard with nervous fingers, "I could not believe it. Are you really dead, Winterton?"

"No, I am not dead," replied Winterton in his usual calm voice. "Of course I am not. That is why I have come here to you. I am certain that I am not going to die. But they are going to bury me."

"Bury you?"

"Yes, bury me alive." Winterton's faded blue eyes held an expression of despair and helplessness.

Hassan knew that the hospital was crowded with cholera cases. The epidemic was reaching its climax, and the doctors and nurses toiled day and night doing what they could for the unfortunate victims. But with about a hundred cases to deal with daily, it was becoming increasingly difficult to find room to accommodate them, and if a few patients were carried to the mortuary before they had actually ceased to breathe, it was conceivable that some of them might indeed be buried alive. He shuddered at the thought.

Hassan regarded his friend's astral double with horror and sympathy.

"Tell me what has happened," he said.

"I admit," said Winterton in a faint voice, "that since I was taken into hospital with the cholera I have been lying on my bed as cold as a corpse, with my eyes wide open, probably looking more dead than alive. But I could see and hear everything that was going on around me. When the doctor came to examine me, I felt and understood what was said and done, although I was unable to speak to him.

"You see, they say that after you die of cholera, your body temperature rises, and muscular contractions cause your limbs to move. And so you can imagine how appalled and horrified I was to learn that the doctor thought I was dead. He told the attendant who was with him to have my body taken away at once for burial. That was when I concentrated all my energies and thoughts on trying to get into communication with you, for I remembered our pact. My thoughts were going through my mind with perfect continuity and incredible swiftness as the hospital orderlies lifted me on to a stretcher and took me to the mortuary.

"Can you imagine what it was like in that mortuary?" continued Winterton. "The twisted bodies—some of them moving, I swear— the distorted faces. There were so many that they piled one on top of the other. Some had no clothes on. Some were unbelievably filthy. And do you know what the smell is like—mixed with disinfectant? And so I had to get out of that awful place. I could not stay there among those who were dead and no longer cared."

Winterton paused for a moment, as though it was becoming a great effort to continue. Hassan watched him helplessly, listening to every word, hardly able to believe that he was in the presence of death, for he was sure now that his friend was on the point of dying, if not yet dead. All the same, he found it difficult to credit that the overworked doctors at the hospital would send a case to the mortuary before life was actually extinct.

"My friend," Hassan said, "may I ask how you managed to come here if you were unable to give a sign to the doctors or the orderlies that you were still alive?"

"I could not move a muscle," replied Winterton. "But I concentrated all the strength I could muster into using organs and powers I had never known I possessed. I knew that my only chance of surviving was by projecting myself outside my earthly body. It was as if a magnet was working inside me drawing out my very soul. An agonizing stress was going on inside my very being, and then I was no longer aware, nor did I care, what was happening in that awful place, for I was here with you, as naturally as if I had just dropped in for a drink and a chat, as I had done so often in the past when . . . we . . . were . . ."

Hassan was aware of a change coming over Winterton. His very substance seemed to be melting and suddenly he stopped speaking as though it was all at once impossible for him to continue. His face turned grey. He seemed no longer aware of Hassan, and it was as though he was unable to hold his earthly substance any longer. Hassan watched, shocked and helpless—yet fascinated—as Winterton's astral body became transparent and then vanished. Hassan was now sure that he must really be dead, and need no longer worry about being buried alive.

After his eerie experience, Hassan went to his cupboard and got himself a stiff brandy, a habit he had acquired through his association with Winterton. He felt very much in need of it after his experience. He made himself an omelet, though he did not have his usual appetite for food. Afterwards he tried to settle down to read, but he found it difficult to concentrate. He kept seeing Winterton's features on the pages, his death-like face disintegrating as it had done before his very eyes such a short time ago.

If it had happened later in the evening he might have thought that he had fallen asleep and that the whole thing had been some fantastic dream, but he had been wide awake and he remembered vividly everything that Winterton had said, and how he had looked. It was a weird but fascinating business. He had always known that Winterton possessed abnormal powers of concentration, but he had never expected to observe such a phenomenon as this.

The question uppermost in Hassan's mind now was would Winterton come again? He could not concentrate on his book. Every time the curtain stirred, or there was the slightest sound, he looked up half expecting to see the ghostly Winterton again. But the evening wore on and Winterton did not reappear.

Hassan began to worry about him. Was he really dead? Or was he still alive, unknown to anyone but himself? This dreadful thought haunted him, and Hassan could understand Winterton's terror at the prospect of being buried alive. It was his awful fear of that which had made him make the supreme effort which enabled him to appear to Hassan. Perhaps he expected Hassan to do something about it. Hassan could not surely assume that Winterton was definitely dead.

What could he do? Urgent thoughts hammered into Hassan's brain. He thought of going to the hospital, but it was now past midnight, and he would not get any satisfactory information at this time of night from the overworked hospital staff, and Winterton had said that he had already been taken to the mortuary. He decided that it would be better to get some sleep and go along to the hospital in the morning.

He was up early, not having slept much, and was fortunate enough to get a few words with the doctor who had been on duty the day before. However, the doctor could not remember much as he had had a large number of cholera cases that day and several had died. They had all been sent to the mortuary, there to await the death carts which would arrive that day to take the bodies away to the pits. Winterton's few valuables, including his medals, were there, having been handed over when he arrived. Hassan asked for the address of the mortuary and then went to see the man who kept it.

The janitor was an old man and had had the job of mortuary keeper for many years. He could remember the Englishman very well and had recognized the body as soon as he saw it. The old man talked about his dead as though they were just so much meat for disposal. The same strong smell of disinfectant surrounded the janitor as had surrounded Winterton.

So there was no doubt about it. Winterton was there. Hassan asked to see the body. He knew he had to, for Winterton's sake. He was well aware of the risks he was taking in that dreadful place of death, for the infection was easily passed on. But he had to be sure about Winterton. It was the least he could do for his old and trusted friend.

He shivered as he stood there among the corpses, with the fetor of death and disinfectant making his spine crawl as though he could feel lice on his body. He would have a hot carbolic bath when he got home, much as he hated the thought of it, for he did not like bathing anyway. He would parcel up all his clothes afterwards and throw them in the river. He had it all planned.

The old man was now looking rather strange. He hummed and hah-ed and explained the difficulties and the risk that would be involved.

"I'll take the risk," said Hassan impatiently. "There's no rule or law against it, is there?"

"It's not that, m'sieur. I——"

"There is a very special reason why I should see my friend's body."

"There was nothing on the body," said the janitor quickly. "Nothing of any value."

"I know that. All I want to do is to look at the body. It hasn't been taken away for burial yet, has it?"

The old man looked decidedly uncomfortable.

"I don't know, m'sieur," he said, dabbing his perspiring face with a red handkerchief.

Hassan grew impatient.

"What do you mean, you don't know? Of course you know. It's your job to know."

"But I don't know, m'sieur, and it's very hard to explain."

"Well, you had better try," exclaimed Hassan. "What has happened? Where is the body of Monsieur Winterton?"

The janitor's wrinkled old face became even more furrowed as he frowned, very worried.

"It has disappeared, m'sieur. M'sieur Winterton's body has disappeared."

Hassan stared at him incredulously.

"Disappeared? What on earth do you mean?"

"I know it was brought here. I saw it with my own eyes. But it was no longer here when I came back."

Hassan looked at the old man intently. He felt strangely excited.

"Go on, explain yourself, man," he said. "When you came back from where?"

"I always go across to the wine shop for a drink after they're brought in. It's all that disinfectant powder. Gets in your throat something awful. Mind you, it's better than——"

"Yes, yes, man—go on," exclaimed Hassan, all impatience to hear what had happened.

The old man looked pained and shook his head as though in the face of some imponderable mystery, which indeed, thought Hassan, might well be the case.

"You see, I'd only been gone a few minutes. Locked the door securely as usual. Well, I have to do that. Rules and regulations. When I came back, he was gone."

"Gone?" Hassan's heart began to beat faster, thinking immediately of Winterton's strange appearance to him the previous evening. "What time was this?"

"It would be about seven in the evening, m'sieur, or perhaps a little after."

That would be about the time of Winterton's visit. Hassan's excitement increased.

"Yes, go on. He vanished. And then?"

The old man looked at him curiously, and then continued.

"Yes, he vanished. I've never had such a thing happen to me before. I just couldn't understand it, m'sieur."

"*You* couldn't understand it!" Hassan's voice rose an octave, sounding hysterical in that horrible, corpse-ridden place. "Are you telling me that a dead man came to life and walked out of here? Or are you telling me that he wasn't dead after all?"

"Oh, yes, he was dead all right. We don't get any but the dead ones here. I can always tell. I've had enough experience of stiffs."

"Well, what are you telling me?" asked Hassan, desperate himself to understand what had happened. "Obviously no one would come in and steal a corpse just dead of cholera. Not even a madman. Are you telling me that the corpse itself got up and walked out?"

The janitor shook his head in bewilderment. "As I said, m'sieur, the door was locked. But the ventilator, which had been closed and bolted when I left, was open when I came back."

"The ventilator?"

Hassan did not know what to think. Had Winterton been alive after all when they had brought him to this place?

"Do you mean to say that the ventilator was big enough for a man to get through?" he asked. "That Monsieur Winterton, far from being dead, was able to escape through it? Where is the ventilator?"

The janitor pointed to it. Hassan examined it.

"He was thin, I know," Hassan said. "I suppose he could have got through."

"That is what I think also, m'sieur. That is the only explanation. But please keep this to yourself. I cannot afford to lose my job now. I am too old to get another. A mortuary keeper whose corpses walk out on him! If the authorities heard about it, I might as well be a corpse myself."

"So you think he was alive after all when they brought him here. Just now you were saying that he was dead. You were certain of it. What do you mean?"

The old man scratched his head.

"When they brought him in, I was certain that he was dead. I mean, I hardly expected otherwise. But strange things can happen, m'sieur. Very strange. Especially with the cholera dead. I've seen them move. I don't pretend to know the answer. All I know is that he's gone. So far as I'm concerned, he came in as a corpse, and as a corpse he vanished. I can't explain it. I can only ask you to say nothing, m'sieur."

"Don't worry. I won't say anything. If there is any fault, it is not yours."

Hassan was glad to get out of the fetid atmosphere of the death house. He had no doubt at all that the old man had told the truth as he understood it.

There would be no point in making a fuss. Winterton was an unusual man. Anything may have happened, and in the Damascus of those days, with the back streets full of disease and death, one more body picked up either dead or dying would occasion neither comment nor inquiry.

Hassan returned to his little shop, still not knowing what had happened to Winterton, and he never did find out. Winterton did not return to his apartment, and was never seen in Damascus again.

In vain Hassan tried to get in touch with him, but was unable to do so—on any plane.

Had Winterton escaped from that place of the dead only to die in the streets of the native quarter of Damascus? He was in an advanced stage of cholera and could not, in the natural order of things, survive.

Or had he, with his abnormal gift of concentration, the power to escape from that awful predicament he believed that he was in—the power to escape from this earth into another dimension?

Hassan always preferred to believe in the latter alternative.

The Vampire of Castle Furstenstein

The castle stands on the top of a sheer rock which drops like a wall
to a brawling torrent in the pine-dark valley far below. The best
commando unit in the British Army would have a job to capture
the place from that side. Only house flies, trained to arms, could
attempt the assault.

Pepperpot turrets, battlements and corner watchtowers crown the
fortress on the rock. It steps straight out of the Middle Ages, a place
of robber barons and ruling princes. Before the war it belonged to
the Prince of Pless, an hereditary German prince who exercised
feudal power over a wild, mountainous countryside of deep valleys,
dark forests and rocky hills. A place of sharp sunlight and sudden
windstorms. Hans Andersen would have peopled it with dwarfs and
gnomes, with witches straight from the Brocken, and warlocks. On
the other side of the valley, on an equally high cliff, stand the ruins
of an even older castle. The legend is that witches hold their sabbats
there. At these festivals, held usually on saints' days, but sometimes
three or four times a week, black magic is practised in every form
of evil and vice. "Presided over by incarnate evil intelligences, a
mob outvying the very demons in malice, blasphemy, and revolt,
the true face of pandemonium on earth".

One of the chief feasts of witches in Western Europe has always
been held on the eve of May Day, 30 April, famous in Germany as
die Walpurgis-Nacht. Oddly enough it takes its name from a Devon-

shire saint, known as St Walburga, who was the daughter of a king of the West Saxons who married a sister of St Boniface. Walburga was born in Devon about the year A.D. 710 and became a nun at Wimborne, in Dorset. She went over to Germany when she was thirty-eight, founded a nunnery, and died at Heidenheim on 25 February, 777. She was regarded as a very holy woman and became one of the most popular saints in England as well as in Germany and the Low Country.

Now May Day was the ancient festival of the Druids. They lit their May-fires and offered sacrifices upon their sacred mountains. These rites were adopted by the witches for their sabbats as part of the blasphemy of God. They also held their sabbats on the nights of saints' days. In Finland, for example, the peasants believed that every hilltop at midnight on 30 April was thronged by demons and sorcerers. The second witches' festival was the Eve of St John the Baptist on 23 June.

At these sabbats the devil was worshipped, virgins were raped, sacrifices of blood, either human or animal, were made and fantastic dances were performed.

Even today peasants in the Carpathian Mountains believe that every evil thing has power at midnight on 22 April, when the Feast of St George is solemnized with honour in the churches. That night the witches hold the Grand Sabbat. In the Balkans farmers and peasants bolt their doors and fasten their windows when night falls and put thorn bushes and brambles on the doorsteps and the lintels and new turf on the window-sills so that no demon or witch can enter. The Grand Sabbat is held in widely different places—an ancient wood, on the top of a bleak tor, in a deep valley, under a blasted oak, in a cemetery, a semi-deserted church or a ruined building. Always they choose a place where they are not likely to be spied on or interrupted. De Lancre says that the Grand Sabbat must be held near a stream, lake, or water of some kind, and Bodin adds that the places where sorcerers meet are remarkable and generally distinguished by some trees, or even a cross.

This brings us to the ruined castle on the estate of Prince John Henry XV of Pless, Count von Hochberg and Freiherr zu Fursten-stein in Bohemia. I was told the story soon after the First World War by the late Lt.-Col. Cyril Foley.

In the spring of 1901 he went to stay with Prince Henry of Pless at Furstenstein. The Prince had just married one of the two very lovely daughters of Mr Cornwallis-West of Chirk Castle, Ruthin.

"Whilst I was there," Foley told me, "I was first of all nearly terrified out of my wits by intense fear of something unknown and then frightened to death by the dark! Nothing quite like these two experiences had ever happened to me before, and I hope to heaven it never does so again. Looking down from my bedroom window on to the top of the tall fir trees, which grew on the steep slopes on both sides of the ravine, one could hear, without being able to see, a swift-flowing stream, which was some 150 feet below. I always somehow connected that side of the castle, which was a turreted one, with Bram Stoker's famous Dracula, and have often, when leaning out of my bedroom window, especially on a moonlit night, visualized that dreadful vampire crawling down the castle wall and vanishing in the gloom of the precipice. It is possible that my subconscious mind was impressed by this, and that it may have had something to do with the very weird and sinister experience that I had on my second visit to Furstenstein.

"We used frequently to go for long paper-chases covering thirty miles or more, the actual distance depending on the energy and enthusiasm of the two people who constituted the 'hare'."

One day, whilst the party was at luncheon just before setting out on one of these mountain paper-chases, Princess Pless said to him: "You know, Cyril, you're sleeping in the haunted room tonight. My old nurse had her bedclothes pulled off in that room and refused to sleep there any more." The "old nurse" had then graduated to being Princess Pless's personal maid. Cyril laughed it off, forgot about the warning five minutes later and that afternoon did well over thirty miles across country on a horse. When the party got back, wind-blown and tired, they dressed, dined and went to bed.

Cyril's room was a very large one. There was no electric light in those days but an oil lamp was set on a table in the middle of the room. His bed was in a corner of the room close to the wall, opposite the door and parallel to it. At the foot of the bed and in the same wall was a long French window. Both sides of it were wide open. The moon shone through this tall, open window and lit up half the room brilliantly just beyond the foot of the bed. The time was half-past twelve.

"I undressed and got into bed," Cyril recorded, "and pulled my sheets up as far as my hips, when I was suddenly struck by what I can only describe as a paralysis, produced by stark and sudden terror.

"Now there was nothing to account for this. I had not given a thought to Dracula that evening, nor had I even remembered the remark which Princess Pless had made at luncheon about the bed-clothes. The stable clock boomed out the three-quarters and then one o'clock. I lay there dripping with perspiration, numb with terror and all volition gone. The slight breeze blew behind the pictures, which hung by long picture-wires, and rattled them against the walls. Between one and a quarter past I heard a scratching on the outer wall. I visualized Dracula descending just outside my window, and I lay frozen with horror in the expectation of a call from him."

When telling this story—and one always encouraged him to trot it out at the dinner-table—Foley always made a point of the fact that another man was sleeping in the room next door and a box of matches was on the table by his own bed. He was on the point of stretching out his left hand for the matches when he suddenly remembered the story of a man in a similar state of terror who put out his hand for the matches—*and they were handed to him*!

"I thought that anything, even a visit from Dracula, would be less ghastly than that," he said. He went on to say that he heard the clock strike half-past one "and realized that I had been under some terrible influence for an hour. I remember firmly clutching the bedclothes, which I was still holding in exactly the same position, to prevent their being dragged away.

"At the first reverberation of the clock denoting a quarter to two, my bedroom door slowly opened. I did not turn my head to see it, but I heard it, and that was enough. *I died.* And the reason I died was not so much because the door opened but because something came softly and stealthily straight across the room towards me. I heard it coming distinctly and, I repeat, I died. At the lowest computation I was dead for over twenty minutes. I know this because when I was brought back to life I lay conscious for about five minutes before the clock struck two-fifteen, and, indeed, if I am correct in this estimate, I was dead for twenty-five minutes, but I will be on the safe side and call it twenty.

"And yet, believe it or not, by twenty past two all fear had gone, and I was able to rise, light the lamp, remove my silk night-shirt, which I threw against the wall where it stuck for a moment, rub myself down with a turkish towel, put on another night-shirt, and sit down to think it over. My bed was sopping wet from where my neck to my hips had been. I lit a candle and went into my friend's room next door.

"To my astonishment he was awake and reading. 'Hallo,' he said, 'I'm sorry if I woke you. I came in for something for my headache, but as you were asleep and I couldn't find any medicine, I went away.' I said: 'I wasn't asleep, I was dead, and you killed me.' I told him just what I have told you, but we agreed to say nothing about it because it would have served no useful purpose to have done so.

"Everything I have related actually happened, and anyone who suggests I went to sleep and had a bad dream is talking nonsense. Does one go to bed on a cold night in Bohemia with no bedclothes over one (especially with Dracula about) with the window open and a silk night-shirt on? No, one does not. Has anyone ever woken up from a dream sufficiently hideous to cause his night-gown to stick to the wall? I do not want to know about that, but I do want to know why I was subjected to the greatest terror that could be inflicted upon mortal man for a period of one and a quarter hours."

Cyril Foley's second experience was more than odd. He decided to explore the deep, dark ravine immediately below the castle wall through which a mountain stream brawled and thundered. So after tea one day he announced that he was going to climb down into the ravine by a steep path which zigzagged down the cliff face. A fox-hunting Englishwoman who was one of the party said: "I'll come with you." That was just after six o'clock. They set off immediately and this, in Cyril's own words, is what happened:

"We found that we had to cross a bridge, follow a path on the side farthest from the castle, and then cross back to a path immediately beneath the very fir trees which grew on the bank upon which the foundations of the castle rested. In spite of it being the month of September it was extremely dark. We followed this path for some little distance, and then retraced our steps as it was getting late.

"When we arrived at the point some hundred and fifty feet below my bedroom, it suddenly became pitch dark. When I say 'pitch', I am not sure what 'pitch dark' means exactly.

"Therefore, in order to convey to your mind the kind of darkness it was, I must add that it descended in blocks, which felt as if they could be pushed about with one's hands. In fact, I realized for the first time that darkness was ponderable. So opaque and menacing was the atmosphere that it was quite impossible to see my companion a foot away, and once I was startled to receive a reply from a yard off in response to my shout of, 'A——, where the devil are you?'

"It was difficult to realize that such a thing could be. We could hear the torrent on our left immediately below us, but to attempt to move along the mossy path, which was about nine feet wide, was out of the question. I tried crawling on all fours, and missed falling over the edge by a bee's knee. I sounded my repeater watch, and found it was between a quarter to and eight o'clock. Some hundred feet above us and on our immediate right were the castle walls, and inside them was dinner, but not for us. I said to my companion, 'We are here till seven-thirty tomorrow.' She said, 'It will be cold; do you wear Jaeger underclothes?' Now did you ever hear such a question as that? And coming, as it did, from a woman who was consistently in the front rank of the Quorn Hunt, it made me very angry. I made no reply.

"No one knew where we had gone, and as dinner was any time between eight-fifteen and a quarter to nine, according to when Princess Pless was dressed, any search-party could not retrieve us before ten o'clock at the earliest. We therefore could do nothing but remain quite still. I was passionately angry. There is nothing more infuriating and humiliating than such a position.

"My companion said, 'It might be worse.' I inquired, 'How?' 'Oh,' she said, 'there might be wolves about.' I said, 'There are; I heard one just now.' That stopped all remarks for half an hour.

"Whether it was the moon which had risen, or that we got more accustomed to the darkness, I do not know, but at about half past nine we managed, moving a foot at a time, to gain the bridge and finally got in at precisely ten o'clock, and walked into the dining-room. 'Where have you been?' everyone shouted. I explained. My explanation was greeted with derisive laughter, among which I heard such remarks as, 'That's a capital story!' and 'Most improper, I call it!' We sat down as we were to dinner, and that was the end of a most unpleasant evening."

These are the considered words of a man who was no fool. Normally, he was scared of nothing and no one. He had been under fire in battle too often. Yet as he frequently told me during that hour and a quarter in a moonlit bedroom and later in the ravine, he felt himself in the presence of something inordinately evil. He wrote the whole experience in an article published in *The Field*.

One theory was that the old castle had been haunted by a vampire. That may or may not be true. Legends of vampires and werewolves are common in the remote districts of Germany, Poland, Austria, Hungary and the Balkans. The belief in lycanthropy and vampirism is still deep rooted.

The horror of the haunted room in Castle Furstenstein may not have been that of a vampire but a mere poltergeist who waited for Cyril Foley to pull up his bedclothes from his hips to his neck so that it might rip them off and scare the Englishman out of his wits.

Whether we believe that the Furstenstein bedroom was haunted or not, what was the cause of the sense of overwhelming fear felt by Cyril Foley and his matter-of-fact fox-hunting woman friend in the ravine at the foot of the castle precipice? It brings us to the legend of the witches' sabbat held centuries ago in the ruined castle perched on its crag on the opposite side of the valley.

That legend, which may have some bearing on Foley's experience, says that a young maidservant, a virgin, was persuaded—or more probably terrified—into accompanying an older woman servant to the sabbat. The older woman was a practising witch on her days off.

When the girl reached the castle ruins she found a mock altar erected within the walls, torches flaring and the place full of witches and demons—in reality men and women both local and from a distance, dressed up in their robes of evil. Montague Summers in his *History of Witchcraft and Demonology* describes such a sabbat thus: "The learned Bartolomeo de Spina, O.P., in his *Tractatus de Strigibus et Lamiis*, Venice, 1533, writes that a certain peasant, who lived at Clavica Malaguzzi, in the district of Mirandola, having occasion to rise very early one morning and drive to a neighbouring village, found himself at three o'clock, before daybreak, crossing a waste tract of considerable extent which lay between him and his destination. In the distance he suddenly caught sight of what seemed to be numerous fires flitting to and fro, and as he drew nearer he saw that these were none other than large lanterns held by a bevy of persons who were moving here and there in the mazes of a fantastic dance, whilst others, as at a rustic picnic, were seated partaking of dainties and drinking stoups of wine, what time a harsh music, like the scream of a *cornemuse*, droned through the air. Curiously no word was spoken, the company whirled and pirouetted, ate and drank, in strange and significant silence. Perceiving that many, unabashed, were giving themselves up to the wildest debauchery and publicly performing the sexual act with every circumstance of indecency, the horrified onlooker realized that he was witnessing the revels of the sabbat. Crossing himself fervently and uttering a prayer, he drove as fast as possible from the accursed spot, not, however, before he had recognized some of the company as notorious evildoers and persons living in the vicinity who were already under grave suspicion of sorcery."

This then was the sort of scene which the terrified girl may have witnessed. It was said that she was stripped, gagged, tied to the altar, raped and sexually assaulted in the most obscene fashion. The black mass was celebrated before her horrified eyes. A live sacrifice, either a goat or a baby, was butchered and offered to the Devil, who actually appeared, horns and all. In reality he would have been a man in disguise.

The wretched girl was released just before cock-crow when all sabbats must break up and witches disperse. She threw herself into the fierce mountain stream, which separates the two castles, and was drowned. Her pathetic ghost haunts the dark valley pleading to return to the safety of the inhabited castle. That is the legend.

Was this the influence which terrified a brave soldier nearly out of his wits?

The Great White Bat

Many strange stories have been told about the powers of the priests of Ancient Egypt, and particularly of the spells which were cast to preserve the sanctity of their tombs. The Egyptians filled their burial places with lavish treasure, and it is not surprising that these places of the dead have been pillaged over the centuries by generations of robbers.

Not the least of these despoilers were the Egyptologists of modern times. They robbed in the sacred name of science, but that made no difference. The curses applied to all who invaded the sanctity of the tomb, whatever their motive. Many strange stories, for instance, were told of the curse laid upon the tomb of Tutankhamen, and the fates of those who excavated it.

The cult of Egyptology was extremely popular in the early days of this century. Diggers of every nationality were busy in the Valley of the Kings exploring the ancient tombs and defying the age-old curses. In the days of enlightenment men of science did not take these old curses seriously. Most of those who encountered sudden and mysterious deaths would have agreed with their colleagues that their demises were unconnected with such superstitious nonsense.

Michael Hendry, however, took a different view. His experience was so terrifying that he was in no doubt that the vengeance of the priests of Ancient Egypt had been visited upon him in the most terrible manner.

Hendry was no professional Egyptologist, and was not a scientist. He was an Irishman who had gone to America in his youth, and made a fortune on the New York Stock Exchange in the days of the Astors, the Rockefellers and the Vanderbilts, when any smart businessman could become a millionaire in the rocketing economy of the nineteenth-century United States.

Hendry made his millions and then retired. He married late in life a widow twenty years his junior. It was no marriage of convenience. He was much in love with her, and she with him. She had not married him for his money alone.

His great passion in life was Egyptology, a harmless enough hobby in the safety of America. But Mary Hendry soon discovered that the nice quiet home in Long Island, of which she had dreamed, was not to be hers. Hendry wanted to spend his retirement pursuing his great passion, and that meant going to Egypt and digging in the forbidden burial places of those unforgettable Pharaohs.

Mary, though a little disgusted, was not entirely discouraged. She thought he would grow out of it, and in any case he was no longer young. The climate of the Nile Valley would do him no good, and she thought she would soon persuade him to settle down in more pleasant and conventional surroundings. She did not mind whether it was Europe or America. She would have settled for somewhere in the British Isles—his homeland—where the standard of living in those days was as high as, if not higher than, in America.

But the trip to Egypt was exciting. They stayed at Shepheard's Hotel, Cairo. This was during its palmy days, a few years before the First World War. Mrs Hendry went to the usual tourist spots, visited the Pyramids and the Sphinx at Giza, rode a camel and sailed on the Nile.

But Hendry had not come to Egypt for these simple tourist pursuits. It was his first visit to the land of the Pharaohs, and he threw himself with passionate interest into the various tomb excavations which were going on in the Valley of the Kings. His knowledge impressed many of the professional Egyptologists and his wealth was a consideration. Most investigations were privately financed in those days, and American millionaires were never discouraged, especially when they displayed such practical knowledge of the subject as did Hendry.

Just about the time that the Hendrys arrived in Cairo some

excitement was caused by the mysterious death of a German archaeologist named Schaffer. He had been excavating the tomb of a high priest of the Royal College of Mystic Priests which was founded by Cheops in the Fourth Dynasty, about 4000 B.C.

The doctors said that Schaffer's sudden death was due to heart failure, but according to the superstitious Arab workers the tomb was haunted by evil spirits which had caused the death of the German.

Only the outer chamber of the tomb had been reached, and the Arabs were certain that the large inner chamber, which contained the high priest's mummy, was impregnated with such powerful evil that it was death to enter.

Hendry determined to take over Schaffer's excavation. He was unmoved by the Arabs' stories of doom and disaster. After all, he held, the ancient tombs had been entered and robbed by innumerable robbers throughout the ages, and if the priests' curses had been so potent the superstitious tomb robbers would have kept away.

And so Hendry obtained official permission to continue Schaffer's work. He left his wife fretting in Cairo while he went to the site in the Valley of the Kings.

None of the Arabs who had worked for Schaffer would go near the tomb and Hendry had to bribe other natives to help him, but they said that they would not enter the inner chamber where the mummy was.

With the aid of his men, Hendry laid bare three chambers, and finally came to the burial chamber, the door of which bore the seal of Cheops, a large winged bat. Beyond this his men would not go.

Fixing a temporary installation of electric light, Hendry continued alone. Entering the inner chamber, he found a superb golden sarcophagus. The chamber was lavishly decorated, for the Fourth Dynasty was a period of great wealth and splendour when artistic grandeur was at its height. Raising the lid of the golden coffin, he saw that the mummy of the high priest was in a perfect state, even his long white beard remaining intact.

On the breast of the mummy was a winged scarab fashioned in the shape of a bat, rather than in the usual beetle shape. The scarab was fixed to the fastenings of the complex bandages in which the corpse had been wrapped after the process of mummification. He picked it up, tearing it from the wrappings, fragile with age. The scarab was a large one and carved with mystic inscriptions.

"It seemed," he said afterwards, "as though a horror of fear descended upon me like a cloud as I touched the scarab. The electric lights dimmed to a faint glimmer. A cold sighing wind filled the tomb, and I heard fluttering shapes passing through the air and brushing my face. I judged them to be bats."

He was filled with panic and fled from the chamber, the scarab grasped in his hand. He had thought that the bats were imaginary, and all he wanted was to get out of the oppressive and macabre atmosphere of the burial chamber into the open air. But he felt ill and faint and quite unable to go on.

He returned to Cairo utterly shaken by his experience. He had read that King Cheops during his reign had been deified as a bat and that he had founded the Royal College of Mystic Priests in honour of his deification. Could he have imagined that there were bats in the burial chamber? It had not presumably been opened for tens of centuries. No bats could have lived there.

When he got to Shepheard's, he found his wife white-faced and in a state of great alarm.

"Michael, I've been so worried about you. I have had an awful feeling all day that something terrible has happened. Thank God you're safe."

Hendry thanked God too. "I don't like that place," he said. "I'm not going back there. Let's go for a trip down the Nile to Luxor. The change will do us good."

Mary agreed, though she would rather have left Egypt altogether. She had never liked her husband digging around in these weird and ancient tombs. She felt there might be something in the stories one heard about the supernatural agencies which were supposed to be at work in these places. Someone had told her that to take a mummy from its coffin was an act of fearful desecration which invited the worst of fates. To touch or even to read the magic inscriptions in the place of the dead could, it was said, have fatal consequences.

The excursion down the Nile was at first a success and Hendry shook off his acute depression. He had foolishly kept the scarab as he could not bring himself to give up this rare and precious treasure from the ancient past. He hid it among his belongings and told no one, not even his wife, about it.

While they were camping on the banks of the Nile not far from Luxor he was awakened by an unusual noise. Peering out of the tent flap he saw a huge bat, snow-white, flitting ceaselessly around the tent, uttering a high squeaking noise. It filled him with the utmost horror. In vain he tried to drive it away, but it circled around, sometimes swooping close to him and staring at him with terrible, piercing eyes. He had never seen a bat like this before. It seemed hardly to be a creature of this world.

He returned to the tent and fastened the tent flap securely. His wife slept on her camp bed. Thank God at least that she had not been disturbed by this fearsome creature of the night.

Hendry himself could not sleep. He lay there for a while, listening to the bat outside the tent circling around uttering its sinister high-pitched noises. Sometimes its wings scratched against the canvas unnervingly as though it was trying to get in.

Hendry noticed that although his wife did not wake, she tossed restlessly in her sleep. When he looked at her closer he saw her face was strained as though in fear and there were beads of perspiration on her forehead. Could that sinister denizen of the night even penetrate human sleep?

After a while the fluttering of the wings ceased, and Hendry cautiously unfastened the tent flap and looked out.

He saw the great white bat make a final circle of the tent then fly away across the Nile in the direction of Luxor. He saw it high up in the chalky light of the full moon winging back to whatever place it had come from. Below it in the distance lay the massive ruins of the Temple of Thebes, erected by Amenhotep III, the father of the heretical Pharaoh, Akhenaton. But between the high priest of Cheops and the Temple of Thebes lay twenty-six centuries of time and hundreds of miles of distance.

It was useless to try to disconnect the great white bat from the scarab he still obstinately clung to, concealed secretly in his luggage.

He returned to the tent and tried to get some sleep. He noticed that since the departure of the bat his wife was resting more peacefully. But he himself got little peace that night. He lay there sleeping hardly at all, a prey to terrible fears. In a half-dream towards dawn he was back in that tomb of the high priest and the place was filled with dark and unspeakable horrors.

In the morning his wife was afflicted by acute depression and melancholy which she was able neither to explain nor to shake off. She had had the most awful nightmare, she said. When he pressed her to try to describe it, she could not, except to say that her dream was haunted by bats, and she had a peculiar horror of bats.

She had had enough of Egypt. The very place seemed to cause her unaccountable mental distress. Hendry also had had enough of the country. He had lost much of his enthusiasm for Egyptology, though he still refused to part with the scarab, the one practical result of his only excavation among the ancient ruins. He did not then believe the thing could harm him in any way, and it never crossed his mind that Mary was in any danger.

So they fled from Egypt, going to Greece and then on to Italy, where he found the remains of the ancient world unclouded by mystery and uncontaminated by the incomprehensible magic of a strange priesthood.

But it was impossible to shake themselves free of the doom which was pursuing them. Mary Hendry never aroused from the strange and suffocating torpor which had first overtaken her that night by the banks of the Nile. No longer her pleasant, cheerful self, she sank deeper into an unaccountable melancholy which affected her body as well as her mind. She grew listless, lost her appetite and physical energy, and wanted to spend all her time lying down.

Hendry took her to doctor after doctor, but while each was full of plausible theories, none could diagnose her trouble or prescribe anything which would improve her condition. She seemed drifting away from him, slipping out of life itself. It did not happen slowly, but in a matter of weeks, so swiftly that he could not take her back to America where he felt there might have been a cure, for the doctors told him that she was unfit for the voyage across the Atlantic.

As for Hendry, his hours of sleep were filled with perpetual nightmare. There came a night following a day in which his wife had seemed considerably better. He had gone to sleep at last with hope in his heart. He had an awful and terrifying dream.

He was passing through great halls and vast cathedral-like spaces in which were colossal Egyptian figures carved on stone monuments. His pace quickened as he progressed through these stupendous chambers of the ancient world of the Nile, and his senses were conscious of a strange aroma, which became more powerful as he continued and began to fill him with overwhelming nausea.

Now the great Egyptian halls had been replaced by endless stone corridors. He thought at first that he was inside a pyramid, but he went on at such a pace through corridors gradually growing smaller and smaller that he knew he was going down into the very centre of the earth. He also knew that he was being pursued. He dared not look round, but he knew very well what it was which pursued him. The aroma, now sickly and overpowering, grew stronger every moment.

At last he came to the end of the passage and found himself in a small stone chamber from which there was no escape. As he stood there sweating in terror, he saw that the chamber was growing smaller and smaller every second, walls and ceiling closing in around him.

He was now down on the floor in unbelievable terror, suffocated by the smell—which was like the concentrated odour of all of Egypt's most ancient tombs. As he looked up there was the ultimate horror—the great white bat settling down on top of him gradually, suffocating the very life out of him.

Hendry awoke with a strangled cry and sat up, bathed in perspiration, with a horrible feeling that something was clutching at his throat.

But the worst terror of all was to discover that waking was no escape, for as he stared across his room, flooded with brilliant moonlight, he saw the great white bat flit across it and escape through the open window.

He jumped from his bed, now afraid not only for himself. His first thought was to close the window and shut the dreadful creature out. As he did so, the bat settled motionlessly against the glass, its pointed ears erect, its bright, malignant eyes fixed upon him. He shrank back into the room, and it lifted itself with a great flutter of wings and sailed away swiftly into the path of the moon, over the houses and tree-tops until it was a speck against the silver orb.

Hendry turned from the window and hurried into his wife's room through the open door connecting with his. As he entered he started forward, her name on his lips, for she was lying in an unnatural attitude in her bed, as though suddenly aroused from her sleep. But she was not awake. She lay there dead, her eyes open wide in terror.

Hendry knew that the white bat, when it had flitted across his room as he awoke from his nightmare, had come from his wife's.

"It was heart failure," said the doctor. "I can give no other explanation. A shock perhaps. Yes, it could, in her depressed state, even be caused by a particularly vivid dream."

Hendry was heart-broken. He loved his wife and they had become closer since the troubles which started in the high priest's tomb.

Everything started to go wrong now. On the day of his wife's funeral he had grave news from New York. Two great concerns in which a large part of his fortune was invested suddenly failed, and he lost heavily in the subsequent bankruptcy. Next, a trusted friend in New York embezzled $50,000 of his money and then committed suicide. His old father in New Orleans suddenly collapsed from an undiagnosed disease and died.

In despair Hendry went from country to country trying to escape the snow-white bat which now continually haunted him. It came with every moon period, and with its coming he had the same nightmare in which he was in the priest's burial chamber where the atmosphere was heavy and stifling and filled with that sinister odour. The chamber grew smaller and smaller, closing in around him while he became choked with suffocation and terror. He awoke with the awful feeling that something was clutching his throat, clawing the life out of him. Always outside the window in the moonlight was the bat, staring at him with those brilliant almost human eyes. Like no other bat he had ever seen, it was ominous, terrifying, and, he was convinced, not of this world.

But despite his nameless fears, Hendry, with obstinate fatalism, still clung to the scarab, heedless of the pleadings of his friends, to whom he told the story, that he should return it whence he had taken it. But Hendry was under a spell. There was no turning back. Everything in life had gone now, and perhaps it did not matter what the white bat did to him.

In London he consulted Egyptologists and students of the occult. The former were sceptical of his story and one told him that scarabs were unknown in the Fourth Dynasty, which was the time of Cheops, or Khufu, and that the scarab found on the mummy of the high priest must have been put there during a later dynasty.

If this was so, Hendry believed that at a later time in Ancient Egypt more deadly and potent spells and curses had been developed by the powerful priesthood, and it was quite possible that, having found the tomb broken into, the priests of a later dynasty sealed it with terrible curses, reinforced by the winged scarab affixed to the mummy. Hendry remembered that he had associated the great white bat with the Temp_ of Thebes, which had been built two thousand six hundred years after the time of Cheops.

The mystery was solved by neither the Egyptologists nor the occultists, who were fascinated, full of theories, but unable to do anything to help him. One borrowed the scarab from him, hastily returning it the next day, saying that he had been troubled with the most ghastly nightmare, after which he had seen a great white bat flitting outside his window. He begged Hendry to take the scarab back to Egypt and return it to the priest's mummy. But Hendry would make no such promise.

Each night he dreaded going to bed and postponed it for as long as he could. After his bat-ridden nightmares he now awoke with his throat stiff and swollen, a condition which the doctor said was probably due to the bite of some poisonous insect.

The end came in Paris.

He was staying in a hotel in the rue de la Fayette when the white bat appeared to him for the last time. A prolonged scream rang through the hotel in the middle of the night. In the morning Hendry was found dead in his bed. The doctor said that death was due to heart failure. The chambermaid said that the dead man had insisted on the shutters being fastened tightly over the windows of his room, but when he was found dead the shutters were wide open and so were the windows.

There was no scarab found among his effects. It had gone, and the great snow-white bat was never seen again.

Let Sleeping Bones Lie

Insomnia is a dreadful thing. Blessed is the rare person who has never suffered from it, even in the mildest form. He is lucky to be unacquainted with those endless dark hours, when no kind of counting, reading, soothing drink or calming pill takes effect; when every striking of the clock is heard and agonizedly counted; when bitter self-analysis and dread imaginings increase in intensity and conviction as the hours pass. He is fortunate indeed if he has never gone to bed at ten, longing to sleep but knowing that it will be one or two o'clock before he will do so: or certain that, however quickly sleep may take him, he will have to endure at least four hours between waking and breakfasting—four hours of cock-crow, and dawn chorus, and, with his resistance at its lowest, imaginings of inevitable death and possible suicide.

At such times sound sleepers in the household are much envied, their taken-for-granted oblivion even resented. Undisturbed by worry, imagination, or fear, they sleep like animals—and who ever heard of an animal with insomnia?

But there have been instances. One occurred in Georgia, in the southern United States of America, where, some fifty years ago, a well-bred farmer with the aristocratic name of Walsingham bought a very reasonably priced farm at Oakville, on the Savannah river. There was a nice house, in that charming Colonial style which rivals much of Europe's small-house architecture in welcoming grace.

With the Walsinghams' many elegant examples of American country-style furniture installed, it appeared both to the family and some of their visitors that here had been a bargain indeed.

The neighbours, too, seemed friendly and were pleased to accept the new settlers' invitations to call and dine. There was a pleasant daughter, Amelia, to be admired: and, for those who liked to contemplate a noble animal, a great mastiff, enjoying the name of Don Caesar. There was also a cat, who, fortunately for his skin, was good friends with the dog who towered above him.

The Walsinghams had been in their new home for some months, and were considered well settled, when Don Caesar began to grow restless. His trouble was insomnia. While the cat would doze happily as before, curled up near his vast friend, the latter could be seen to be disturbed by something which caused him to shift about, and lift his head to look round, and get up and prowl, and flop uneasily down again, only to be up once more within a moment. He was not his old self at all, and more than once he was seen to lunge testily at the unoffending cat, as if jealous of its serenity. Night-time was his worst. Instead of dreaming away the hours, sighing and twitching in pleasurable imaginings, he could be heard prowling about, not knowing what he wanted but unable to compose himself to rest. Sometimes he would growl, long and low, and bark: but there seemed to be no cause beyond his own discomfited state.

The Walsinghams heard all this because they, too, were no longer enjoying nightly oblivion. One by one they had first been awakened by noises, as though there might be intruders about the place. Mr Walsingham had gone down and looked around, but had found nothing stirring except the unhappy Don Caesar. Another night there had been long, insistent peals at the door-bell. Hurrying to answer them, the farmer had found no one there—but some pieces of furniture in the downstairs rooms had been shifted and one or two overturned.

The house-sounds soon became a nightly occurrence, often accompanied by the ringing of the bell. The family began to suspect that their neighbours might not be as friendly as they seemed, or had found out how little they had paid for the house and farm and were resentfully trying to drive them out; but they were intelligent people and soon dropped this notion as absurd.

The noises continued. Furniture was now being moved or

knocked over nightly, and several pieces had suffered damage. What with this, the ringing of the bell and the barking of Don Caesar, no one could get a night's sleep. Of them all, the poor dog seemed to be the most affected by insomnia. He slept neither by night nor by day. Sleepless dogs do not develop bags under the eyes, but their nerves and tempers are just as vulnerable as any human insomniac's. One morning the family hastened downstairs towards his frenzied barking, coming from the hall. They halted on the stairs as they caught sight of him, his great legs braced, coat bristling, neck straining forward, eyes staring, as he barked incessantly at nothing.

Suddenly, the huge dog's last restraint seemed to give way. With a snarling roar of rage he sprang, as if at an invisible throat.

Then the watching family saw a remarkable and terrible thing happen. At the height of his lunge the dog was stopped. For a moment he writhed in mid-air, threshing his limbs and body, twisting his head this way and that. He might have been gripped about the throat by someone stronger than he who was holding him aloft, throttling him. Yet there was no one in that hall except the strangling dog and the horrified watchers on the stair.

With a gurgling cry, Don Caesar was suddenly propelled backward. He thudded to the floor and lay still. It was some moments before the family dared approach him. Their fear that he might spring up at them in this madness was unnecessary: Don Caesar was dead—of a broken neck.

Now, it is a well-known fact that animals can see and sense things which humans cannot. We ourselves have seen dogs and cats bristle and widen their eyes at an empty chair or corner of the room, and slowly follow with their gaze the movement of something which, long to discern it as we will, we cannot. What the Walsinghams had watched that morning went beyond this, though; and yet, in that disturbed household, where a gigantic dog had been terrified frantic and then throttled by nothing more tangible than the air around him, the cat continued to behave as serenely as if he were perpetually surrounded by doting admirers. He sat on empty chairs, purring and closing his eyes and smoothing back his ears as though invisible hands were stroking him from head to tail. He leaned against nothing, and rubbed against it, and curled his tail round it, and smiled and purred. He was the one easy member of that household: and his calm gave the rest of them optimism that their troubles were due to quite ordinary causes, and would soon pass.

In this frame of mind, Amelia Walsingham was perhaps shocked more than she might otherwise have been when one evening, as she sat at her dressing-table preparing for bed, she felt a touch on her shoulder, and, glancing into the mirror, saw a hand there. The hand was a man's, coarse and gnarled. It was covered with black hair—and there was nothing attached to it at all.

Once more the family managed to come to terms with a horror which would have driven many people out of the house on the instant. Most of us will put up with a great deal before we will subject ourselves to the upheaval of removal. Though Amelia's screams had been dreadful to hear, she was persuaded to believe that she had dozed briefly at the dressing-table and, waking with a start, had been frightened by a movement of reflected shadow or light.

Whether Mr Walsingham was really convinced of this, or whether he was putting up a show of confidence for the benefit of his women-folk, an event a few days later left him in no personal doubt that something rather nasty was afoot on his property: afoot literally, for at the time he was strolling across the dewy grass of his garden, which fell away to the Savannah river. It was a perfect morning, a time when man might least expect to encounter the supernormal. Yet, as Mr Walsingham walked and glanced down at his feet, he saw, forming themselves in the soft, dewy ground beside him, a parallel line of footprints—and they were of the naked feet of a man.

This was the last but one experience Mr Walsingham or any of his family underwent at this place. The last one of all they shared with a number of neighbours. After it, there could be no more self-delusion.

It was that same evening, and the neighbours had come in for a meal. Despite their ordeal of late, the Walsinghams were entertaining their friends cheerfully and a relaxed mood prevailed. If the cat, on a chair in the corner, was apparently being stroked, to its visible and audible delight, by someone who was clearly not there, this was merely put down to eccentricity—"his game".

Conversation was proceeding spiritedly and gaily at the table when suddenly it was interrupted by a loud, long groan. Assembled diners do not normally pay obvious heed to sounds which might be due to one of their number's digestive misfortune; but this was so obviously a groan, and so loud, and so located in the room above the dining-room, that everyone stopped speaking at once and stared at the ceiling.

As they stared, a bead of red was seen to form on the plaster. It grew, elongated, and fell. And where it landed on the tablecloth it made what for all the world looked like a bloodstain. Almost at once another drop followed it, and then another. Gesturing to the other men present, Mr Walsingham leaped to his feet and dashed from the room. The men followed him, leaving their ladies to stare as though hypnotized at the falling drops and the spreading red stain.

Reaching the top of the stairs, Walsingham flung himself into the bedroom above the dining-room. It was empty. Hurrying to the middle of the floor, he knelt to examine the close carpeting. There was no mark on it. He only hesitated a moment, then told the men who had followed him to rip up the carpet along the walls while he moved furniture aside to let it be turned back. They heaved the carpet back together and exposed the wooden flooring. It was unmarked. A film of undisturbed dust was plainly visible on the varnish.

Running downstairs again, the men found the women standing round the table, hands to their mouths, watching the inexorable drip from above. The stain had now spread on the tablecloth and was a foot or more across. Then, as they watched, the dripping ceased. The men rushed upstairs again. The bedroom was as empty and quiet as they had left it, the dust on the floorboards still undisturbed.

Walsingham went down and ripped off the tablecloth. In the morning he took it to a local physician for an opinion upon the stain. A microscope soon settled that. It was human blood.

That was the end of the Walsinghams' sequence of unnerving experiences, for they left the house soon afterwards. No one else moved in. There had been too many guests at that final supper for any part of the neighbourhood not to hear of what had occurred.

Some years passed. The pretty house remained empty and deteriorating. The horrific tales became local legend, scarcely credited by the more cynical, younger members of the Oakville community. One of these was Horace Gunn, a particularly sceptical young man.

He hesitated when offered a worthwhile bet that he wouldn't spend twenty-four hours alone in the house: but he accepted, and, thinking to get quickly over the worst of the ordeal, went there just after sundown and settled in for a night's vigil.

Next morning, his wagerers decided to check on him. They drove out to the farm and hooted for Horace as they approached it. He did not come to the door. They knocked, then peered through windows: there was no sign of him. Triumphantly, they prepared to go back to town, seek him out and make him pay up. Someone suggested that, since they were there, they might as well go inside the house and have a look round. Forcing a window, they clambered in.

In what had been the dining-room they found Horace Gunn. He lay spread-eagled on the floor, his throat swollen and terribly bruised with the distinct marks of long fingers

Horace Gunn was not dead. But he was never the same man again; though he was able eventually to tell what had happened that night.

His first act on shutting himself into the farmhouse had been to light an oil lamp: or rather to *try* to light it. Each time he struck a match it was puffed out sharply, as though by someone standing at his shoulder. Giving this up after many exasperating attempts, he knelt to the grate and tried to kindle the fire laid there. Again, every match was extinguished before he could touch it to the paper.

Feeling by now a deal less sceptical than before, he considered going home; but the wager and his not inconsiderable courage determined him to stick it out.

He sat down in the dark and waited. For long there was no sound, save what might be attributed to the creaking of wood and the patter of small creatures in an abandoned house. Suddenly, from below where Gunn was sitting, there resounded a blood-freezing scream. It was followed by sounds of hysterical pursuit up and down stairs and through other rooms, with the bursting open and slamming of doors, as though someone were after another for his very life.

The din ceased at last, and Horace Gunn breathed again, believing that perhaps he had now come through all the ordeal he would have to endure, and need only sit through the remaining hours to his reward. He was never more wrong in his life.

As he crouched there in the pitch dark, he became aware that at one point on the wall opposite him a speck of light was beginning to appear. He stared as it grew and spread into a ball of light, in the midst of which there slowly materialized a man's head. It grew more and more distinct. There appeared long, grey hair, staring eyes of misery and madness, and a bloody temple lacerated by a gaping wound.

The worst thing about it, however, was that it was starting to move, at about the height of a man's head from the ground—and it was coming his way.

Terrified, Horace Gunn backed away, groping into the darkness behind him. Suddenly the head vanished, as though extinguished by a switch: but Gunn had had enough. He stumbled towards where he believed the door to be. Whether he tripped, or whether, as he swore afterwards, a hand grasped his ankle and jerked him to the floor, is not known: but there could be little doubting the truth of his description of the unseen hands which grasped his throat and choked him, until he lost consciousness. For there were the finger-marks for his friends to see next day.

This latest horror at the Oakville farmhouse was widely reported and discussed in the newspapers of the South and elsewhere and many theories were put forward. The most interesting detail to emerge was that some weeks after Walsingham had bought the farm a quantity of bones had been unearthed in a corner of one of the plantations. Dismissing his farmhands' assertion that they were human remains, the farmer had had them destroyed.

Although the farm had stood for seventy years before that without any sign of supernormal disturbance, trouble in plenty had broken loose afterwards. The moral, clearly, is to let sleeping bones lie: and to note that brave dogs do not get insomnia for nothing.

Sung to His Death by Dead Men

Human bones littered the worn stone floor of the college cloister. Grey with the dust of centuries, and almost paper-light, they might have been Norman, since this part of the college was built between 1175 and 1230. Lying there in the distilled sunlight of a summer afternoon, the hum of bees coming from the Master's Garden, doves cooing on the jumble of college roofs, an undergraduate in cap and gown talking in low tones to another in rowing shorts, this spectacle of dead bones was grotesquely incongruous. Utterly out of place on an afternoon of summer peace in Jesus College, Cambridge.

It was soon after the end of the First World War. The last guns had thundered into silence on the fields of Flanders. The last star-shell had flickered into nothingness in a velvet sky above the fields of dead. No longer the green fields of England or quiet college gardens of Cambridge shuddered to the tremors of box barrages and exploding mines far off across the waters of the North Sea. We had come home to pick up the threads of learning. Even thus young soldiers, home from the wars of Napoleon, from Agincourt or the trenches before Sebastopol, had come back from the stench of death, the sight of dead bones, to learn afresh the lost paths of peace. Odd how history timelessly repeats itself.

I thought I had seen enough of blanched bones that afternoon when the workman, grubbing away like a dust-covered mole in a shallow trench behind a rampart of upheaved stones, threw out the bones.

"Funny, ain't it, Guv," he grinned. "Shan't never know 'oo they b'long to, shall we? Hundreds o' years old. Might be one o' the nuns what liv'd 'ere before they turned the place into a college. Every time us chaps do a bit o' excavatin' 'ere we allus turn up somethin'—old bones, bits o' carvin'—Gawd knows—if it ain't nuns, it's monks or dead dons. They do say some of 'em died o' the plague. I reckon there's more spooks walk about in this college o' nights than anywhere else in Cambridge. Reg'lar rabbit warren it is—one warren on top of another." He went on digging.

Now I was not a member of Jesus College. Young, hard-up, eager, just out of the army, anxious to be in the cut-throat world of journalism, but avid also for that deeper learning which only an older university can give. I was extra-mural, combining journalism on the local newspaper with English Literature which meant sitting at the feet of that master of English, the late Sir Arthur Quiller-Couch.

I climbed the bare, open staircase to the long panelled room in which he received the privileged few. I told him of the bones tossed out of the shallow grave on to the paving stones of the cloister.

"Ah! Probably the bones of Anthony Ffryar, a Fellow of this college who was sung to his death by dead men," he remarked gently.

"Who on earth was Anthony Ffryar?" I asked. "Q" gave me a quizzical smile.

"He might have been the greatest name in medicine—the man who discovered the cure for all ills, but he was sung to death at the wrong moment. I can't tell you any more than that. You like listening to nightmare stories. There's one for you. Ask the Master. He tells the tale better than I can."

Now the Master of Jesus College at the time was the late Arthur Gray who, for esoteric amusement, delved into the dusty bones of college history. Arthur Gray recorded some of his findings, and buttered them with his fancy, in a series of papers which he wrote for his own amusement, and that of a few friends, under the pen-name of Ingulphus, which was the name of the far-off author of the *Saxon Chronicle*.

Jesus College is not quite the oldest college in Cambridge since

Peterhouse was established as such in 1281, eleven years after the first statutes of Merton College, Oxford, but Jesus was the Benedictine nunnery of St Radegund before that time. When the nunnery declined to only two nuns, one of them being called *Infamis* in the reign of Henry the Seventh, Bishop Alcock of Ely got leave from the King to suppress the nunnery, take over its buildings and revenues and replace it as Jesus College. Parts of the nunnery survived.

So many odd architectural survivals of different periods are embodied in the present fabric of the College that it has become, as the workman said, a rabbit warren, one warren on top of another. You never know what will turn up. It is full of bones, of history known and half-known, of ghosts and dim legends of horror.

So we come to the strange, blood-chilling legend of Anthony Ffryar. Arthur Gray, the Master, sorted it out and put it together. What is known for undoubted fact is that Anthony Ffryar matriculated in 1541/2 when he was between fifteen and sixteen years of age. He took his B.A. degree in 1545 and his M.A. in 1548. He became a Fellow towards the end of 1547 and died in the hot summer of 1551. The Master of the College during the whole of his Fellowship was Dr Reston, who died in the same year as Ffryar.

Ffryar, like most Fellows of his time, was a priest, but he was no dedicated student of theology. He was an alchemist. This does not mean that he was a magician or a dubious dabbler in the occult. He was a serious, utterly dedicated student of the science then known as alchemy from which spring the physics and chemistry of today. Alchemy was a recognized subject of university studies in the sixteenth century.

Anthony Ffryar was undoubtedly as serious a student and as honest in his beliefs as the famous Dr John Dee. Like Dee he may have stumbled upon a discovery in alchemy which could have revolutionized the well-being of mankind. He died in a moment of unbelievable horror on the threshold of that discovery.

Ffryar ate, slept and worked in a panelled chamber with a stone fireplace on the first floor of the oaken staircase at the west end of the College chapel. That staircase is now absorbed in the Master's Lodge but you can still see its doorway in the cloister. The windows of Ffryar's room overlooked the tombs and green mounds of a graveyard then called "Jesus Churchyard" since the nave of the chapel was used as a parish church at that time. The graveyard is now part of the Master's garden and part of the Master's Lodge is built into what was the nave. Professor Pevsner says: "The chapel is much smaller than the church had been. It is shorn of part of its nave, both have aisles and both chancel aisles." He goes on to say that parts of the old chapel have been uncovered and that "the cloister floor was originally lower than it is now".

Imagine Anthony Ffryar at the age of about twenty-six, hard at work in his lonely chamber at the west end of the chapel looking on the graveyard. He worked for nothing less than the discovery of a master-cure for all the diseases which afflict mankind. Dr Gray has written of him: "To the study of alchemy he was drawn by no hopes of gain, not even of fame, and still less by any desire to benefit mankind. He was actuated solely by an unquenchable passion for inquiry, a passion sterilizing to all other feeling. To the somnambulisms of the less scientific disciples of his school, such as the philosopher's stone and the elixir of life, he showed himself a chill agnostic. All his thoughts and energies were concentrated on the discovery of the *magisterium*, the master-cure of all human ailments."

For four years young Ffryar pored over his books, compounded his concoctions, distilled the results, studied his alembic, compared results, was lifted by sudden hope and dashed by despair. Time after time he thought he had found the secret. Time and again, since he was a perfectionist, a cold scientist, he admitted bitterly to himself that he had not found it. The *magisterium*, the great secret which was to save mankind infinite pain and suffering, was always just round the corner.

Then, in the summer of 1551, he was suddenly sure that he had found the answer. The final experiment promised glorious success. A new passion arose in his heart—"to make the name of Ffryar glorious in the healing profession as that of Galen or Hippocrates". Those are the words of Dr Gray. Ffryar was certain that within a few days, even within a matter of hours, the fame of his discovery would burst upon the world of Tudor England and re-echo round the known world overseas.

That summer was hot. A still, oppressive, tropic heat. The drains and sewers of Cambridge, never a rose-garden, stank. The fetid smells which arose from the crude lavatories and horrible drains was overpowering. More, it was killing. Then came an outbreak of that fatal epidemic known as "the sweat" from which, as Fuller says, "patients ended or mended within 24 hours". It was a form of plague. When it struck, the inhabitants of Elizabethan London and of every other afflicted city, town or village, died like flies.

Thirty feet beneath the oaken floors and stone pavements of Jesus College there ran a dark, Stygian sewer known as "the kytchynge sinke ditch", foul with filth and scum from the college kitchen and lavatories. It was a breeding-place of disease unbelievable. When, in 1642, it was opened up and cleaned out they discovered a complete human skeleton buried beneath the slime of centuries. Nobody knew how it got there or whose it was. That grim monastic mystery remains unsolved to this day. There is little doubt that the "kytchynge sinke ditch" was the main cause of the plague which struck Jesus College in that hot summer of 1551.

First to die was little Gregory Graunge, a thirteen-year-old school-boy and chorister, who lodged in the College school in the outer court. He died on 31 July, and was buried the same day in Jesus Churchyard under Anthony Ffryar's windows. Ffryar knew the boy by sight. The burial service was held that night in the chapel and Ffryar heard the singing of the choristers and the solemn words of the Requiem. Funerals at night were the common practice and burials in college were not uncommon. The death of this poor child, alone among strangers, touched even the cold obsessed heart of Anthony Ffryar. Not only the pity of it struck his heart. The scene in the dim chapel that night, the Master and Fellows shrouded in their hoods, standing darkly in their stalls in the faint, flickering light of candles, the long-drawn chanting and the childish singing of the other boys who had been Gregory's friends, struck cold into his mind.

Three days later another child chorister died. The College was immediately cut off from the town and the fields which surrounded it. All gates were locked and guarded. No messages were allowed except by a chosen messenger. Jesus College was a place of terror, isolated from the outside world. Barred gates and banned visitors were no proof against the plague. Mr Stevenson, the choristers' usher, died on 5 August. Two days later one of the junior Fellows, named Stayner, died. Each night by the dim chapel candles, the bodies were laid on a bier draped in black cloth, whilst on either side the miserable chants rose up to blind Heaven and the solemn Latin phrases were intoned. Each night, under Ffryar's windows, a grave was dug in the green churchyard and the bodies were lowered under the stars to the hooting of owls.

Then on 8 August, that gaunt, severe man, Dr Reston, the Master, died also. The Plague was no respecter of academic eminence. Next day, 9 August, a Master of Arts died. Night after night the grim scene was re-enacted in the chapel.

All scholars had been sent home on 6 August, and some of the Fellows had left the College the same day. The terrified few who remained met on 8 August and declared that the College should be closed until the pestilence had passed. This meeting was held after the Master's death that same day. The meeting decreed that Robert Laycock, a college servant, was the only person to remain in the College and that his only word with the outside world should be through his son who lived in Jesus Lane, then a rough country road, tree-shaded. A hard and bitter sentence of death on Goodman Laycock. We may picture him as a simple rustic, unable to read or write, in awe of the learned men who were his masters. He was to be the human sacrifice.

Anthony Ffryar defied this inhuman decree. Come what may he refused to leave the College. His research was on the threshold of success. If it succeeded he could present this pestilence-stricken world with the magic *magisterium* which would put an end to all such terror of disease. His laboratory was in his room. Without it his work would stop. It is likely also that he considered himself immune from the pestilence. "Solitude for him was neither unfamiliar nor terrible," as Dr Gray wrote.

Anthony Ffryar declared that he would bar his door and unlatch it only to take in the supplies of food which Laycock was to leave for him on the staircase landing.

For three days, Ffryar and Laycock lived their solitary lives apart in the empty College. Each day Laycock left his food outside the barred door. Within the room Ffryar worked consumedly, frantically, without fear, oblivious of the dying world outside. Only in the evening did he unlock his door to take in his food. August 12th was to be his day of victory over disease.

On that night he began his last experiment. It would take some hours. He had not eaten since dawn. He opened the door and peered out, but there was no food on the landing.

He waited. No footsteps came. He shouted for Laycock. No answer came. Finally, he crept downstairs in the dark, groped his way to the Buttery where Laycock lived and slept, and beat on the Buttery door. There was no reply but the pattering feet of rats. He went to an open window by the hatch beneath which Laycock had his bed. He called again. No answer came. Cautiously, he slipped through the window and groped towards the table where he knew that his food should be set out on a tray. In the dim light he saw a truckle-bed. Upon it lay Goodman Laycock, corpse-white and dead.

Terrified, Ffryar groped back to his room. Hungry and frightened, he must still get on with his great work. When it was ended he would have the answer to all disease and could walk boldly into the town. He lit the brazier used for his experiments, put it in the fireplace and placed on it the alembic which was to distil the *magisterium*.

In the darkening chamber he sat and waited, watching the wavering flame feverishly. A nameless fear stole over him. Outside, the College and the town lay still as death. At each hour the College clock, last wound up by Laycock, struck the passing hours. It was as though the old college servant was speaking his last words. Midnight was to be the magic key to it all—the final moment of solution. Somehow, Ffryar fell asleep although he tried desperately to beat off the weariness, born of hunger, fear, silence, heat and the presence of the dead. When he woke, the clock struck one.

The moment of truth had passed. Had he lost his chance? His brain beat feverishly within his head. Yet the fire still burned, the alembic simmered quietly. All might still be well. Then the clock boomed another stroke—another, and yet another.

Anthony Ffryar opened his door and listened. The clock toiled out its solemn notes. Was this a funeral toll? His mind flew back to that first night when the bell tolled for little Gregory, the choirboy. Were unseen hands now tolling for the dead man on his truckle-bed in the Buttery?

Ffryar was a brave man. He went in the dark down the stairs. The night was hot and still and the cloister as black as death. He looked towards the chapel. A faint light from within lit the windows. The door was open. He went in.

By the chancel door a man, black-gowned, his face shaded, pulled silently at the bell-rope. A solitary candle in an iron bracket gave

dim light. Ffryar, with fear in his heart, was bold enough to
and look the man who tolled the bell full in the face. It was Goodm
Laycock.

Anthony Ffryar walked into the chapel to his own stall in the
choir and sat down. Four candles burned about a figure draped in
black lying on the bier. A chorister stood on either side of the dead
body. In the dim candle-light Anthony Ffryar saw four tall figures,
hooded and erect, in their stalls. One was in the Master's place. It
was the figure of Dr Reston.

The bell stopped tolling. The funeral service began. It was the
Roman Mass for the Dead, forbidden in England at that time. The
voice of Dr Reston intoned the solemn introit, the voice of Stevenson, the usher, responding. Ffryar, the living man, sat rooted in his
stall whilst the dead conducted the funeral.

The sad chanting ended. The four dead men in the stalls descended
to the pallid figure lying on the bier. Anthony Ffryar, the cold
scientist who knew not fear, and had faith in his own claim to
immortality, rose from his seat and, half certain what he would see,
joined the four mourners. He drew the black cloth from the face of
the dead man on the bier and saw the face of Anthony Ffryar.

At that instant the choristers put out the guttering candles one
by one.

"*Requiem aeternam dona ei, Domine.*" The four hooded dead men
chanted the words. The first taper went out.

"*Et lux perpetua luceat ei,*" came the childish treble of the two
choirboys. A second light went out.

"*Cum sanctis tuis in aeternum,*" replied the four hooded dead. One
candle alone remained alight.

Dr Reston, his face corpse-white, tossed back his hood and turned
his fearsome eyes upon the living Anthony Ffryar. He stretched out
his dead hand across the bier, grasped the hand of Anthony Ffryar
tightly and unyieldingly. "*Cras tu eris mecum,*" he said.

The last candle went out.

The Man who Hated Cats

Why do some men hate cats?

The inbred fear in Man of certain animals, insects or reptiles is fully explicable. The rat, the snake, the wolf, the scorpion—even the gentle useful spider—are all creatures of open or implied menace. But the cat cannot be ranged with them. Pest-destroyer, companion of the lonely, he wants only to enjoy himself and to let others do the same. He is beautiful with a boneless grace that belongs to no other species; his kittens are the most charming of all young animals. Yet history is black with cat-persecution; one meets people who say with an affected shudder that they cannot stand cats, cannot bear one in the room. We suspect that cat-hatred proceeds from Man's lower depths of subconscious jealousy and resentment of a small creature so much more essentially civilized and elegant than himself.

Such a one was Lionel Earnshaw. A bachelor of comfortable means, he enjoyed the good things of life and was known among his friends for a dandyish fastidiousness in dress. He maintained a dignified flat in London, where his domestic life was organized by an even more dignified manservant; for these were the years following the First World War. In fairness it may be said that he worked quite hard as the head of a small but distinguished publishing firm.

As a single man he was always much in demand to make up numbers at dinner-parties or at those weekend gatherings in country houses which have provided a wealth of material for the authors of detective fiction. He revelled in these gatherings, and was particularly pleased when an invitation arrived from Jack Vaughan, a friend since Cambridge days, to spend a weekend at his house near Eastbourne. The Vaughans' entertaining was very much to Earnshaw's taste: besides, he had had a hard week of it in Bloomsbury, for the autumn publishing rush was gathering momentum, and he was in the later stages of a heavy chest cold—the sea air would do him good. He accepted with gratitude, telling Pearson, his manservant, to lay out the tweeds as well as his evening clothes.

The door was opened to him by the Vaughans' butler. The butler admitted him deferentially, taking his hat, coat and bag. Behind him, Jack Vaughan was emerging from the drawing-room.

"Lionel, my dear fellow! Come in. We'd no idea you were catching the early train, or we'd have sent the car."

"I couldn't be sure of catching it. Besides, there are always plenty of cabs. How are you? All well, I hope?"

"Absolutely top-hole. Eve's just seeing about dinner arrangements —she'll be delighted to see you so early. What about a drink?"

"Think I'll freshen up first, Jack." Earnshaw was unpleasantly conscious of the miasma of the Southern Railway about his beautifully tailored suit. He was about to move in the direction of the staircase when there appeared, as if at a summons, a large black cat. It matched briskly past Vaughan, tail perpendicular with well-being, its face wearing that smile which a pleased cat assumes: a remarkable feat, considering the flatness and inflexibility of its features. Straight up to Earnshaw it went, encircled his legs with affectionate rubbings, then stood up with its claws kneading his shins as though inviting him to pick it up. Earnshaw started back. Vaughan saw his repugnance, and laughed.

"Stop it, Blackie! Sorry about him, old man—I know you hate them. Here, Blackie." He clicked his fingers. "In there with you, and don't pester people." But the cat remained near Earnshaw, looking up at him with the light of love in its golden eyes. He set off upstairs, and it followed dog-like at his heels, undeterred by its master's calls. Earnshaw decided to ignore it, rather than start the weekend off with an awkward scene. Having ascertained that he would be occupying his usual room, he entered it and shut the door firmly, resisting the temptation to lock it; washed, changed, applied a little discreet Cologne-water, and prepared to go downstairs.

The cat was sitting outside the door, not washing itself or studying birds through the landing-window, but upright, intent, immobile, a watcher on the threshold. When he appeared it rose promptly, paid brief homage to the turn-up of his trousers, and set off downstairs with him.

In the drawing-room an inviting tray of drinks was waiting. Earnshaw chose one of Vaughan's special cocktails, admired his golf trophies, complimented Eve on her healthy bloom and her daughter Joan on being "quite a young woman", and sat down. Blackie unhesitantly jumped on his knee, and Earnshaw unhesitantly pitched him off.

"Really, that cat," said Eve. "Jack says he followed you upstairs. I don't know what's come over him—he's not that friendly with everyone."

"I appreciate his civility, but I wish he'd chosen a more receptive subject," replied Earnshaw, downing his drink more quickly than usual, for his nerve was slightly shaken by Blackie's attentions. The cat was turned out, and the cocktail hour proceeded with pleasant chat, the exchange of news, and the arrival of two couples who were the Vaughans' other guests.

Dinner was, as ever, excellent. Earnshaw thoroughly relished the rich, creamy *oeufs cocotte*, the *truite meunière*, the early grouse sent down from Aberdeenshire. It was unfortunate for his appreciation of the rest of the meal that the arrival of the savoury was coincidental with that of Blackie. The cat entered eagerly, "Ah, *there* you are!" written all over his face; and came to sit by Earnshaw's chair. He was turned out at once, amid general laughter and much chaffing about Earnshaw's power over animals. Wryly he joined in, but he did not enjoy the delicious savoury.

When he went to bed, that night Blackie accompanied him and was carried downstairs by a maid, unprotesting but casting yearning looks over his shoulder at Earnshaw's relentlessly closed door. Sunday found him again on watch outside it. For the entire day, from the bringing to Earnshaw of early tea and the Sunday newspaper, a battle of wills took place. Wherever Earnshaw went Blackie would go. Only after luncheon, when the men took a stroll, did he abandon the chase: and on Earnshaw's return, as he was changing his shoes, he felt to his horror a stout form clamber on to his shoulder from the back of his bedroom chair and wreathe itself round his neck. He was quite glad when bedtime came and he was secure. Still, the day had been pleasant otherwise, the food perfect, the company bearable, the air stimulating. His cold was better. He slept soundly and dreamlessly.

It was morning when he awoke, to his agreeable surprise, for he had recently been in the habit of finding himself awake in the dismal hour before dawn. Something more than the light had roused him, he felt—what could it be? He lay there, recovering consciousness, gradually aware of an unpleasant sensation. It was almost a feeling of illness, of breathlessness, as though he were breathing with only one lung. He thought of his chronic chest weakness, of his recent bad cold, and wondered whether yesterday's walk had brought it on afresh. Perhaps he had better go to sleep again. Soon they would bring him nice hot tea which would dispel the congestion, or whatever it was. He felt very languid, almost faint.

It was a sharp pain somewhere in the region of his heart which brought him fully awake. He clapped his hand to his side, to meet something warm and soft, like a large hot-water bottle in a velvet cover. But last night he had not asked for a hot-water bottle. He realized with unspeakable revulsion that the object lying so close and warm against him was the cat. It was purring loudly, almost stertorously.

Half rising in the bed, he made a frantic effort to push it away, though the contact of his hand with its fur almost turned him sick. It clung like a burr, and he realized that it was licking the jacket of his pyjamas, just below his left arm. He was disgusted to feel a large wet patch on the material. Then he looked down, and saw that the wet patch was blood. The sharp teeth and sandpaper tongue of the feline vampire had penetrated the cloth and his flesh. His pyjamas were soaked, and the sheets stained bright scarlet.

Somehow he managed to get out of the bed, half-jumping, half-falling, casting the cat from him. It retreated, startled, and crouched on the floor at the end of the bed. He began to scream abuse at it, and to throw article after article from the bedside table in its direction—a book, a tumbler, his cigarette-case, a camphorated-oil bottle. The cat took cover under the dressing-table and huddled there spitting at him, its eyes enormous with fear. He picked up the bedside lamp, wrenched it from the socket, and advanced on the cat. If he had reached it he would have battered it to death. But one of its nine lives came to the rescue: before the blow could fall Earnshaw had collapsed across the blood-stained bed, unconscious.

The servant who brought his morning tea received a shock unparalleled in his experience. It served him right, as Eve Vaughan severely pointed out, for he had been the guilty party. He had got up that morning an hour too soon; had taken in Earnshaw's tea at six instead of seven, and had then realized, glancing at Earnshaw's watch in its case, that he had made a silly mistake. He had noticed Blackie sneaking in at his side, but not wishing to make a noise and waken Earnshaw, thereby drawing attention to his own foolishness, he had let the cat remain.

For an hour and a half it must have clung leech-like to the sleeping Earnshaw's side, causing him to lose a good deal of blood. The horrified Vaughans called a doctor as soon as he was discovered, and the wound was pronounced unpleasant but not dangerous. Earnshaw, pale and bandaged, in clean pyjamas and sheets, demanded hysterically the immediate destruction of the cat.

"Have it killed! Send for the vet! Drown it! It's not fit to live, filthy thing!"

The Vaughans, although they had been apologizing until their throats ached for the grotesque accident to the guest in their house, looked sideways at each other, for Blackie was a family favourite and they were not in any case fond of having animals put down.

"He didn't actually do any *harm*," Eve ventured rashly.

"Harm?" Earnshaw's voice rose to a shriek. "Half-drained me of blood and probably ruined my nerves for life? What do you call harm, then? The thing's mad as a hatter, and evil as well."

"He's always been an amiable sort of cat," said Jack defensively. "Never scratched or bit anyone, lets children pull him about—doesn't even go on beds, never mind in 'em."

"Then if he wasn't mad before, he is now," Earnshaw snapped. "I shall report the whole thing to the health authorities—they'll soon put him out of the way."

"Dammit, Lionel, you can't do that!" Jack protested. "He's our property, after all. The doctor says you'll be all right, clean wound and all that."

"I'm the best judge of whether I'm all right. Before I leave this house—which I shall do the minute I feel strong enough—I'm going to telephone the police."

Eve was almost in tears. "If only we knew what made Blackie do such a thing," she said. Earnshaw gave a strangled scream and pointed to a corner of the bedroom.

"It's got in again! There it is, waiting for another chance! Get it out! Get it out!"

There Blackie undoubtedly was, apparently over his fright, and at his former game of licking and purring like a small sawmill. "What an earth has he got?" Eve wondered. "Blackie! Puss! Come out from under there." But Blackie paid no attention, and she bent closer.

"Why, it's a medicine bottle!"

"It's my camphorated oil. I threw it at him," said Earnshaw sullenly.

Enlightenment dawned on the faces of the Vaughans. "Do you rub it on your chest, by any chance?" Eve asked. Earnshaw looked surprised at the apparently irrelevant question.

"I have been doing," he said shortly. "It helps my breathing at night when I've got a chest cold." To his intense annoyance, his hosts began to laugh, simultaneously, with a note of hysteria in their mirth.

"But he—simply adores it!" Eve managed to gasp out. "He used to lick it off Joan's chest when she had bronchitis."

"Of course he did," put in Jack, wiping his eyes. "I'd forgotten that. And the time he got at the bottle in the medicine cupboard! So you see, old man, it wasn't vampirism or anything like that. He simply liked the way you smelt—and tasted, I suppose!"

Earnshaw's face was a pale mask of umbrage.

"If you find it amusing," he said icily, "I congratulate you. And now if you'll kindly go, taking that fiendish animal with you, and telephone for a taxi to take me to the station, I'll dress. I have no intention of staying in this house a moment longer than I need, ill as I feel."

His fury was justified, for it was many years before he could sleep without the subconscious fear of waking to find his dreaded succubus beside him. It was the most ghastly experience of his life, outdoing anything that had happened to him during his spell in the trenches. But Blackie, the cause of it all, never knew to the end of his long life that he had for a short time been a vampire.

Accusing Eyes of Vengeance

The head! A woman's head, severed at the neck. He knew he must get rid of that tell-tale piece of evidence without any further delay. Eight full days had passed since he had struck his victim down, and since then her corpse had been hidden in a small locked room in the bungalow on the shingle between Eastbourne and Pevensey Bay.

He had rented the place, furnished, for two months in the assumed name of Waller. No one knew him in the district; he was unlikely to be disturbed. That was why he had felt perfectly safe in deliberately shelving the problem of disposal while he devoted his energies to building up a foolproof alibi. He had gone about this boldly, day after day. No haste, no panic, but with complete self-possession. Indeed, every stage of his crime had been planned in advance with calm, calculating precision.

Now, with most of the dead woman's savings in his possession, her absence accounted for in circles where she might have been missed, and with his alibi established against emergency, he felt safe to dispose of her remains at leisure.

It was Tuesday, 22 April, 1924, and he resolved to get rid of the head that night. He had a twofold reason for making this a priority. First, it provided an infallible means of identification. Second, there were injuries to the skull from which the manner of her death might be deduced. Complete destruction of the head, therefore, was a logical move, and destruction by fire seemed the most practical and immediate way.

The sitting-room grate was the largest in the bungalow and he soon had a fierce fire blazing away there. While it was burning up he unscrewed the door of the small spare bedroom in which the partly dismembered remains had lain concealed since he had dragged the body there from the sitting-room on the night of 15 April.

He grabbed the severed head by the fair hair without hesitation, carried it through to the front room and dumped it squarely in the very heart of the flames. Then he returned to resume the work of dismemberment, which he had begun on the preceding Good Friday.

Three pieces remained. The torso and the two legs which he had cut off from the hips, using a cook's knife with a ten-inch blade, and a small meat saw.

Outside the bungalow a fierce storm was starting up, with great flashes of lightning and reverberating peals of thunder that seemed to rock the small building to its very foundations. He had taken the precaution of seeing that all curtains were tightly drawn, but every now and then the lightning flashes would penetrate the smallest chinks to illumine the gruesome scene. Not that Waller felt the slightest squeamishness or entertained any compassion for the victim of his blood lust. She was a former mistress who had become an incubus and he had planned her destruction in coldly matter-of-fact detail.

Between the thunderclaps other sounds began to assail his ears and, as he worked, he could hear a disturbing sizzling, spluttering, and crackling coming from the burning head in the next room.

A sudden feeling that it might fall out upon the hearthrug and perhaps set fire to the place smote him so forcibly that he rushed into the sitting-room to see what was happening, his hands still blood-smeared from his unfinished butchery. He recoiled in the doorway as his nostrils were filled by the stench of burning flesh and singed hair. And, while he stood there, hesitant upon the threshold, there came an extra-loud crash of thunder. A moment later the noise of spluttering in the grate increased in volume, so that Waller's gaze was automatically attracted to the fire.

What he saw there filled him with unspeakable horror, for that very instant the victim's eyelids popped up suddenly and it seemed the woman's eyes were staring straight into his with a light of intense reproach and hatred. It may only have been that they burned with the reflection of the flickering flames; but the effect upon Waller was devastating.

For one instant he stood there as if rooted in an agony of abject terror; then complete panic engulfed him and he dashed for the front door and, slamming it behind him, plunged out into the storm. He was in shirtsleeves, and the fury of the storm was increasing. In a few minutes he was soaked to the skin; but he was oblivious of all external feeling. Seared into his mind as with a white-hot iron was the frightening spectacle of that blazing head and his victim's staring, accusing eyes, seeming to reflect a light of terrible, undying vengeance. Even when the murderer clenched his own streaming eyelids tightly, the haunting vision could not be shut out; it was still vividly real.

He began to pace to and fro upon the sodden shingle like some caged beast of the jungle who knows that he is trapped. But here were no restraining bars save those of abject terror. The sea pounded just beyond the low garden wall; the wind roared; the rain lashed down unmercifully; lightning flashes grew fiercer; the reverberating thunder lasted longer.

Waller became chilled to the bone and a prey to uncontrollable shivering fits as his panic mounted. And all the time those relentless, searing eyes were burning their image into his teeming brain, an image he found it impossible to eradicate.

The cumulative effect was completely demoralizing. That haunting vision had reduced him from the ice-cool, calculating schemer of iron nerve and no human feeling to a shattered, gibbering creature, the terrified wreck of a man. How long he remained pacing the shingle out there in the raging storm he never knew; but thereafter a sudden flash of lightning or a peal of thunder was sufficient to make him turn white and to shrink back, cowering in obvious terror.

Yet, somehow or other, he eventually managed to force himself out of his present consuming panic and to steel himself to face the dreadful ordeal of venturing back into the bungalow. But the moment he stepped inside he found it a haunted place, and he moved from room to room with shaking footsteps, prey to a mounting agony of terror.

He stayed just long enough to scramble into some dry clothes and to screw up the spare-room door again. His hands were trembling and he cut himself slightly when his screwdriver slipped, but he was too shattered to worry over that. He fled from the bungalow and caught the first available train for London.

For the next three days Waller went through life as in a nightmare from which there is no waking. By some superhuman effort he contrived to put up an outward appearance of near normality at his home in Richmond and also at his place of work. As a sales manager he enjoyed some freedom of movement, but he could not avoid meeting people. Inwardly he was in terrible torment, still haunted by the memory of those staring, accusing eyes; and he must also have been secretly appalled at the realization of what still remained to be done if he were to cover up all the traces of his ghastly crime.

The only comfort he can have drawn must have lain in the knowledge that his prefabricated alibis were pretty well cast-iron. Five days before the murder he had started to cultivate the trust of a new mistress, a Miss D., and had impressed upon her that she could expect to hear from him quite soon. The day before the murder he had encouraged his victim to write letters to two of her intimate friends confiding her intention of going abroad, first to Paris and then to South Africa, and that it might be some time before they heard from her again. This trip had, indeed, been the dream she had long entertained, so the letters, dated from her London lodgings, had an authentic ring and could be calculated to allay suspicion should her friends miss her.

On the day of the murder, 15 April, Waller had sent a telegram to Miss D., asking her to meet him in London on 16 April. They met and dined together at the Grosvenor Hotel and Waller invited the unsuspecting young woman to come and spend Easter with him at his seaside bungalow. He said he would telegraph her fare and let her know the most suitable train for her to catch.

Waller stayed in London that night and took the opportunity of posting his victim's letters before returning to Eastbourne the following day.

On that same day he had wired the fare money to Miss D. as arranged and had stipulated that if she came down on an afternoon train on Good Friday he would be able to meet her.

He had actually spent the morning of Good Friday in his "Blue-beard's" chamber and had made a start upon the gruesome task of dismembering his victim, severing the head at the neck and removing each leg at the hip. He had expected the pieces to fit very compactly into his victim's cabin trunk, but the torso had proved too long. Further dismemberment was going to be necessary. He had locked the room and had gone to keep his tryst with Miss D.

When she arrived Waller took her out to dinner at an hotel. At that time he had still been complete master of himself. Nothing in his demeanour had suggested that he was under any kind of stress. And at 10 p.m. he had boldly escorted his companion back to the bungalow, and they had actually slept together in the principal bedroom—only a few yards from the locked room with its grisly secret.

Next day they had spent the morning together in Eastbourne, but Waller had gone off to Plumpton races in the afternoon, leaving Miss D. to her own devices in Eastbourne but arranging to meet at the station at about six o'clock.

There had been a chance encounter with a neighbour on the race track, and Waller, scared that the neighbour might mention the fact to his wife in Richmond, had to do some fast thinking. Before leaving Plumpton he had sent a telegram to himself in yet another assumed name, supposedly calling him back to London for an early morning appointment on the following Tuesday.

This message he had read out later for the benefit of Miss D., feigning great disappointment that this would mean cutting short her stay. They would have to return on Monday so that he could be available for that early appointment on the Tuesday.

Meanwhile, there had been Easter Sunday to get through, and while Miss D. had cooked lunch for them and had dusted and tidied generally, Waller had spent a lot of time trying to fix a Yale lock to the spare-bedroom door, making the excuse that he was storing some very valuable books there for a friend. But his skill as a carpenter and locksmith had proved unequal to his zeal. Unable to fix either the Yale or another form of lock he had by him, he had compromised by screwing up the door, saying that he would hate anything to happen to his friend's property.

For a second night he and his unsuspecting companion had slept together in the murdered woman's bed in the main bedroom; and next day, Easter Monday, the attentive Waller had escorted Miss D. back to London, having set up a further useful alibi against future emergency.

All this, of course, had been thought out and carried through with calm deliberation and, up to the dramatic incident of burning the head, Waller's iron nerve had never once failed him. Now, however, his ability to think clearly or to plan with the same detached precision was gone. His mind was in confusion. He knew only too well what dreadful tasks still had to be completed, but for the first time he must have begun to doubt if he would ever be able to see them through. Only the powerful spirit of self-preservation can have sustained him through those three nightmare days when he was keeping up appearances at home and at work.

His sole thought now was to brace himself for a final trip to that haunted bungalow, to clean up there as rapidly as he possibly could, and then to leave the wretched scene for ever.

On the following Saturday, 26 April, he travelled down to the bungalow, still a prey to feelings of revulsion, yet resolved to destroy all remaining evidence of his crime. His first consideration was to examine the ashes in the front-room grate. Naturally, he approached them with some qualms, but when he probed the charred skull with a poker the point went right through and he found that the bone, now brittle, snapped off under light pressure.

Perhaps a trace of his former ruthlessness was revived as he realized that the disposal of the remains of the skull would pose no difficulty. Even as he lifted it from the grate a fragment snapped off, so he carried the whole thing into the garden and, breaking off small pieces with his finger and thumb, scattered them casually over the low surrounding wall on to the shingle as if scattering crumbs for the gulls. No one would ever be able to re-assemble those minute fragments, even if they could be discovered and collected. He felt quite safe in scattering the last few fragments into the dustbin.

He went back to the bungalow, determined to burn the rest of the corpse. He got fierce fires going in two grates, unscrewed the spare door and selected pieces for burning. But when he embarked upon this piecemeal incineration the smell so disgusted him that he feared the neighbours in adjoining bungalows would come round to complain.

When he looked at the rest of the remains in the spare bedroom his heart must have quailed. It was obvious that they could never be burned in a single day, even on two fires. In his panic he thought of boiling as an alternative.

He found a small portable bath, and, selecting the largest saucepan he could find, began to boil water on the kitchen stove. He was desperate now, still suffering from shock and horrible revulsion. Immediately the water came to the boil he dumped in dismembered portions of his victim. It was not a success. As the water bubbled and seethed the stench was even more sickening than that set up by the burning.

If he had felt the bungalow to be haunted before it must have seemed doubly so now. When that dreadful day ended the place was in an appalling state, with evidence of his abortive efforts in every room.

What terrors assailed him during that night, which he spent in an hotel, can only be imagined. He was back in the bungalow early next day to resume his losing battle. Completely demoralized, he was reduced to an insane recklessness that contrasted strikingly with his deliberate preparations before the crime.

He abandoned all efforts at further burning or boiling. Instead, he bundled boiled portions of the corpse into the murdered woman's undergarments, wrapped each item in brown paper and tied each package with string. These he crammed into a Gladstone bag, and the fact that he tossed in the cook's knife suggests that he had no stomach for further dismemberment. He also included the dead woman's racket case which had become bloodstained in his panic.

The place was now a shambles. He left some pieces of torso in the cabin trunk, put some into a biscuit tin, some into an old leather hatbox. He had to leave the big saucepan on the stove, a layer of horrible congealed fat lining the bottom. The bath, now on the floor beside the stove, was half full of blood-tinged water, covered by fatty scum. But Waller, incapable of coping, grabbed his bag and dashed for the London train.

His mind in undisciplined turmoil, all he could think of was to toss his sinister parcels out of the carriage window. But no opportunity for this arose on the journey to Waterloo, so he pressed on to Richmond. He did manage to get rid of a few parcels on that short run, then he decided to go on to Reading.

When he came back to London next day, after spending the night in a Reading hotel, his bag was empty, save for some bloodstained rags, the bloodstained racket case and the cook's knife.

Carefully locking the bag, he put it in the left-luggage office at Waterloo, intending to pick it up at the weekend, when he hoped that one more visit would enable him to clear up the mess and resume his new method of scattering his victim's remains in different parts of the country.

But a net was closing in. His neighbour who had spotted him at Plumpton races mentioned the fact, and Waller's wife, suspicious, searched his pocket and came upon that cloakroom ticket. A former railway policeman with whom she was friendly managed to take a peep at the bag. He couldn't open it, but by slipping the swivelled catches at the end of the bag, on either side of the lock, he was able to sight enough to justify a word with the police. They advised the wife to say nothing; to replace the ticket in her husband's pocket, and leave the rest to them.

Thus, when Waller arrived to claim the bag he was challenged by the police. The bag was opened and its contents brought to light. The bungalow was searched, and the grisly finds there spelled murder with a capital M.

An attempt to bluff by pretending that he had been carrying meat for his dogs was shattered when the stains on the bag were shown to be human blood.

Moreover, Waller's fingerprints were on record at Scotland Yard and he was eventually brought to trial at Sussex Summer Assizes in his true name of Patrick Henry Mahon. His victim, whose initials were on the cabin trunk and the racket case, was Emily Beilby Kaye, with whom he was known to have been consorting for some months, and who was found to be pregnant.

Mahon tried to brazen things out, concocting as his defence a story that the woman's death had been the result of an accidental fall during a quarrel. She had died, he contended, after striking her head against a coal cauldron. This was produced in evidence, as was a model of the bungalow, the roof of which could be removed to show the whole interior, complete with miniature furniture which included a Lilliputian coal cauldron.

It was a most ingenious defence; but Mahon found himself faced with too many unanswerable questions.

He had bought that cook's knife and saw just three days before the death of his mistress, and with them some special cleaning powder, traces of which remained on the knife when recovered from his bag.

He had bought those locks, with screws, a chisel and a screw-driver, on the eve of Emily Kaye's death.

His carefully prefabricated alibi of arranging the visit of the innocent Miss D. destroyed itself when it was proved that he had wired to her on the afternoon of the murder, thus betraying that he fully expected to be free to meet her in London next day.

But it was really the last of nearly fifty witnesses for the prosecution—Sir Bernard Spilsbury, famous Home Office pathologist—who shattered Mahon's story of the accidental fall. He stated flatly that the victim could not possibly have received rapidly fatal injuries from falling upon that cauldron, a flimsy article, as jurors saw when it was passed round for their inspection.

The presiding judge, Mr Justice Avory, with his characteristic needle-sharp alertness, underlined this vital piece of evidence in a flash.

Turning upon Sir Bernard, he asked:

"Do I understand in your opinion a fall upon that coal cauldron would *not* cause her rapid death?"

"That is so," replied Sir Bernard.

"*That is what you mean?*" repeated Mr Justice Avory with great deliberation.

"*That* is what I mean," Sir Bernard insisted.

Thus, by obtaining triple reiteration from this eminent, expert witness, the astute judge saw that a devastating spotlight was sharply focused upon the weakest part of Mahon's story. The dullest jury-man could scarcely fail to grasp the significance. Just a flimsy old cauldron, Exhibit 15, and by far the smallest item in that faithful scale model; yet perhaps the biggest factor in sealing Mahon's fate that day. As members of the jury had handled the original cauldron for themselves they could appreciate Sir Bernard's opinion.

There is a touch of irony in the fact that by destroying his victim's head, Mahon had also destroyed the possibility that anyone could confirm the nature of the injuries that had caused Emily Kaye's sudden death. It never could have supported his "accidental fall" line of defence.

The actual murder weapon, an axe, had been found in two pieces.

The head and a snapped-off haft were discovered in an outside coal-shed—buried under about ten inches of coal. The rest of the haft, which fitted exactly, was found in an old breadpan in the larder.

The jury took barely three-quarters of an hour to reach its verdict of guilty, and only after sentence did its members learn that Mahon had already served a term of penal servitude for a murderous attack upon a young woman who had surprised him in the act of robbing a bank!

The Walking Dead

One spring morning many years ago the labour manager of a big American sugar plantation and factory in Haiti was puzzled to see shambling towards him a line of ragged, miserable-looking people. They neither spoke nor gestured, but shuffled along with sightless eyes like people walking in a dream. Indeed they seemed not to be part of the bright, sunny Caribbean world as they lined up to be registered. There were nine of them.

On the American manager they had a strangely depressing effect, and as their shadows fell across the registration book he shivered unaccountably.

In charge of this band of unhappy-looking creatures was a gnarled old coal-black Haitian named Ti Joseph, a headman who came from Colombier, and who pushed them into line like so many cattle.

He explained that they were simple, ignorant people who came from the wild regions near the Dominican border. They did not understand the local Creole language and were frightened by the noise of the great sugar factory.

But they were good workers and if they were put in the cane field as far from the factory as possible, they would, under his direction, work well.

Hands were in great demand. The cane season was at its height, and any labour was welcome. Joseph and his wretched company of workers were assigned to fields distant from the factory, and Joseph and his wife, Croyance, set up a camp for them. They kept strictly to themselves, and indeed were left to themselves.

The other West Indian workers would not go near Joseph and his wretched companions, for they knew they were Zombies whom Joseph had, by diabolical sorcery, raised from their graves and endowed with a mechanical semblance of life.

Zombies are neither ghosts nor persons, but soulless animated corpses who are used to perform dull and heavy tasks. A Zombie must be procured from a fresh grave before the body has begun to decompose. Only exponents of Voodoo can animate a corpse in this way. The stories of Zombies have been dismissed as superstitious fantasies, but the authorities in some West Indian islands took it so seriously that they passed laws forbidding the practice.

The West Indians themselves were so afraid of their relatives being turned into Zombies that even the poorest put themselves in debt to bury their dead beneath solid tombs of masonry. If this was not possible, they put them in graves in their own gardens when they could continually watch over them. Others mounted guard over their relatives' graves with shot-guns day and night until they were sure the body was decomposed and safe from the Voodoo men.

Zombies move like automatons, like people asleep with their eyes open. They will toil like obedient machines all day in the hot sun without rest. They must be given tasteless, monotonous food, for if they are allowed salt or meat they are aroused and become conscious of what is happening to them, and realize that they are the dead who should be at rest. Those who are using their toil for their own ends then lose control over them.

The strange story of Ti Joseph and the Zombies was told by William Seabrook in *The Magic Island* (1929). It is a story to make the flesh creep.

Day after day the Zombies toiled dumbly in the cane fields under Joseph's supervision, and if they did not move fast enough he whipped them on. At their shunned camp Joseph's wife Croyance each night cooked two pots of food—an unsalted, meatless mess for the Zombies, and a more tasty dish for herself and Joseph.

Every Saturday Joseph collected all their wages, and of course he kept it all himself. He was on a good thing. It was no business of the sugar firm whether the money was divided among Joseph's working party. In any case the Zombies had no use for money. All they wanted, did their dimmed consciousnesses but know it, was rest from the toil of the world—the peace of the grave.

If Joseph was hard-hearted, Croyance was not without pity for these poor creatures. When she suggested to Joseph that perhaps some more flavour should be put into their tasteless food, he scolded her, and warned her of the danger of thus arousing the Zombies.

The carnival which preceded Lent was a weekend holiday for all the workers. Old Joseph went off to Port-au-Prince to enjoy himself, his pockets stuffed with the money the Zombies had earned him. Croyance had to stay behind to look after the Zombies, to prepare their food and to ensure they did not stray, for they were without volition or purpose, and had to be urged and guided in everything they did.

"Be careful with their food, even though it is carnival," Joseph warned her. "And don't let them wander. They mean good money to us. I'll be back on Monday night so that you can go to Mardi Gras on Tuesday."

And so Croyance was left to spend the lonely carnival weekend with the forlorn Zombies with whom it was impossible to have the slightest social contact. It was depressing in the empty fields, with the silent sugar factory in the distance. Everyone was at the carnival, even the white folk who worked in the factory. She began to feel unnerved, for it was worse than being alone, having the company of these empty folk, these walking dead with neither souls nor minds. But she was not afraid. With the loneliness, her pity for the Zombies grew, for Croyance was at heart a kindly old soul and was sorry for what she and Joseph had done to the poor dead folk.

Monday night came, but no Joseph, and when he had not returned on Tuesday, the day of the Mardi Gras, she came to a decision. She would go to see the processions at Croix de Bouquet and take the Zombies with her. There could be no harm in it, and it might do something to cheer up what spirits they possessed to see the gay crowds and the brightly painted religious effigies.

And so she aroused the Zombies from their sleep, which differed little from their waking state, and after giving them their tasteless breakfast of cold, unsalted boiled plantains, Croyance tied a brightly coloured handkerchief around her head, and set out for the town with the dumb obedient Zombies walking behind her in single file in the manner of country people.

The Zombies had originally come from one of the villages on the slopes of the Morne-au-Diable, and she knew that the people of these mountain villages always returned home for the Mardi Gras celebrations, so there was no danger at all of the Zombies being recognized by relatives who had recently buried them.

Obediently the nine Zombies followed Croyance towards the town. She paused at the great crucifix just beyond the railway crossing, knelt on the hot, dusty road and crossed herself. The Zombies did not cross themselves, but stood patiently waiting, staring with their unfocused, unseeing eyes into a fathomless distance which neither Croyance nor indeed any other living person could comprehend.

When they reached the town, Croyance took her charges to the market square and found them an empty bench among the gay crowds watching the procession. While Croyance gazed entranced at the purple-clad processionists, the great gold crucifix, the bells, the swinging incense holders, the images and the sacred tableaux, the Zombies sat there with their dead, unseeing eyes fixed on nothing, shunned by the gay groups in the square.

After the procession, vendors came by selling savouries and sweet-meats. Croyance bought a salted herring for herself. It tasted so good that she wanted the Zombies to enjoy such a delicacy, for they had worked so well and so hard for her and Joseph. But she knew that she must not let them taste meat or salt.

All the same, she was determined to give them something to eat a little more palatable than the tasteless food they had been having. When a woman came by selling candy made from cane sugar and pistachio nuts, she thought there would be no harm in giving this to the Zombies.

So she bought the candy and divided it among the nine Zombies who began to eat it. Almost immediately a dramatic change came over them. They got to their feet with terrible cries. The people in the market square fell back, knowing very well what they were, and there was a dreadful silence as the Zombies with cries of anguish turned and pointed towards the sunlit slopes of the distant Morne-au-Diable. The Zombies then walked out of the market place and out of the town.

No one attempted to stop them or speak to them, least of all Croyance, who stared at them with a quaking heart, knowing the terrible reckoning to come.

The Zombies walked on, looking neither to left nor to right—"with no soul leading them or daring to follow". The sun was going down before they reached their village on the slopes of the Morne-au-Diable where the festivities of Mardi Gras were at their height in the market place.

When the villagers saw the Zombies walking in single file through the warm twilight, their festivities suddenly stopped. Many recognized their relatives and loved ones whom they had buried recently, and most instantly guessed the bitter truth, that they had been taken from their graves by Voodoo and forced into this dreadful semblance of life. In fact the disturbed state of some of the graves, with the hastily replaced earth, had already aroused suspicion. But others thought that perhaps a Lenten miracle had been wrought, and rushed to their loved ones with arms opened in blessed welcome.

But the Zombies walked on with their strange, mechanical step, straight through the market place, recognizing no one, and made for the path which led to the graveyard.

Their harrowed relatives followed. One woman, whose daughter was in this tragic company of the walking dead, threw herself screaming at the girl's feet, begging her not to go back to her grave. But the girl's cold feet passed over her unheeding as she lay in the dust, as did the feet of the other Zombies whose steps quickened as they came to the graves. Then each Zombie rushed back to his own despoiled grave. They threw themselves down among the stones and earth, clawing at the ground with their fingers, then lay there at last, still, silent and at peace, while tearfully, reverently, their relatives, their simple hearts broken afresh, took spade and shovel and restored them to the soil where they belonged.

One of the men of the village set off down to Croix de Bouquet to find out who had done this thing. He returned to Morne-au-Diable with the name of Ti Joseph.

Croyance stayed in the market place all night, not daring to return to the haunted cane fields, nor to seek out her doomed husband. She had learned that the pistachio nuts which had been put in the candy she had given the Zombies had been well salted before being stirred into the candy mixture.

The man returned to the village beneath the Morne-au-Diable with a shirt he had stolen from the camp in the cane fields. The shirt belonged to Ti Joseph and was stained with his sweat.

The relatives of the Zombies took this shirt to a Voodoo man in the mountains who made a deadly concoction of dried goat's dung and cock's feathers dipped in blood. Pins and needles impregnated with this were thrust into a wax image of Joseph to the accompaniment of many fatal imprecations.

But the villagers knew that Ti Joseph himself was steeped in Voodoo, or he could not have raised the Zombies from their graves in the first place. It was thought that he might have counter-magic which would nullify any spell put upon him.

And so they drew lots, and one night one of the men went down the mountains and lay in wait beside a path where it was known Joseph would pass. The following day Joseph was found with his head completely severed from his body.

The West Indians accepted Zombies as a matter of course. To refuse to believe in them was to be ignorant of the facts of life. The Zombie belief is not encountered anywhere else in the world, which has puzzled some people.

But it is not surprising that the West Indian's idea of a very particular kind of hell is to continue working in the cane fields after death. The origin of the belief is buried in the horrors of centuries of West-Indian slavery. The slaves' only release from a life of brutal labour in which they were literally worked to death in the cane fields—considered the most economic way of using slave labour—was in death. The great horror was that they should continue this life afterwards. Thus the Zombie was born in their haunted, superstitious minds, and has lingered on long after slavery came to an end. Even today West Indians are known to guard the fresh graves of their relatives for fear of their being turned into Zombies.

From the Zombies have originated the Jumbies, who are walking dead not enslaved to the cane fields as the Zombies, but who go abroad and cause mischief. Jumbies were supposed to have been responsible for the disturbances among the coffins in the vault of the Chase family in the Barbadoes during the early years of the nineteenth century. This is one of the world's most mysterious happenings, and one which was fully authenticated and witnessed by several responsible persons.*

The negroes did not share the baffled bewilderment of their white masters at what had happened in the Chase vault. They believed the Chase family had offended one of their powerful spirits, who might have been an ill-treated slave during his or her earthly travail.

The negro, uprooted from his native home in Africa and transported to slavery in the West Indies, took nothing with him to the Caribbean except his burning hatred and the embers of a fierce religion, the animism of the great forests, inextricably intermingled with strange and terrifying mysteries which came from the remote heart of the vast continent. This religion had been welded into the simple negro mind by the rhythm of the drums.

In the Caribbean the slaves were immediately exposed to Christianity. The colonists had snidely pleaded with a conscience-stricken Europe that slavery was an infallible way of converting Africans to the Christian faith. And so the slave trade, which brought prosperity and vast fortunes to slavers and colonists alike, was permitted and flourished for centuries.

The Africans, like the pagan Europeans before them, just added Christianity to their old religion and developed a mixture of both. In the same way the old paganism lived on in Europe for many centuries. It just went underground and later emerged as witchcraft.

Thus Voodoo was born in the West Indies. It was a force which unified the negroes and came to be much dreaded by the white people, for it was behind the bloody slave revolts at the turn of the nineteenth century, just after the French Revolution, when in Haiti particularly the slaves massacred their former masters wholesale and subjected them to terrible tortures, such as sawing them in half.

Voodoo, with its roots in the ancient gods of pagan Africa, embraced Christianity in a way which struck Christians as extremely sinister. Human sacrifice was part of Voodoo practice, but its adherents could point to the embarrassing precedent of Abraham and Isaac.

Voodoo has no philosophy, no ethic, no dogma, or theology, but it has a vast jungle-rooted mythology, and a long and complicated

* It is told fully in *Fifty Great Ghost Stories*, edited by John Canning (Odhams, 1966).

ritual, the details of which have shocked and horrified generations of Europeans. The missionaries were especially scandalized by Voodoo, for, in the words of Père Labat, "they couple the Ark of the Covenant with Dagon and secretly preserve all the superstitions of their ancient idolatrous cults with the ceremonies of the Christian religion".

There were whispers of human sacrifice and cannibalism as well as the cruel slaughter of animals, to say nothing of dancers maddened by the rhythms of the drums tearing off their clothes, biting themselves in frenzy and then indulging in promiscuous sexual orgies.

The West-Indian negroes retained their faith in their witch doctors while they paid lip service to the Christian priests, as was illustrated in the story of Croyance and Ti Joseph. The Zombie superstition still lingers, and so does belief in the power of Jumbie dust, which is a powder made from human bones, a pinch of which put into a person's food is said to bring about a slow and painful death.

The raw material of Jumbie dust has always been easy to obtain in the West Indies, where slaves who died were buried, not in stone vaults like their masters, but just under the top soil in the garden. They say you can dig around any old house in the West Indies today and find the ingredients of Jumbie dust.

In matters of morbid superstition we were not in those days much different from the ignorant savages we kidnapped from West Africa and made slaves in our colonial plantations. In England we were making potent love charms out of the charred ashes of witches who were burnt at the stake, and excellent ale was said to be made from the ashes of human bones. The flesh of malefactors whose bodies hung on gibbets was stolen and sold at inflated prices in the market places of England as it was supposed to possess especially magical properties.

Perhaps we should not smile therefore at similar things the West Indians did, such as leaving a matchbox containing a small dead lizard on your doorstep in order to bring about your demise. This symbolized you in your coffin.

There is evidence that these magic spells worked. Many people who have lived in the West Indies have had personal experiences of the strange power of the malign spirits which the Obeah men of Voodoo seem to command. Natives who have fallen under the power of the evil eye have been known to lie down and die, without any physical cause.

Voodoo also concerned itself with the converse of the dreaded powers by which the peaceful dead were turned into unhappy Zombies. To avoid such a thing happening and to ensure the liberation of the spirit so that it might join the spirits of its ancestors, Voodoo prescribed that certain rites and ceremonies be performed upon the dead body. The first part of the ceremony was performed by the practitioner sitting astride the corpse and plucking the spirit from its prison of clay. For a year the spirit dwelled upon the waters, when another rite finally liberated it from this world.

If the spirit was not liberated in this manner, it joined the company of earthbound ghosts which in the Voodoo belief are always malevolent and dangerous, no matter what their temperaments might have been during life. This was apart from the danger of the dead person being turned into a Zombie by such villainous practitioners of Voodoo as Ti Joseph.

Of course it was not always possible to get hold of the body in order to liberate the spirit. But the rite could be performed just as well by sitting astride the grave. This had to be done at night and in great secrecy and it was strictly forbidden by the authorities.

Whatever might be said against Voodoo, it was the slaves' only way of escape from the desolation of their lives. It unified them. To them Christianity meant the hell of servitude, and it is not surprising that they turned it upside down in their black rites. Their daytime was spent in inhuman toil in the cane fields under the lash, and so Voodoo became a thing of the night, a secret world in the darkness, illuminated with the blood and cruelty which the white man had made part of their lives. The drums and dances had the most elemental appeal to the African, and without their fierce rhythms Voodoo would have died, for Africa soon became a dim memory and faded into wondrous legend. Voodoo lives on today with undimmed vitality, and it means far more to most West Indians than the Christian religion they have been taught.

Visit from a Vampire

In 1284, Hugh de Balsham, Bishop of Ely, seeking a solution to the disciplinary problems which involved the inhabitants of the town with the unorganized gown, founded at Cambridge a house for the scholars on the lines of Merton's College, now at Oxford. Naming it Peterhouse—sometimes it is known as St Peter's College —after one of the patron saints of his own cathedral, de Balsham, by his act of benefaction, to all intents and purposes founded the University of Cambridge, though this claim is not mentioned in any of the history books.

Still one of the most distinguished of the Cambridge colleges— there are those who would say with pride, "the most distinguished" —Peterhouse can count among its dons and alumni eminent scholars and potentially eminent scholars in a ratio challenged by no other collegiate body. This was equally true forty years ago, when among its undergraduates was one Peter Grimes.

Over the centuries Peterhouse has undergone many vicissitudes. Its original exposed position on the edge of Coe Fen has been dissipated by the busy modern traffic in Trumpingdon Street. But this process of hemming the College in has been a long and progressive one. In 1816, for example, the College deer park fell under the shade of the Fitzwilliam Museum. But hundreds of years before that, on the other side, one of Cambridge's most beautiful churches,

St Mary the Less, was built, the boundary of its graveyard marching with the walls of the principal court of Peterhouse.

In one of the sets of rooms in the north range of this court lived the poet Thomas Gray, who wrote *Elegy Written in a Country Churchyard*. Gray had a horror of fire, and the young gentlemen of eighteenth-century Peterhouse, discovering this, frequently diverted themselves by calling "Fire" up his staircase and watching their victim clamber down a rope he had fixed to a bar across his window. The time came when he could no longer support the emotional shock which their joking caused, and he crossed the road to Pembroke College, where he spent the rest of his life.

Not far from Gray's room, though on the ground floor, in the late 1920s Mr Peter Grimes had his rooms. They were on the western corner of the block. Over them was the Junior Common Room, while the staircase led to three sets of rooms to the east, the J.C.R. and a set above the Common Room.

They were splendid rooms, particularly the sitting-room, which was long and proportionately lofty, and lit by two windows overlooking Little St Mary's now disused graveyard. Because of this prospect, despite their splendour, they did not appeal to many young gentlemen, though the rent asked for them by the Bursar was a very moderate one.

But there was another point about them, too, which did not attract some. Because the windows gave easy access to the outside of the College, to prevent their being used as illegal exit or entrance for law-breaking undergraduates during curfew hours, the College authorities had had bars fixed across the windows. These bars, by giving the sitting-room a cell-like aspect, combined with the graveyard outlook to depress the more freedom-conscious.

Mr Grimes, however, was quite unmoved by either tombstones or iron. A classical scholar, he proclaimed that as to the graveyard, its antiquity was modernity when compared with the objects of his study, and did not therefore impress him; while if a man set his mind to work he should be undistracted by his surroundings.

I was not a scholar of the foundation and so was not entitled to "keep"* in college during my first year, and as I was reading English I did not come into contact with Grimes at lectures. We did, however, both have an interest in music and met regularly on

* To keep=to live or to lodge.

Sunday evenings at the College music club, and at rehearsals of the Cambridge University Musical Society. Still, we could not claim to be intimate, though we greeted one another briefly as we passed through the court.

I had rooms in Tennis Court Terrace, and as I attended only one nine o'clock lecture during the week, I breakfasted at eight, worked from half-past eight to half-past nine in dressing-gown and slippers, at half-past nine dressed and left for my ten o'clock lecture, calling in at the J.C.R. on the way to collect any letters and have a quick glance at the newspapers. This had been my procedure one morning before our freshman term was half-way through.

The J.C.R. was strangely deserted. The only other occupant was the Music Scholar, who was also reading English. He was sprawled in a chair immersed in *The Times*, while I sat on the arm of a chair not far from him reading a letter from an old friend from whom I had not heard for several months.

We were both absorbed in what we were doing, and I personally did not hear anyone else come into the room, until I heard an exclamation and on looking up saw Peter Grimes by the letter-rack frowning at a letter. He was in his pyjamas and dressing-gown, and had not bothered to comb his hair. His face was white, and there were dark smudges below his eyes, as though he had spent the night on the town.

Normally I would not have spoken to him, but I was so struck by his pallor that a remark slipped out before I was aware of it.

"Are you all right?" I asked him. "You look as if you haven't slept all night."

"I haven't," he said.

"Finishing an essay?"

"No," he said.

He came and sat in the chair next to mine and continued to read his letters. Clearly he was not in a communicative mood and, though I must admit being curious, I decided that if he did not wish to talk, I would not pry.

However, when he had read his last letter, he said, "No. As a matter of fact this is the third time it's happened in the last ten days."

"What has happened?" I asked.

"I've been kept awake by something scratching on the windows," he said.

"All night?" I exclaimed.

"That's what it amounts to," he replied. "I go to bed soon after eleven. I need a good eight or nine hours sleep. I read for a short while, then get my head down. After about an hour or so this scratching noise wakes me up. As soon as I go to see what it is, it stops, so I go back to bed and go to sleep again, and I haven't been asleep long when I'm wakened again by the same noise. When this has happened two or three times, I can't get off to sleep again, and lie twisting and turning and sleepless until my gyp brings my breakfast."

"And there's nothing which could account for the scratching outside the windows: a tree or shrub?" I asked.

"No. There are one or two small trees not far away, but none of them touches the windows. Besides, last night there wasn't the slightest breath of breeze to stir even a leaf."

"Does the scratching continue while you're at the window?"

"No, as soon as I switch on the light it stops. Do you think it could be fellows from the town making a nuisance of themselves?"

"Could be, I suppose," I said.

"No. It'll be the vampire!"

The Music Scholar had put aside *The Times* and was gathering up his books. He was smiling at us as he spoke.

"The vampire?" I said.

"What do you mean—vampire?" Grimes asked. "Do you mean bats?"

"No, I mean vampire," the Music Scholar said, "Little St Mary's churchyard reputedly houses a vampire. The only one in England, and I believe I'm right in saying, one of just seven still active in Europe."

"You don't really believe in that sort of nonsense, do you?" Grimes asked.

"Perhaps," the Music Scholar replied. "I know that nothing on earth would persuade me to have your rooms, Grimes. Good morning."

When he had gone, Grimes said to me, "You don't believe in vampires, do you?"

"I've not given it any serious thought," I said. "I didn't even know that any are supposed to exist outside the pages of Bram Stoker."

"Oh yes," said Grimes. "There is a tradition coming from quite ancient times, and having its origins in the belief that the corpses of people buried without the proper rites are unable to rest and are reanimated. Though I am not absolutely sure, I think the blood-sucking vampire only emerged towards the end of the seventeenth century. The classics contain several accounts of dead people return-ing bodily and molesting relatives. But it is a myth founded on superstitions surrounding death and arising out of not knowing what really happens after death. But since I don't believe in eternal life, naturally I can't believe in vampires and all that rot about ghosts."

"Well," I said. "I think I should find it a bit eerie living in those rooms of yours, knowing the story."

"I still think it may be hobbledehoys from the town," Grimes smiled. "If it happens again I shall go and have a word with my tutor."

"I must be off," I told him.

"I'm going to cut my lecture," he said, "and go back to bed as soon as my gyp has finished."

I suppose it must have been the Music Scholar who spread the story about Grimes's scratchings, though I had never thought of him as a college gossip. Or it might have been Grimes's gyp, if Grimes had confided in him, which it never occurred to me to discover. At all events, by "first hall" that evening it was clear that a large proportion of the College knew, for I overheard in the J.C.R. after dinner several of the tough rugger and rowing freshmen teasing Grimes about it.

He did not appreciate the ragging, I could see, for he presently left hurriedly, exclaiming sharply, "I don't believe in the existence of vampires or in ghosts of any sort, and I wish you'd all shut up."

Believing he might think that it was I who had spread the story and so was the cause of his embarrassment, I went after him. I heard him slam his door as I came out on to the landing. It had made such a noise that I thought he might have sported his oak,* and I was relieved on reaching the foot of the stairs to see that he had not.

* The entrance to all sets of rooms in Cambridge have an outer as well as an inner door. The outer door is referred to, in university parlance, as "the oak". It has a latch on the inside. If a man "sported his oak", i.e. closed the outer door, one under-stood that he desired no visitors, and one respected his wishes.

I knocked, and when he called, went in. Still wearing his gown, he was kneeling on the hearthrug putting a light to his fire.

"Sorry to trouble you," I said, "but I wanted you to know that I haven't told anyone what you said this morning in the J.C.R."

"That's all right," he replied. "It hadn't occurred to me that you might have. I suppose Jackson (the Music Scholar) must have said something. No reason, of course, why he shouldn't. It's that rugger-playing numskull of a Chapman who riles me. We were always falling foul of one another at school. I can't think why Peterhouse ever accepted him. My heart sank when I heard he was coming here."

"They need some beef in the scrum," I smiled.

"I wouldn't know about that," Grimes said, "but it must be the only reason for taking him, because he hasn't one pennyweight of brains in his thick head."

He asked me to have coffee and took up the kettle from the hearth and went out to fill it and put it on the gas-ring.

While he was gone I went over to one of the barred windows and peered out into Little St Mary's graveyard. It was well kept. The grave mounds, if there had ever been any, had been flattened and the turf between the headstones was kept in good order. In fact, but for one or two somewhat dilapidated tombs, all was neat and tidy, though there was about it an atmosphere of latent foreboding which made me feel a little apprehensive. I was probably imagining most of it, because in the darkness—the only light came from the low stars and the glow of the town against the sky—I could see nothing very plainly except the dark forms of the tombs and headstones.

I checked to see whether there was anything outside which could cause the scratching on the windows, and confirmed that Grimes's denial was well founded. The nearest shrub was a good seven or eight feet from the windows, while a tree that was closer than the shrub was outside the reach of any of the windows, and in any case, if its branches were to touch any window, it would be on the first floor.

I was still standing looking out when Grimes returned and began to get cups from a cupboard.

"I'll admit it's not a very attractive outlook," he smiled, "but quite honestly, it doesn't worry me. After all, in the country people go and sit in churchyards because they are peaceful and quiet."

"Are you quite sure," I said, "that the noises you hear are made by something scratching on the windows?"

"I'm not absolutely sure," he replied, "because the noises stop as soon as I switch on the lights, and by the time I have reached a window there is nothing there. But I can only describe the sounds as being like those you can produce if you tap with fingernails on glass or draw some sharp instrument over glass. That is, they are both tapping and squeaking noises."

"But have you tried to find out whether they could be made by some other combination?" I asked.

"Such as?"

"Well, an old iron bedstead will both rattle and squeak," I said. "Supposing you were restless in your sleep?"

"It's not the bed," he said. "I brought it from home because the one provided by the College was a bit dilapidated."

"What about mice in the skirting? Mice squeak and their gnawing could sound like tapping," I suggested.

"I had thought of that, too, but I've lain listening before switching on the light and I'm convinced the sounds come from the windows in here, and not from the skirting."

"I give up, then," I said.

"I'm sure it's the town boys."

"Perhaps you're right," I agreed.

I did not see him again to speak to for more than a week. I saw him in the distance in hall, but he was never in the J.C.R. when I was there, and we never met at lectures. I could have called on him, but I did not really know him well enough and he might have thought I was being a busybody and been resentful.

We met coming out of chapel after eight o'clock Communion, and, on an impulse, I asked him to come and have breakfast with me. He said he would like to, and we went to the Buttery to cancel his and to order an extra breakfast to be sent round with mine.

Tennis Court Terrace was only a few minutes from the College, and it was not worth while getting his bicycle from the sheds, so I wheeled my machine and we walked. Mrs Turrell, my landlady, was a little put out: not so much, I think, because of my having a guest to Sunday breakfast, but because she had not tidied my room while I had been out.

Grimes was in an expansive mood. He did not seem to have many friends, at least not in college. At all events I found him very easy to get along with.

Over breakfast we plied one another with questions about careers and our aspirations. Towards the end of breakfast, however, I took the bit between my teeth and asked him about the scratching.

"I haven't heard it since the evening you came in for coffee," he said. "I'm quite sure it was someone having fun."

"Good," I said. "I must admit that I was in two minds about the vampire story. I keep meaning to look it up, but never remember when I'm in the library."

"Well, I deny their existence utterly and completely," he said. "I find superstitions of that kind irrational."

He went soon afterwards, and I wrote some letters before going to chapel to sing matins. He played Chopin's *Grande Valse Brillante* magnificently at the music club that evening.

Thursday that week was All-Hallows Day, and in the evening I dined with friends in Jesus College and afterwards went to a concert with them. We had exeats until midnight, so after the concert we went to the Waffle in Petty Cury, and stayed there until a few minutes to twelve. I left it a bit late and reached Tennis Court Terrace as Pembroke clock was striking the witching hour. Mrs Turrell let me in with good-natured scolding.

I went to bed in an unusually contented frame of mind, absolutely unaware that while I was, in fact, taking off my clothes something was happening in the College that neither I nor Grimes nor anyone else has ever been able to explain. It was almost to be the death of Grimes, and certainly converted him from an unbeliever in the occult. At the same time it almost sent him out of his mind.

Despite the unaccustomed lateness of my going to bed I awoke at my usual time—quarter past seven. Pulling on shirt and trousers, and my thick dressing-gown, I collected my washing-case from the washstand, went downstairs and cycled round to the College.

One of the customs of the University which in those days puzzled the visitor most was the habit of undergraduates clad only in pyjamas and dressing-gown pedalling vigorously between their rooms and their colleges between seven and half past eight in the morning—

rain, sun, frost or fog—merely to take a bath. Our foolhardiness in doing this makes me wonder now why we did not catch our deaths of cold. Then, however, we thought nothing of it. Only very few official lodgings in those days had bathrooms; but there were blocks of bathrooms in the colleges; one had been brought up to bath on rising; so the prophet went to the mountain.

Tony Reford-Jones, bleary-eyed and uncommunicative as usual when he first got up, was at the basin next to mine. We grunted at one another and shaved in silence. We made for adjacent showers simultaneously and it was not until he had turned the hot jet of water to icy cold and emerged with a good deal of spluttering that Tony said to me, "You know that fellow Grimes, don't you?"

"Only slightly," I said. "Why?"

"They took him off to Addenbrookes in the middle of the night."

"What's wrong with him? Appendix?"

"Bit of a mystery. Some of the chaps on his staircase heard a scream come from his rooms, rushed down and found him collapsed and gibbering on the floor. One of his windows was open and there was a red band round one of his wrists that Dick Carpenter says was raw flesh. They fetched the Dean, and the Dean sent for the ambulance."

"Do you know how he is now?"

"'Fraid not. It's a jolly rum business, though. You know he's been complaining about scratching on his windows at night and the chaps have been teasing him about the vampire?"

I nodded. "He wasn't impressed by that story. He believed town boys were playing him up. But he told me only a couple of days ago that the scratching had stopped."

"It certainly looks as if it began again last night," Reford-Jones said. "Dick Carpenter says one window was certainly open. It's a rotten trick if someone was playing the fool with him."

On my way back to breakfast I called in at the J.C.R. and telephoned Addenbrookes hospital. The sister told me that Grimes was suffering from serious shock, but was recovering. However, it would be a day or two before he would be able to leave hospital. I inquired about visiting hours and was told that I could see him between three and four that afternoon.

The college authorities, I learned later in the morning, were taking a serious view of the incident, and had begun to make discreet investigations. They had not been able to question Grimes yet, but the Bursar and the Senior Tutor had inspected the room and the churchyard, and the story going round was that someone had clearly been at the window, since the paintwork was very scratched. On the other hand, they were mystified by the total absence of any footprints in the soft earth outside the windows. Speculation was naturally rife, and the College was divided into two camps—those for and those against the vampire theory.

When I went to the hospital a few minutes after three, a very pale Peter Grimes was sitting propped up on pillows. He smiled and thanked me for the fruit I had brought him.

"It was good of you to come," he said, and I could sense that he meant it.

"I was sorry to hear about your accident," I told him.

"It wasn't any accident," he said.

"Look," I said, "you don't have to talk about it."

"I want to," he replied. "The Tutor and the Bursar are coming in later, and it would be a help in sorting out my thoughts if you'd let me tell you. You'll probably think I'm off my rocker—though I don't know. You weren't really with me when I maintained the scratching was done by town boys having a rag."

"Well, if you're sure you want to tell me," I said, "I'm ready to listen."

Grimes, it appears, had gone to bed a few minutes after eleven, having finished a particularly exacting Greek Prose for his supervisor of studies. He was very tired, and put out the light as soon as he got into bed, instead of reading for a while as he usually did. He had the impression that he had fallen asleep at once.

He had no idea how long he had been asleep—actually it must have been a little more than half an hour, for it was about ten minutes after midnight when his screams brought his neighbours on the scene—but presently he was awakened by scratching noises on one of his windows.

"They seemed much more persistent than the previous scratchings, much more urgent," he explained. "I automatically switched on my bedside light, though I had decided not to do so if I ever heard the scratching again, and I was surprised when the noise did not stop, as it had done on earlier occasions.

"I was feeling particularly peeved when I got out of bed, because

I was very tired and knew from what had happened before that I probably wouldn't get to sleep again.

"The noise was coming from one of the sitting-room windows, so I made my way there. As I went into the room the scratching grew louder and increased in speed. It was as if whoever was there was getting more and more excited as I came nearer.

"I peered through the window nearest the door, but could see no one outside. The noise was not very loud and I could hear moans as well. Grunts would really be a better description. It was the sort of sound one might make if one were physically exerting oneself more than ordinarily.

"Both the noise on the window and the grunts were disturbing me, I found. I felt cold and a bit faint, and I would have gone back to bed without more ado if I had been able to. But I couldn't. I was drawn irresistibly towards the other window, and vaguely I realized I was no longer in control of my movements.

"As I came level with the window I could see quite clearly, though the room light had the effect of making the dark outside seem darker than it was, a figure moving about excitedly, all the time drumming on the window with its finger-tips.

"My immediate thought was that it was some silly ass dressed up and trying to frighten me. In hall that stupid fellow Chapman had brought up the subject of the vampire again, and it passed through my mind that this would be his idea of a practical joke, because he, or one of his friends, had said, 'You ought to be specially careful tonight. It's All Souls Eve, when the dead come out of their graves.'

"I shouted to him to go away, and that I would fetch the Porter if he didn't stop fooling about. The effect of my voice was to make him more excited still. He was hitting the glass so hard now that I thought he must break it, and the noise he made as he swayed backwards and forwards across the window grew louder. When I was a kid I got cornered up a tree by a copulating couple—they didn't know I was there—and the man had made just such a noise, presumably as he began to approach his climax. The whole incident had scared the wits out of me, but it had been the noise the man made that had frightened me most. I felt the same awful fear now. Yet I couldn't move myself away.

"I only realized what I was doing when my hand was actually

on the window-catch. I tried to draw it back, but couldn't. Without any willing from me, my hand began to loosen the catch, and all the time the figure outside was rocking and tapping and groaning.

"As the catch came off, he lurched at the window, which flew open, catching me on the forehead." (He touched the strip of plaster over his right temple.) "He lunged against the bars with such force, I swear they shook, and he thrust an arm through the window and seized hold of my right wrist.

"I tried to prise his fingers off my hand, and as I did so noticed how long they were and that they did not look like fingers at all, but an eagle's talons. The pain in my wrist was awful.

"As I struggled to get free I happened to glance up. The violence of his movements had made the hood fall back over his shoulders and what I saw made me panic. I renewed my struggle to get free from his grip, and when I realized I couldn't I let out a mighty shriek and passed out. I don't remember any more until I came round in this bed."

"What did you see?" I asked.

"His eyes were bright as though they were burning coals—I'm sorry, but only clichés will serve—and his lips were drawn back from his teeth. And from each corner of his mouth protruded a very long, sharply pointed . . ."

"Fang?" I suggested.

"Yes, fang. The classical description of the vampire."

"No wonder you passed out," I said. "Could it have been a mask?"

"No," he replied.

We were silent for a moment or two. Then he drew his right hand from under the bed-covers and held it out towards me. The flesh around the wrist was livid still, and there were four distinct scars that could have been made by sharp and abnormally long fingernails.

"What are you going to tell the Tutor?" I asked.

"What I've told you. I may as well. They can sort it out. But I'm not going back to those rooms."

I couldn't blame him.

The doctors apparently advised that he should go down until the beginning of next term, and he took the advice.

A mathematics scholar volunteered to change rooms with him. He was a level-headed, down-to-earth young man, but if you asked him if he heard any scratchings on his windows, he would say, with a smile, "From time to time, But they don't worry me. The Bursar has had shutters fitted on the inside."

It was nearly a year before the marks of the vampire had entirely disappeared from Grimes's wrist, and until he eventually graduated and went down, he was as nervous as a highly strung hare.

The Exorcising of the Restless Monk

The Abbot of Durham looked round the silent circle of his brethren, cowled, their hands clasped within the wide cuffs of their habit sleeves. All eyes were downcast; not one, he noted, looked even in the direction of their brother, who stood alone (truly alone, for God had forsaken him surely) in the middle of the floor of the Chapter House. Was it compassion, he wondered, that made them keep their gaze upon the tiles? Or was it shame that one of their number could have found it in his heart to shame the abbey's good name? Or was it humility—that there but for God's special grace it might be almost any one of them standing in Brother Simeon's place?

When his eyes had travelled the complete circle of *sedilia*, he turned towards the accused on whom they had only moments ago pronounced a unanimous verdict of guilty. With a firm voice he commanded Brother Joseph to hand him his crozier; and in equally firm tones, chin held high, he began to pass sentence.

"Brother Simeon," he began. "Though why I should continue to address you as brother I know not, since you have forfeited all relationship with us here. Simeon, you have been tried by us in conclave, and we have found you guilty of a gross breach of one of your solemn vows.

"When you were admitted to our Order, you made God and us promises which you swore to keep until death took you from this earth. One of those promises was that you would renounce the lusts of the flesh and keep yourself pure and chaste.

"Though we are aware that some are tempted by the workings of their bodies more than others, and can understand how you might be afflicted in this way, what has grieved us most in this sordid affair has been your utter lack of confidence in us. Had you come to us and told us that the temptations of St Antony were no less plaguing you, we would have prayed for you and done all in our power to help you overcome them not merely by advice, but by practical means. For the body can be tamed—this *I* tell you in all certainty. It is not easy, but it is possible.

"But what have you done? Except for an initial weak and feeble struggle, to which you soon surrendered, you have done nothing to curb your natural concupiscence—it is not for that concupiscence I condemn you—but you gave it full rein.

"Even in falling from grace there are degrees. Had you taken for your paramour some slut from the kitchens of one of the city's inns, it would have been bad enough. But that you should seduce a sister, only lately a novice, in the care of our Mother Superior, my kins-woman, at Blanchlands, is too horrible to contemplate. But what is even more horrible is that having got her with child, you encouraged her to conceal it, and when it was born, that you took it, strangled it and cast it into our River Wear.

"You are guilty, then, not only of breaking your vow and persuading one who looked to you as her mediator with Our Heavenly Father to do likewise, but you deliberately took the life of the child sprung from your own loins.

"Had you shown any degree of penitence since the discovery of your abundant crimes, we might have had pity for you. Yet even now we have a kind of pity, not for you but for the weakness with which you were endowed, and which you flaunt as strength.

"But the pity we have is not such that tempts us to be merciful, for we recognize that your mentor and master in all that you have done has been Lucifer, the Prince of Darkness. You have boasted to us that what the Devil bade you do, you did willingly.

"Since we have no part in the service of the Devil, we owe no allegiance to his servants. Indeed, we are as much his servants' enemies as we are his, and we see that it is our duty to root out his minions as pitilessly as we would cast him out.

"Our sentence on you is, therefore, that you shall be immured. You shall be provided with bread and water sufficient for your needs for seven days, after which may the all-merciful God take pity on you. We impose this sentence in the hope that the period of grace thus afforded you will work repentance in you, and that when you finally expire, it will be into the arms of our most Blessed Saviour."

The chorus of Amens had scarcely died away than with a scream the young man threw himself forward and flung himself at the feet of the Abbot, clasping that stern man's ankles.

"Not that, Reverend Father! Not that!" he shouted. "Throw me from the rock! Burn me at the stake! Be merciful, let me die quickly."

"What I have decreed must be done," the Abbot told him, "so that you may have time to reflect and seek forgiveness for your sins."

He made a sign to two of the brothers, who came forward to seize the abject man and pull him to his feet. But before they hauled him away there was one final degradation to be performed. While the two held their prisoner one by each arm, a third approached and taking hold of the condemned man's habit ripped it from top to bottom and let it fall about his feet.

And the Abbot, looking upon the beauty of the young man's nakedness, sighed inwardly at the waste of it, and then quickly turned his eyes away.

For three weeks the screams of Brother Simeon in the torture of hunger could be heard by those who passed along the far bank of the river at the foot of the high rock, and those who heard it crossed themselves and hurried on their way.

On the seventh day of silence Simeon's brother-judges sang a Requiem Mass for the repose of his shriven soul, not knowing that with his last breath the young man had cursed them all and vilified God, execrating Him for His inhumanity to Man.

By the turn of the present century that part of the monastic buildings in which Brother Simeon had been walled up and left to starve to death had been converted into a dwelling house for the convenience of one of the Canons. In 1931 Canon Y and his wife and daughter came to live there.

They had been warned by other inhabitants of the Close that the shrieks of Brother Simeon rising from the cellars might disturb them, but they had smiled, thanked those who warned them and, in the business of moving in, put it out of their minds. They had not been in the house more than three months, however, before Brother Simeon made himself known, and they had to agree that while it lasted the experience was not very pleasant. But when they were left in peace for the next six months they began to feel that if he visited them only two or three times a year he would not disturb them too much.

But Brother Simeon was not content to be an infrequent visitor and began to draw attention to himself almost every night. By degrees what had initially been a rather whimsical feature of their new abode became a downright annoyance. The Canon, lost in scholarly contemplation of the Epistle to the Romans, was aware of the restless monk's intrusion only vaguely. His wife and daughter, however, and particularly the former, increasingly found the moans and shrieks difficult to tolerate.

Brother Simeon decided one evening to pay his call earlier than usual, and made himself heard just as the Y's and their dinner-guests were taking coffee in the drawing-room.

Mrs Y, at the first shriek, exclaimed with some heat, "Really, that young man is becoming quite objectionable. It is getting extremely difficult for me to keep a servant longer than a week, and you must admit that the noises he makes do not tend to endear him to one."

"I understand," said Dr Mannington, the down-to-earth medical officer at the gaol, "that he has been stepping up his appearances since you arrived. Previously, I believe, though I did not know the Canon's predecessor, Simeon attracted attention to himself only once or twice a year."

"So we have been told," Mrs Y agreed. "What have we done, I wonder, to merit his more frequent calls? For the last three or four months this has been happening almost every night, and I am beginning to find it very wearing."

"Have you ever thought of exorcism, Mrs Y?"

The speaker was a tall, thin young man with the high cheek-bones and pointed nose that reminded one either of an eagle or of a North-American Indian. His clerical evening clothes sat awkwardly on him, while his pinched figure proclaimed a certain asceticism.

"It had occurred to me, and I mentioned it when I was at tea at the Archdeaconry the other day," Mrs Y admitted. "But old Mrs Proudfoot said that the Mortimers had tried it when they were here just before the war, but it hadn't worked."

"Would you allow me to try?" Father de Montmartin asked. "If the Canon had no objection, I would be very happy."

"I have no objection," the Canon said. "Perhaps I ought to mention it to the Dean, but I don't imagine he would forbid it."

"Do you have to get the Bishop's permission?" Dr Mannington asked.

"Oh, no," Father de Montmartin said. "If it were a public ceremony, it would be a different matter. But here, with no one the wiser but the Y's, his lordship would probably prefer not to know."

"Well, I think it's a very good idea," Mrs Y said. "When will you do it?"

The priest took out his diary.

"Thursday evening of next week I'm free," he said. "How would that suit you?"

"I shall be in London," the Canon said.

"I have bridge in the afternoon, but the evening would be all right," Mrs Y remarked.

"I shall need assistance," the Father said, "someone to hold the candle and ring the bell."

"Would you oblige, Dr Mannington?"

"Pleased to."

"Then you'd both better come to supper."

So at ten o'clock on the appointed evening, just as Brother Simeon began his shrieks, Father de Montmartin, accompanied by the doctor carrying a candle in a silver holder in his right hand and a hand-bell in his left, set out for the cellars of the house, the priest in amice, alb and purple stole, and holding a gilt bowl of Holy Water and an aspergillum. Father Roderick Scott followed carrying aloft a large electric torch to light their way.

As soon as they came to the cellar entrance the two priests began to chant the Litany, Dr Mannington supplying the responses. This was followed by the Fifty-fourth Psalm—"Save me, O God, for thy Name's sake: and avenge me in thy strength . . ."—which brought them to the bricked-up doorway reputed to be that of Brother Simeon's grave-cell.

Making the sign of the cross with Holy Water on the ancient bricks, Father de Montmartin cried out in a loud voice, "I exorcise thee, most vile spirit, the very embodiment of our enemy, the entire spectre, the whole legion, in the Name of Jesus Christ, to leave and flee this place.

"He Himself commands thee, who hast ordered those cast down from the heights of heaven to the depths of the earth. He commands thee, He who commanded the sea, the winds and the tempests.

"Hear therefore and fear, O Satan, enemy of the faith, foe to the human race, producer of death, thief of life, destroyer of justice, root of evils, kindler of vices, seducer of men . . ."

As he spoke these last sentences a strange invisible presence filled the narrow dank corridor in which they stood, and a howl, unlike any they had heard, swept round them, deafening them and completely drowning the voice of the priest. Father de Montmartin held his ground, however, and shouted in stentorian tones, "Depart in the Name of the Father, and of the Son and of the Holy Ghost; give place to the Holy Ghost by the sign of the Cross of Jesus Christ our Lord, who with the Father and the same Holy Ghost liveth and reigneth one God for ever and ever, world without end."

As his voice came thinly through the bellowing and the commotion of the atmosphere all round them, Dr Mannington who at each mention of the Trinity had rung his bell, suddenly felt a tremendous, breath-stopping blow between his shoulders, and at the same moment the candle-holder was knocked from his hand. Almost simultaneously the torch was struck from Father Scott's hand and the passage was plunged into darkness. Both Scott and Mannington related afterwards that as they were attacked they were enveloped in an icy, foul-smelling atmosphere which brought up goose-pimples on their flesh and made their stomachs writhe with nausea.

Above the roaring, which filled the passage-way, they heard Father de Montmartin shout, "We must retreat," and together they stumbled in darkness out of the cellars.

When they emerged into the light of the house, they saw that de Montmartin had not escaped attack. His amice had been wrenched from his throat and hung down his back in tatters, his stole was no longer crossed upon his breast, but all awry, one end touching the ground at his feet and the other in the small of his back, while his Holy Water bowl was empty.

"I had thought he might be very strong," he said breathing heavily. "I have brought with me a reserved Host. I warn you that this is a most drastic measure and will meet with even greater opposition than what we have already met, but if you are willing I will try again."

Both his assistants declared their willingness, and once more they set out down the cellar steps. This time de Montmartin, elevating the Host above a portable ciborium, led the way.

In contrast to the confusion they had left, the passage-way was utterly calm.

"Don't be deceived!" de Montmartin warned them. "And hold fast, whatever happens."

"Why, truculent one, dost thou refuse to depart? Why rash creature, dost thou withstand the adjurations of the Almighty?

"Thou art accused by God whose statutes thou hast transgressed. Thou art accused by his Son, Jesus Christ, our Lord, whom thou didst tempt and presume to crucify. Therefore I adjure thee, most wicked dragon, in the name of the Immaculate Lamb, who trod upon the asp and the basilisk, who trampled the lion and the dragon, to depart from this place.

"The Word made Flesh commands thee. He who was born of a Virgin . . ."

Once more the three men were aware of the unseen presence, once more the atmosphere of the passage-way became clammy and dank, once more they were buffeted. But the voice of Brother Simeon was weaker than it had been and the voice of Father de Montmartin dominated it as he cried, "In the Name of the Host I hold in my hand, depart from this place."

The doctor felt the bell being pulled from his hand, but summoned up all his strength and held on, and though the flame of the candle danced and left the wick, it returned.

A great wind filled the passage and above the wind came the tormented howl of Brother Simeon.

"Depart, depart from the presence of the Host!" Father de Montmartin cried. "Depart monk, receptacle of Satan! Depart seducer of women and taker of life! Depart Simeon, in the name of the Trinity I command thee!"

Suddenly all was quiet. The air was calm, the light of the candle burned upright, the invisible presence was gone.

Father de Montmartin heaved a sigh.

"Praise be to God!" he exclaimed.

But even as he spoke, all heard a voice cry out in agony, "Father, forgive me. Father, receive my soul. Father, give me peace."

The next moment all was darkness, and the darkness lasted it seemed for several seconds. Then the Host held aloft by the priest glowed in the darkness, and a voice answered Brother Simeon's, "Son, We forgive thee. Come into Our bosom and be comforted."

And the darkness became light again, and with a moan Father de Montmartin fell to the ground.

As Mannington and Scott carried him out of the cellars, he recovered his senses.

"The Host," he said urgently.

But though they searched until they knew their search was hopeless, they did not find the Host.

And Brother Simeon was heard no more.

The Recluse of Kotka Veski

When the former Baltic State of Estonia was a Russian province the whole country was divided into 274 great estates, each owned by a member of the Baltic-German nobility. Until the beginning of the present century, a feudal system was in force. Each baron had the power of life and death over all who lived on his estate, and the peasants, in the position of serfs, were bound to him and could not move from the estate without his permission, which was seldom, if ever, granted. Inevitably there were good landlords and bad ones who treated their serfs accordingly. Unfortunately, however, the time came when no distinction could be made between bad and good; and it is pleasant to be able to record the humanity and kindness of one good Baltic baron.

The geographical position of the three Baltic States—Latvia and Lithuania were the other two—placed them at the point where East and West met. In the centuries-long clash it was they, therefore, who bore the brunt of the tug-of-war between East and West. For seven hundred years from 1219 they were occupied by the Danes, the German Knights of the Sword, the Swedes, the Poles and the Russians. But somehow they managed to keep alive their national identities, their languages, their cultures and their aspirations for independence.

When the Bolshevik Revolution broke out in Russia in 1917 they believed that at last the moment had come when they had more than a sporting chance to achieve their great ambition. They declared their independence, put armies, composed half of fifteen-year-old schoolboys, in the field against the Red Armies and, with a little help from the Western Allies, defeated them. In 1920 Soviet Russia recognized their independence and the *de facto* recognition already granted them by most of the western powers was converted into *de jure* recognition, and the three republics of Estonia, Latvia and Lithuania came into being.

The natural resources of the three new countries were small. About one-fifth of Estonia consisted of forests, which provided her with a thriving but not extensive trade in pit-props. Apart from this there were small flax and cement industries. The basis of her economy, therefore, had to be agriculture; and this meant that the land could no longer be left in the hands of 274 families who, in any case, were as strongly opposed to the independence movement as the Russians had been.

The first piece of legislation passed through the new Estonian parliament was an act dispossessing the Baltic-German landlords and nationalizing the land. Latvia and Lithuania followed Estonia's example in this respect, but whereas Estonia allowed her Baltic landlords to retain one small house and five hectares (roughly twelve acres) of land surrounding it, the other two countries provided no indemnity at all.

The nationalization of the land was a major national upheaval. It brought into being an entirely new national structure. The former peasants now became farmers and smallholders, and the former landlords, unable to support their extensive families on the proceeds of twelve acres, were forced to send out their dependants to fend for themselves, which they did eventually in the professions, in industry, in the schools and behind shop counters.

One of the barons so affected was Admiral Baron Fersen, who had had the double distinction of being His Imperial Majesty's Naval Attaché in Washington and the only Russian commander to save his ship in the Japanese attack on Port Arthur in 1904, which he achieved by running her aground. In the middle 1930s, Baron Fersen, then well on in his seventies, lived with the Baroness in a small *datcha* (country cottage) in the middle of a vast pine forest at Kotka Veski, some thirty-five miles east of Tallinn, the capital.

The little house had five or six rooms and a garden room, where the seventy-year-old Baroness tended hundreds of potted plants. Fifty yards or so from the house ran a swift stream owned by the Estonian Anglers Club who had stocked it with fat salmon to provide sport for its members.

The old couple subsisted on the produce of a patch of land cultivated for them by a seventeen-year-old grandson, Baron George Fersen, the milk of a goat, the eggs of a dozen or so hens, a few *krona* rent from seven or eight acres which they let to nearby smallholders, and salt and sugar and ten *krona* a month from a German charitable organization. They were in fact living just above the starvation level, and to add to their resources they used to rent the *datcha* for the summer months. During this occupation they themselves lived in considerable discomfort in the inevitable *sauna* (bath-house) which was situated some forty or fifty yards from the *datcha*.

For two or three years in the middle thirties their summer tenant was the American Consul and Chargé d'Affaires in Tallinn, Harry C. C's wife, two small children, their nannie and the cook moved to Kotka Veski at the beginning of May and remained there until mid-September. C himself stayed behind in the Consulate in Tallinn, and joined the family at Kotka Veski from Friday afternoon until Monday morning, spending most of his time in waders in the Kose River casting flies for hours on end, and never making a single strike. (Young Baron George, on the other hand, was adept at tickling salmon, and whenever Mrs C wanted a fish for supper would readily and rapidly oblige to the great chagrin of C.)

The Cs' first tenancy of the Fersen *datcha* was in the summer of 1935 and it was on this visit that the following incident occurred.

Though the winters in Estonia are almost arctic in their fierceness, the summers rival those of the Mediterranean. Between mid-May and mid-September a cloud is a rare sight and the sun beats down with a brazen warmth. From early June to late August is the period of the "white nights", when it never gets darker than dusk and the temperature falls little, making bed before midnight purgatory, if one is foolish enough to go there.

One evening, not long after their arrival, Mrs C and Nannie were sitting on the veranda of the *datcha* a little after midnight, chatting. Suddenly, as they talked, they both saw a man's figure appear from the trees at the right side of the "lawn"—which ran down from the house to the stream—and move with an awkward limping gait, but with considerable speed, across to the trees on the other side, where he disappeared. Mrs C broke off in the middle of a sentence.

"Was that George?" she asked.

"Too tall for George," Nannie replied. "Besides I was talking to George just before supper and he wasn't limping then."

"Who can it be, then?" Mrs C exclaimed.

They had understood that only the three Fersens lived at Kotka Veski. The nearest houses were five or six miles away.

"A prowler?" suggested the nannie.

"Must be," Mrs C said. "I think we ought to go inside. I'll have a word with the Baron tomorrow."

So they went into the house and carefully locked the doors, bolted the windows, and went to bed.

Mrs C came upon the Baron as he took his mid-morning stroll. His tall, upright figure, despite the slightly bowed shoulders, gave him a dignity which the little white round sun-hat with its brim turned up all round—his habitual covering indoors and out—did nothing to lessen. He smiled and bowed as they met.

"Good morning, Madame C," he said. "I hope you are enjoying our retreat and that you are not finding the solitude boring?"

"Why no, Baron," she smiled ."It's not easy to be bored with two young children about. Besides, the quiet of this lovely place is heaven after the dust and fumes of Tallinn."

"Yes, Tallinn is no place to be in the summer. You will tell us if we can help you in any way. Not that the Baroness and I can do much, but young George is very resourceful and always willing—or perhaps I should say, nearly always willing."

"Thank you, Baron. If there is anything. But Nannie and Lii are very willing, too, as you put it."

"Still, a household of women sometimes has need of a man."

Mrs C laughed. Then she remembered the experience of last evening.

"Baron," she said, "I think perhaps I ought to tell you that while Nannie and I were sitting on the veranda last night before going to bed we saw a man run across the bottom of the lawn."

"That was probably George," the Baron said. "Out poaching, you know. I suppose I ought to forbid him, but it's hard to remember that the fish in the Kose no longer belong to me."

"No," Mrs C told him. "We both agreed it wasn't George. It was too tall for George, and besides he dragged one leg."

The old man smiled, indulgently Mrs C thought.

"Are you sure it wasn't a shadow, Madame? At night the eyes play tricks."

"If just I or just Nannie had seen him, I might agree with you," she replied. "But we both saw him together."

"Well—I can't think who it can have been, Madame, but I'm sure you need have no worry. No one round these parts would think of harming you or trying to frighten you. They know who you are, and are proud that you have come to live among us for a short time. However, I'll tell George to pass word round the village and you'll find you won't be troubled again."

"Thank you, Baron," Mrs C smiled, and continued, not quite truthfully, "I'm not worried for us. Each of us is quite able to look after herself, but I thought I ought to mention it in case someone might be after something in the house."

The old man's eyes creased in a grin. "Have no fear on that score, Madame. Everyone knows that we have nothing worth taking."

A week or more passed and Mrs C had forgotten the incident until it was brought back to mind by a more frightening experience.

Summer was now coming to its climax. The ground, the foliage, the house—everything exposed to the heat of the sun during the day became so impregnated with it that the short hours of night-time did nothing to alleviate it, and long after the sun went down everything invisibly glowed.

"I must call Harry tomorrow," Mrs C remarked to Nannie as they sat on the veranda after supper fanning themselves with elegant lace fans which the Baroness had suggested they should borrow. "He must bring us some electric fans."

"But we shouldn't be able to work them, Mrs C," Nannie pointed out.

"Wouldn't they work off car batteries?"

"Oh, goodness! I don't know. I don't know anything about electricity, I'm afraid."

"Surely there must be some way of doing it. Anyway, I'll call him; perhaps he can think of something. It's funny how one takes electricity for granted, isn't it? Not until you haven't got it do you realize how much you rely on it."

"I was thinking only yesterday what a blessing the white nights are out here. At least we don't miss the electric light so much as we would if it got really dark."

They sat for a moment or two in silence, fanning themselves and looking out across the lawn to where the Kose rushed over the stones and small boulders in its bed, even its fast-moving waters lukewarm after the day's sun. Opposite the house the stream ran into a deepish pool some twenty feet long and eight feet wide, dropping away to a depth of four or five feet.

It was there that Mrs C, on her first morning at Kotka Veski, had come upon the young Baron swimming. He greeted her with a kind of merry dignity, told her in answer to her question about the temperature of the water that it was pleasantly fresh, and when in reply to his inquiry about the time she told him it was seven o'clock, he swam with two vigorous strokes to the bank and climbed out. As he reached for his towel she realized for the first time that he was naked, and she felt the blood rushing to her throat. But with a nonchalance that came from honest shamelessness as he dried himself, he said, "I'm going to Tallinn on the seven-thirty bus. Can I get you anything?"

"Why yes," she said. "Could you get some chocolate for the children from Stude's? Plain chocolate. We forgot to pack any."

"Certainly," he said, pulling on shirt and trousers. "How much, a hundred grammes, two hundred, a pound?"

"A pound. I haven't any money . . ."

"Pay me this evening, Madame," he called over his shoulder, and was gone.

She stood looking after him, smiling at her own calmness. She had heard that except in the enclosures in front of the pavilions on the fashionable beaches they swam naked here, but had forgotten until the young Baron had risen out of the pool like a Nordic Apollo. When she had first heard she had wondered how she would take to it, which she would have to do according to the British Consul's wife, who had told her, "If you wear a costume, my dear, they think you've got some loathsome disease." But if they all behaved as naturally as George, she thought now it wouldn't be difficult, and in an attempt to prove it took off her clothes there and then and plunged into the pool.

It had taken Harry a day or two to pluck up courage to swim

when she and Nannie and the children did. He had even proposed speaking to George and telling him not to go near the pool when they were there. But eventually he took the plunge.

For some reason that first morning passed through her mind as she sat fanning herself on the veranda, and she smiled; for all this had happened only a few weeks ago, and yet this morning she had not hesitated to swim before breakfast even though young Fersen and his best friend, Baron Willi Steinbock, who accompanied George on his poaching expeditions and often spent the night in a hammock slung alongside George's in the little clearing behind the bath-house, were already in the pool when she got there. In fact she had seen them from her bedroom window. If Frances Cooke, back in Palaski, Virginia, could have seen her, she would have had her membership of the Daughters of the American Revolution withdrawn before you could say Boston Tea Party.

"I'm going to have a swim," she told Nannie. "Coming?"

"Oh, yes, I think so. I'll get towels," Nannie said.

As she walked across the lawn towards the stream she looked up at the sky, and then at her watch. If she lived here until she was a hundred, she told herself, she would never get used to the almost broad daylight of an Estonian summer evening at quarter-past ten.

Arrived at the pool, she kicked off her sandals, unhooked her frock and let it fall about her feet. Within seconds she was free of the two undergarments, which, light as they were—and no lighter had been devised—were too cumbersome for this climate.

As she stood naked on the edge of the pool, the warm air caressing her too-warm skin, she caught sight of her reflection in the surface of the water, which, though moving as the Kose tumbled north-eastward to the sea, was still mirror enough to let her see that figurewise she had nothing of which to be ashamed.

She sat on the edge of the pool, waiting for Nannie, trailing her feet in the water, which was cooler than the air admittedly, but warm as though it had been standing all day in a pipe. She sighed with pleasure at the relief.

Presently Nannie came up behind her, silent except for the swishing of her feet as she walked through the longer grass on the stream's banks.

"Does it get much hotter than it has been today?" Mrs C asked.

"A little," Nannie said. "But not much. After Jaanipäev (St John's

Day—midsummer's eve) it begins to get cooler. Which reminds me. Jaanipäev is only a fortnight away. We shall be expected to provide food and beer and a bonfire, I'm afraid."

"What for?" Mrs C inquired.

Nannie sat down beside her on the bank, and explained that on midsummer's eve everyone stayed up all night, feasting and dancing, and at midnight they jumped through the bonfire and wished for luck. In the past on that night any man could make love to any woman he chose, whether she was married or not, and she could not refuse him, unless it was her husband who wanted to lead her into the forest or the cornfields.

"In a lot of country districts they still do," the girl said.

"Here?"

"Perhaps."

"Harry won't like that."

"As a foreigner I suppose you could refuse."

"And upset the whole countryside!" she laughed.

The uncertainty of her laugh made her conscious of the nervousness which Nannie's matter-of-fact tone had made her feel. The girl was not having a joke with her, that was certain.

"I'm going in," she exclaimed a little too loudly, and pushed herself into the pool.

Only the surface inches of the water were warm. Below it was cold and, in contrast to the upper warmth and the night air, felt almost glacial. It caught at her breath and she turned on her back and splashed vigorously with a scissor-movement of her legs.

"At last I'm cool," she called to Nannie, who followed her into the pool.

She was tingling with freshness now, and stopped the flailing of her legs, except for an occasional movement to keep her buoyant.

"This is better, isn't it?" Nannie said.

"It's the first time I've been cool today," Mrs C declared.

But the girl could not have heard her, for she let out a cry which ricochetted over the surface of the water, startling her.

"What's the matter? Cramp?" Mrs C asked, swimming to the girl's side.

"No," the girl whispered. "Look by the side of that wild plum bush. To the right. There's someone watching us."

"Oh no!" Mrs C exclaimed softly.

Whoever it was, was crouched in the long grass beside the bush. Whether it was a man or woman, she could not tell, though the hair was short like a man's.

It took her several seconds to realize what was frightening her, because after her experiences with the two young barons in the last weeks, being seen swimming naked should not have disturbed her. Nor was it the fact that the watcher had hidden himself, had cast himself in the role of a vulgar Peeping Tom, that was the cause of her alarm.

It was the eyes peering at her. The sky reflected in the water caught them, making them glow. Nor was it only the gleaming eyes, but the fact that they peered from slits in a black mask that completely covered the face from hair-line to throat.

"Come quickly!" she said urgently to the girl. "Back to the house!"

As she spoke the figure moved, and the girl, thinking it was making towards them, screamed and swam hastily to the bank, and scrambled out. Heedless of her clothes lying in the grass, she ran across the lawn to the house, Mrs C close on her heels.

Inside the house, they bolted the doors and, hurrying to the windows, closed and fastened them, and then looked out across the lawn beyond the pool. A movement in the trees to the right of the lawn caught their attention.

A figure, which though bent was obviously tall, moved unevenly between the trees.

"The man we saw the other evening," Nannie said.

"It certainly is," Mrs C agreed. "I shall go to the Baron immediately after breakfast. I'm sure he knows something. If he doesn't come clean I'll call Mr C and insist he does something, otherwise I'm not staying here another day. He can go fish somewhere else."

Next morning, Mrs C did not go to swim before breakfast. She had just finished dressing when Nannie came to her room, carrying her clothes, which she placed neatly folded on a chair.

"Oh, thank you," Mrs C said. "I'm not too keen on swimming till this business is cleared up. Have you been down?"

"No," Nannie said. "I found our clothes in two neatly folded heaps on the veranda."

"Where?" exclaimed Mrs C.

"On the veranda."

Immediately after breakfast Mrs C went over to the bath-house, taking Nannie with her.

The old Fersens greeted her with their customary dignity. Somewhat brusquely she turned their politeness aside, and bluntly told them what had happened.

"Nannie saw him, too," she said. "Two of us cannot be imagining it. I think you should inform the police at Võsu."

"I am sorry to have to disagree with you, Madame," the Baron replied with equal firmness. "I am quite sure that what you saw was a hallucination."

"How could both of us suffer from the same hallucination, Baron?" she demanded.

"Oh, it has been known, Madame. Mass hallucination."

"So you will do nothing?"

"What can I do, Madame? The police would merely laugh."

"But our clothes!" Nannie said. "I found them neatly folded on the veranda."

"George went to swim this morning," replied the Baron. "I suppose he found them where you left them, and brought them back."

"Let's ask George."

"He has already gone. He is spending the day at Loksa with the Steinbocks. But I will certainly ask him when he returns. In the meantime, I beg you, ladies, not to worry. No harm will befall you. Of that I am certain."

"Perhaps not, Baron. But I prefer not to be frightened," Mrs C exclaimed, and unceremoniously turned her back on them. "Come along, Nannie."

They had planned a picnic by the sea for the day. Cook was having the day off to visit friends in the neighbourhood of Võsu, and they were to drop her on the way and pick her up as they came home.

"I'll telephone Mr C from Võsu," she told Nannie. "Do you know what I think? The old couple are keeping something from us."

"Perhaps they are. But what?"

"That Mr C must find out."

By ten o'clock they had loaded the picnic-basket and the children's toys, and themselves and Cook into the Buick and were setting off. As Mrs C drove along the track through the forest to the road they caught up with the old Baron taking his morning walk. He stepped aside and halted, and as they passed he bowed to them. Mrs C ignored him.

By half past eleven they were in Võsu, where Mrs C pulled up outside the post office. She returned twenty-five minutes later.

"Just like a man!" she said to Nannie.

"What did he say?"

"He said what did I expect? Going native was inviting . . ." She stopped abruptly, embarrassed. "I'm sorry, Nannie," she said. "I shouldn't have said that."

"Why not? Following local customs is going native, isn't it?"

"Yes, but we use it in a rather derogatory sense."

"I'm sure you didn't mean it like that. Don't worry. What else did Mr C say?"

"I had forgotten tomorrow is Friday. He says he will speak to the Baron when he arrives."

The worst of swimming off the north coast of Estonia is that if there is no jetty to help bathers out into deep water, you have to wade almost to Finland before you are up to your waist. Võsu has no jetty. Nevertheless, merely to sit or lie in the water a dozen or so yards from the beach took the burning rim off the heat.

The children, who had only rarely visited the sea—for five years before coming to Estonia Mr C had served in Berne—amused themselves with what was practically a new experience, and even rejected the offer of Nannie to play with them. So the two women passed the time between lying in the sea and sprawling on the beach, and since they were the only people in the bay except for half a dozen or so teenage boys and girls who only most of the time lay on the sand earnestly discussing the fate of the German Jews, Mrs C told herself that this was the nearest she was likely to come to Paradise. In fact, looking at the naked party a couple of hundred yards away, one could imagine oneself in Paradise. If only our young people could do this at home, she thought, the psychiatrists would soon be extinct.

At four o'clock they packed up, dressed and returned to the car. Cook was waiting for them where they had put her down, and as she had friends with her they had to pause for a few moments' greeting. However, it was only a little after half past five when they drew up before the *datcha*.

338

While Mrs C, Nannie and the children unloaded the car, Cook went into the house to start preparing the children's supper. She had been inside only a few seconds when Mrs C and Nannie were startled by a piercing shriek.

"Stay with the children!" Mrs C called to Nannie, and ran towards the house.

As she reached the steps leading up to the veranda, in the doorway appeared a grotesque figure. Mrs C stopped short, her limbs refusing either to carry her on or take her back. All feeling seemed to desert her but for the ice-coldness of the fear that coursed down her spine, tightened her throat and contracted the skin over her skull so fiercely that she was conscious of pain. As in a nightmare, she opened her mouth to scream; but her throat was seized in an invisible vice, so that no sound broke from her lips except for strange little retching noises.

And all the while her eyes were riveted on the hideous figure above her.

It could once have been a man. Now it was a monster.

It had no ears, frightened eyes glared from lidless sockets, sunken holes took the place of a nose, teeth were bared in a lipless mouth, and where once there had been hands were but the stumps of wrists.

For a full minute Mrs C and It stood gazing at one another both immobile with fear.

Then the sound of voices penetrated the numbness of Mrs C's consciousness; the voices of the old Baron and Baroness hurrying towards the house as fast as their age would permit, calling: "Petya! Petya, come here! What are you doing there?"

Nannie picked up the little girl, seized the boy by the hand, and hurried with them down to the stream.

The figure in the doorway, hearing its name, seemed to come to life. It lurched forward, dragging a leg behind it, indescribable animal noises issuing from its throat. Half-falling down the veranda steps, it brushed Mrs C aside.

As it touched her with the stumps of one of its arms, she lost control and with a small moan crumpled to the ground. When she came round, she was lying on a *chaise longue* in the house and Cook was holding brandy to her lips. Nearby the young Baron and the old Baron were standing.

"I told you, *Dadushka*!" George was saying. "I told you something like this would happen!"

"It would not have happened if he had obeyed me," the old man replied. "What did he want in the house?"

"He was in my room," Cook said.

"He left some things in the room," George explained. "He did not expect Mrs C to return so soon."

As Mrs C stirred the old man stepped nearer.

"Madame, can you ever forgive me?" he said. "It is my fault that this has happened. I should have told you, but I imagined that by keeping it secret I was doing the best for that poor creature."

"Who is he?" Mrs C asked.

"He was my servant when I was in the navy, Madame. No man had a more faithful servant. He had been with me less than a year when the Japanese attacked us in Siberia. He was nineteen. He was on an errand from me to the army headquarters ashore one day, when he and his companions were ambushed by a party of Japanese.

"Three weeks later he was released in a counter-attack and returned to me as you see him now. Those fiends had removed his ears, his nose, his eyelids, his lips, his hands and the attributes of his manhood; and they had also broken both his legs.

"Since that day we have looked after him, the Baroness and I, and if he survives us—he is just past fifty—the family will protect him until he dies. Madame, what can I say?"

"It would have been better to have told us," Mrs C smiled. "But say nothing more. I understand."

The Secret Agents and the Corpse

The scene, despite the elegance of the great drawing-room, had about it an air of wild dissipation in suspense. Curls were tangled, coiffures were awry, one or two ladies, who had allowed prowling fingers too near to bosoms, yet seemed unaware of their nakedness and unresponsive to their partners' explorations. No one spoke, and there was scarcely a movement in the room except for the hands of the two who sat at the table surrounded by their passively unruly guests.

The man and woman faced one another across the table, the heap of cards, face down, in a disorderly muddle in front of them. The man's face was flushed and his lips were set in a stiff smile. His opponent's cheeks were whiter even than the lawn handkerchief with which she dabbed her moist upper lip from time to time. Her hands fluttered nervously, while his moved with calm deliberation, when he moved them at all.

"You have won all my fortune, my lord," Mrs Hetherington said. "You have won all my jewels, my carriages and my horses. I'll wager you now, sir, the whole of my estate—farms, woods, streams, houses, all—against the return of my fortune, my jewels, my carriages and my horses."

Lord Harcop, still smiling, looked across at her, his eyes twinkling.

"Madam," he said. "You are a pleasure to game with, but are you really sure you want to risk *everything* you possess?"

"What good are houses, farms, woods and streams if I have no money to maintain them, sir? At this moment I am the loser and therefore the challenger, and I challenge you now, my lord—all I still possess against the return of what you have won from me this evening, to be decided on the turn of two cards."

Lord Harcop looked down at the cards sprawled across the table. He did not speak, neither did his challenger, nor yet did anyone else in the room.

After a silence that seemed to last an hour, he looked up.

"Madam, are you quite sure?"

"For the last time, my lord, yes!"

"Very well, madam. I accept your challenge. Shall ace be high or low?"

"High, my lord. I always have luck when the ace is high."

"Will you do me the honour of drawing first, madam?"

"Certainly, my lord."

Mrs Hetherington of Thame Park, widow at forty-eight, a handsome and attractive woman, one of the richest women in the Eastern Counties, held out her hand above the cards and closed her eyes. The guests crowded round the table were motionless, the only sound in the room the stertorous breathing of the Honourable Clive Morton, old before his time, sick of disease contracted in the pursuit of lust, alive only by the grace of a Providence which had endowed him with the renowned Morton constitution.

Breathing deeply, Mrs Hetherington lowered her hand to the table, and rested the tip of an elegantly poised forefinger on a card. Opening her eyes, she slipped the point of her finger-nail under the edge of the card and flipped it over, disclosing the black visage of the king of clubs.

A burst of exclamations came from the watchers. Sir Jeremy Makepeace, an amateur mathematician, wondered briefly how one might calculate the odds against Lord Harcop turning up an ace. His lordship, though in different terms, was wondering the same thing.

Again silence fell on the immobile company as Harcop gazed at the cards as though trying to read their faces through the backs. After what seemed an interminable pause, with a movement so sudden that it drew a brief, startled cry from one of the ladies, his hand shot out and turned over a card on the far right of the heap.

A moment of stunned silence followed, and then all Babel was let loose. For there on the table lay the shining red ace of hearts.

Realizing that she was now absolutely penniless, and the realization depriving her temporarily of speech, Mrs Hetherington pushed back her chair, rose, dropped a curtsy to his lordship and, turning, made her way with dignity through the path made for her by her awed guests.

Harcop managed to scramble to his feet.

"Margaret," he called after Mrs Hetherington, but if she heard him she did not acknowledge it.

By the time he reached the hall, brushing aside the congratulations of the company, his hostess had disappeared from sight. Unable to face the half-inebriated fatuities of his fellow-guests, he hurried to the library. There for a full quarter of an hour he paced up and down, then, suddenly resolved, he pulled up a chair to the writing-table and for five minutes wrote.

"My dear Margaret," (Mrs Hetherington read some moments later) "I know that as one who sets such store by gaming you will insist upon honouring your debt to me. I wish you to know that it is not my desire that you should be cast upon the world without prop or support. Tell me how I can make this possible without wounding your *amour propre*."

He was still in the library when Mrs Hetherington's maid brought her reply.

"Dear John, Kind and considerate as ever. Breakfast with me tête à tête and we will talk about it. I shall expect you here in my room at nine o'clock. God bless you."

When Lord Harcop was admitted to her room next morning she greeted him with a cheerful smile. What an extraordinary woman she was, he thought, and dam'd attractive, too! Had there been no Lady Harcop, the solution would have been obvious.

"I didn't congratulate you, John," she said. "Luck was certainly with you yesterday."

"Don't embarrass me, Margaret, please!" he protested.

"How can I embarrass you? It's you who embarrass me by your kindness."

"What can we do, Margaret? Have you given it any thought?"

"Yes. I have a proposition. I have nothing so I cannot challenge you, but I can ask you to agree to cut the cards with me one last time. If you will, gambler that I am, I promise you that I will never again game or wager so long as I live."

"You really mean it!" he said, looking at her intently.

"Yes, I really mean it."

"What are to be the stakes, then?"

"If I lose you will settle £5,000 on me and I will go into some religious retreat. If I win you will not call in your winnings so long as I remain above ground."

"Done!"

"Gallant as well as generous, John. Here is a new pack. Break the seals and let us get it over with. Then we can enjoy breakfast."

He shuffled the cards briefly, and balancing the pack in the palm of his left hand he held it out to her. Calmly, deliberately, she cut and showed him the ten of diamonds. Equally deliberately he cut, and turned up the seven of spades.

With a laugh he let the cards fall on the coverlet of the bed, and bent and kissed her cheek.

"I have never in my life been so relieved," he said. "Have your lawyers draw up a deed."

"But there is no need for that between friends, John."

"I insist. I may be thrown and break my neck out hunting tomorrow, and Robert could—and would—claim Thame at once. For once we must be business-like."

"Very well, if you insist."

"I insist."

Ten years passed before Lord Harcop was reminded of these events, and it was Mrs Hetherington's death that recalled them. In those ten years a series of small catastrophes had greatly reduced his resources, and he had to admit that he would find the Thame estate and Margaret Hetherington's fortune very welcome. Still, he was sorry to lose an old friend, and on the day of the funeral he was driven over to Thame to pay his last respects.

A private chapel had been built in the grounds by Mrs Hetherington's late husband's great-grandfather, and all the Hetheringtons since then had been buried in the small graveyard on the north side of the tiny church. Lord Harcop, who had been expecting Margaret Hetherington to be laid beside her husband there, was surprised to learn, on arriving at Thame, that in her will she had instructed that she should be "laid to rest" in the chapel itself.

He had heard that she had built a miniature chapel in the north-east corner of the chancel, and that she had told friends that she had done so as an act of penance. Since she had kept her part of the bargain meticulously, and had never wagered again in any form, he had accepted this statement in good faith. Now he learned that she was to be buried in this chantry. Well, she was an extraordinary woman from every point of view, and who was he to look too closely for the reason for this break with Hetherington tradition.

He was shown into the pew behind that reserved for the family. Before he went away the usher told him that the late Mrs Hetherington had left a communication for him, and that Mr Robert Hetherington would be grateful if his lordship would call at the house after the obsequies.

The mention of Robert Hetherington started a new train of thought. The young fellow must know that when his mother died Thame was to pass to Harcop. He had made some very discreet inquiries and it had been reported to him that on hearing what had happened Hetherington had said, "Well, that's a relief anyway. I never did want to be a country gentleman." Apparently old Hetherington had settled a nice sum on the boy when he had entered the diplomatic service, and report had it that young Robert was already ear-marked for high advancement. So perhaps he really did not care what happened to Thame.

The congregation rose to its feet as the parson's voice broke the rustling silence—"I am the Resurrection and the Life, saith the Lord."

Borne on the shoulders of six men from the Thame estate the coffin containing Margaret Hetherington's body came slowly down the aisle. Immediately within the chancel two trestles had been set up, and on them the bearers lowered their burden and removed the pall.

It was as the coffin was uncovered that Harcop received his first shock. The lid of the casket was a sheet of glass, and below it one could see the body richly gowned, jewelled and ringed, the features set in the repose of sleep.

If one could judge from the smile faintly curling the lips, Margaret Hetherington had died during a happy dream.

When the committal was reached, the bearers took up the coffin and carried it to the chantry chapel. There they placed it on a stone catafalque, the parson scattered a handful of dust upon it, read the sentences and it was over.

"Rum goings on!" Harcop said to himself. "Why not put her directly in the stone thingumajig?"

Robert Hetherington was waiting outside the chapel.

"Did you get my message, Lord Harcop?" he asked, and when Harcop nodded, went on, "If you don't mind going over to the house, I'll be with you presently."

"I'm in no hurry, Mr Hetherington," Harcop said.

The servant had just placed the decanter of marsala beside him in the library when Robert Hetherington came in.

"I have to admit to being embarrassed by this affair, Lord Harcop," he said.

"Embarrassed? Affair? What affair?" Harcop said, puzzled.

"But you've heard the terms of my mother's will, sir?"

"No. I arrived back from the continent the day after her death and I've heard nothing."

"You saw where her coffin was placed, sir?"

"Yes. When are you planning to bury it?"

"That's just the point, sir. She left instructions that she was not to be buried. She was to be placed in an air-tight coffin with a glass lid, and the coffin was to be put on the stone platform prepared in the chantry chapel, so that she would remain 'for ever above ground'."

" 'For ever above ground'," Harcop repeated quietly.

He was silent for a moment or two, regarding the glass of marsala he held up to the light. Then suddenly the corners of his eyes creased and he gave a loud laugh.

"What a remarkable woman your mother was!" he exclaimed. "Damned clever! Don't you think so, sir?"

"I admired my mother greatly for all her faults," Hetherington replied. "But you understand what this means, sir?"

"I understand perfectly well. That fellow in the chapel said something about a letter. May I see it?"

Hetherington drew the letter from his pocket.

"I have it here, sir."

Harcop broke the seal. It was a short message.

"Dearest John, I have kept my part of our wager. I know you will keep yours. My love from eternity—Margaret."

"So I will," he said.

"Will what, sir?"

"Keep my part of the wager," Harcop said. "I won't deny that Thame wouldn't be dashed useful at the moment, but . . ."

"Sir, I have already spoken to the lawyers. There would be ways and means . . ."

"Robert, my boy, your mother was a gambler born. There have been few to equal her. She was absolutely scrupulous in settling all her gambling debts. I should despise myself if I did not as scrupulously honour the terms of our wager. We'll say no more about it."

"So I'm to be saddled with Thame?"

"I'm afraid so."

"Would you buy it from me for a sovereign?"

"No, sir. That would be cheating. Would you be good enough to have my carriage called?"

It was Harcop himself who put an end to the affair. He drew up a simple document repudiating all claim to Thame for himself and his heirs.

"It's the only sensible thing to do," he explained. "How could the place be managed under such conditions? There would always be uncertainty in the minds of the owners, and the place would go to rack and ruin."

His action, however, did not entirely preserve Thame. The estate passed out of the Hetherington family, and after many vicissitudes, shortly before the outbreak of the Second World War, it was bought by a wealthy industrialist as a wedding present for his son and heir. By this time the house had fallen into disrepair, but money and skill soon restored it and the young couple moved in. They had not been in residence long, however, when the War Office decided it would make excellent temporary quarters for one of their establishments. In 1940 Special Operations Executive, that strange organization which put secret agents into Occupied Europe, was operating it as a training school.

It is not known what the plans of the new owners had been with regard to the chapel. This building had suffered far more than the house, and was, in fact, in a state of almost complete dereliction. Parts of the roof had caved in, the plaster had fallen from the walls leaving disfiguring scars, the pews were little more than heaps of broken wood. Rats and mice and bats had their home there.

Only Mrs Hetherington, in her glass-lidded coffin in the chantry, was untouched and practically unchanged. Her gown had perhaps faded somewhat, but her features were as fresh as ever, and the jewels on breast and fingers still sparkled brightly.

To Thame Park during 1942 there came for training a number of young French agents. Among them were Anton and Pierre, only just out of their teens, replete with vigour and vitality remarkable when one remembered that they had escaped from the Gestapo in Paris, walked across the Pyrenees in mid-winter and spent eight months in a Spanish concentration camp.

It was probably the hardships and deprivations of their escape experiences which made them somewhat wild when they came into contact with the atmosphere of wartime London, gay compared with Occupied France. It did not take them long to discover that the "appeal" of their nationality was an open sesame in certain circles, especially if they had well-lined purses, and they found the discreet anonymity of the blacked-out capital overpoweringly alluring.

S.O.E. was extremely understanding of the personal needs of its agents, and allowed them a freedom of movement while training probably unique among clandestine organizations. Saturdays and Sundays were free days, and the young men who would shortly be thrust into close quarters with death, were encouraged to relax in the way that suited them best, provided no breach of security was committed. Since London was chockablock with thousands of foreigners of all ages, and the great majority of them were in uniform, unless the agents themselves betrayed their status there was little reason for anyone who met them to suspect that they were rather special.

Every Saturday morning after breakfast, therefore, Anton and Pierre made a bee-line for the London train, and from midday until Sunday evening they delivered themselves over to their animal cravings.

Unfortunately, these activities cost money. More unfortunately, the rates of pay which S.O.E. accorded its agents under training, while generous if tastes and needs were not excessive, were not such as to allow even a mild Lothario to have his head without running into financial difficulties. One could always tell when pay-day was approaching by the number who decided to spend a quiet weekend in the country.

Anton's and Pierre's requirements were much greater than their allowance could support. When, because of lack of funds, they could not finance a London weekend, they suffered from acute boredom. They were so bored, in fact, they developed an obsessive horror of boredom, and this increased as their training approached completion and the entry into the field became daily more imminent. It was their appreciation of what lay ahead that made their weekend diversions even more essential to them than the requirements of their instincts. There is no other rational explanation of their behaviour, which ended with Anton being so emotionally disturbed that he had to be discarded by the organization.

Like most students who visited Thame, the two young Frenchmen explored the ruins of the chapel. They had heard of the old woman who, richly gowned, jewelled and ringed, lay embalmed in her glass-lidded coffin on the north side of the sanctuary. They had clambered over the broken pews and heaps of rubble, and had viewed the sight, shuddered and hurried away.

In three weeks they could expect to be dispatched on their mission. In fact, on the Friday evening they had been virtually told that this time next month they would be back in their own country.

They had drawn their pay shortly afterwards and had made up their minds to forget the future by seeking something extra special in the way of diversion. In this they were very successful. They found just the partners they had hoped for.

The weekend made such an impression on them that before they took their way to Marylebone station to catch the last train for Thame, they promised their friends they would repeat the experience the following weekend.

It was only when they counted up the remains of their pay during their lunch-hour on Monday that they realized that even if they pooled their financial resources there was not enough for one of them to divert himself at half the cost that this weekend had entailed, let alone both. The discovery threw them into the depths of depression and they cast about in their minds for means of raising the money they needed.

They were discussing what they could do as they strolled in the grounds after dinner that evening. In the course of their walk they passed the chapel, and Anton suddenly had an inspiration.

He stopped short in his tracks and gripped Pierre's arm so tightly that his friend gasped in pain.

"The old woman!" he exclaimed in a dramatic whisper.

"What about her?" Pierre demanded.

"One of those rings or a brooch would be enough," Anton replied.

"You mean, rob a corpse?" Pierre was genuinely horrified. "It's sacrilege."

"She wasn't a Catholic."

"What difference does that make? Do you think religion counts in heaven?"

"She hasn't had the benefits of the rites of the Church. Anyway, you know I'm an atheist."

"Well, you can do what you like," Pierre told him. "I'll have nothing to do with it."

"But I shall need some help."

"Find someone else."

But Anton knew that no one else would help him.

So for the next two or three days he tried to wear down his friend's resistance, attempting to dispel his scruples by argument and cajolery. To talk about a corpse bringing bad luck was sheer superstitious nonsense, he maintained. No one would miss a ring. What a waste of all those valuable jewels, just tarting up a corpse!

Pierre was strong-minded, but by degrees Anton's persistence wore him down, and, much against his better judgement, he agreed to help.

They planned the operation for after midnight on Friday night. Anton had wanted to make it Thursday in case anything went wrong, so that they could have a second chance. But Pierre rejected this, saying that if they failed at the first attempt he would take it as an omen, and there would be no second attempt by him.

There was no very particular reason why they should fail, since there were only two obstacles to be overcome: getting out of and back into the house without being seen (in case if and when one of the jewels were missed they should be connected with the theft), and avoiding the patrol which made the rounds of the grounds at intervals during the night (for the same reason). Since much of their training had been devised to make them expert in this kind of activity they did not expect to have any great difficulty in defeating these obstacles.

And so it happened. In battle-dress, gym-shoes and gloves, balaclava helmets pulled down over blackened faces, they reached the ruined chapel without incident. Negotiating the piles of rubble and broken furniture noiselessly they found more difficult. Disturbed rats scurried away with sinister squeaks, and at each squeak a shiver of disgust tinged with fear shot down Pierre's spine. Bats swooped with swift silence in fantastic figures of eight, sometimes coming so near that they could hear the draught of their wings. However, they reached the chantry successfully.

At the catafalque, Anton drew off his gloves and took from his pocket the screwdriver and chisel he had borrowed from the workshops that morning, and by the light of the torch held by Pierre he went to work on the screws securing the lid of the coffin. Time had corroded them and they would not respond to the screwdriver, but he found he could ease them out of the wood by inserting the chisel between lid and coffin and gently easing the lid up.

He worked deftly, silently and with concentration. Pierre watched him with admiration, and not only for his skill, but because he was clearly unmoved by the close presence of the old woman's corpse. Pierre himself was trembling a little, and began to wish he had not agreed to the plan. The light of the torch produced macabre shadows over the corpse's waxen features, so that the face seemed to be alive.

"For heaven's sake, Pierre, hold the torch steady!" Anton whispered.

"How long will you be? I don't like this," Pierre whispered back.

"Two minutes—there."

Putting the chisel back into his pocket he took hold of the lid with both hands and very slowly began to raise it. Suddenly, immediately overhead, an owl hooted raucously, startling Pierre so much that he dropped the torch with an exclamation. Fortunately it did not go out, and to Anton's curses he quickly retrieved it.

Once more Anton began to raise the lid and, holding it open with his left hand, he slipped his right between lid and coffin. But as he stretched out his hand towards the corpse's hand, the beringed fingers began to move.

He saw them moving, but could not draw back his own hand,

and with a convulsive movement the dead hand seized his wrist and held it tightly. With an exclamation of horror he pushed back the coffin lid and it fell to the ground with a crash of broken glass. Desperately he tried to pry the lifeless fingers from his wrist, his horror mounting with each second of failure. Then suddenly, with a loud cry, he fell forward over corpse and coffin, senseless.

Pierre had watched the scene dumb with terror, but as Anton fell mobility returned to his limbs, and calling for help he clambered with noise enough to be heard in Thame over the debris of the chapel.

His cries brought the patrol. Scarcely articulate, he managed to convey to them that Anton needed help.

When the soldiers reached the chantry, Anton was still sprawled over the coffin unconscious. But the fingers that encircled his wrist were a fleshless skeleton. Gone, too, were the waxen cheeks and the carmined smile. Only a grinning hair-crowned skull gazed up at the stars.

Two days Anton lay unconscious, and when, after several weeks, the doctors pronounced him physically well, they reported that mentally he would be unfit for many months.

So Pierre went into the field alone, and was grateful.

The Bath of Acid

John George Haigh and his pal, Donald McSwan, were characters of a type found in all the big cities in England during the Second World War. Both were avoiding military service. Both were on the fiddle, dabbling in the black market and in business of varying degrees of legitimacy. Haigh had served prison sentences—one for pillaging houses bombed in the London Blitz.

McSwan ran a pin-table saloon and Haigh had a workshop in the basement of 79 Gloucester Road, South Kensington, where he repaired pin-tables. It was not a very profitable business. Nevertheless, Haigh lived in style at the Onslow Court Hotel, South Kensington. He had an interest in a light engineering firm in Crawley, owned by a man named Stephens, and was very friendly with the proprietor's daughter Barbara.

Haigh had known Donald McSwan and his parents for years; they had then been at Wimbledon and owned a modest amount of suburban property. Young Donald McSwan's main concern in 1944 was to avoid the call-up. The military authorities were already seeking him and he was partly in hiding, avoiding all contact with strangers. He hadn't seen John Haigh for several years, and was pleased to encounter him in the saloon of the "Goat" in Kensington High Street. It was probably no accident. Haigh had had his eye on his old friend Mac, and had plans for him.

Mac knew he could trust John Haigh not to betray him to the

police. He took Haigh to see his parents, now living in Pimlico, and there was a pleasant reunion. Haigh was his old, affable self, and seemed to be doing well enough. He said nothing about the military authorities looking for him for having dodged an Army medical board after his release from prison in September 1943. Haigh was no fool. He did not talk about his murky past.

He noted that the McSwans had not changed. They kept to themselves and had practically no friends. He invited Donald McSwan to the Onslow Court Hotel for an evening. Mac would do for a start—the first experiment.

Haigh told him about his girl friend, Barbara Stephens, and offered to show him his pin-table workshop in Gloucester Road. The two young men spent a pleasant evening at the Onslow Court on 6 September, 1944, during which Mac wrote a light-hearted postcard in shorthand to Miss Stephens who was holidaying at Weymouth, adding a postscript to the effect that John had let his cocoa get cold. Haigh had other things on his mind while Mac was thus innocently engaged.

Haigh was thinking about that fascinating experiment he had done in the tinsmiths' shop at Lincoln Prison when he had put the body of a mouse in its own volume of concentrated sulphuric acid. The acid went cloudy and became hot. In half an hour the mouse had completely disintegrated, leaving nothing behind but black sludge. This very interesting and instructive chemical phenomenon had given him much food for thought. He had no animosity towards either men or mice, but a fellow had to live, and his bill at the Onslow Court was mounting up. Mac's pin-table saloon was making a handy profit, and Mac had told him that he would rather go into hiding than do his national service. He had told his parents the same thing.

His was a perfect case of victimology.

On 9 September, three days after their cosy evening together at the Onslow Court, Haigh took his pal to see his workshop in the basement of 79 Gloucester Road. As Mac was examining the equipment, Haigh picked up a cosh and hit him on the head with it. Taken by surprise, Mac succumbed immediately, and Haigh hit him until he judged he was dead. He experience, he later confessed, a "slightly squashy sensation".

Haigh then lifted McSwan and, folding him turkeywise, fitted

him into a forty-gallon tank. It was hard work, for Haigh was not
a big man.

In the workshop he had a carboy of concentrated sulphuric acid
which he used in his sheet-metal work, and which he was able to
obtain without difficulty. He then started pouring buckets of the
acid into the tank on top of Mac. Choking fumes arose and he had
to keep going outside for fresh air. At last it was finished. Mac was
completely covered by the acid, and all that remained now was to
wait for corrosion to work and obliterate the body.

He knew this would happen. There was not only the evidence of
his experiment with the mouse in Lincoln Prison. He had read about
the case of Georges Sarret who was sentenced to death at Aix-en-
Provence in 1933 for murdering three people and dissolving their
bodies in a bath of sulphuric acid. Sarret was given away by his
accomplices. No trace of the bodies of his victims was found. Haigh
was not such a fool as Sarret. He would have no accomplices.

After thus disposing of Mac, Haigh went to the "Chepstow",
a pub in Bayswater. Usually very abstemious, he found himself
greatly in need of alcoholic stimulation. After all, it was his first
murder.

He had been brought up in a strict, religious home, his parents
being devout Plymouth Brethren. He had abandoned religion long
since, but it was nevertheless deeply ingrained in his mind. He was
imaginative, romantic, with a love for music. When he was a boy
he sang in the choir at Wakefield Cathedral and played the organ
there. He developed a passion for the ritualistic cathedral services,
rather to the sorrow of his Calvinistic, anti-clerical parents. Such
was his religious zeal in those days that he left home at five-thirty
every Sunday morning to walk three miles to the Cathedral to act
as a server for the early Communion. He used to gaze upon the
images of Christ's bleeding on the Cross and dream strange dreams
of blood.

But long ago he had forsaken the Church and the religious life.
The Plymouth Brethren had expelled him from their community
in 1934 when he had been sent to prison for fraud, forgery and false
pretences. The teachings and the ways of the Brethren had made
a deep impression on his life. As a boy his parents had shielded him
from the sinful outside world, and his home had been almost like
a monastic establishment. It had been a shock when one of the

Brethren had initiated him into homosexual practices. Another shock had been when the Brethren excommunicated him.

But it was not any of these things that had made him into what he became. Many survive both bigotry and corruption to live useful lives. No one really knows what makes a man murder in the way that Haigh did.

He himself found his first essay in murder sufficiently disturbing to spend the evening drinking heavily. He went to bed drunk, a rare experience for him.

The following day, when he returned to the basement at 79 Gloucester Road and looked into the acid bath, he found Mac had completely dissolved into a mass of dark sludge. He gazed at this convenient miracle of chemistry with rare satisfaction, and then disposed of the sludge down a man-hole which led directly into the drains.

Mac was gone, vanished, obliterated, and there was not a tell-tale trace of him left. It worked beautifully. Haigh's heart beat faster at the exciting prospect which now opened before him.

He believed that murder could not be proved unless a body could be produced. There would be no *corpus delicti*. This was an old and favourite theory of his, and he had expounded it to his fellow convicts at Dartmoor, where Mr Justice Charles had sent him in 1937 for a series of swindles. At Dartmoor they called him "old Corpus Delicti". No one told him that his theory was quite wrong and that *corpus delicti* does not mean the body of a murder victim, but the facts which establish the commission of a crime. Haigh made the mistake which a number of murderers have made.

All the same, he was no fool, and he now went about things with both cunning and skill. Mac had already set the stage for his own disappearance by saying he would go into hiding to avoid national service. Haigh went to his parents and told them that this was exactly what their son had done, and they believed him. He told them Donald was in Glasgow, and would be writing to them.

In his diary he put a cross in red under the date 9 September, 1944, and then took over Mac's pin-table saloon which provided him with sufficient ready money to solve his immediate financial problems. He was nothing if not thorough in convincing Mr and Mrs McSwan that their son was still alive. He carefully forged letters in Donald's handwriting and then went all the way to Glasgow to post them.

Mr and Mrs McSwan he planned to be his next victims, and he plotted their destruction with both cunning and imagination, keeping them primed with forged letters from Donald, in which reference was made to his good friend, John Haigh, whom the supposedly alive young man trusted implicitly, and who was looking after his interests at the pin-table saloon during his enforced absence.

Haigh bided his time, perfecting his murder technique. The fumes of the acid had disturbed him somewhat, but that was simply overcome, he found, by donning a civilian gas mask, readily available in those days. Also he discovered that the best and, for him, safest way of transferring the acid from the carboy to the bath containing the victim was by means of that familiar wartime fire-fighting device, the stirrup pump. Later he wore a special murder outfit for the task of dissolving the bodies of his victims—reinforced gloves and an old jacket and trousers.

It was not until early July, 1945, that he was ready to dispose of Mr and Mrs McSwan. He made one of his periodic visits to Glasgow and posted a letter from Mac, saying that he was coming to London, but as he was on the run he could not visit their home. Only his loyal and true friend John Haigh knew where his place of hiding would be, and they must let him take them there.

Haigh took the McSwans there separately. The place, of course, was the basement in Gloucester Road, where Haigh coshed them, beat them to death, trussed them up, put them into the tanks, pumped in the acid and left them to dissolve.

He later admitted that he was not sure whether or not they were dead when he put them in the acid. If they were alive, their agonies when immersed in the vitriol can hardly be imagined.

Later he swilled the sludge down the basement man-hole into the sewers, tremendously pleased at his success in completely obliterating the McSwan family so that not a trace of any of them was left. No one asked where they were, for they had no friends or close relatives. There was never any evidence against Haigh of these murders, apart from his own confession, and he was never in fact charged with them.

He then set about the important task of appropriating their property, which was the object of the exercise. He found this remarkably easy. He went to the McSwans' solicitors in Glasgow and told them he was Donald McSwan. He forged Donald's signature in front of their eyes, and granted power of attorney over the McSwan possessions to John George Haigh, who was authorized to deal with the McSwan property in the London area. The property included four houses, and there was about £2,000 worth of gilt-edged securities which Haigh also got.

It was calculated that he made about £4,000 out of the slaughter of the McSwans. Some estimates put the figure as high as £7,000, for nearly that sum was paid into his bank between 1945 and 1947, most of it, it is thought, from the McSwan loot. His fraudulent power of attorney seems never to have been questioned. No one asked where the McSwans were. Their disappearance was never reported to the police.

John Haigh was on top of the world. Murder was good business. He was in the money. Christmas 1945 was a good one for him. "A right Merry Christmas to all," he wrote expansively. "I am feeling content with the world."

He lived the life of a normal, prosperous young man. He drove his car on black-market petrol. He took Barbara Stephens to Beethoven concerts. He talked politics and war, and discussed Hiroshima in the Kensington pubs.

For two years he lived on the McSwan loot, and by the August of 1947 it had all, like its legitimate owners, gone down the drain. Haigh believed in spending, and he was a gambler too. After all, there were other fish in the sea. The world was full of unwary people ripe for an acid bath, Haigh-style. No one suspected him. He had hit on a foolproof murder system. He was, he thought, rather clever, brilliant in fact. He had outwitted them all.

It was a wonderful life, with everyone thinking him a hell of a good fellow. He had a pleasant, platonic friendship with his attractive girl friend, Barbara. Haigh wasn't one for sex. He had tried it once and, as he put it, soon got tired of it. There were more important things in the world.

By August 1947 Haigh was again desperately in need of money. He was overdrawn at the bank and his bill at the Onslow Court was mounting up. It was getting time for someone to have an acid bath.

At first he was not rash in his choice of victims. He did not pick rich or conspicuous people, or people who had a lot of friends and relations. In September he met the Hendersons, who, as the McSwans had been, were well suited to his purpose.

Dr Archibald Henderson's first wife had died in 1937 in circumstances so sudden that Bernard Spilsbury was called in to do a post mortem. But Spilsbury found nothing wrong with the death, and the coroner gave a verdict of natural causes. The first Mrs Henderson left her husband quite a lot of money. Rosalie Henderson was the doctor's second wife, and Haigh met them through answering an advertisement for the sale of their house in Ladbroke Square, W.11. They seemed to like him, and throughout the autumn and winter of that year a friendship developed between this ill-assorted trio.

Haigh often visited them at their Fulham home, and during one of these visits he stole Henderson's revolver and ammunition. He had come to the conclusion that using a cosh was an untidy method, and there was no reason at all why Henderson should not provide the means of a clean dispatch for himself and Rose.

By now Haigh had his famous experimental workshop at Crawley. He had fitted it up for what he humorously called "conversion jobs", and his equipment included large metal drums and a stirrup pump. Just before Christmas he ordered three carboys of concentrated sulphuric acid to be delivered to the workshop. He was not wishing everyone a right Merry Christmas as he had done two years previously. His mood was vitriolic rather than expansive. His overdraft was building up. So was his hotel bill. A financier was pressing him for £400. It was time for his friends the Hendersons to come to his assistance.

In the February of 1948 Haigh joined the Hendersons at Broadstairs where they were staying, and then drove on to Brighton with them where the trio stayed two nights at the Hotel Metropole.

Brighton is handy for Crawley, and while they were there Haigh persuaded Archie Henderson to go to his experimental workshop where, in addition to the carboys of acid, two forty-gallon tanks were waiting to receive him and his wife. The tops of the drums had been removed in order to facilitate Haigh's "conversion job".

Haigh shot Henderson with the man's own revolver, removed his gold watch, his cigarette case, wallet and loose change from his pockets, trussed him and then put him in the tank. Leaving him thus, he went out to get a gas mask, trusting to providence, as he put it, that he would not be discovered. Haigh believed that he was under some kind of divine protection.

Donning gas mask, gloves and leather apron, he filled the drum from the carboy with a stirrup-pump, and leaving Archie to the unbenign processes of chemistry, returned to Brighton and told Rose that her husband was ill and she must come at once. Rose lost no time in accompanying him to Crawley, where he promptly shot her, removed her rings and jewellery, put her into the second tank and filled it with acid as before.

It was 12 February and in his diary of that date he wrote "A.H., R.H." and made the sign of the cross.

The first thing he did was to realize on their personal jewellery. This netted him some £300. He sold this in Horsham. He went to Brighton and paid their outstanding hotel bill. He then made off from the Metropole with all their effects, including their dog.

By the time these essential matters had been completed, Archie and Rose had been reduced to sludge in their respective acid baths. When Haigh tipped the residue out in the yard of his Crawley workshop he noticed that Archie's foot still remained, but so supreme was his confidence that he just left it there.

The next important thing to be considered was the question of Rose Henderson's relatives. He dealt with this problem by writing to them in a fair imitation of her hand to say that difficulties had suddenly arisen and they were emigrating to South Africa.

After that Haigh seems to have had little difficulty in disposing of their property by means of forged deeds. He spent the year 1948 doing this, and by Christmas he had paid more than £7,000 into his bank, mainly from these proceeds.

It worked perfectly. He had killed five people, appropriated their not inconsiderable belongings, and not a shred of suspicion devolved upon him. No one had asked where the McSwan family were, and only half-hearted inquiries were made concerning the disappearance of the Hendersons. Mr Arnold H. Burlin, Rose's brother, was anxious about his sister, but it is not likely that his inquiries would have uncovered the truth.

Haigh was still friendly with Barbara Stephens, and although he thought himself the cleverest and most accomplished murderer of the century, if not of all time, he nevertheless considered the possibility of being caught. Miss Stephens was secretary to a psychiatrist, and they had long discussions on the subject. Although Haigh ridiculed the whole thing, and regarded it as a lot of nonsense, he listened intently to what she had to say about such things as paranoia and schizophrenia, realizing that here might lie the way out for him if he was ever caught. He might laugh at psychiatry, but a lot of people took it very seriously, including the modern school of criminologists.

It was out of these innocent conversations with Barbara Stephens that was born his plan to pose as insane and not responsible for his actions.

By 1948 he had made something like £15,000 out of his five successful murders. If he had retired on his ill-gotten loot, he might have got away with it. But Haigh was not the sort of person to rest secure upon his homicidal laurels.

Again all the money went down the drain and by early 1949 he had squandered the thousands he had realized from the Hendersons' property, much of it in gambling. He owed his bookie over £300, had business debts of more than £500, an overdraft approaching three figures, and a big bill owing to the Onslow Court Hotel.

And so he committed his last and least clever murder—that of Mrs Durrand-Deacon, the sixty-nine-year-old widow of an Army officer, who also lived at the hotel, was often seen in his company and had many friends. After five perfect murders, Haigh now went all to pieces. He could hardly have made a more unwise choice than Mrs Durrand-Deacon, who was instantly and urgently missed, and whose property, apart from such things as were on her person, was inaccessible to him after her death. He was desperate for money, and a more clever rogue would have conned the susceptible Mrs Durrand-Deacon, who was quite well off. Haigh might even have married her, for he always got on marvellously with elderly ladies, and then disposed of her later at his leisure. But for all his self-confessed cleverness, all he could think of was her jewellery and her fur coat, which would provide only a modest amount of loot.

He lured her to the Crawley workshop on the pretence of discussing the manufacture of plastic fingernails. A day or two previously he had gone to Crawley with a "shopping list", later recovered, on which were noted such items as H_2SO_4, a drum, a stirrup-pump, gloves, apron, a cottonwool pad, some red paper, etc. Also written down was the address and phone number of the London firm which supplied the sulphuric acid.

On 18 February ten gallons of acid was delivered to the store-room at Crawley, and the following day Haigh drove Mrs Durrant-Deacon there on the pretext of discussing the plastic fingernails project. He shot her in the back of the head while she was examining the red paper which was supposed to be the colour to be used for the fingernails.

Haigh then stripped her of her Persian-lamb coat, her rings, necklace, earrings and jewelled crucifix, and then put her into a forty-five gallon tank.

It was hard work, so at this point he adjourned for refreshment to a local café. He no longer required the consolation of a booze-up as he had done after his first murder. A nice cup of tea now sufficed the experienced Haigh, and was more in keeping with his abstemious tastes. He then returned to the workshop, donned his murder clothes and gas mask, and filled the tank with the stirrup-pump, until the lady was completely covered by the acid.

The afternoon's work thus completed, he repaired to Ye Olde Ancient Priors Restaurant in Crawley and had an egg on toast and a pleasant chat with the proprietor. Later on he had dinner at the George. It must have been hungry work.

It was certainly a disastrous afternoon's work. Mrs Durrand-Deacon's friends went straight to the police when she did not return to the Onslow Court Hotel. The police questioned Haigh, and became insistent when they found that not only did he owe a big bill at the hotel, but he also had a prison record. Haigh, with his habitual contempt for authority, just talked himself into the dock with remarks of classic stupidity like, "How can you prove murder if there is no body?"

Finding that his *corpus delicti* theory was all wrong, he tried to put his ill-digested psychiatric theories into practice and to make out that he was mentally irresponsible for his actions, adding naively the now famous question to Inspector Albert Webb: "Tell me frankly, what are the chances of anyone being released from Broadmoor?" He told wild stories of drinking his victims' blood and his own urine, judging that only a real nut case would do such things.

At his trial at Lewes in July 1949 the whole edifice of his insanity defence was shot to pieces without difficulty by Hartley Shawcross. The jury found him very sane and very guilty and Mr Justice Humphreys sentenced him to death. To the grim and solemn sentence, Haigh replied with a cool and insolent smile, "Thank you very much indeed, my lord." It was said that he met the hangman on 6 August in similar mood.

Two women stood by him to the last. Barbara Stephens, despite many temptations, refused to write her memoirs for the Sunday papers, and was always loyal and restrained in her comments about their relationship. He wrote to her from the condemned cell, saying he was proud that their association had always been an honourable one.

When his broken-hearted mother learned what kind of monster had sprung from her womb, she gallantly tried to shoulder the blame by saying that it was not his fault but, rather, hers, for when she was carrying him her pregnancy was accompanied by the most acute anxiety. Her husband had been unemployed at the time and it was a period of great privation for them.

However that may have been, Haigh went to the scaffold—a grim warning that, though there may well be the perfect murder, there will probably never be the perfect murderer.

The Girl in the Train

The story was told to me one evening by Professor X, whose name, though he insists on this anonymity, is almost a household word. Since shortly after the war he has been Professor of Gynaecology at a teaching hospital in London and we meet from time to time at our club. When he told me this story it was late and we had dined well. I pressed him to go on with an episode which had started off as a remark about railways in general and he courteously carried on—perhaps because he felt he owed it to his host of the evening. I soon regretted my insistence: Professor X told it as if he were re-living some dreadful, personal experience, which of course he was. His hand shook as he re-lit his cigar; he crossed legs awkwardly and nearly knocked over the table.

"You know," I said, "you don't *have* to tell me—if it upsets you."

"I must, I'm afraid—now it's come back. But I've never told a soul before. Not a soul."

And slowly, haltingly, with a complete absence of the well-chosen phrase and *savoir-faire* for which he is renowned, Professor X limped on with his story. I have his permission to re-tell it as best I can, on condition that I alter the names of all concerned.

The year was 1945, the month December. The war was not long over and he was travelling north to give some lectures at the University of Edinburgh. Already his fame had spread, though knighthood was still some five years off. He had caught the 4 p.m.

364

train, as it then was, from King's Cross, due at Waverley at midnight. Though comfortably off, he was hard-headed in money matters and had bought himself what in those days was a "third class" ticket; there being, for some unfathomably British reason, no "second class". The train—it was a Wednesday—was fairly empty, and in fact the compartment when he entered it five minutes before departure was completely so. He put a wooden chest of books and instruments and his small suitcase on the seat immediately opposite, by the window, with the frank and antisocial intention of discouraging others.

A girl ran in, breathless, just as the train was pulling out. Annoyed, he shut the door behind her while she stood in the centre of the compartment for a moment, getting her breath. Then she dumped herself exactly in the centre of the opposing seat, small overnight case beside her, handbag on her lap, staring fixedly over his head at a faded reminder of the joys of Clacton-on-Sea.

She leant towards him.

"I wonder if you'd mind moving your cases?"

The Professor frowned. She could scarcely be more than nineteen, and she had a choice of at least four other seats. For that matter, she had a choice of other compartments, some of which must be empty. He grunted and with perhaps a greater show of exertion than was needed, lifted the cases to the rack above.

"Thank you," said the girl, moving up to the window. She was, now he looked at her, rather small and rather pretty, with thick blonde hair and a full red mouth—which was black in the dim lighting of the compartment. Her face seemed very pale. She was wearing a brownish coat-and-skirt which seemed well cut and probably expensive, a modest string of pearls round her neck, and shoes which he recognized as Army—A.T.S.—Issue. Obviously the clothing coupons had run out before she got down to her feet.

And of course, she would be wearing hideous Army Issue undergarments. Pants, Woollen. He found himself deciding that her pelvis was small, and tried to concentrate on the *Evening Standard*. This was absurd, because effort was needed even to see where the pictures had been put on each page.

He looked up to see her smile at him and move to stand against the half-opened window. She leant her head half out and the wind ruffled the blonde hair. Their compartment was near the front of the train; a hot reflection from the cab, inferno from the firebox, were reflected in a thin bank of fog, a transparency of hell superimposed on the passing, darkening, landscape of north London. It was cold, and the fog would increase. He hoped the train would not be delayed: he would need all his sleep before tomorrow's round of lectures and interviews.

She seemed to be staring at the dreary urban landscape, as if she were leaving it for the last time, trying to soak up each detail, impress it for ever on her mind. The red glow from in front caught the blonde hair, turned it pink.

She turned to him, was about to speak, then turned back to the window. He made another attempt to deal with the *Evening Standard*, then closed his eyes.

He must have slept for some time, because he was woken by her voice: "Oh darling—do you think so?" He jerked himself into wakefulness, found the train halted. As he sat back, eyes half closed, trying to remember where he was, who would be making such a remark, he was dragged into wakefulness by the train re-starting. Engine wheels slipped and raced, there was frenzied snorting and puffing from the steam-box, and then they were under way. As he sat up and looked into the darkness, he saw the sign: "Peterborough". He had slept for two hours.

The girl pulled her head in, went back to her seat. Odd that she should have found a friend on the platform. He smiled, but she seemed not to see him. The eyes were wide; like her lips they seemed black in the near-darkness of the compartment, but they would of course be blue or grey to go with her colouring. They were staring at him—through him.

She spoke and he was shocked to find her almost in tears. "What —what shall I do?"

"*Do*, my dear? What do you mean?"

"He wants me to get off the train."

"*Who* wants you to get off the train?"

"My fiancé."

"I see." (What else could one say?) "I see."

"He said so, just now. At that last station."

"He was there, was he? At Peterborough?" The Professor sat up, tried to take in the situation.

"Yes. You didn't see him, you were asleep."

"I suppose I was."

"He came right up to the window—fairly close, anyway, just before we moved off. And he told me to—to get off the train."

"You don't think you could be imagining it, do you? What would your fiancé be doing on Peterborough platform? You're going to meet him at Edinburgh, aren't you?"

It was a guess, and it was right. "Yes—he'll be waiting for me. In Edinburgh." She smiled suddenly, seemed to have forgotten her worry.

"No, I'm sure you were imagining it. Fog does strange things sometimes. We see things in it that aren't there, we even hear them. Tell you what—let's get along and have some dinner. At least it'll be brighter in the dining car."

She agreed and they got up and went slowly back along the bending, rolling train.

An hour later they were back at the door of their compartment, and as they slid it open the train began to slow down. Soon it had stopped. It was Grantham; though the fog was now so thick that the Professor had to rely on private knowledge of the route. It had been, despite shocking food—nameless "fish" in a gluey sauce—a pleasant meal. Mona Sinclair, for that was her name, had opened like a flower in the light and warmth of the dining car. He plied her with questions, because he was genuinely interested. She was Scots, but working as a secretary in a London office, living in "digs" at Highgate. She was indeed engaged and wearing a small solitaire diamond which he duly admired. Her fiancé was a lieutenant in the Black Watch. From the photo which she produced from her handbag he was a personable young fellow—very young—a bit on the stocky side, with a well-meant, patchy moustache. Like her, he had fair colouring with yellow, sandy hair. They were an unusually handsome couple: they would have masses of handsome children. As for the pelvis, that need not matter.

Suddenly she let out a cry and jumped to the window. "Yes—yes. I can hear——"

This was too much. "There is *nobody* there," he said. "Nobody at *all*."

She ignored him, went on talking to someone outside, and after a moment the Professor began not to trust the evidence of his eyes and ears. He sat up and stared through his window. There were shapes moving about in the fog, fish in a muddy pool.

She pulled her head in again, eyes staring. It could have been another person altogether from the delightful creature he had talked with in the dining car. "I must go, must go. He's insisting——"

He seized her wrist as she made to open the carriage door. "You're imagining it. There isn't a soul out there, and certainly no one has said a word."

She tried to break free. "You're hurting me."

"Not as much as you'll hurt him, hurt Angus, if you get off the train here. He's waiting for you at Waverley Station, you said so yourself. How can he possibly be *here*?" He let go the wrist.

"But can't you *see*?" She turned to the window and pointed. "He's there—just there. In his uniform, see?"

There was no one. Even the fish in the muddy pool had swum off.

She picked up her overnight bag, made to open the door, and he literally shouted at her. "*Sit down!* D'you hear me? *Sit down.*" The Professor knew about hysterical women.

As if in a trance, she did so, and the train moved off. He stood up, back to the door, just in case.

For a few moments she seemed calm, and when at last he caught her eye he smiled. "My dear, if you'd got off there, in thick fog in the middle of Lincolnshire, you'd never have reached Edinburgh. Or Angus."

She stared at him.

He sat down and soon was dozing again. Once again he awoke, just as the train was entering a station. This would be York. "It's only York," he said. "We'll be off again in a moment."

But now, when the train halted, there was no holding her. She leapt suddenly to her feet, pulled the window wide open and started to talk hysterically into the night. "Oh, darling, of course I will, I *will*——"

"Miss Sinclair," said the Professor. "We will get out together—and have a chat with Angus."

"Oh. Oh, all right. We'll get out together. Of course."

He got to his feet, opened the carriage door with one hand and held her firmly with the other, letting her lead him a few yards along the platform. Then she stopped.

"Well, my dear?"

"He went."

He wished he'd never clapped eyes on the girl. "Dammit," he said, "can't you see the whole thing's imagination? You're over-excited, that's all. Angus is waiting for you *in Edinburgh*. Whatever happens, you've got to get there. Come back on board, and I'll give you a sedative to calm your nerves."

"No. *No*. I'm getting off. You hear me?—I'm getting off. Angus said so." She turned to go back for her luggage.

"All right. If you feel so strongly about it, it's as well that you do. But you're making a big mistake."

She had her overnight case, her handbag.

"What are you going to do? It's late. Have you any money?"

"I shall be all right, thank you. I'll find a hotel. And I've got lots of money." She jumped down from the carriage. "Goodbye—and thank you for—for being kind."

"What do I tell him if——?" But she was gone. And when he got back to the compartment it was with annoyance that he saw her seat occupied by another young woman. He glanced up at his luggage, confirmed that he was in the right compartment and leant back, closed his eyes.

He slept through Newcastle, wasn't conscious of Berwick or the border. And somewhere between the Scottish border and his destination it happened.

He awoke to feel the train lurch beneath him, to look into the staring eyes of a girl, the dark-haired girl opposite. Her mouth was open and as he dragged himself into consciousness she screamed. At that moment the carriage lurched over on its side. He could see earth and stones through the window which now splintered into a million fragments, and he was flung like a cricket ball across the compartment as the carriage decelerated from sixty miles or more an hour to zero. Somehow he almost managed to avoid the girl as he crashed. She was still screaming, but he heard no noise: it had been drowned in the other screams, of splintering wood and glass, of tortured metal. She was forced back in her seat by the same momentum that impelled him towards her, and as his head struck a panel exhorting him to spend holidays on the Isle of Wight, he lost consciousness in a thunderous stab of pain. Just before he did, he heard the wooden case, with his books and instruments in it, shoot across the compartment.

He had no idea how long he could have been unconscious, but woke to find himself lying on the splintered door. It was absolutely dark. There seemed to be blood—it was hot and sticky—all over him, and yet he could feel no pain. He moved his limbs one at a time. Only one, the left arm, seemed under control, prepared to do what he told it. The other arm was pinned under another body, as was his right leg. The left leg, from the excruciating pain it now gave him, must be broken in more than one place. Compound fracture. Hell.

With his free left arm he fished out a lighter, flicked till it lit. What he saw filled him with such horror and confusion that when it blew out he made no attempt for half a minute to re-light it. The dark-haired girl had been badly hurt and there was nothing he could do for her. Blood from a wound in the head had drenched them both and she was unconscious, quite possibly dead, with an arm twisted grotesquely around behind her back and her neck at an impossible angle. With a gasp of horror he realized that probably his own heavy case had done it. It lay there in two halves, hinges broken, books and instruments flung grotesquely round the compartment. Obstetrical forceps lay across the girl's stomach.

He could hear moaning, a dreadful moaning, from down the carriage, and with an effort he lit his lighter again and struggled into a more or less kneeling position. Gently he touched the blood-smeared head.

It dropped, like a heavy vase from a mantelpiece, and hung at another sickening angle. The Professor had seen death in many guises, but now he retched.

It was an hour before firemen hacked a way into the carriage. By this time he had laid the body out, closed the staring black eyes, made an attempt to "tidy up". With his tie and handkerchief he had splinted his leg so that he was able to drag himself about the compartment without too much pain. The ambulance men were cool, efficient and complimentary: "Mon, that's a grrrrand job ye've done on yersel'."

The pair of them, dead girl, crippled doctor, were loaded on stretchers and carried a hundred yards in darkness—the fog, ironically enough, had cleared completely since the crash—to carriages on a siding. In a minute he was on the carriage floor beside a man on another stretcher who was moaning softly to himself. He thought of volunteering his services, then realized that without drugs or equipment, but with a compound fracture of the femur, he would be more nuisance than help. He refused the offer of morphia and a little later the relief train chugged off.

The accident had taken place very near Edinburgh, for it was only minutes before they arrived at Waverley. A section of platform had been roped off, there were a hundred photographers with flashbulbs at the ready just behind the barrier. There were also a great many agitated men and women.

His stretcher was unloaded and then, because one ambulance had departed and another not yet returned, he was placed on the platform near the barrier. A man in overalls, perhaps a mechanic from an all-night garage, leant over and put a lighted Woodbine between his lips. "Thank you, thank you, how very kind——" he mumbled.

Then suddenly his mouth fell open, the cigarette rolled to his chest. Staring past the mechanic, he fumbled for it, burnt his fingers and got it back into his mouth. "Ye're a'right?" asked the man.

The Professor ignored him. "I say," he said, very loudly. "You there, in the Black Watch——"

"Yes, yes——" said the young kilted officer. "Can I help you, sir?" He elbowed his way to the barrier and leant over, addressing the older man on his stretcher. "Can I get you anything?"

On a night like this, the Professor hardly dared trust himself. He looked up at the friendly, worried face, its straggling moustache, and spoke. "You're Angus?"

"*Yes*, sir."

"And you have a fiancée. Miss Sinclair?"

"Oh *yes*, sir. I *have*. Can you—can you tell me about her?"

This was more like it: this was the only pleasant thing that had happened for hours. "Yes—I have good news for you. She wasn't on this train. She was in my compartment, but she got out at York. She'll be in a hotel there."

"Oh, thank God. Thank God."

"I thought you'd like to know," said the Professor with becoming modesty.

"Oh, thank you, sir. What a relief." Then the young face looked puzzled. "I wonder why she got off?"

"She seemed to have some strange feeling that you—yes, *you*—

were calling to her, asking her to get off. Perhaps some premonition of this whole ghastly affair." His leg was beginning to ache terribly: he wished he'd had the morphia. "I——" He thought better of telling the young man he had gone to great pains, trying to *stop* her getting off the train.

"Good night, sir. And God bless you." The squat, manly figure strutted off in its dark-green kilt.

Someone offered him a swig from a quarter-bottle of whisky, but he politely refused. Really, it had been an astounding affair. Enough to make one believe in second sight. He wondered whether the young man had been really wishing her off the train, whether either or both had felt premonition of disaster.

The ambulance came, he was loaded into it, and a few minutes later unloaded at the Casualty section of an Edinburgh hospital. Probably he knew the hospital well, but Professors, particularly of Gynaecology, seldom enter Casualty, and certainly not horizontally. He wondered whether the staff might recognize him. Probably not: he was still caked brown with blood. Blood from that tragic creature who had so unwittingly entered a doomed compartment, sat in a doomed seat.

He seemed to be spending the night on floors. Once again his stretcher had been dumped at floor level and he was beginning to get annoyed. In a minute he would struggle to his feet and demand attention. As he pondered this, he caught sight of a shoe projecting over the edge of a rubber-covered couch near his head. The shoe was half on, half off, a female foot.

Something about it made him catch his breath.

But this was ridiculous. A.T.S. Issue shoes would be worn by half the young women of Britain for the next five years. A doctor and nurses were fussing about this one, giving a plasma transfusion. He sat up on his elbow to see.

"Yes?" said the nurse.

"Shut up," said the Professor. Then to the horror of all around, he pulled himself up by the frame of the rubber-covered couch till he was standing at the end of it, standing unsteadily on his one good leg.

"Ohhh!" he said.

"Keep quiet!" said the doctor. "Very ill—fighting chance——"

"Miss—Miss Sinclair! Mona! You—*you got off at York!*"

The eyes half opened, then closed and a faint smile lit the ivory features. "Changed mind—last—last minute. H-had to run——"

Whether Mona Sinclair died in that moment or later the Professor never knew. He hoped it was then—for she was smiling. The next evening when he was comfortably settled in a private room at the Infirmary, with doctors young and old fussing over the enormous cocoon of his leg, he read the List of Dead in the paper. He got to the Ss, failed at first to see it, and took heart.

Then—there it was: Sinclair, Miss Mona. Highgate, London.

"What a dreadful story," I said. The old man's face, despite half a bottle of vinage port, had gone suddenly white as he came to the end of his tale.

He sat silent for a whole minute. Then he said, "You know what *really* upsets me?"

"No."

"Just can't get it out of my head. What *can* that young man think?"

The Black Dahlia

When a crime of peculiar horror is committed, there is often a rush by unbalanced people to confess to it. In the case of the Black Dahlia murder, which took place in Hollywood just after the Second World War, no less than thirty mixed-up people, including one Lesbian, confessed to the crime.

But not one of them had done it. The crime remains unsolved to this day.

The victim's name was Elizabeth Short, and she was born in 1925 at Medford, near Boston, Massachusetts. The name Black Dahlia was not given to her until much later.

There were five daughters in the Short family, and Elizabeth, or Betty as she was called, came in the middle. When she was six years old her parents separated. Her father, Cleo Short, went to the West Coast to live, taking Virginia, the eldest daughter, with him. Phoebe Short and her four other daughters remained in Medford.

It was the middle of the depression, and they did not have an easy life. Betty had a difficult childhood. She was insecure, neurotic, discontented and restless.

She grew up into a beautiful girl—tallish, with a lovely figure, delicate skin, raven-black hair, and blue provocative eyes. In 1942 she was seventeen. America was at war. Business was booming and there were jobs for all.

Betty left school and went to Miami where she became a waitress in an Army Air Force centre.

She started her love life at an unhappy time. An exceedingly attractive and susceptible girl thrown among hundreds of young servicemen—men who were here today and gone tomorrow, perhaps to their deaths—she was bound to get hurt.

In the Second World War the flying-men were the most glamorous and sought-after heroes, and were often spoilt, and selfish in their treatment of girls. It was the old, old story of war, of brief, passionate love affairs in which the girl was expected to give herself completely to the man. The gift of her body was a little thing, for he was giving his very life to his country. The man was the hero. The girl, as often as not, was held in contempt, not only by society, but by the fighting-men themselves. In the United States they called them Victory Girls, and the term was meant as no compliment.

Betty soon tired of the life and became bitterly disillusioned with men. She wrote to her father, who was working in the Navy Yard in Richmond, California, and asked him for help. He sent her fare and in 1942 she went to live with him in Vallejo, a town on the north side of San Francisco Bay.

Virginia, the eldest daughter, was married by now and living in nearby Berkeley. Cleo Short was anxious to do his best for Betty. He knew she had had a rough time since the family break-up. His idea was for her to go back to school and keep house for him. He was earning good money in the nearby shipyard at Richmond.

But Betty had been too spoilt by the loose, free-and-easy life at the Florida Air Force centre to settle down to the humdrum existence her father wanted. California was full of young servicemen bound for the Pacific and, of course, she was soon seeking their company.

Despite her father's protests, she was always out with soldiers. It led to endless rows between father and daughter. In 1943 she was caught in a police raid on a café which was serving liquor to minors. She was booked as a delinquent, and her father, fed up with her behaviour, offered no objection to the Californian authorities putting Betty on a train and ordering her to return to her mother in Medford, Mass.

But Betty had no intention of returning to respectable Medford, which was no place for a good-time girl. She left the train at Santa

Barbara, a few miles outside Los Angeles, and got herself a job at Camp Cooke, as a civilian employee in the post exchange. She stayed there quite a long time, and it was apparently the happiest period of her tragic young life.

She lived with a sergeant for a while, and then fell passionately in love with an Air Force major—Matt Gordon, Jr., of Pueblo, Colorado. But he was drafted to India and killed in an air crash.

Meanwhile she had an affair with another young pilot, Lieutenant Joseph George Fickling. But early in 1946 she did finally return to Medford to visit her mother. She stayed there several months, waiting in vain to hear from Matt Gordon, not knowing until August that he had been killed.

It was Lieutenant Fickling who could not get this tragic, lovely girl out of his mind. In April he wrote to her at Medford:

"I have always remembered you. I can't deny that I get awfully lonesome sometimes, and wonder if we haven't been very childish and foolish about the whole affair. Have we?" He suggested that she returned to the West Coast, saying that no one would be happier to see her than he would.

But Betty stayed in Medford too long making up her mind, hoping against hope to hear from her real love, Matt Gordon. She finally returned to California, only to find that Fickling had changed his mind about her and had already left for Texas to be discharged from the Air Force.

She wrote to him, and received this reply: "You say in your letter that you want us to be good friends. Are you really sure what you want?" He told her bluntly that marriage, or even engagement, was out of the question. "When I get out of the Army my plans are very indefinite and uncertain."

This was after she had heard of Matt Gordon's death, and it was an added blow. She was utterly down, neurotic, depressed—the good-time girl reaping what she had sown during those gay wartime years.

Things were different now with the coming of peace. Betty must live as best she could, and that meant making full use of her abundant physical charms.

She had now become Beth Short and hoped to get into pictures. She went to Hollywood and teamed up with a girl named Lynn Martin, who was only fifteen, but described as hard and practical where men and money were concerned. Together they haunted the cafés of Hollywood trying to make contact with the right people.

She soon discovered that Hollywood was full of girls with looks but no talent, and that it is the most cruel and heart-breaking place in the world.

The net result of their campaign to get into pictures was that she and Lynn became "party girls" at certain Hollywood gatherings which the film city preferred not to talk about.

It was at these erotic revels that she became known as the Black Dahlia. This name was given to her not only because of her mass of magnificent black hair, but also because she always wore black clothes, black underwear and black nylons. Pictures taken of her at this time showed her as a provocative-looking sex-pot.

Poor Beth was now on the edge of prostitution, if not there already. She pulled herself up suddenly, parted company with Lynn Martin and became friendly with twenty-two-year-old Ann Toth, a screen extra who had had a small part in *The Razor's Edge*. Ann Toth introduced her to a middle-aged theatre owner, Mark Hansen, who invited Beth to live with him, which she did.

From the cosy hospitality of the Hansen apartment in San Carlos she made dates with innumerable men in an almost frantic attempt to find what she wanted—love, security and understanding, perhaps. Who knows what she did want? But whatever it was, she did not find it this way, and suddenly she threw everything up and returned home to Medford—right across the continent.

Disappointment awaited her there as well. She did not fit in. All her sisters were respectably married. The glamorous Black Dahlia was completely out of place in the cool and rarefied air of suburban Boston.

In December 1946 she was back again in Los Angeles. She was twenty-one, lonely, embittered, perhaps frightened. Life held nothing for her. Hollywood was the only place she knew and the only place where she had any friends. But she knew it was the one place where there was utterly no future for her. There was no hope of getting into pictures, nor much hope of marriage. The place was full of pretty faces and provocative figures, and the men she met were after only one thing. What else could she do but go back to the bed-hopping party life?

But she teamed up again with Ann Toth, still scratching a living as an extra, and tried to make a go of things. Beth worked as a waitress, posed in the nude for photographers and haunted the Hollywood cafés.

On 6 December she left the boarding house where she and Ann were living, saying she was going to visit her sister. Two days later she turned up in an all-night movie in San Diego. What she was doing those two days is a mystery. The police wondered if she told a deliberate lie to throw someone off her trail. They thought it might cast a light on the motive for the murder.

Mrs Vera French of San Diego met Beth at this all-night movie, and the girl told her a pathetic but untrue story that her husband had died in the war and the baby she bore him had also died. Mrs French was greatly sympathetic with the lovely, lonely girl and invited her to live with her and her daughter. Beth stayed with them through December and over Christmas and New Year.

She became friendly with a man whom she introduced to Mrs French as a "business associate". This man was six feet tall, with red hair. On 8 January Beth received a telegram which said: "Wait. I'll be down for you."

This telegram threw her into a state of excited expectation. She packed her things and in the evening the red-haired man arrived in a car. As they got in there was an argument. She wanted him to drive her to Los Angeles to visit her sister. Mrs French heard him protest that he could not do this as he had business in San Diego in the morning.

But Beth was insistent and said that if he would not take her, she would go by bus. The man then agreed that business could wait. They drove off.

That was the last that was seen of her until her body was found.

Finding a body is always a shock, but the man who found the body of the Black Dahlia was horror-stricken.

He lived in a housing estate on the outskirts of Los Angeles and on the morning of 15 January 1947 he saw the body of a woman lying just off the sidewalk. When he approached it, he was shattered to discover that the body had been cut cleanly in half at the waist.

Poor Beth had fallen into the hands of a sadist who, before killing her, had tied her up, gagged and tortured her. Her mouth had been slashed, her breasts had been mutilated and her skull had been smashed in. The lower part of her body had been cut open. There was evidence that she had been suspended upside down while this torture was performed.

Afterwards the murderer had cut the body in half so cleanly and skilfully that not one vital organ had been damaged. Then both halves of the body had been washed and drained completely of all blood and fluids. It was estimated that she had been dead between eight and fourteen hours before she was found.

She was identified through her fingerprints, as she had been a government employee at Camp Cooke.

Detectives deduced from tyre marks on the little-frequented road where the body was found that the murderer had brought the body by car from the south, that is from the direction of San Diego, that the body was dragged out of the car, left on the lot and then the killer continued his journey northwards. The tyre marks were of a common pattern.

A man who lived close to where the body was found said that on the night before it was discovered he saw an old battered four-door sedan, about a 1935 model, parked near the spot. There was a man near the car who presently got in and drove off.

Ann Toth told the police she last saw Beth in the company of an Air Force lieutenant early in December.

Another friend. said that Beth had left her trunk at Los Angeles Union Station when she returned from Medford, as she did not have the money to redeem it from the railway express office. The police examined the trunk, finding many pictures of men in uniform, ranging from privates to a lieutenant-colonel. They found letters from Lieutenant Fickling.

Fickling was traced to Charlotte, North Carolina, where he was working as a pilot for a commercial airline. He was able to convince the police that he had not seen Beth since April of the previous year. He said he was never engaged or married to her.

A great murder hunt was now on. Squads of detectives combed the Los Angeles district asking endless questions. They knew there was a dangerously homicidal psychopath at large, and one who obviously had a knowledge of anatomy. But they discovered no clues which would lead them to any such suspect.

Not that clues were lacking. A number of people came forward with what seemed like promising leads.

A man who worked in an apartment house where Beth had once lived said that on 11 January he heard two women quarrelling in the building. He believed one of them was the dead girl. Beth's hairdresser said she had told him that she had been afraid of a red-haired Marine and only went out with him because she was afraid to say no. The description of the Marine tallied with that of the man who had called for Beth at Mrs French's house.

This man was eventually traced. He was twenty-five-year-old Robert Manley of South Gate, California, a salesman, married, with a young son. He said he first saw Beth when she gave him the eye at San Diego bus station on 8 December. When he left Mrs French's house with her on the evening of 8 January they drove to a motel where they booked in as man and wife. But apparently Beth was sick that night, and Manley had a disappointing time. She sat up in a chair all night wrapped in blankets. The next day he drove her to Los Angeles, where he left her at the Biltmore Hotel waiting for her sister who had not turned up. That was the last he saw of her.

Manley said that there were some scratches on Beth's arms which she told him had been inflicted upon her by an Italian boy friend in San Diego who was jealous and mean to her.

Manley convinced the police that on the night of the murder he was at home with his wife and child. He submitted to a lie-detector test and was completely cleared of suspicion.

In the same way every other clue, every other lead was carefully pursued, without any results.

The lack of clues was made up for by the rush of crackpots to confess to the crime. Each phoney confession had to be carefully examined by the patient, if harassed, Los Angeles police department.

The murderer still had the final touch to make to this gruesome crime.

Ten days after the murder, on 24 January, an unsealed envelope reached Los Angeles post office. On the envelope were pasted letters cut from magazine advertisements, which read: "To the Los Angeles *Examiner* and other papers: Here is Dahlia's belongings. Letter to follow."

In the envelope were Beth's birth certificate, a cutting of the death in India of Major Matt Gordon, a social security card, her identification card, some snapshots, a membership card of the "Hollywood Wolves Association", her comb, her make-up and the little black address book she had acquired from Mark Hansen, with one page torn out.

Three days later a second Los Angeles paper received another note of cut-out letters which read: "Here it is. Turning in Wed. Jan 29, 10 a.m. Had my fun at police. Black Dahlia Avenger." A second note posted in Pasadena said: "Dahlia killer cracking. Wants terms." Three hours after the 29 January deadline, the Los Angeles Homicide Squad received another note which read: "I'm afraid I won't get a fair deal."

That was the end of it. All the rest is theory and phoney confessions.

The police believed that the girl was held captive somewhere in the Los Angeles area in some isolated shack all that week. Her eyebrows had been bleached and her hair hennaed. This, it was believed, was done by the murderer to conceal identification, as Beth herself never used such things.

The police had three theories. Beth was not difficult to pick up, and she might have found herself unwittingly at the mercy of a sadistic sex killer, a complete stranger to her. The second theory was that she was killed by someone she tried to blackmail, who then mutilated her to make it look like a sex crime. The third theory, and a favourite one, was that she was killed by a vengeful lesbian whom she had repulsed—though not the one who confessed.

The first theory is certainly the most probable. She was just the sort of girl who would get herself into that position. On the other hand, no one could say that the kind of life which she led was the cause of her appalling death. The most innocent and virtuous girls sometimes fall victims to these sadistic monsters, despite the saying that a nice girl is never found in a trunk.

It must not be forgotten that many men, too, had been victims of bestial sadism of this type during the Second World War, at the hands of both the Germans and the Japanese. It is within the region of possibility that a man, unhinged by experiences of this kind, might have committed the Black Dahlia atrocity.

The police believed that this was a solo effort on the part of the murderer, who was never caught, and who did not repeat the crime. This is unusual, because murderers of this type usually don't stop once they start. There could be many reasons why this murderer only struck once. He or she, could have been convicted for another crime, or have gone into an asylum, as Jack the Ripper was supposed to have done, or even have been killed in a road accident.

The depressing thing about this crime, apart from the phoney confessions by mentally disturbed would-be murderers, was the fact that during the next year six more murders of the same type were committed in the Los Angeles area. Some of these murderers were caught, and the police were certain that none of these crimes had any connection with the Black Dahlia atrocity, but were merely inspired by it.

Scent of Death

Madame X looked round the sitting-room of the small flat into which she had moved only a few days ago, and was pleased. She wondered once more, as she had many times since she had seen the results of the labours of carpenters and interior decorators, why she had not thought before of converting these five rooms at the top of the old Marylebone house into living-quarters for herself, and so saving the expense of leasing the fashionable flat which she had felt she must have as a symbol of her business success.

Here she was not only saving money. The connoisseurs of the service she offered—and only connoisseurs could afford her fees—were more than willing to come to the quaint house despite the slight drabness of its situation. And if they had no hesitation in giving chauffeurs and taxi-drivers the address, surely they would not look down their noses when they knew that she lived on the premises. Her professional reputation was such that had she lived in a Soho garret her clients would still have clamoured to come to Marylebone.

At all events, her French sense of waste was appeased. The rooms, which were above the consulting and treatment rooms, had been unused except when cartons of lotions and creams were dumped in one of them on the rare occasions that the stockroom became over-crowded. Now they were being put to good use; and they obviously appreciated it, for they seemed to be preening themselves. Besides having the sheen of freshness on them, which was reflected in the two or three antique pieces of simple taste, they had the faintly scented aura of feminine beauty provided by the perfumes that wafted up the staircase from the professional rooms below.

Madame X glanced at the French ormolu clock on the mantelpiece. Her guests would be arriving in ten minutes, and she decided that there would be just time for a martini to complete her feeling of well-being. She mixed her drink and then, hearing the movements of Mrs Alexander in the kitchen, poured out a glass of sherry and carried it through.

"Everything under control?" she asked.

It was a rhetorical question, she knew, for Mrs Alexander always had everything in the kitchen under control. She was a treasure, and Madame X after five years could not visualize what life had been like in the pre-Alexander era.

At sixty-two, and a widow—and therefore without ties, for her son and his family lived near Birmingham, and her daughter in married quarters at Portsmouth—she was as vigorous as a woman twenty years her junior. She was not a *cordon bleu*, but only because she disdained paper qualifications. When Madame X had once asked if she had not thought of becoming really professional, she had bridled a little and said, "Would a diploma hanging on a wall make me cook any better? The proof of the pudding is in the eating." And Madame X had to admit that she was right.

"Is everything to your satisfaction, Mrs Alexander?" she went on. "I mean the equipment and the way it's arranged?"

"Oh, yes, madam, thank you—perfect. But so it ought to be since you asked my advice, didn't you?"

"I'm glad," Madame X said. "Sometimes things come out differently from the way they are planned on paper."

"Are you pleased with the rest of the flat, madam?"

"Very."

"I think it's all lovely. And one of the nicest things about it is the beautiful scent that comes up from downstairs."

"I'm glad you approve."

"Oh, I do. And I'm sure your friends will be very envious when they see it. You'll eat at half-past eight, madam?"

"If you're ready."

"I shall be ready on the dot, madam."

A bell rang in the passage outside.

"Ah, the first arrivals!" Madame X exclaimed, and finishing her martini in a gulp, went to answer the door.

The next five minutes were spent, amid exclamations of wonder and delight, in showing her guests round the flat.

"My dear, it's wonderful!" Signora Capucci declared again and again. "Is it not so, Freddie?"

Freddie was more laconically English in his response.

"Very satisfactory, *cara*," he agreed.

"But everything fits in so well! Doesn't everything fit in well, Freddie?"

"Very well," Freddie Palmer acquiesced.

"How ingenious you've been! I think Rosa has been very ingenious, don't you, Freddie?"

"Very ingenious."

"And that delicious scent!" Signora Capucci said, drawing in a deep breath of it.

"From the salons," Madame X explained.

"Exquisite! It is exquisite, isn't it, Freddie?"

"Exquisite," Mr Palmer agreed.

"Sherry or a dry martini?" Madame X asked.

She had just handed them their drinks when the doorbell rang again.

At the door George Statham greeted her with a kiss and a bouquet of freesias and white camellias.

"Darling!" she exclaimed. "You're naughty! They must have cost the earth!"

"Not quite," Statham smiled, pleased by her genuine pleasure. "I couldn't really afford the earth."

"Still . . ." she smiled, squeezing his hand.

"Who are the others?" he whispered as he hung up his coat.

"Maria Capucci and Freddie Palmer," she told him.

"Good," he said. "Fun . . ."

"If Freddie can get a word in, darling!"

"He will," Statham assured her. "Hasn't everything turned out well!"

"You like it?"

"Very much. Strange how spacious it seems."

They passed into the sitting-room, and he greeted the others. Madame X mixed and poured him a dry martini.

"Hasn't Rosa been clever, George?" Signora Capucci remarked.

"Very."

"And don't you agree that the finishing touch is the scent?"

Statham sniffed.

"From the rooms below, I suppose."

Madame X nodded.

"You could make a fortune if you put it into an air-spray," Freddie Palmer said.

"One would never get the blend if one deliberately tried," Madame X replied.

"No, I suppose not," Freddie Palmer agreed. "Well, dear Rosa, cheers and every happiness during your sojourn here."

They drank and the conversation turned to other subjects.

Presently, as they talked, Madame X became aware of a strange unpleasant smell which seemed to be increasing in volume every minute. At first she could not identify its sickly pungency, which bit sharply into the lining of the nostrils and caught at the back of the throat, and yet she was sure that she had smelled something like it before.

Then she told herself that she was imagining it. It was a reaction to Maria Capucci's harping on the perfume coming up from downstairs. She drew in a deep breath, hoping to dispel the horrid stench, that she felt almost to be choking her, by a draught of the pleasantly scented air that was not Maria Capucci's imagination. But instead, the acrid mephitis almost overcame her, and she found herself controlling her troubled stomach only with difficulty.

She jumped to her feet and going to the drinks table began to mix more martinis. Glancing up, she saw in the mirror above the table that Maria Capucci was holding her handkerchief to her mouth and nose, and was signalling to Freddie Palmer   o nodded in response.

"My God!" she exclaimed, swinging round, the ice in the mixer clinking like a leper's bell as she did so. "Can you smell it too?"

"But what is it?" Maria Capucci almost choked. "A few moments ago this room smelled delicious, but now . . ."

"Let me open a window," Freddie Palmer suggested.

He crossed to one of the windows and threw up the lower sash.

"Do you smell it, too, George?" Madame X asked Statham.

"I'm afraid so," he said.

"But where is it coming from?" Maria asked. "It's like rotting corpses!"

Rotting corpses! Maria was right, Madame X told herself. Now she recognized the smell and remembered where she had encountered it.

Shortly after VE-Day she had gone to visit her parents who had remained in France throughout the Occupation. The village in which they lived had seen some of the heaviest fighting around Caen, and very few of the houses were habitable. Though the work of clearing away the great mounds of rubble was being pressed forward, there was still, even after several months, much to be done, and every mound moved revealed skeletons of men, women and children, or fragments of them.

This was disconcerting enough, but what had impressed itself upon her most was the smell of rotting human flesh that hung over the village like a pall still, though not one shred of sinew clung to a single bone uncovered. It was as if Death was determined to set up a permanent memorial there. For weeks after her return to England she found her nostrils assailed by the sweet-sharp sickly odour every time she thought of the village.

The opening of the window in no way reduced the smell in the room, which seemed to be swirling about them in noxious gusts like the hot mist above a tropical swamp. Every minute it seemed to increase in strength.

"What can it be?" Madame X asked.

"A dead rat under a floor-board," Freddie Palmer suggested.

"Could be," George Statham agreed.

"But why should it suddenly begin to smell now?"

"Gases and all that sort of thing," Palmer said.

"If it is a rat, the trouble will be locating it."

"Well, we can't stay here. Dinner will be ready in five minutes. Let's go into the dining-room," Madame X suggested.

"Let me offer you coffee at my flat," George Statham said.

"Would you?" Madame X said gratefully.

"Of course." To the others he said, "I'm only just round the corner."

"What a shame, madam," Mrs Alexander commiserated, when

Madame X told her what had happened. "Well, I'm ready when you are."

As always, Mrs Alexander's dinner was impeccable. Smoked salmon, followed by casseroled pigeons on red cabbage, a Milanese soufflé and an exactly ripe camembert washed down by Veuve Clicquot 1959 temporarily put all thoughts of the fetid atmosphere of the sitting-room out of their minds.

It was almost a quarter to ten before George Statham suggested they should adjourn to his flat for coffee, and only then was the earlier experience of the evening recalled.

"I must get my handbag from the sitting-room," Madame X said.

"Let me get it for you," George offered.

"Oh, would you? I don't think I can bear to go into that room again this evening," she said.

Seconds later they heard George calling to them.

"It's gone," he was saying. "Completely gone! How odd! Come and see for yourselves."

They went into the room reluctantly, and stood, with nostrils twitching, sniffing the air.

"You're right, George!" Freddie Palmer agreed. "It can't be a rat, then. Where do your drains run, Rosa?"

Madame X laughed.

"Goodness, I've no idea."

"I should get the plumber in tomorrow, just to be on the safe side, dear," Maria Capucci suggested. "One can even smell the perfume again. It is very strange."

"I'll tell Mrs Alexander we'll have coffee after all," Madame X said, and went to the kitchen humming happily.

It was almost midnight before her guests eventually took their leave, loud in their praise and sincere in their thanks.

"Don't forget to have the plumber round in the morning," Maria Capucci reminded her from the doorway.

"I won't," Madame X promised her.

But she did forget. The schedule for the day was a particularly heavy one, and at half past eight an assistant telephoned to say that she was ill and would be unable to work. Consulting the programme, she decided that it could not be adjusted and that she would have to take the absent girl's place herself.

By six o'clock in the evening she was so weary that she cancelled a visit to the cinema and supper with one of her woman friends and asked Mrs Alexander to leave her something cold on a tray. She told herself, as she lay thawing the weariness out of her body in a warm bath, that no one who did not actually give beauty treatments realized how physically exhausting it could be. For a brief moment she wondered if she were paying her assistants enough —and sensibly decided that she was.

When eventually she emerged from her bath she put on a house-coat and went into the kitchen. On the tray Mrs Alexander had left her cold breast of chicken with coleslaw and watercress under a silver entrée cover. By it was a cup of cold consommé, and on a dessert-plate a delicious-looking pear.

She carried the tray into the sitting-room. She would eat as she watched the television.

She turned on the set, and while it was warming up mixed herself a martini. She sipped it, her feet curled up under her on the settee.

When she had finished her drink, just as the eight o'clock pro-gramme was beginning, she drew the table on which she had put the tray towards her and picked up the cup of consommé. She had taken no more than three or four spoonfuls when she became aware of the rotten stench, faint at first, but momently growing stronger, which had disturbed them the previous evening.

Her reactions verging on terror, she waited. As the raw, tainted odour grew in volume, a sensation as of a hand clutching at her throat almost suffocated her. Her heart began to pound and swell until she felt that it must burst. She wanted to rush out of the room, but her limbs refused to obey the commands of her brain.

Breathing heavily she drew the fetid atmosphere of the room down within her, until it seemed to her that she was actually con-suming decomposing flesh. Her stomach revolted and she retched, vomiting into the handkerchief she managed to hold to her mouth, a quantity of the martini she had lately drunk.

By a superhuman effort she managed to get to her feet and make her way from the room. The atmosphere had turned icy cold, yet under her house-coat her goose-pimple-studded skin was moist with perspiration. As she reached the doorway she staggered under what seemed to be a blow in the small of her back; as if some presence in the room were pushing her out of it.

Sobbing she hurried into her bedroom and telephoned George Statham. Fortunately he was in.

"It's happened again," she told him. "May I come round?"

"Of course," he said. "I'll come and fetch you."

"Angel!" she said. "Come quickly, please. I can't stay here!"

She dressed hurriedly and arrived at the street door just as he drew up.

"Would you like me to go and investigate?" he asked.

"Oh no! Take me away from here," she begged him.

"Have you eaten?"

"No. I was beginning my supper. But I've no appetite now."

"I haven't eaten yet, either," Statham told her, "so perhaps you won't mind keeping me company?"

"Whatever you say, George," she agreed.

She ate a little supper after all and when Statham asked her what she would like to do she had recovered sufficiently to tell him that she would go home to bed.

"Sure?" he asked.

"Quite sure," she said. "I suppose I was overtired. I've recovered now, thanks to you, dear George. I won't go into that room. I'll go to bed."

At the house Statham said he would like to go up with her and see if the stench was still invading the room, or whether, as had happened yesterday evening, it had by this time retreated.

When he went into the room all he could discern was the faint perfume ascending from the rooms below.

"I don't know what to say," he confessed. "Personally, I'm beginning to wonder."

"About what?"

"I won't say at the moment," he said. "But have the architect in, and if he can't suggest a solution and it happens again, then I'll tell you what I think."

The architect came almost as soon as she telephoned him next morning. He discounted the dead-rat theory, not only because a dead rat would stink all the time, but because when the conversion was carried out all the floor-boards had been taken up and the gaps between the joists had been packed with glass fibre.

"Insulation, you know," he explained. "No rat would stay there."

He said, too, that no drains of any description ran anywhere near the room, and in any case, a faulty drain, like a dead rat, would smell permanently and not between eight in the evening and whenever it was the stench departed.

"Except for pulling the place apart, I must confess myself defeated," he admitted. "But if it goes on, that is probably what we shall have to do."

She thanked him and at lunch-time telephoned George Statham.

"I'll come round a little before eight," Statham said, "and if it happens again, I'll tell you what's in my mind."

It happened again. By quarter past eight the stench was so overwhelming that they had to leave the room.

On the way to the Café Royal Statham said, "I think it's something supernatural and the only chance of finding out is to ask a clairvoyant to help."

"Do you really believe . . ." Madame X began.

"Yes. Think what you like, but I've had a couple of very odd experiences I'll tell you about some time."

"Do you know a clairvoyant?" she asked.

"Yes. There's one not far from you in Marylebone High Street. If you agree, I'll ask her to come and investigate."

Statham and Mrs L arrived at quarter to eight the following evening. Mrs L refused a drink "until afterwards", but chatted easily and pleasantly while Madame X and Statham sipped their martinis. Looking at her and listening to her, Madame X thought, she seemed no different from any ordinary comfortably built middle-aged woman.

The clock on the mantelpiece said three minutes past eight precisely when the odour became faintly perceptible. Simultaneously with Madame X's exclamation, Mrs L stood up, saying, "It's beginning. I can see it coming in at the door."

"You can *see* it?"

"Yes, quite clearly. A yellowish emanation which increases in volume with the strength of the smell. It is quite a large cloud now. As large as that gold cushion on the settee. It is beginning to move about the room. It is making in your direction, Mr Statham. Don't move! I want to see what happens."

Statham's instinct had been to duck. But he stood his ground and almost immediately was aware of being enveloped not only in the most nauseating smell but in a current of air so cold that it made him shudder. A shiver of tangible apprehension rippled down his spine, causing him automatically to tighten the muscles in his buttocks as it seemed to attack him there.

"There, it's leaving you now," Mrs L said. "Do you experience any difference?"

"Yes. The smell isn't quite so bad, and I don't feel so cold," he replied.

"It's going towards the window. You are quite right. It is a terrible smell."

"What can it be?" Madame X asked.

"Any one of half a dozen things," Mrs L told her. "It's leaving the window now and crossing to the fireplace. Now it's making in your direction, Madame X. Don't be frightened. I want to see what it intends to do. It has almost reached you. There . . ."

"I can feel it. It's very cold, like last night, and the smell . . . !" Madame X broke off, desperately trying to control a desire to retch.

"It's leaving you," Mrs L said, "and coming towards me. It is as if it's searching for something, someone. Perhaps . . . Ah!"

She stood rigid and quivering for some seconds, not speaking, her hands clasped so tightly below her bosom that the knuckles strained white against the skin.

Presently she sighed and her body relaxed. "It's making for the door," she said. "It has reached the door. Now it is coming back towards me. It is passing behind me."

Suddenly she staggered forward half a pace.

"It is pushing me," she said.

"That happened to me yesterday," Madame X said.

"Perhaps it is trying to tell me to follow it. Let us see. It's going to the door again. Now it's coming back."

Once more she lurched forward, and when she had recovered said, "Yes, it wants me to follow it. It seems to understand what I'm saying, because it is waiting by the door. It's really quite uncanny."

She went to the door and opened it.

"What shall we do? Wait here?" Statham asked.

"I think it would be advisable if you followed me," Mrs L replied. "I may want to ask Madame X something about the house. Do you mind, Madame X?"

"I'm not very happy about it," Madame X began, smiling uncertainly.

"Oh, you won't come to any harm, I assure you."

"Hold my hand," George Statham said, "and I'll lead the way after Mrs L."

"Right!" said Mrs L. "Shall we go? It's leading us down the stairs. I shan't speak any more at the moment, but you will know I am following it."

So in silence George Statham led Madame X after Mrs L down the two flights of stairs to the ground floor. A passage-hallway led from the street door to the stairs and round them to a back door, which opened on to a miniature paved garden. The reception room and the consulting room both opened off the passage—the treatment rooms were above on the first floor—but Mrs L ignored them and turned towards the back of the house.

Half-way between the staircase and the back-door, however, she stopped.

"I presume this door leads to the cellars, Madame X," she said, pointing to a door under the stairs.

"Yes," Madame X told her, "but we don't use the cellars, and I've no idea where the key is."

"The door isn't locked."

"Not locked!" Madame X exclaimed. "But I am sure it has been locked ever since we moved in."

"I am beginning to receive very strong vibrations," Mrs L said. "I think it will be best if you don't come any farther. Will you wait here for me, but whatever you may hear don't come down. Especially you, Mr Statham."

"Don't you need a light, Mrs L?" Madame X asked.

"No thank you. I shall see perfectly well, unless I am very much mistaken. I don't know how long I shall be, but don't be alarmed. Perhaps you could make yourselves comfortable in one of those rooms."

She opened the door leading to the cellar stairs, and as she passed through it Madame X heard the sounds of knocking.

"There is someone down there," she said to Statham. "Do you think it's safe?"

"Why do you say there's someone there?" Statham asked her.

"Didn't you hear the knocking as Mrs L opened the door?"

"No, I didn't," he admitted.

"I heard it very plainly. I think she ought to have left the door open. Supposing whoever—or whatever—is down there attacks her?"

"She told us not to go down whatever we might hear," he reminded her. "She knows what she's up to, and it might be dangerous for her if we did anything she told us not to."

"George, darling," Madame X persisted, "I'm not at all happy about it, all the same."

"Perhaps the knocking you heard wasn't in the cellar at all," he said. "Let's go and make ourselves comfortable in here, as she suggested."

And he took her arm and led her into the consulting room, opposite the cellar door.

But Mrs L heard the knocking as she felt her way carefully but deliberately down the cellar steps, following the shapeless emanation which swayed and eddied before her.

By the time she had reached the bottom of the stairs the vibrations which she had begun to experience as she opened the cellar door had increased, and she knew that any moment now she would come face to face with whatever force it was that was attracting her into this dark, dank, subterranean room. What it was she could not guess.

The fetid smell of the emanation still attacked the inner membranes of her nose and throat. She was icy cold from head to foot, yet she was conscious of moisture trickling down her cheeks from her temples, and irritating the flesh of her armpits. Her head throbbed in rhythm with the knocking, which became louder with every step she forced herself to take.

At the foot of the stairs openings led off to left and right. It was from the right that the sounds of the banging were coming and she felt herself being drawn that way.

As she turned she saw before her a small basement room. She had only a fleeting glimpse of it for the emanation now disappeared and the cellar was plunged in darkness. But though the emanation had gone the sickening odour remained more powerful than ever.

She longed to cover her nose and mouth with her hands, but her elbow joints were locked so that she could not move them. Convinced that she must collapse at any moment, she struggled for breath, her stomach revolting from the assaults of the stench. The knocking, which seemed to be coming from the far end of the cellar, suddenly ceased, but the throbbing in her temples was no less insistent.

Trembling from head to foot, she waited. She knew from long experience that this was all she could do.

Presently the knocking started again, and an aura began to form at the far end of the cellar. It developed rapidly and from little more than a circle of light no bigger than a saucer in seconds it was illuminating the whole place, and by it she saw standing at a bench, hammering at a shoe on an up-ended last, an old bearded man.

He seemed unaware of her as he beat at the sole of the shoe with his hammer, and she had time to note that he was wearing a black long-skirted coat, green with age, and breeches buttoned below the knees; but she saw, too, that his thin shanks were uncovered by stockings, and that his feet were bare. With each blow on the shoe his sparse beard jerked up and down.

Suddenly he turned his head and saw her, and his features became suffused with a malevolence such as she had never before encountered. Slowly and painfully, it seemed, he moved from the bench and began to shuffle soundlessly towards her, the hammer raised threateningly in his right hand.

And as he moved his coat gaped open and revealed that he was shirtless. He was no more than a skin-covered skeleton, every rib plainly discernible. He was so thin as to be obscene, and yet it was not his thinness that shocked her.

In the arch of his ribs a large vivid lump gaped and throbbed, while a similar lump protruded just below his left knee-cap.

She recognized the source of the odour which had been given off by the emanation in Madame X's sitting-room as soon as she saw the suppuration oozing from both. She recognized, too, the disease of which the lumps were symptoms—the plague.

As the old man dragged himself towards her, her impulse was to turn and flee, but she knew that if she did she would have failed in the undertaking she had given George Statham. "If there is anything there," she had told him, "I shall find it and dispel it."

He was very near her now. If she stretched out her hand she would almost touch him, but her arm would not move.

Summoning up her last reserve of courage, she looked at him steadily. "Go in peace!" She forced the words from her quivering lips. "In the name of God, go in peace!"

He stopped in his tracks and lowered the arm brandishing the hammer. For a brief second a smile flitted across his lips—and then he was gone.

In the black darkness of the cellar, Mrs L felt her limbs loosened. With outstretched arm she found a wall and began to make her way back to the stairs. The air in the cellar, she noted, was cool and fresh. With the old man, the stench had also disappeared.

"Are you all right?" Madame X demanded as she emerged from the cellar door.

"Quite all right, thank you," she replied, "except that I am very tired. But that is usual."

"Come upstairs and I will make a cup of tea," Madame X urged her.

"That would be nice," she said, taking Madame X's proffered arm.

It was George Statham who shed the light of history on the whole episode.

At Marylebone Town Hall he was told that in 1665 a shoemaker had lived in the basement of the house which had stood on the site of the present house, and there alone had died of the plague. Not until some time after the emergency was ended were his remains found.

I say remains advisedly, for little flesh clung to the skeleton; the rest had been gnawed away by rats. For some reason, by order of the authorities the bones were denied Christian burial, and were taken at once to the charnel-house where they were burned, with no prayer said over them.

Clearly the old man's soul had longed for the solace of eternity, and this Mrs L seemed to have given him for never since that last evening, now several months ago, has the perfumed pleasantness of Madame X's sitting-room been disturbed.

The Face of Mrs Cartwright

It all happened to Roger Morgan's cousin. It was a story very close to him, and he was reluctant to tell it. I don't suppose he did so more than a dozen times in his life—and on three of those occasions I was present.

Each time, my blood ran cold.

He didn't meet her, this beautiful cousin, until he was eight. Then, as an adoring young boy, he was confronted by an ecstatically beautiful young woman who came all the way from America and yet shared his family name. Not a very striking or unusual name, but at the age of eight Roger Morgan had believed it unique.

She was welcome to it, welcome to anything, everything, Roger could provide—for he loved her, really loved her, at first sight.

When he first met her, Constance Morgan was a gay, fun-loving creature of eighteen, who spoke in a strange, soft, exciting way and had chestnut hair, green eyes and a most entrancing smile. Her home was in Virginia, where a branch of the family had emigrated generations before. I think it was Arlington, but it makes no difference. They were very, very rich, from tobacco. They had now decided to bring their eighteen-year-old daughter to "do Europe".

Constance made much of Roger and was adored in return. All too soon she disappeared from his young life. But when he saw her for the last time, two years later, when he was a man of ten and she a woman of twenty, she had become Constance Cartwright,

397

changed from youth to age, from dazzling beauty to a pale, trembling infirmity that distressed him utterly.

Roger, when he died last year, was a man in his late sixties, so his friendship with, love for, Constance, must have occurred some time during the first decade of this century. He never married and there are no members of the family still living. His father was a prosperous solicitor with rooms in Lincoln's Inn in London—rooms in which Roger himself, until he retired a few years back, was to work for many years.

And it was during her stay in London, those few weeks that Roger always remembered, that his young cousin fell in love. Not, unfortunately, with Roger. Constance fell in love with a man she met at a week-end house-party, a Major Cartwright, officer in some yeomanry regiment. Roger met him and instantly struck up a dislike for the man which he would maintain throughout the time they shared on earth. You must judge for yourself whether this was simply the result of Roger's infatuation with Major Cartwright's wife, or whether there was more to it than that.

For Major Cartwright, aged just forty, met and proposed marriage to his Connie while on home leave from India. And while Connie fell head over heels in love with her much older suitor, Mr and Mrs Morgan from Virginia were considerably less enthusiastic. The details are not clear in my mind, and with Roger gone they never can be. Major Cartwright of the deepset eyes and fierce military moustache pursued his love to Virginia and there, with reluctant blessing from her parents, succeeded in marrying her. A few days later they sailed for England. The Major never went back to India; it was said Connie would hate the climate. After a few months' service in England he retired.

A few months later he bought a surprisingly large farming and shooting estate in Yorkshire. Major and Mrs Cartwright pointed out to their friends that Standings and its three thousand acres had been bought for a song. Perhaps this was in order to convince them that the Major had bought it from his pension and his savings, and not Connie from her capital.

It was at Standings that young Roger next, fleetingly, met his beautiful cousin. He had been invited with his parents to spend a few days, had been met at the little country station by the Major in his large and noisy Daimler and whisked off over moorland roads in a gale of laughter and wit and good fellowship, as if they had known him all their lives. The Major was a charming fellow, and Roger hated him.

Three miles of moorland, then a wooded drive, and suddenly the great bulk of Standings House framed in its trees. She came out as they thundered in, stood with arms wide in greeting as the Daimler halted. Green eyes flashing, she kissed them all, and Roger—still only eight-and-a-bit—almost fainted with the ecstasy of it. The usual, banal things were said, but somehow it seemed as if the company of players, all five of them, had been dropped gently into an eighteenth-century salon, where each phrase they uttered was a jewel, each thought new, exciting. Yes, the train journey had been fun; yes, they had been exactly, surprisingly, thrillingly, on time; what a glorious, surprising place Standings was; how lucky Connie was to have such a domesticated husband, so readily able to beat sword into ploughshare and make a showplace from a run-down estate which he had cleverly bought cheap.

And the neighbours, the other county folk, were delightful. Connie knew her cousins would love them. Some were coming to dinner this evening.

They did, and although Roger was—protesting—in bed, they greatly pleased his parents. Connie was a lucky girl, and they were delighted.

The weekend, for Roger, passed in a haze of love. It was as if Connie knew his feelings (Roger was certain she did) and was anxious to fan them, for she seized so many opportunities to take his small hand in hers and lead him here and there to see paintings or goldfish or ornamental birds. At one stage she rested her cool hand on the back of his neck as she gently propelled him across the lawn to study a pond and its lilies, and it was all he could do not to spin round, fling his arms about her, bury his schoolboy head at the point where it reached, somewhere below her bosom, and tell her he loved her.

However, Roger did none of this and the weekend passed off with decorum. He saw her again in London when she came up for shopping and was as overcome as before by her beauty, her vivacity, her kindness. He wanted of course to go shopping with her, help her round Harrods and the Army & Navy, but that could not be.

That autumn day, in perhaps 1908, was the last time he saw his laughing, lovely cousin. The next time, a year and a bit later, she had changed beyond recognition. Had she placed her hand on the back of his neck he would have been shocked and frightened.

But Connie remained lovely and gay till the end of the year and into the next. It was her occasional letter to Roger's mother which first hinted at something wrong. There was an unfamiliar note of sadness, a hint that the wild winds of Yorkshire, the loneliness, were no longer entirely pleasing to her. It was only a hint, but it was there, and the letters from Constance (as Roger's father continued to call her) began to be dissected at the breakfast table, in front of the children, in an attempt to find out what was wrong.

Then, in a way, they had confirmation. Connie's father wrote from Virginia and asked urgently that investigation be made. He was worried, over there, about the strange note of distress in the letters sent home. He had persuaded other Americans, touring Europe, to call on Major and Mrs Cartwright. These had known her at home and now were shocked by what they saw. They reported that she looked pale and ill, had lost a great deal of weight and hardly ever spoke or smiled. She never laughed. As for poor Major Cartwright, he was obviously very worried about his wife.

Roger's father caught the first train to Yorkshire.

Two days later they were discussing it, while Roger, eyes like organ stops, sat and listened. Yes, Mr Morgan reported, the Major (David, but no one seemed brave enough to use the Christian name) was indeed distressed over the change which had come over his young wife. But the reason seemed absurd: Connie had dreams. In them she would see a face, bearded and cruel, which stared at her. Occasionally, whether her dream discovered the face in Yorkshire, or a London street or even Virginia, the cruel eyes would flash at her, the sneering lips would open slightly as if about to address her.

Then it would simply vanish, as if in a puff of smoke.

Of course, it was all nonsense, and Connie would just have to snap out of it. A holiday abroad had been suggested. This would be bound to do the trick.

"It *was* odd, you know," Roger's father said at the breakfast table, "that face she keeps seeing, the face which seems to terrify her, is one she's seen before, in real life. She *knows* it is——"

And at this point we must stop seeing our story through the eyes of a ten-year-old boy, and piece it together, as Roger did later, to make a continuous narrative.

David Cartwright and his wife sailed for France, on the Dover–Calais steamer, in the spring of 1910. It would be a "rest" for Connie. In easy stages they made their way south across France to Nice. They moved into the Hôtel des Anglais, and the weather was kind to them, for early spring on the Côte d'Azure can be as unpleasant as anywhere else, with icy winds and stormy sea. Day after day, through March and April, the sun shone down, and David and Constance were able to go for walks along the front. By the end of April Connie seemed back to her old self. Certainly she was as beautiful as ever, and crowds of people turned to stare in admiration as she walked by. The roses were back in her cheeks, and she smiled —though not as often, perhaps—as dazzlingly as ever. The green eyes shone.

In the middle of May they left Nice and went to Paris, *en route* for England and home. There had been no dreams at all to disturb Mrs Cartwright's repose. The bearded, cruel face had been forgotten.

They made their way north by easy stages, staying briefly with friends outside Lyons and in Clermont-Ferrand. Everyone agreed that both Cartwrights looked younger, more handsome than anyone remembered them. The Major, at forty-two, had mellowed from peppery soldier to genial gentleman farmer, and Constance, though still showing even less than the twenty-one years or so she had attained, had matured into a beautiful and gracious lady.

They reached Paris on the first of June and moved back into the Ritz. They had spent a night there on the way south and the hotel staff seemed as delighted as their friends to see the change the Riviera had wrought.

Then it happened.

David had gone off early for the day, to talk business with someone, and Connie, after a late breakfast by herself, went out for a stroll in the *Bois*. It was the most heavenly of days, not a puff of cloud in a violet sky, the birds singing lustily, as if their little hearts would break for love of Connie.

An old couple with a dog were pottering along, fifty yards behind her, when they heard a piercing scream and saw the young woman fall to the ground.

They hobbled to the spot and gently turned her over. As they did, her eyes opened and stared at them with an expression of utmost horror. Her mouth fell open.

Very faintly she asked, "Who—who are you?"

So—it was an *Anglaise*: that would account for her behaviour. "Me, *chère Mademoiselle*, I am Monsieur Laufrage. But you, you 'ave just fainted——"

"*Alors*," said Madame Laufrage, gasping with excitement, "*alors*, you 'ave fainted, you 'ave fallen, you 'ave hurt?"

For answer, Connie closed her eyes and Madame Laufrage, certain she had now expired, burst into a shriek even louder than Connie's. A gendarme appeared and asked briskly irrelevant questions of Monsieur Laufrage and wrote in his notebook. Connie opened her eyes and got to her feet, helped by a dozen gallants from the crowd.

To her husband that night she confessed that she had seen the cruel face—the same bearded, deep-eyed face—in the *Bois*. It had appeared from behind a tree, had stared at her. It had been about to rush on her, she had known it. She had fainted.

"But—but Connie darling; you were seeing things."

"No, David. I *know* it was there. I saw it——"

"*Darling* Connie. It could only have been an illusion. This hateful face, a figment of your dreams, could only have impressed itself on you while you slept. And now you imagine you can see it——"

But as the days went by Connie recovered her strength and her courage. She began to realize that he must be right. There had been no one else in the *Bois*—apart from the old couple behind her with their dog. She had made a fool of herself, an utter fool.

And David, when she apologetically mentioned this to him, smiled wryly and agreed. Never mind, it was over now, and they would get back home. Unless of course she would like to stay away a little longer.

Suddenly Connie trembled, without knowing why. It had perhaps been the thought of Yorkshire, a dim reminder of the situation in which she first dreamed her dream. Perhaps it had been David's unsympathetic reaction.

They decided to stay in France a little longer. As the holiday—if one could call it that—had cost a lot of money, Connie got her broker to sell some shares, shares which David had advised her to part with. How fortunate she was in having so loving, so clever, a husband: others might have jibbed at spending three months away from home, nursing a neurotic wife back to health. Others might simply have bundled her off to a nursing home.

They had been happy in the south, and they went back there, to Cap Ferrat. An American friend owned a villa, overlooking the sea and a stone's throw from the lighthouse, and they gladly accepted her kind offer of it for a month. The friend wrote from New York that she had got in touch with all sorts of nice people, from as far apart as Monte Carlo and Cannes, to call on them. The Cartwrights in turn would be able to visit them. Obviously, the change, the meeting with gay, sympathetic people, would work wonders with Connie.

And certainly the poor girl needed it. The shock in the *Bois* had reduced her in an instant to the trembling wreck she had been, leaving England.

Kind people called, brought gifts, good humour, to the Cap Ferrat villa, and again Connie mended.

One day, when David was out, a certain Count called. He had been written about the Cartwrights by a dear friend, Mrs Bamberger of New York, and he duly presented himself at the villa and rang the bell.

As he was standing there, waiting for a servant to answer his ring, a tall man in a stove-pipe hat, dressed entirely in black, came up the stone steps and stood beside him. Embarrassed, *Monsieur le Comte* nodded, and the man, at least half a head taller than himself, smiled gravely behind his dark beard and nodded back.

A maidservant appeared, the Count spoke, and the two men followed her towards the drawing-room. The Major, she pointed out, was away, but *Madame* Cartwright would be happy to see them.

The Count always remembered that long, clattering walk along cool marble floors, through the long hall to a winding staircase which the three of them ascended in silence, only the cadence of their three sets of footsteps audible and echoing.

A little way along another wide passage and the maid pushed open a door.

The Count just had time to take a step forward, to smile, and see the beautiful young face turn to him as his hostess got up, when to his horror—*no*, he remembered, not horror, but *terror*—young

Madame Cartwright flung a hand up over her mouth and fainted dead at his feet.

The maid had not gone far and he shouted for her. The two of them lifted the unconscious girl to a sofa. It was only when they had done so that the Count noticed the other visitor had gone. Had he in fact ever been there at all? After all, no words had been exchanged from the moment they met on the doorstep: had it been his imagination?

But when poor Mrs Cartwright had come to her senses, he asked the maid. *Oui*—another gentleman had come in, *à la meme fois*. She had thought they were together.

That night David was firm: they would get a doctor, even a French one, and abide by his decision.

The doctor listened patiently, then agreed it was all most unfortunate. *Madame* Cartwright must stay indoors, in a darkened room, for at least a week. He would call again.

The Major went away on business connected with his farming, went back to England for a fortnight, leaving instruction to the servants to take good care of their sick, mentally disturbed, mistress. And while he was away, a friend of theirs from Yorkshire, a Mrs Slater who was staying at Menton, called.

She was aghast at what she saw. Poor Connie was a thing of skin and bones, blue patches under her once-lovely eyes, cheeks sunken, hair dishevelled. When Mrs Slater came into the darkened room, Connie took her by the arm and dug her nails into it.

"Mrs Slater—oh, thank God you've come. I'm so frightened——"

Mrs Slater, who could scarce keep the horror out her own voice, tried to smile. "Why—whatever for, dear? In this lovely house?"

Connie buried her head in the older woman's bosom and wept piteously. Mrs Slater led her to the sofa and they sat down.

When at last she was able to speak, she said, "I—I haven't dared tell David, he thinks I'm being wicked. But I see the dreadful thing *every night*! Oh God—what shall I do? I can't close my eyes for fear of dreaming——"

"Why, my dear—you mean that silly old face you worry about! Listen; next time it appears, speak to it. It'll probably speak back very politely."

But Mrs Slater was trembling as she spoke.

So distressed was she that she postponed a return to England to call on Connie every day for a week. Her solicitude was rewarded by a steady improvement. The French doctor called, pronounced himself delighted with the change, and when introduced to Mrs Slater beamed and said he would like to take her into partnership. On the other hand, she would deprive him of a livelihood, so he would not: she would make all his patients better.

Connie wrote her husband about the kindness of the English visitor and Mrs Slater in Menton was delighted to receive a letter from him, posted in London. How thoughtful she had been!

And David Cartwright appeared ten days later, decided his wife was well again, and took her back to England. Not at first to York-shire: a few days on the south coast, at Bournemouth, would put the finishing touches to her cure. They went via London, however, and it was there that ten-year-old Roger caught one final, horrifying glimpse of his cousin. They arrived just as he was being sent to bed, and he looked back over the bannister as the door opened. The sight of Connie, elderly—or so it seemed to a ten-year-old—ill and frightened, terrified him and instead of coming back in his pyjamas to say good evening and good night, he crept to his bed and wept.

They were gone by morning.

That day the Major booked her into the Grand Hotel in Bourne-mouth and left almost immediately again for London. He would be back for her in ten days.

The kindly and persistent Mrs Slater decided to break her own journey home by a few days in Bournemouth. What more con-venient than the Grand Hotel? She moved in, too. Connie was delighted and promptly wrote the glad news, yet again, to David at his London club.

Mrs Slater had been out for the day, had just returned to the hotel and gone to her room, when there was a knock on the door. She opened it and Major Cartwright appeared. He seemed distressed and perhaps a little puzzled. (At least, these were the emotions she fancied, in retrospect, she had seen.) He looked down at her.

"Where is she?"

"Your wife?"

"My wife."

"But—but I assume she is here. I've been away——"

"She is not. The hotel manager tells me that when the maid went to her room this morning she wasn't there. The bed had not been slept in."

"But my dear Major Cartwright, I have no idea. She must have gone to spend the night with friends. I'm sure she has many friends in these parts."

The Major turned on his heel and left.

Mrs Cartwright, the beautiful, green-eyed Connie, was never seen again. But the owner of a little antique shop near the hotel, a shop which Connie had several times visited, *had* seen her, he was certain, and he lost no time in telling the story. It was exactly half past seven on the evening of 9 May, a clear and lovely evening with a red sun poised above the sea. She had driven past, deathly pale, in the back of a large black car, a sort of limousine with a driver in front. The man had seen her for only a moment as she passed, but that face would always stay in his mind. The mouth was half-open, as if to scream, the eyes caverns in her face.

And beside her, bolt upright, like a policeman beside his prisoner, was a tall man with black beard and stovepipe hat. The antique dealer had heard all about Mrs Cartwright's fears: this was the man! He flung open the upstairs window, his bedroom window above the shop, and leant out to see where the car was going.

At that moment it vanished round a corner.

Major Cartwright, though everyone could see he was beside himself with grief, kept under control. He returned to Yorkshire, avoiding people for a month. Meanwhile, the police of every European country were alerted: the search for Mrs Cartwright went on.

She was never found. (And of course, if she were still alive today, she would be an old lady of almost eighty.)

Some wag suggested later that not only had the bearded man been a figment of imagination: so had Connie Cartwright. After all, there were no children or anything to prove the Major had ever married.

A year later Cartwright sold the place in Yorkshire and emigrated to British Columbia.

My friend Roger—who died last year—had the opportunity as a young man of visiting western Canada. He wrote Cartwright, asked if he might visit him. There was no reply. When he reached Vancouver he made inquiries and learnt that Colonel Cartwright, as he now styled himself, had sold his large farming interests and emigrated the year before. It was believed he had gone to South America. A nice guy, a good egg: his stay in Canada had been tragic in that he married an attractive girl, daughter of rich prairie people, and she had gone out of her mind. Soon after, she died. The Colonel, heart-broken, had been unable to go on living in Canada, and he sold up. Such a good, kind man: he had waited till the age of fifty before marrying—only to have this happen.

And now, with Roger gone, and with him the tales of his beautiful cousin, I find myself wondering if Cartwright ever existed. In a year or two, I shall have convinced myself he never did.

The Events at Schloss Heidiger

Karl Heinz was an orphan, and an extremely fortunate one, for he was brought up by a great friend of his late father—a father Karl never remembered—who was very rich indeed. Old Baron von Heidiger had his *Schloss*, his castle, a few miles from Brunswick, in the foothills of the Harz Mountains, one of the loveliest parts of Germany. Sadly, the present-day border between West and East, the "Iron Curtain", passes within a mile of Schloss Heidiger, leaving it that distance behind the East German frontier.

And though the huge castle with its vast grounds has probably been converted into a People's Funfair, a Collective Farm or a Warehouse, and will be impossible to visit without a fistful of documents, these are not the reasons for Karl's refusal to go back and see it. His last, dreadful, visit was 1938—and wild horses will not drag him there again.

But for twenty-odd years, starting more or less as the First World War began, it was home, and a heaven on earth. The Baron was a childless widower and he doted on the small boy whom fate had provided. The best tutors and instructors in all Germany were assembled to teach Karl literature, languages, science and art, to make him proficient with the sabre, the saddle, the rifle and even the tennis racket, so that by the time he arrived at Heidelberg University he so far outshone his fellows as to be an embarrassment.

Not surprisingly, Karl Heinz grew up a conceited prig. But that need not concern us here. He went on to join the German Diplomatic Corps, where he shone in half the capitals of the world, keeping in touch with the old Baron from places as far apart as Tokyo and London.

He was genuinely heartbroken to learn of the old man's death.

He was also highly annoyed at not being informed sooner. For by the time news reached him in Paris, from which he could easily have returned, the funeral had already taken place. He was sent a newspaper cutting with a picture of weeping peasants at the grave-side. It had been the biggest, most moving, funeral for years. Schloss Heidiger had been inherited by the Baron's nephew, Georg, a young man Karl vaguely remembered and now hotly resented. He made a point of not writing to commiserate, a point of not returning to that part of Germany. He had a distant cousin in Dresden whom he would now visit occasionally, but for the most part Karl Heinz would reside abroad, dazzling lesser breeds with his ability and his charm.

But two years after the Baron's death he got a letter from Georg. Georg and his wife had thought so often and so much about Karl: he must come to stay. They knew how much the old Baron had loved him and they would do everything in their power to make him feel at home again.

Karl regretted, crisply, that he was unable. He would be returning to Germany on leave very soon, but his plans were made.

To his surprise, an urgent letter came back: please, please—*do* come and stay. It would mean so much to me and my wife. It would fill our hearts with joy if you could spare only a few days to be with us here at Schloss Heidiger.

Annoyed, but feeling that perhaps he owed it to the memory of the old man, Karl accepted. He would spend three days.

He arrived late in the afternoon, and they were delighted—just as they had threatened—to see him. There would be a large dinner party that evening, a party for him to re-meet some of his old friends and make the acquaintance of some of Georg's new ones. It would be, as Georg felicitously put it, quite like old times. Karl nodded gravely and went upstairs to change.

And the party was pleasant. There were many people he remembered, and a number of other charming folk. Almost too charming, he thought, to be friends of Georg and Anni. They seemed interested in him, and from time to time, as the servants milled about with fresh courses, new wines, he fancied he saw guests looking quizzically at him. It occurred to him that Georg might have assembled this gathering in order to prove to neighbours, whom he wanted to become friends, that Karl was a good friend. For as everyone present must know, Karl and the old Baron had been extremely close for many years: Georg had probably not met his uncle more than a dozen times before he died.

The party broke up a little after midnight and, after an unwanted nightcap with his host, Karl made his way along the echoing stone corridor to his room. Carefully, as he had been taught all those years ago, in this very house, he hung up each article of clothing as he took it off. He noticed dust on the mantelshelf as he placed collar-stud and watch on it, and he frowned: the old Baron would turn over in his grave.

He would visit that grave first thing tomorrow.

He had been asleep for perhaps an hour when a sound woke him. He roamed the corners of the room with one eye, saw nothing, then sat up.

A man—or at least something—was squatting in front of the fire. It was still glowing faintly, and the shape was outlined against the grate. He watched, and the creature crossed its arms and shivered.

Karl sat there for what seemed hours, wondering what to do. He could see, as his eyes adapted themselves to the darkness, that the apparition was a very old man with white hair down to his shoulders. His clothes were ragged and clearly insufficient. Obviously it was some old, underpaid servant of Georg's, a still-room attendant, or a man who lit the fires every morning before anyone else was up. Equally obviously, he had no idea that anyone was using the room.

Slowly, very slowly, the man got up and Karl saw that he was bent almost double and that he had a long white beard. His feet were bare and, as Karl watched, they started to move in his direction.

The figure halted at the foot of the bed.

Never at a loss in any situation, Karl opened his mouth to utter a firm but friendly *"Guten Abend"* which would frighten the old fellow out of his wits: but nothing came out. And to his horror, the figure started to move towards him, got right up to the bed and clutched at the eiderdown.

The old fool was trying to get in! This was too much, and Karl found his voice, roared at him. "*Halt!*"

The old man had just lifted one leg to clamber in, when the sound knocked him off balance. He let out a feeble scream and collapsed on the floor.

Karl switched on the light.

There was utter silence for a few seconds as they stared at each other. Then the old man spoke, so feebly Karl hardly heard him. "*Karl, Karl—was tunst Du hier?*"

But this was impossible.

"And you have come back, dear Karl—oh, how happy I am, how happy."

"But—but you are *dead.*" And even as he spoke, the trained diplomat was aware of having made the stupidest remark of his life. "You are dead—they *said* you were."

"No, my son, I am not dead. I am here, alive, feel my flesh." And the old Baron, a thin, wasted, unrecognizable Baron, stretched up a skinny arm. Karl took it and helped him to his feet. Then they sat together on the bed.

"But there was the funeral—though I could not come. No one told me until it was too late—but I saw pictures, I read of it in the newspapers. You had a very grand funeral."

The old man smiled and now Karl saw that he was indeed the Baron he had known and loved. "I am glad my funeral was grand. A—a pity I was unable to attend it."

Karl gently wrapped the eiderdown round the old man's shoulders, then went over and put coal on the fire. As he did, the old man began his story and kept it up, without pause, for half an hour. Karl rejoined him at the edge of the bed and listened.

"But how *could* they have a funeral—without a body?"

"I am sure they could have done it in many ways. They could have put stones in the coffin, buried an empty coffin, anything. No one asks questions at Schloss Heidiger. But I believe that it was made easier for them because a servant was ill at the same time as I— old Schutzmann, you remember him—and whereas I, to their distress, got better, Schutzmann died. It was Schutzmann they buried."

"Surely no doctor——"

"He was a new doctor. I never knew him—and no doctor attended me during my illness. Only good Georg and his wife, who *so kindly* rushed over to nurse me. And I imagine that poor Schutzmann, in my clothes, would look very much like me, in death. Particularly to someone who had never seen me."

"But——"

"I can tell you no more, Karl—and perhaps what I tell you is not altogether accurate. For I have been locked in my room, a room not far from *yours*—which used to be *mine*, Karl, since somewhat *before* my funeral."

Karl sat in stunned silence.

"How long ago did I die, Karl? One has no idea of time, in a darkened room. When was my funeral?"

"Two years ago. Almost exactly two years ago."

The old man cackled with laughter. "Then if these two years have been the life hereafter, I need hardly have bothered to say my prayers. Hell would have been more comfortable. And warmer."

Karl was hardly listening. The story was obviously true—and he had only a few hours, before daybreak, to work out an ending.

"I must go back to my room now. I did not know it was you that released me: now I see it was. For, in the confusion of planning that big party for you—I think it is about the only time they have had people here—they forgot to lock me in after they gave me yesterday's food. They will be back soon—and I must go."

"You cannot go. You are free. I shall see you remain free—that the wicked pair who have imprisoned you go themselves to prison. Or worse."

The old man got up from the bed—oh, how bent he had become! —made a little gesture of farewell and went out through the door. Karl was about to dash after him, but as the bare feet padded away down the passage he thought better of it. The poor old fellow was half out of his mind, quite reconciled to his prison. If he went back to it and nothing was suspected it would give Karl more time to think, to plan.

A door clicked shut in the distance.

He was up early for breakfast and Georg and his wife came down to find their guest happily reading a newspaper: he got to his feet as they came in. Yes, he had slept magnificently. What a wonderful party it had been—how kind, how thoughtful, of them. His face almost cracked with its ambassadorial smile, and Georg and Anni beamed back, delighted.

After breakfast he insisted on going for a long walk by himself, a walk to relive memories, and as soon as he was out of sight of Schloss Heidiger he broke into a run. In the village he found a telephone and got through to Berlin. No, there was no time or opportunity to explain: they must simply recall him, immediately, for consultation. He would expect a telegram from them by midday.

"But this is dreadful," said Georg when it had come and been opened. "We have seen so little of you. You cannot go."

A wry smile. "When duty calls, dear Georg, we go. And I must go now. This afternoon."

They drove with him to the little railway station and waved affectionately as the train pulled away, taking the indispensable diplomat to Berlin. What exciting new crisis could have burst upon the Diplomatic Corps? If only he had been able to tell them.

But Karl Heinz went nowhere near Berlin. At Brunswick he got off and went straight to the police station.

"I see, *mein Herr*," said a patient official who obviously did not see or believe. Karl had just finished his story, fully conscious that no sane man would believe it, and now he was determined that action be taken, however unwillingly.

"Let us get this quite—er—clear in our minds, *mein Herr*," the official smiled bravely. "This Baron von Heidiger—indeed, I remember his funeral, a very great occasion—did *not* die, but was imprisoned in a room of the Schloss, by his nephew, in order, no doubt, that the nephew could inherit the estate?"

"That is so."

"And the nephew was able to do this after coming from afar, to nurse the Baron during an illness?"

"Correct."

"There was a mock funeral. Something, or someone, was buried. And since then the Baron has languished in a locked room of his Schloss. Until last night when he was—er—inadvertently allowed to escape from it and you discovered him. One wonders, *mein Herr*, why you allowed him to go back to it?"

The man was a fool. "Really, my good fellow, I have no time to answer foolish questions. I demand that a police party go, now, to Schloss Heidiger. I will direct them to the Baron's room, and when they have released him and arrested his nephew and wife, they can ask all the foolish questions they wish. I demand as a citizen of the Reich—*and* as a senior member of the German Diplomatic Corps—that an armed party be sent there immediately."

The man was cringing now. "Yes, *mein Herr*. Certainly, *mein Herr*."

And after what seemed an outrageous and inexcusable delay, a party of six policemen under a sergeant set off for the Harz Mountains in a lorry. Karl sat in front with the driver, biting his lip, cursing officialdom.

Then he smiled, brightly and suddenly. (And the driver, turning to look at him, nearly drove into the ditch.) What a stir this would cause! A senior member of the German Diplomatic Corps had rescued a German nobleman—from the grave!

"*Alles in Ordnung, mein Herr?*"

"Yes. And keep your eyes on the road."

In an hour they had reached the gate of the Schloss, a minute later the clumsy gang of police were thundering on the door while their sergeant stood importantly apart, holding a warrant. Georg himself answered the door. "What is the meaning of this? Oh, Karl, *you* are there? What has happened?"

"These men have a warrant to enter your property. I wish them to investigate a certain room."

There was no use protesting, and Georg opened the door. Embarrassed, the constabulary trooped in and Karl led them up the winding stair, along a passage, then up another stair and along a short corridor.

The Baron's door, as he had foreseen, was locked again. "We shall require a key." He found himself shouting. "If there is no key we must break the door down." He raised his voice still further. "Baron von Heidiger—answer me please."

There was no reply.

"It is I, Karl, again. Please answer. We have come to release you."

Still no answer. Poor old man, half out of his mind, he would be too frightened to speak, terrified lest it be some sort of trick. Never mind, within moments they would have him out.

"But of course there is a key," Georg said. His voice was calm. "It hangs here, on a hook with these others. We often lock the door because there are valuable bits stored here." He pushed his way through a crowd of now very apologetic policemen, inserted the key and turned it.

Slowly, creaking, the door opened. Karl pushed by everyone, went in and switched on a light.

The room was empty, apart from a bed without bedding, a table, and some trunks. Could the old man be hiding, in terror, inside one of the trunks?

As if to answer the unspoken question, Georg went over and opened each trunk. There were furs, other items of clothing, inside. "I have no idea what you gentlemen are in search of—but this is all we have to offer. Perhaps you will be good enough——"

"You know perfectly well what we are looking for."

"If I did, Karl, I would hardly have asked the question."

The man was so calm with it; Karl could have hit him.

"The—the search, then, is over, *mein Herr*?"

"No, it most certainly is not. We will search every room in the Schloss, until we have found him."

" 'Him', Karl? Just whom have you in mind?"

"You know perfectly well. Your uncle, the Baron von Heidiger. The wretched creature whom you locked in this very room two years ago in order that you might inherit the estate."

"Oh dear! Poor, poor Karl! You have taken leave of your senses."

But at Karl's insistence the search began, of every room in the building. As there were rather over a hundred of them, the prospect was daunting.

Suddenly, Karl had an idea. As the search party clumped away down a passage, he dashed back to the room he himself had occupied during the night. It was unlocked and he pushed open the door. The sheets had been removed from his bed but, apart from that, no cleaning seemed to have been done: the wastepaper basket was full of the old newspapers he had dropped in it the previous night.

Wildly, he looked round the room. Surely the old man must have left some trace, a few white hairs, perhaps?

He found nothing.

And then, just as he was about to leave the room, he found exactly what he needed—proof that the whole episode had not been a dream or figment of his imagination. There, at the corner of the fireplace, was a pair of thick brown woollen socks, with large holes. The old man had taken them off in front of the fire, taken them off to warm his feet better, and he had forgotten to put them on again. Karl went over, fought back his revulsion—for they smelt—and picked them up.

"Stop!" he roared down the passage. "Stop, all of you. Here is proof, positive proof, of what I have been telling you."

The party emerged from a room. "Yes, sir?"

"Look—look, all of you. This is a pair of socks."

"No one would question that, *mein Herr*."

"But they are *the socks of Baron von Heidiger*. Don't you see?"

Georg laughed gently. "I must say, dear Karl, they seem hardly the sort of garment my uncle would have worn. They are the socks of some servant, some peasant. You surprise me—that you would think my uncle capable of owning such a pair of socks as these."

God, how he hated them. "*Carry on the search!*" he said.

An hour later it was over: nothing had been found. Nothing, that is, apart from one pair of evil-smelling socks. "You wish to keep those socks, Karl? Pray do. If a servant complains you have stolen his, I will buy him another pair."

"And now we must exhume that body from the churchyard."

"That, *mein Herr*, we cannot do. We need another Order for that, another warrant."

"I shall see that you get it!" Karl was beside himself with rage and frustration.

And within twenty-four hours he had done so. This time it was with another party of police, and a doctor, that he drove up, in the same lorry, to the churchyard. Silently, they trooped across the grass to the large cross which marked the grave they now planned to open. There was an awkward pause, for no man wanted to be first in such desecration, and Karl angrily seized one of their spades, drove it deep into the soft earth. The others followed suit.

In ten minutes they had tired themselves sufficiently to need a rest, but Karl, sweat pouring down his face, went on digging, and the men were shamed into joining him. In half an hour they had uncovered the coffin and a man was down the hole unscrewing the lid.

With a creak it came off, and they peered down.

Karl let out a whoop of delight, and the doctor stared at him. "Look, my God, *look!*" It was better, far better, than he had hoped. He had expected to find the skeleton of a man, who would then have to be proved other than Baron von Heidiger. Dentists would have to be called in, doctors would remove bones. But here, six feet below him, was exactly what was needed to prove him right, the others fools.

"There you are! What did I tell you, you fools? Now you will know that Karl Heinz, senior member of the German Diplomatic Corps, is no fool but a wiser man than all of you. Look down there, fools."

"There is hardly a need for such abuse, *mein Herr*. We have only been doing our duty."

"*Duty!* Fool. What, tell me precisely *what*, you see in the coffin below us?"

"A few stones, *mein Herr*. Certainly the matter will be reported; there has been some miscarriage somewhere."

The idiot. "I demand that you return immediately to Schloss Heidiger and place its present occupant under arrest, with his wife." If the fools refused to do that, he would do it himself, in his official capacity.

Without committing itself, the party drove back to the Schloss and knocked again on the front door. There was no reply. Further knocking on other doors, all of which were locked, produced nothing, and at last the police broke one of them down and rushed in.

The house was deserted, with signs that Georg and his wife had made hasty exit. Had the servants gone with them?

And it was as Karl, still triumphant—for he had been proved right, even if the malefactor were never brought to justice—as Karl pushed open the door of the room he had slept in, that he screamed.

There, lying on the bed he had slept in—the bed which he remembered clearly had belonged to the Baron, in the Baron's own room—was the little old man, spread-eagled like an early Christian martyr. The throat had been cut from ear to ear, the mattress was crimson. There was a steady drip, drip, drip, as blood soaked through it to the floor.

The Birthday Gift

It was front-page news in its day, and still sufficiently recent for us to alter the names, set the scene on a different stage. For the family was not called Macalester—and it did not happen in Glasgow.

But happen it did, in the first few years of the present century. And the players in the drama were—exactly as we shall represent them—all Scots.

In "Glasgow" lived the "Macalester" family: husband and wife and their children, a boy and a girl. Also resident with the Macalesters was old Mrs Paton, Mrs Macalester's mother. Mr Macalester was a big silent, man of moods and red hair; his wife a small, dark, pretty thing of thirty or so, a few years younger than her husband. The two children, Helen and Philip, were exactly the sort of children one would expect, and respectively twelve and seven years old. Mrs Paton was an old woman of fifty-five, with arthritis, short sight, a whining voice.

She was also very rich. She had property (slum property, the neighbours said) in three large cities of Scotland, and the money from their rents was kept closely in a metal strongbox under Mrs Paton's bed, its key for ever round her neck on a dirty string.

The old lady made a small contribution each week towards the cost of housekeeping, but was hardly a generous guest. Occasionally she gave coins to the children and they accordingly loved her deeply. Philip in particular was devoted to his grandmother and happiest sitting beside her, when even school homework became bearable.

And as our story begins, he is sitting beside her, practising hand-writing and composition in a little pencilled essay entitled "What I Did Yesterday". It is Saturday morning, and a coal fire is burning merrily in the grate, for this is winter. There is an antimacassar on each chair and three chairs are occupied, the third one by Mrs Mac-alester, who is knitting. Granny Paton is trying to see what the boy has written, her brow wrinkled and the spectacles perilously balanced on the bridge of her long, thin nose. Several strands of her white hair have come out of the bun at the back of her head, and they project in all directions.

Having set our scene, we will go back to the past tense. Philip finished his essay, slammed shut the exercise book, walked over to his mother.

"Well done, darling. Let me have a look." Mrs Macalester opened the book and began to read, while Granny Paton beamed at the boy and rubbed her old hands.

"Philip, this is good. A very good essay indeed—but you've made one silly mistake."

"Oh, mother?"

"The date, silly boy. Today is the 8th. You've signed it, 'Philip Macalester, 9th November, 1904'. That's bad luck, you know, for nobody knows what tomorrow will bring. But of course, I see why you did it."

"'Cos tomorrow's my birthday and I was thinking about it, I "spose."

Old Granny cackled in the corner. "Heh, heh, that's why you did it, Philip, that's why you did it."

'S'pose I'd better rub the date out."

"Don't you do anything of the sort. You tear that page out of your exercise book and let your old Gran have it. And if they ask you about it at school, say your Gran wanted it because it was such a good essay; and they'll have to do without it."

Philip carefully tore out the page—it wasn't a long essay—and handed it to his grandmother. Then he left the room to find Helen, while the old lady, still cackling, settled down behind her spectacles to read it.

When she had done so, she looked up. "You know, my dear," she said to her daughter, "he's a very clever boy. This is a lovely little story: 'After breakfast, which was porridge, I walked in the snow to school——'. I like that, don't you?"

"Well, it's quite clear," said Philip's mother. "Very explicit."

"You know, my dear," Mrs Paton said again. "You know—I'm going to give him a surprise." Her strongbox was beside her, she had brought it down to do her accounts, and now she carefully opened it and took out a gold sovereign. As her daughter watched, she folded the little essay around the coin, made a parcel of it, and then wrote, in her shaky hand, "For my dear grandson Philip, on his eighth birthday—and *what* a good essay!"

Then, to her daughter's irritation, she put the packet into the strongbox and carefully locked it. The task complete, she looked up. "Tomorrow morning I'll give him that."

"I'm sure it's very kind of you, Mother."

The old lady grunted.

Mrs Macalester was glad her husband was away. He had gone to Dundee on business—though he might return this evening—and if there was one thing more than another which annoyed the red-haired Macalester, it was the fuss his mother-in-law made over the strongbox, opening it, relocking it, half a dozen times a day. His business had been less rewarding this year than usual: they had all felt the pinch. All the old miser-woman had to do was give them a wee bit out of the box.

And there was always the fear at the back of Macalester's mind that the old woman might not remember them in her will.

It was, as we have seen, a Saturday, and, as long promised, Mrs Macalester took her two children to the circus in the afternoon. It was really a birthday treat for Philip but, as circuses do not play on a Sunday, he would take his treat a day early. They made their way by tram, enjoyed themselves thoroughly among elephants, clowns and acrobats. At five the circus was over and they made their way home. There was the chance that Mr Macalester would be back from his trip, perhaps with a special present for the morning.

They got to the house, opened the door, and went in. "Robert," called Mrs Macalester. "Robert—are you back?"

Obviously, Robert was not.

Gran hadn't spoken—which was unlike Gran. Probably she was asleep in her chair by the fire. "Don't make a noise, children. Granny's asleep."

"No, Mother, we won't." She led the way upstairs to the sitting-room. It was a tall old house, designed for more servants than the Macalesters could afford, with kitchen in the basement, dining-room and little boudoir on the ground floor, sitting-room and a bedroom above that, and three bedrooms on the next floor, one each for Helen, Philip and Gran. Above that, on the third floor above ground, were four little servant's-rooms, huddled under a sloping roof. Only one of these was used, for the family could afford only one servant. And today was Jennie's day off.

Helen was just behind her mother, nearly at the top of the stair by the living-room door, when the door slammed shut in her face, her mother on the far side. She heard a stifled sob, the key turned in the lock.

"Mother, Mother—what *is* it? Open the door——"

The only answer was her mother's weeping—deep, frightening sobs of a kind Helen had never encountered.

"Oh, Mother, what's *wrong*? Don't cry, Mother. Open the door, please, please, open the door."

"You—you can't come in. Go downstairs, both of you, and I—I'll come down. Oh my God, my *God*——"

It was many years before Philip found out what had happened. Though Helen, who was older and read the papers when she could find them, and had even older schoolfriends who read more papers, knew everything within two days. As far as Philip was concerned, his grandmother had suffered a terrible accident, had fallen into the fireplace, killed herself.

A little later, while the children were locked into the little boudoir on the ground floor, an ambulance came. The body of Mrs Paton was removed, under a sheet.

An hour after that, Mr Macalester arrived. He was in a good mood, though he seemed to have been drinking, for he smelt of whisky. They heard his cheery voice—it was a cheery voice tonight —shout, "Ahoy! Anyone in?"

"Yes, Robert. Wait a minute, Robert. Stay there." And Mrs Macalester ran down the stairs to meet him.

"Darling—what's wrong? You've been crying."

"Oh Robert, Robert darling——" and the frightened children heard her burst again into deep, terrifying sobs. She was unable to speak for a bit, then they heard her gasping in whispers, and they made out one word in ten. "Terrible, terrible—poor mother—blood, blood—who could have—oh Robert——"

The next day the news was all over town and in all the Sunday papers. Someone had broken in—there were clear signs of the lock having been tampered with—and gone upstairs. There, with some blunt instrument, he had beaten Mrs Paton's head in, smashed it to a bleeding pulp. Her brains, one paper pointed out, were "exposed to view".

The motive for the crime was obvious: the old lady's strongbox had gone.

Amid the excitement, the horror, young Philip almost forgot the imminence of his birthday. But he went to bed, and the next morning it came, just as planned. He got an air-gun, a fountain-pen and a football.

It was a week before the sitting-room door was unlocked, and when the children went in, it was to discover a new carpet, new wallpaper. Within another week neither of them could remember what colour the old ones had been. A week after that, poor Gran had been all but forgotten. Only the daily visits by policemen and others, the endless muttered consultations all over the house, the tramp of strangers' feet, reminded them that something strange and unpleasant had happened.

Six months later the police had their man. A blacksmith, a notorious fellow who had already served two sentences in prison, had broken in. It was proved that he knew the servant-girl Jennie, and though the weeping child denied having done so, no one doubted that she had, quite inadvertently, paved a way for the crime. She had told him the day each week she had off, had mentioned Philip's birthday, the fact that he would go with his mother and sister to the circus the day before it. She had told him of Mr Macalester's business trip to Dundee.

And the man—this was the final, damning piece of circumstantial evidence—the man had lived, recently, in a Gorbals hovel owned by Mrs Paton. He fell behind with the rent, and she—quite correctly, of course—had got him evicted.

It was front-page news, and it remained front-page news for many months. The trial began and continued for weeks, but the outcome was a foregone conclusion. In October 1905, almost a year after the crime, the murderer Reid was hanged, protesting to the end that he had not even been in Glasgow on the day of the crime. The law knew better.

By this time Macalester's business had improved considerably—which was as well, for though the old lady's will was gratifyingly made in their favour, the missing strongbox had contained not only all her money, but the deeds to her property. Until title was re-established, no rent could be demanded, and the process took many months. But business flourished and Mrs Macalester was even able to indulge her dream of moving from the house, with its dreadful memory, to another in a more fashionable part of town.

The years went by and with Philip seventeen, his sister twenty-two, a great war broke out. Mrs Macalester heaved a sigh of relief that her husband was too old, at forty-three, to join up; her son was too young. It would all be over by Christmas.

A year later the war was still very far from over, and Philip was on Salisbury Plain learning to be a soldier. Helen was already a V.A.D. Their father, anxious to do his bit, had applied to join the Army, been rejected.

But fate had more cards to play. While Mrs Macalester prayed daily for Philip's safe return, he came back, time after time, from the front, while one by one his contemporaries were killed. And Mr Macalester, going peacefully each day to his place of business, was knocked down and killed by one of the new motor-cars just as he got off a tram. Helen married a doctor, and Philip returned triumphant and bemedalled from a war which had just been won. He was conveniently able to go into his late father's business, where the partners made great fuss of him. The Macalesters' life had been full of tragedy; it was everyone's duty to brighten it up for them.

A year later, in 1919, Helen came to spend a few weeks with her mother. She now had a daughter of her own, whom she brought from Leicester, where her husband practised, to show the child off. Her mother seemed to have recovered from both major tragedies of her life, could look at the handsome photograph of the late Mr Macalester on the mantelpiece without weeping. She was much like her former self.

One evening as they sat round the fire—mother and Helen—the girl spoke. "I was going through some old papers of Father's this afternoon——"

Her mother stiffened. "Oh really? And why were you doing that?"

"Oh come on, Mother—you don't mind, really, do you?"

"I suppose not. But where did you find them?"

"In the cupboard in my bedroom. Didn't he use it as a dressing-room once?"

"Yes, he did."

"Well, at the back of the cupboard there was a great pile of papers. Receipted bills, letters from various people——"

"Really——"

"Didn't you know they were there?"

There was a pause.

"Well—didn't you?"

"Yes, Helen, I did. But I never went through them. I tied ribbon round them—I suppose you found that, and undid it—and I left them there, just as he would have wished."

"Oh, Mother! What a silly, sloppy, sentimental thing to do! They might be important, might tell us all sorts of things."

"I don't think there's anything I want to know, Helen."

"Look—let me go up and bring them down. You *ought* to see them. You're his widow, you should see everything he left behind, absolutely everything."

"Very well, then. If you insist. Go and get them."

"All right." Helen got up, and as she did, there was a wail from upstairs. "Coming, darling, don't cry, darling——" It was five minutes before she got back, but then she was holding a crumpled heap of papers in both hands. A long bit of red ribbon hung down from them, and Mrs Macalester frowned.

"Mind if I put them on the floor? Or are they too precious for that?"

They spread them out on the floor.

Grudgingly, Mrs Macalester admitted to herself the idea was worthwhile, not a sacrilege. There were many old bills—goodness, how cheap things had been!—a few bank statements, a few typed, official-looking letters. They went back for almost twenty years, to a few years after their marriage.

One thing she found puzzling was the state, at any given moment, of her husband's business. There were balance sheets, which she half understood, seeming to show that the business had almost gone bankrupt in 1903 and again in 1904. There was an ominous letter from a bank manager pointing out that the maximum amount of overdraft had already been exceeded.

Somehow, there had been an injection of capital into the business in early 1905, some sort of a loan, for there was a letter from another partner congratulating him on managing to raise privately a sum which the firm had been unable to get by itself. "With this, we may well have turned the corner." And yet, on almost the same date, there was this letter from the bank manager, pointing out that no more money was available.

Oh, well—she had never understood business matters. She put the papers down.

Helen was scuffling through others, a terrier at a hedge, separating them in little piles. She came to a small piece of crumpled paper, more crumpled than the rest, and ironed it out flat with her hand. There was ink on one side, almost illegible pencil on the other.

"Look, Mother—this looks interesting. Not just a silly old bill, or a business letter. Real handwriting—only I can't read much of it. The ink says 'For my dear something, on something——'"

Mrs Macalester's heart sank, then she smiled at herself for being a foolish, jealous woman. At first it had seemed this must be a love letter. Robert had been attractive to women, and not entirely uninterested.

"See if you can read it." Helen handed over the scrap of paper.

It was funny—something was definitely, *oddly* familiar. She held it close, straining her eyes, then she got up and went over to a lamp on the table and studied it in the light. But her eyes were old and weak, and she called for Helen. "Come here and have a good look, in this light."

Helen came over, took the paper and stared at it again. Now, in the bright light—the new electric light, for it had only been installed a few weeks back—she could read both sides, and she did so. Then she laughed out loud.

"What is it, dear? Tell me."

"It's some sort of an essay written by Philip. Years and years ago. What he'd been doing the day before—the day before 9 November, 1904."

Her mother had paled and suddenly Helen knew why. "That—that was the day after Granny died. Wasn't it?"

Mrs Macalester nodded.

"But—but this is extraordinary."

Her mother leant forward. "What is, dear?"

"The writing on the other side is obviously Granny's. I can read it now, and it says, 'for my dear Grandson Philip, on his eighth birthday—and *what* a good essay!' And I think there were coins wrapped up in it."

"Well?"

"But don't you see, Mother—Philip wrote the essay on his birthday, 9 November. He's written the date on it. And Granny has written on the other side, 'what a good essay'."

Suddenly Mrs Macalester felt ill, desperately ill. Things, terrible things, were falling into place and as yet she had not understood. "Yes, dear?"

"But on Philip's birthday in 1904, Granny was dead. She—she died—the day before. Didn't she?"

Her mother seized the piece of paper from her, stared at it in horror. Her face was ashen. Helen had never seen her like this before. "Oh, Mother, Mother *darling*—what's wrong?"

For answer Mrs Macalester took one last anguished look at the scrap of paper, screwed it up in a ball and dropped it into the back of the fireplace. Then she fainted.

"Philip, Philip, are you in? Come quick, *quick*!"

He was, he arrived. Together they carried Mrs Macalester to a divan, laid her gently upon it. Philip telephoned for the doctor, and in a few minutes he came. Still she lay unconscious, and Helen tried to explain what had happened.

With smelling salts, she was revived, and within an hour she was up, despite doctor's orders, looking pale and very ill. She had made a fool of herself, that was all. It was just the sudden reminder of how poor Granny died, that had done it. That was all, just thinking about that.

Helen never brought the subject up again: the mystery, both of the strange date and the real reason for her mother's fainting attack, would remain for ever unsolved. In any case, the mysterious paper was gone. And the following day, as planned, Helen and the baby would go home. The episode was closed.

But when Helen next came to visit her mother, she noticed the handsome photograph of her father had gone. She asked why.

"Oh, I don't know, dear. It's just that I think it's sort of mawkish, looking at the dead. That's all."

The Attic Room

Slowly, they climbed the creaking stair till they were in a dust-filled attic. At one end were two closed doors, and Alastair led the way towards them, picking a footing carefully along a sort of catwalk laid above the joists. The doors were both ajar, and he gave each a shove. "Make yourself at home," he said, waving them into the right-hand one. "Next door's a maid's bedroom, too—but Mother uses it for storing junk. You can inspect that one as well, if you like."

Inside, the room—his room for the night—was almost entirely dark, with a pale winter light oozing in through a single tiny window. He walked over to it, raising big arms as he did so, feeling the pitch of the roof slope down from a highest point of seven feet at one side of the room to four feet at the other. The window was at a gable end, and now, as he looked through, he could see the sheen of water, the open sea.

As if reading his thoughts, Alastair bent beside the bed and switched on a reading-lamp. "The only light," he said. "I hope it's bright enough for you."

He put his suitcase on the bed.

"And there's a radio for you. May cheer you up."

"Thanks." He eyed the dumpy, old-fashioned, bedside radio.

"Anyway, come on down and have a dram before dinner. Mother's dead keen to meet you—the man who's going to defy the

Ghost of Drumkattle. Or do you want to inspect the place first?"

"I'll inspect it." He went over to the door and its huge keyhole, key on the outside. Inside was an even larger, very rusted, bolt. He examined the cupboard in the corner, which was part of the wall and almost the size of a man. He reached in, felt the boards at the back, and they were firm. He sat on the bed, bounced up and down, looked underneath. "O.K.," he said. "That'll do."

"Fine. Let's go downstairs——"

"We've forgotten something," said Duncan. "The bell——"

"Lord, yes." Alastair reached up and felt for a rope hanging a few inches down from the roof, took a length of coarse twine out of his pocket and joined the two. "This is your signal, Kevin old man. I'll leave the end of the twine here beside the bed, and if you give it a tug the wee bell above will ring. It's been there for ages—but it still sounds."

"Ha," said Kevin. "I won't be needing your bloody bell, mate."

"All right, then: you won't be needing it."

"Wait," he said. "I think I'd better tell you one thing." He opened the suitcase, felt about inside and produced a pistol. "This Smith and Wesson is loaded." He put it on the bedside table. "And any ghost that appears is going to get a slug in the guts. Thought I'd make that clear before we start."

"You heard that, Ghost?" said Alastair to the roof. "If you pop out, you get a slug in the guts."

They descended from the attic, made a way along dark corridors, down a spiral staircase and into the drawing-room. Alastair's mother, a small, delicate-looking creature, was sitting in a corner of the large, ill-lit room, reading under a brass standard lamp.

"Mother, this is Kevin Donaldson. From Australia."

She smiled, said she was glad to meet him; once upon a time she had visited Australia, when her husband was alive, and had liked it. And now—what was all this about defying the Drumkattle ghost?

Alastair explained. It was all a bet, made at University, during the last hectic, end-of-term week at St Andrews. Kevin, brave man from down under, didn't believe in ghosts; Alastair's house had one: it was as simple as that. No one had slept in the ghost's room for a hundred years, not since the night the long-remembered house-maid, in the days when people had housemaids, had been assaulted in her bed, and murdered. Kevin would sleep—or try to sleep—in that room.

"Fifty pounds is a lot of money," said Mrs Moncrieff.

"It would be, for me," said her son. "But Kevin's rich—and he's the one who's going to pay."

Kevin smiled. "I doubt that."

And now it was past eleven and he was alone in the attic room, the door locked, the key taken away. He for his part had closed the bolt, so as not to be taken unawares by some fancy-dress ghost in the small hours. It was a moonless December night, and the room, if he switched off the bedside lamp, was as dark as it was possible to imagine. Only the window, a small rectangular eye peering over the North Sea, made a pale patch.

He lay on the bed, fully dressed, staring at a paperback, but his mind was full of the wager. Nine hours and it would be over. If he hadn't rung the bell—how ridiculous of them to think he would, and advertise his alarm to the neighbourhood!—by eight in the morning, they would let him out and he would collect fifty quid.

On second thought, there was no one to whom one *could* advertise an alarm: Drumkattle was the only house along this deserted bit of coast. Only those inside it—Alastair, Alastair's mother, and Duncan—would hear the ringing. Not that there would be any ringing.

He grew tired of his book, switched on the bedside radio so thoughtfully provided and listened to a bit of "Music at Night" on the Home. He fiddled it round to Light and got jazz, eventually settled for Hamburg playing waltzes, sat up and began to undress.

He took pyjamas from the case, put them on, folded clothes neatly over the singleton hard-back chair, went over to the cupboard, opened it again, felt inside, closed the door.

The Smith and Wesson was by the bed, and he flicked it open, saw the cartridges in place, shut it. Then, getting into the narrow wooden bed—perhaps the discomfort was intended to help drive him out before dawn—he turned off the light.

The radio played softly in the dark for a few minutes; then, with a yawn, he switched it off.

He wasn't sure whether he had dozed and woken, but he heard a sound, according to the luminous dial of his watch, at 1 a.m. He could not analyse it at first. Then, slowly, it began to seem as if the roof were leaking and water dripping on the floor. He listened, then switched on the light.

No sound now. No water on the floor. He switched off.

This time, half an hour elapsed before he heard it again, and it was distinctly louder, as if water were dripping steadily into the centre of the room.

He fancied he heard a sound near his head and, to his annoyance, he turned and his heart began pounding, blood thundering through his temples. The sound of liquid went on as counterpoint to the rhythm of his bloodstream, and then suddenly the dripping seemed to switch position, as if a new leak had sprung in the roof. He turned on the light, and the noise stopped.

He got up, looked through the window, opened it, and put out a hand: it wasn't raining. In any case, there was no water on the floor. He went to the cupboard, flung it open, half expecting to find Alastair or Duncan crouched inside, making noises. It was empty.

He lay back in bed with the light, and all was quiet and calm. He stole a glance at his watch, which said half past three, and carefully put out the light.

He must have dozed, for he woke suddenly to the sound of a voice, and jerked upright, pulse beating hard. The voice was a female one, a girl's voice with a Highland lilt, and, as he strained ears to listen, it seemed to say, very softly, and very distinctly, "Kevin——"

This was absurd. He would *not*, decidedly not, make a fool of himself by answering. He turned the light switch again—and this time nothing happened.

He cursed. The bulb must have blown. A lump had crept into his throat now, the pounding in his ears had grown, and he felt quickly for the pistol on the table beside him.

"You are lying," said the voice, "in a pool of warm, red blood. *My* blood, Kevin."

He opened his mouth to make flippant reply, and nothing came out. At last, and in a voice quite unlike his own, he said, "D-don't be a drongo——"

"Keep quiet, Kevin. I have come to kill you."

He forced a laugh. "Good on you, mate. And why?"

"Because, Kevin, this room, the bed you lie on, are mine. I died in that bed, Kevin."

There was a pause and the thumping in his ears grew almost unbearable.

"I died in that bed, Kevin, at the hands of a man. He killed me when I cried out——"

This was too laughable for words. "Ha," he said. "Confucius say, when rape inevitable, lie back and enjoy. Ha——"

"I do not understand, Kevin. I have come here for you."

A thought flashed suddenly through his mind and he found the switch of the radio. It was off.

The girl's voice began again. "Make peace with your Maker, Kevin Donaldson, for you have only minutes to live. Can you hear my blood dripping past you to the floor? Soon it will be *your* blood, Kevin."

Confound it—the dripping *had* started again. If only one could see: curse the broken bloody light bulb. And why, oh why, hadn't he brought a torch?

He remembered his lighter. It took courage, and he cursed himself for the fact, to get from the bed and over to his jacket, but he forced himself and got there, took the Ronson from his pocket and flicked it on. In the oily light, there was nothing.

But now the voice was closer. He felt again for the radio and was certain the voice came through it, even with the switch off. After all, Alastair did amuse himself with electronics, had a workshop somewhere in this vast and hateful house. In a sudden rage he banged the top of the radio with his clenched fist. The voice went on, but now, perhaps because he was excited and breathing hard, he could not make out what it said. But it *must* be the radio. With frantic fingers he felt at the back for the mains cord, followed it to the plug it shared with the bedside lamp, wrenched it out.

That was more like it: the voice receded. Now it was near the wall. The sound of dripping was there, but it was no longer beside his bed, it, too, was by the wall. Then, with a new and awful panic, he realized it was still in the room, and he seized the radio, flung it to the floor and heard the case crack. Then he reached down and battered it with his shoe till it broke in a dozen bits.

The voice was even clearer. "That did no good, Kevin Donaldson. You cannot alter fate—and your fate is death. Death tonight, Kevin."

He flicked the lighter, and the room was empty.

Suddenly, there was a wild commotion in the corner. The dripping had become a torrent, a deafening Niagara, and he sat up, appalled, to stare through the dark at the spot.

He must have stared half a minute when he felt a draught, and as he swung round to it he was certain he saw something. Frantically he spun the wheel of the lighter; spun four times till it caught fire.

He called out in horror, then caught his breath. The light was feeble, but just strong enough to light up a figure, a shape near the cupboard. The face, if it were a face, was ashen, and the clothes, if one could call them that, were dark—perhaps blood-red. It spoke to him—the same, girl's, voice—but the lips didn't move. He was too terrified now to hear what it said, conscious only that it was moving nearer.

He fought off an urge to hide in the bedclothes and sat bolt upright. "*Right*," he said—but it was a scream—"*Right*, mate, whoever you are——" He had the revolver in his right hand, he pulled back the hammer with a click.

"Put that down, Kevin. It will do no good."

"I'm—I'm going to shoot, d'you hear? *You hear me?* I'm going to shoot! Going to kill you, mate. This is the last—last warning——" His voice was astonishing, a high-pitched scream. "*Last warning*——"

"No bullet can penetrate me, Kevin. A man did once, Kevin. Penetrated me as I lay where you lie now, but no man will again, And no bullet——"

"Last warning!" he screamed.

He fired, straight into the figure, and the report deafened him.

As the cloud of smoke swept away he made out the white face, still there.

He screamed, fired again. And again, and again. Through acrid gunsmoke he could see the creature, getting closer. He screamed again, felt with his left hand for the bell-pull he had sworn not to use. As he did, he fired, again and again, with the right, till there was only a dull click on an empty chamber. The figure was on him now and he tried to hurl the spent revolver, but it fell from his hand. He was soaked to the skin: it wasn't sweat, it was blood; he knew it was blood.

His hand found the bell-pull, the end of twine, and pulled it with all his strength. A bell, a tiny, tinkling Scots kirk bell, sounded somewhere above him, and as he tugged again and again, the creature lunged and suddenly everything went black. Mercifully, silently, black.

They were sitting, the pair of them, in Alastair's club—and what now follows is still told in that club, though its name, of course, is not Green's. Nor do the three chief characters in the sad, true story own the names we have given them. The two had kept in close touch—and today would bring reunion with the third. They looked forward, almost like schoolboys, to the meeting. After all, it had been an easy matter for Duncan and Alastair to keep up a friendship; both had moved south after University, both were in London, Duncan in Fleet Street and Alastair, rich, dilettante Alastair, with a comfortable, convenient job, producing something or other for the BBC, on steam radio. They met at least once a week, and often in Green's, for Alastair enjoyed entertaining there, and Duncan, impoverished journalist, was grateful that club rules forbade him to buy a drink.

Today—at long last—they would catch up with Kevin, or he with them. Good old Kevin—he had taken the "ghost" ordeal quite well, even though the poor chap had passed out at the end. He had recovered, deathly pale, and scribbled a cheque for £50 which they had torn up, and he had merely shrugged his shoulders without showing any interest in how they had done it. He left that morning, a few hours earlier than planned, to spend the Christmas vac with some obscure relative in Cornwall; and they had put him on the train at Leuchars.

They hadn't seen him since: he never turned up for that term in St Andrews. Weeks later, Alastair got a letter from him, posted in Australia. He had been ill, nothing serious, but to cut a long story short he'd gone home. After all, a B.A. (St Andrews) wasn't all that important to a bloke who'd be growing wool in New South Wales. He'd be back one of these days and they'd have a yarn.

Two years and a month later, he made it. He'd kept in touch and he was arriving in London this very afternoon from Cornwall, where he'd been staying, it seemed, with the same obscure relative. His father was with him, on a first visit to the U.K., and they were both coming up to town for a few days. Yes, they'd enjoy coming to Green's Club, and they could arrange a further meeting then. Kevin would arrive at six, and his old father, who had something else to do in London, would arrive a bit later.

The hall porter came in, handed Alastair a letter. "Alastair Moncrieff, Esquire" was on the envelope, in a thin and spidery hand, "Green's Club, St James's, London." In the top left corner was the word, "Urgent".

He was used to this sort of correspondence, and he tucked it away in his breast pocket.

Kevin arrived punctually and was ushered to the bar. They got to their feet, genuinely delighted at seeing him again, so little changed. Three old members in the corner watched as the three young men shook hands.

Drinks came and they began to talk—of everything but Scotland. Kevin was happy in Australia, there were things in Britain he missed, but on balance he knew he was glad to be living in his own country. And how were his two friends making out? Pretty well, it seemed.

As Alastair got up to get drinks, he heard Duncan's voice behind him: "And now—shall we tell you about the Drumkattle ghost? Would you like to hear, Kevin?"

There was a pause, then the Australian voice, "I would."

And so the story unfolded. It had been too, too simple—given Alastair's house and Alastair's interest in electronics. There'd been a loudspeaker in the wall, behind the paper—you could only see where it had been glued in the brightest of sunshine. And the bedside radio, of course, had been wired along its cable so that it, too, was in circuit with microphones and things downstairs, whether switched on or not. Given this, and Alastair's young sister—who'd wanted to meet him the next day, but he'd fled to Cornwall—it had been easy to produce a vivid "stereo" effect, so that voices, the dripping of blood, and the rest of it appeared to emanate from any point in the room. And—though this was the least ingenious part of all, for every old house had loose panels—it was a simple matter for a man to get into the bedroom cupboard from behind. It made a noise, of course, but if a hellish din came from elsewhere—like a Niagara of blood in the corner—it was easy. A man—Duncan—could get into the cupboard, dressed as a rather unconventional ghost in an old blue overcoat, and come out through the front.

"I see," said Kevin, still grinning. "I must have upset your sound effects when I smashed the bloody radio. If I remember rightly,

I beat hell out of it with my shoe. I suppose I really owe you a new one."

They all laughed. "Yes, you certainly smashed it with that bloody great shoe. And so the stereo effect was gone—but by that time it didn't matter, the speaker in the wall was good enough. You were pretty damn scared by this time."

"Too right."

Duncan was enjoying it. It was nice that the big Aussie—and he seemed even larger than at their last meeting—was being so pleasant, understanding, about it all. Some chaps might have taken it the wrong way.

The big man spoke again. "Just one thing I'd like to know."

"Anything you want, old man."

"You remember I—I shot at the bloody ghost. At *you*, I suppose, Duncan?"

"You did. I was terrified."

The smile had gone. "Then, Duncan, why didn't I *kill* you, Duncan?"

There was a longish pause as the two young Scotsmen contemplated the changed demeanour of their friend. Then Alastair spoke. "That was the smartest bit of all. You remember when my mother went to bed after dinner?"

"Yes."

"Duncan walked out with her. You maybe didn't notice; you and I were stuck into the Glen Grant, arguing about something. Well, anyway, he just sprinted up to your room, chum, and——"

"And what?"

"And—and just *emasculated* your wee gun, Kevin."

"What—what d'you *mean*?"

Duncan was laughing, almost uncontrollably. "Yes, if I'd been able to put my hand on some blanks, I'd have put them in. When you told us you'd got a gun, I don't mind telling you I was scared. I suppose I could have emptied the thing, but you'd have spotted that."

"I would indeed."

"So I—and, God, how I had to race—I hacked the bullets from the cartridges with a knife."

Alastair had got up again with the glasses. He just reached the bar when there was a strangled shout from the far end of the room and he turned to see the oldest member on his feet, eyes on stalks, pointing.

"Gawd—oh my *Gawd*!" screamed the barman.

Even before he spun round, he knew what he would see. He dropped the glasses and sprang, but it was too late. Duncan was on the floor, the huge Australian straddling him and stabbing, again and again, with a short, red-bladed knife. A sea of blood was gushing out over the carpet, and as Alastair flung himself on them he saw, with a strange lack of emotion, that Duncan's throat had been cut from ear to ear.

It was midnight of the most dreadful day Alastair had lived through, and he was back in his small flat off the Edgware Road. Duncan had died instantly, that was the only mercy; died perhaps without knowing what hit him. Alastair had gone with him in the ambulance to Charing Cross, but it had been only a gesture.

Kevin Donaldson had been led away, silent, mystified, by a dozen policemen.

He was taking things out of his pockets now as he prepared for bed. Heaven only knew whether one would sleep, whether one would ever sleep again.

He found the letter, the letter from the club, and now he opened it and sat on the edge of the bed to read. He dropped the crumpled envelope to the floor, screwed up his eyes and began.

"Dear Mr Moncrieff," it said. "What I have to write is important. I am Kevin Donaldson's father, and as I write this tonight, you will be meeting my son tomorrow. I implore you to read this carefully. You have never known, Mr Moncrieff, what you and your friend did to rry boy. Perhaps you never will. All I can say is that he has been ill, very ill, and he is still very sick. He is unable to travel by himself, Mr Moncrieff, that is why I am here. It is impossible for my Kevin to go anywhere alone. Now perhaps you will see what I am driving at. I have promised him to let him meet you, without me, for a little while, for a yarn, a little while only, before I join him. He loves you two boys, Mr Moncrieff, though only the Lord knows why.

"And now I *implore* you, Mr Moncrieff"—and the word "implore" was underlined half a dozen times in ballpoint—"I implore you on no account to bring up the matter of the house in Scotland. Kevin will not do so himself, he never, never, will, and I *implore* you, from the bottom of my heart, not to do so."

The paper fell from Alastair's hands and he sat, white-faced, aghast, staring in front of him.

Footprints in the Dust

"Would you like me to call you a cab?" their host asked as he led them to the door.

"No, thank you, sir," Lieutenant-Commander Gerald Merriment R.N. said, then turning to his companion, "Unless you would prefer to ride, Martin."

"It's such a beautiful night," Lieutenant Martin Rodes answered, "I'm game to walk."

"After all, it's not far," their host smiled. "Thank you for coming."

"Thank you for having us, sir," Merriment said. "We've enjoyed ourselves immensely."

"The hospitality we are given in Malta is quite different from anywhere else, sir," Rodes said. "Somehow you don't seem to make a duty of it."

"A duty? Certainly not! We really enjoy it. When one lives on a small island, you know, one's friends and acquaintances are naturally restricted. New faces, new ideas become very important."

"Well, goodnight, sir, and thank you again for a most pleasant evening," Merriment said.

"And thank Mrs Blank for us, too. Goodnight, sir," Rodes added.

Under the midnight-blue, cloudless, star-encrusted sky a slight breeze took the oppressiveness out of the Mediterranean heat, yet was itself edged with a soft warmth of its own which reduced the contrast between day and night to a kind of sensual caressing that set the seal on the evening's pleasure.

The two men had been sincere in their appreciation of their evening's entertainment. The food and wine had been impeccable, their hostess and her daughters had provided beauty as well as intelligence, their host and his son had led the way with good talk.

As they walked past the few late promenaders in the narrow Valetta streets on their way back to their ship, for Merriment and Rodes life seemed to be particularly pleasant. Side by side, their footsteps on the singing stones the only noise they made, they headed for the Grand Harbour.

Presently, however, Merriment paused at the entrance to a narrow side-street.

"I think if we go up here," he said, "we shall cut out those tiresome cobbles at the top of this street."

"Right," said Rodes, and they turned together into the darkness of the side-street.

The buildings here seemed to be mostly dwelling-houses, though there were small shops on the ground floors of one or two. Their tallness, the narrowness of the street and the absence of street-lighting, except for a lamp at each end and one in the middle, made it appear that the ribbon of sky above the roof-tops was a candelabrum of winking lights, giving a powdery, diffused illumination to the confined space of the road-level.

They were half-way up the street when they noticed a woman trying to open a window to the left of the entrance to one of the houses. It was a large house, and had a door-frame of carved stone surmounted by an ornate fanlight.

"We'd better see if we can help," Merriment said.

So they crossed over to her. She heard them coming a dozen yards away, and turned to them. She was dressed in a long black lace gown which almost swept the ground and her head was swathed in a black lace mantilla, which she had lowered to cover her eyes and nose.

"Can we be of any assistance, madam?" Merriment asked.

"I should be very grateful," she said, and they noted the rich, full maturity of her voice.

"I have foolishly left my keys inside," she went on, "and my servants are attending a wedding-feast in Mdina, and will not be home until the small hours. But I notice that this window, by some good fortune, is unlatched."

Rodes had already stepped forward. The lower half of the window had obviously not been raised for some time, but exerting all his strength he eventually raised it and with an agile leap climbed through.

By the light that had been left burning in the hall-way, he found the front door, turned the lock and opened it.

"I am most grateful," the woman said. "I hope, gentlemen, that you will allow me to offer you a drink?"

"You are very kind, madam," Merriment said. "But we are on our way . . ."

"But I insist," she said. "I am sure that officers of His Majesty's Navy will not reject a lady's invitation."

"Madam, how can we?" Merriment smiled.

"Good," she said. "Please come in."

Though from the outside the house looked substantial, neither of the men were prepared for the vast hall into which they stepped. Flagged with large white and black marble slabs, it ran to the back wall of the house, and rising from the middle of it was a large curving double-staircase whose delicately intricate wrought-iron balustrade gave it the appearance of floating.

Leading the way across the hall, their hostess went before them up the stairs, the steps of which were also of alternate black and white marble. At the top of the stairs she took them into a small room, whose door was exactly in the centre of the landing.

It was a kind of casual sitting-room, perhaps serving as ante-room to the two large reception rooms which opened one each side of it. It contained only three or four easy chairs and a small settee with a long low table before it. In contrast with it and the completely empty hall-way, the glimpses the two officers had of the reception rooms, through their open doors, showed them to be sumptuously furnished in the Italian and Spanish *fin-de-siècle* styles. The owners were obviously wealthy and cultivated people with the quietly flamboyant taste which one finds in the Mediterranean.

"Please make yourselves comfortable," the woman said, "while I get the drinks."

They thanked her and sat down, not knowing quite what to make of it.

In a moment or two she returned carrying a tray on which were decanters and glasses.

"I fear I can offer you only a choice of madeira or marsala," she said, putting the tray down on the table.

They both took madeira, which she poured for them, afterwards pouring for herself half a glass of marsala.

"To your good health, gentlemen," she said, raising her glass. "And my gratitude."

"We were happy to be of assistance, Madame—er—Madame— er . . ." Merriment said.

She ignored his obvious wish to know her name, and though he had been on the point of introducing himself and Rodes, her desire not to reveal her identity was so clear that he decided it would be ungentlemanly to embarrass her by telling her their names.

"Are you in port for long?" she asked.

"Until next Monday, madam," Merriment told her.

"Is this your first visit to our island?"

No, they said. They had been here frequently. They found the island extremely interesting and the Maltese generous and hospitable.

For half an hour they exchanged this kind of conventional small talk, and, refusing a third glass of madeira, they presently rose and said they must be going.

She led the way down the stairs, and at the door once more thanked them.

"It was a pleasure, madam," Merriment said. "Thank you for the wine."

He held out his hand. She could not have failed to notice his gesture, but she made no attempt to respond to it.

"Goodnight, gentlemen," she said. "*Bon voyage.*"

They put on their caps and saluted her, and turned into the street.

"That was a bit odd, don't you think?" Rodes said after a moment or two.

"How do you mean?" Merriment asked.

"Well, she practically refused to tell you her name; then she wouldn't shake hands. And another thing—the key was already in the lock inside, and the door was locked. How did she get out?"

"By the servants' door?"

"How did she lock that door then? Besides—did you notice how our voices echoed, though there were rugs on the floor and heavy curtains at the windows? It was just like talking in an empty house."

"Yes, I'll admit it was a little strange," Merriment agreed. "But we're not at home, you know."

Rodes, however, could not dismiss the strangeness of the encounter so easily.

Next day, with colleagues, they were lunching with a member of the Executive Council and to make conversation with the guest on his right Rodes recounted what had happened. The guest was interested and puzzled, and when he had asked Rodes to identify the house again, he said, "But I think you must be mistaken, Lieutenant. That house has been empty for the last twelve or fifteen years. In fact, it has been allowed to become derelict."

"I assure you, sir," Rodes insisted, "that my friend Merriment will vouch for what I have told you. Two of us could not have been deceived."

"And I assure you, sir," said the guest, "that the house has not been inhabited since Miss . . . was drowned. If you can spare an hour after luncheon, I will prove it by taking you there."

So after luncheon Merriment and Rodes allowed themselves to be taken to the scene of the previous evening's incident.

"You are absolutely certain this is the house?" their guide said.

"Absolutely," Merriment told him. "I remember that shop there and the name over the window."

"Well, you can see for yourselves that you must have been deceived," the man laughed. "Wine can work miracles, you know."

"You forget we are hardened sailors, sir," Rodes grinned. "Do you think it's possible to get inside?"

"Let's try."

So they went towards the house which was indeed derelict. The beautiful fanlight over the main entrance had no glass in it and several spines of the "fan" were broken, while the window through which Rodes had climbed had been roughly boarded up to keep out curious children.

"I do not understand it," Merriment exclaimed, and putting his shoulder against the door, he pushed. It gave suddenly under his pressure and he lurched inside.

As he stood looking about him, the others joined him. Light poured through a hole in the roof; the walls were cracked; and a very thick coating of dust covered everything.

"Good God! Look!" exclaimed Rodes, pointing at the dust on the floor of the hall. "Footprints! Two men's and a woman's."

He strode forward and put his foot in one of the smaller of the men's prints.

"It fits exactly!" he exclaimed. "Mine!"

They followed the footprints up the stairs into the ante-room. It was empty save for the table, and in the dust that covered it they saw the marks of two glasses.

And as the three men stood looking down at the marks in benumbed silence, suddenly the air about them became disturbed. At first it was a slight draught, but in seconds it rose in a violent crescendo, with a roar which made their ears throb.

Instinctively they covered their faces with their hands to keep swirling dust from eyes, noses and throats. As the dust eddied about them it pecked at the skin of their hands and faces, like spiteful birds.

Then as suddenly as it had risen, it died away.

Cautiously they looked about them. Nothing seemed to have been disturbed, even the carpet of dust on the floor.

But as they looked at it they saw that the three sets of footprints which had been there when they had entered, had gone—only the prints they had just made remained.

A shiver of apprehension ran through Rodes' body.

"God!" he exclaimed. "I'm getting out of here!"

And he fled down the staircase, the others at his heels.

Amazonian Horrors

The difference between nature in England and nature in Amazonia is that people escape to one and flee from the other. No one in South America talks of "getting away from it all". Nature is a thing to be feared. Escape lies in the cities, despite the fact that a person is just as likely to be killed by a motor-car in Rio de Janeiro as by a bushmaster on the banks of the Amazon.

But in Amazonia nature is gigantic, malignant, full of horrors which man could never invent. In no other tropical country is nature more inimical. The most ferocious shark of the Pacific has nothing on the vicious little piranhas who will eat alive the unwary swimmer in the Amazon, and nowhere else on the face of the earth is to be found such a loathsome fish as the candiru, which burrows its nose, with its terrible barbs, into the natural orifices of the body and causes indescribable agony.

It is not surprising that nature of this sort should bring out the worst in man. More horrors were perpetrated in the Amazon than were ever told to a shocked world by such investigators as Sir Roger Casement. It is not illogical to suppose that the horrors of nature conspired with the evil in man to bring out the worst in him.

The hostile nature of the flora and fauna created a deep impression on Europeans when they first entered Amazonia centuries ago. It was the origin of many legends and tall travel tales.

Brazil was exploited by both Spain and Portugal in the great centuries of the Latin-American colonial empires, and adventurers of both countries penetrated into the interior with a reckless courage which claims our admiration, even though we criticize their methods and motives.

The first descent of the mighty river from the Andes to the Atlantic was made in 1541 by Francisco de Orellana, a Spanish soldier, one of Pizarro's gang of robbers and murderers who looted and destroyed the empire of the Incas in the name of the Emperor Charles V. Orellana is reported to have encountered a tribe of female warriors and this inspired him to name the river *Amazonas*.

The horrors experienced during those early voyages of exploration soon entered into legend, and fearsome stories of monstrous animals of nightmare appearance, of terrifying powers and ferocity, appeared in supposedly authentic travel tales until well into the nineteenth century.

But no more hideous fish than the piranha was ever invented by the feverish imaginations of the writers of ancient travel books. Size was usually considered an essential attribute of piscatorial horrors. But the piranha is not a large fish. It is in fact relatively small, though not as small as some travellers have reported.

The full-grown male is eight inches long and the female ten inches. Sometimes they grow to two feet in length and a two-foot-long fish is not small.

Piranhas are peculiarly vicious flesh-eaters, excited and attracted by blood which they can scent through the water for great distances. They have ugly, bulldog faces with massive jaws and mouths equipped with razor-sharp teeth which make a continuous cutting edge. They can excise a piece of flesh cleanly at one bite. They have large eyes and their incurving vicious teeth are prominent. The piranha's body is brownish silver with dark patches, its fins grey-brown with black borders. The body gives the impression that it has been compressed. It has a keel on its back and its belly, and its caudal fin is broad and blade-like, enabling it to swim at great speed.

The piranhas have a savage and fearsome reputation and will attack animals of every kind, including man. There are stories of men being literally stripped to the bone in a few minutes when attacked by a pack of these predators.

Fording a stream in the Amazon is always hazardous unless the absence of piranhas is established.

These remarkable fish have recently been kept in captivity and are greatly prized by aquarists on account of their evil reputation, a piranha being a real show-piece. But they are difficult to keep and require a high protein diet—meat, liver, fish and any flesh. They savagely rip and tear their food, dead or alive, to pieces. They are impossible to breed in captivity. Attempts at mating usually result in one fish killing the other.

The unpleasant habits of the piranha were put to practical use by unscrupulous men in the bad old days of the Amazon when the authority of the central government did not reach the hinterland. One practice was to tie your enemy to a stake, make a small gash in his stomach and then immerse him waist-deep in the river and await results. The piranhas would soon be attracted by the blood seeping from the wound, and if they came in a swarm the unfortunate victim would within minutes have every inch of flesh torn from that part of his body which was immersed in the river. This was a particularly horrible and agonizing death. When the body was pulled out of the water, the lower half would be practically all skeleton—a remarkable sight, even for those times.

Similar atrocities were perpetrated during the savage war between Paraguay and Brazil which lasted from 1865 to 1870. Both sides played the apparently amusing game of "feeding the little fishes" with prisoners of war staked in the river and bloodied to await the piranhas, which infested the River Paraná and its tributaries as well as the Amazon.

In this war, which was over boundary disputes, Brazilian mulatto troops invaded Paraguay. Not only the Paraguayan men, but also the women, and boys of twelve to fourteen, fought in the field. So great was the slaughter in this terrible conflict, that the population of Paraguay, which had been 1,337,439 at the beginning of the war, was reduced to a quarter of a million of whom less than thirty thousand were men.

Nothing else can produce a skeleton from living flesh as quickly as the piranha. Even crocodiles fear them, for their tough armour is no protection against the razor teeth of these terrible fish.

When cattle are being taken across a river infested with piranhas, the practice is to put a freshly-killed crocodile in the river downstream, and then get the cattle across while the piranhas flay the crocodile. Failing a crocodile, one of the cattle has to be sacrificed.

The Amazon is the world's most dangerous river to swim in, but of course many brave the perils from the necessity of crossing the innumerable streams and tributaries. Men examine their bodies carefully before entering the river to ensure that they have no cut or open sore which would attract the piranhas, and in the Amazon, with the steamy air infested by vicious flies and insects, unbroken and unbitten skin is uncommon.

In the ranches near the Paraguay the slaughter-houses of the canned-beef factories were beside the river bank. Not only did these places reek with the smell of burnt bones and decayed flesh, but the river itself was tainted, and swarmed with piranhas feeding on the abattoir waste which went into the river.

No one dared to venture into the river at these places. A peon, fishing for piranhas (which are considered a delicacy), fell into the river. Instantly he was set upon by swarms of the fish he was trying to catch. The following day his skeleton was recovered, picked clean.

Travellers in these malignant regions reported that not the slightest sympathy was ever expressed for victims of these misfortunes. On the contrary, the sight of a man struggling in the river and fighting for his life against the vicious creatures which attacked him, from crocodiles to piranhas, was usually treated as great entertainment. Crowds would gather on the bank cheering the man on, bets would be wagered on the chances of his coming out of the river alive, but no attempt would be made to assist him.

It seemed that it was quite a laughable occurrence when a man, unable to get his leg quickly enough out of the piranha-infested water, should have every shred of flesh torn off his foot in less than a minute.

There was the case of the Brazilian soldier fishing from a canoe in the upper reaches of the Paraguay. He caught an extra-large fish on his line, and its violent struggles upset the canoe and he went into the water. He caught hold of the stern of the canoe and shouted for help. Rescue came in the shape of another canoe, the occupants of which, instead of taking the soldier out of the water, towed his canoe to the bank with him holding on to it.

When they pulled him ashore they found that he was dead, though his fingers remained tightly clasped to the canoe. The piranhas had flayed him alive below the waist, where not one particle of flesh remained on his bones. This was considered one of the best jokes on the Paraguay for months.

Another fish of peculiar horror in Amazonia is the candiru, which infests the tributaries of the Madeira on the borders of Brazil and Bolivia. This piscatorial terror is no more than two inches in length and a quarter of an inch thick. It has a hard, piercing snout, knife-like teeth and swept-back barbs on its body. Its habit is to burrow itself into the natural orifices of the body and once it gets inside it cannot be taken out on account of the barbs. The pain and suffering involved in having one of these little horrors inside your body can be imagined. The prize exhibit of a doctor who practised on the Tambopata River in the early years of the century was a candiru he had extracted from a man's penis. The man, as well as the candiru, died under the operation.

Other perils of the Amazon are electric eels, a single shock from which is sufficient to paralyse and consequently drown a man. This particular eel, the puraque, which is about six feet long, makes sure of its victim by returning to the attack and administering repeated shocks.

The banks of the Amazon swarm with snakes and reptiles of legendary ferocity. A fearsome snake is the bushmaster, which sometimes grows to a length of fifteen feet and may be a foot in diameter at the thickest part of the body. Bushmasters are very fierce and will attack human beings at sight in the mating season. It has been known to hunt a man down. Death rapidly follows one single bite from its double-fanged jaws. Another terrifying snake is the nacanina, a large creature which attacks on sight without provocation. It is extremely savage and moves at a frightening speed.

Death lurks for the unwary walker in these snake-infested regions, and some of the most deadly snakes are very small. Those who go barefoot expose themselves to great danger.

Another legendary terror of the Amazon is the anaconda, the largest of all living snakes. Travellers have reported anacondas of up to sixty-five feet in length, though naturalists doubt this.

The anaconda is a creature of the rivers and is semi-aquatic. It is sometimes called the water-boa. It feeds on mammals and birds that frequent the river banks, stalking its prey through the mud and water. It is olive or greenish brown with large roundish black spots scattered along the body. Anacondas sometimes fight other reptiles such as the caiman—a kind of antediluvian nightmare in which the anaconda usually manages to crush the caiman to death.

Anacondas are greatly feared on account of their strength and terrifying size. There is a story of a party of travellers who camped near the river bank where they could sling their hammocks. One man, who could not sleep on account of his companions' snores, had the habit of slinging his hammock a little distance away so that he was out of earshot. During the night he was heard to utter a shriek which was suddenly stifled in a manner which suggested that his windpipe was being squeezed. His companions rushed over with a lantern to find the solitary sleeper encoiled, hammock and all, by the body of a huge anaconda. They opened fire on the monster, which released his victim and beat a retreat to the river. The man was dead and there was not an unbroken bone left in his body.

It was customary for rubber gatherers to work in pairs in the forests, so greatly feared were the anacondas. Many lone workers mysteriously disappeared.

Anacondas are said to give off a penetrating and very unpleasant odour. This is said to come from their breath, which is believed to have the effect of stupefying their prey. There is a curious belief in the Matto Grosso that if a man is bitten by one and survives, then he is immune from the bite of any poisonous snake. Anacondas are prolific breeders. An Amazonian hunter once shot one and opened it up to find no less than forty-five young ones in its body.

Everything about the Amazon river life is huge and, to all but the natives, demoralizing. Bees are enormous and make a noise like a small motor. The insects bite ferociously and there are enormous spiders whose bite can mean death. Large spotted catfish make strange grunts under water. Ants are so big you can hear them.

Soldier ants are a much dreaded peril. They march in countless millions and you can hear their approach—a deadly whisper of sound which grows into a kind of hissing, weird and fearful. They eat everything in their path, humans not excepted. If you do not get out of their way the consequences can be horrible in the extreme. Many an unwary sleeper has been woken by the torment of a million bites to find himself being eaten alive, and of course being staked on an ant-hill was a well-known form of torture.

Soldier ants are huge and are so named because they march in columns, about eight or nine inches wide. They breed at a fantastic rate and an invasion of countless millions of them is difficult to repulse. One way is to pour petrol over the vanguard and set light to them. For a time they will still come on, marching blindly suicidal, into the flames; then eventually they retreat, sometimes to reform their ranks and return to the attack.

Habitations are often abandoned at the approach of the ants, which go through the dwellings, picking everything clean, and annihilating all the insects and vermin, which is not unwelcome.

In Africa it is said that soldier ants are the only creatures that lions are afraid of, and that these insect predators will climb up the trunks of elephants and drive them mad with fright and pain as they consume the brain.

In Amazonia the Brazilian fire-ant is the most vicious of the ants, and has an extremely painful bite. It inhabits a certain tree, the *palo santo* (the holy tree) which grows on the river banks. If you touch the tree, the ants rush out from holes in the trunk, and even drop down from the branches above, to attack with great viciousness. Indians sometimes tie their enemies to these trees and leave them to die in indescribable torment, a particular piece of unpleasantness which some white men who came to Amazonia were quick to imitate.

The Amazonian forest itself is dark and steamy, and beneath the high-flung tree tops, aflame with brilliant orchids, it is a place of death and decay. From the rotting tree trunks, stagnant pools and black mud arises a suffocating odour. Even delicate, lacy creepers give off dank perfumes. The foot sinks into green, stinking slime which clings sickeningly so that every step forward is an effort that pulls at the leg muscles. Among the slime, beneath the thick screen of creepers, lurk the anacondas.

Under this vivid canopy of bright green which faces the sky and is laced with riotous colour, there is the silence of death, amid which nature is engaged in a perpetuated death struggle. Everything that grows climbs straight up, desperate to get to the blazing light of the high-flung forest roof, where its leaves and flowers can luxuriate in the sun while its roots are fed by the odoriferous compost below.

The trees' most deadly enemy is the liana, an enormous vine-like creeper which grows swiftly, and seems to leap from tree to tree, curling around them like deadly snakes, covering them with thick green drapery. Some lianas are of enormous size and they spiral around the trees like boa-constrictors, feeding on them, suffocating them, and finally crushing the very life out of them, dying themselves as they do so. The tree then falls to become home and food for swarming insects, the steamy damp and spreading fungus rapidly rotting it into rich, malodorous decay.

The lianas seem to have a life of their own, growing beneath the trees in strange, tangled patterns, turning first one way then another, threatening this tree and then that. Finally several lianas at once attack one tree in a concerted effort, leaving the others untouched.

There are none of the delightful pleasure-giving flowers of the temperate regions in these savage forests. No nightingales sing. There are no restful gardens or pleasant landscapes. Everything is bold and savage. Flowers drug each other with poisonous odours, and seem to engage in strange cannibalistic sexual rites.

This habitat brought out the worst in man. In an air laden with disease and decay life was short, with the highest mortality in modern times.

The horrors of Amazon river life were enormously increased in the early years of the century by the activities of the rubber companies who forced the natives to work for them by atrocities which shocked and scandalized the civilized world. Slavery was openly practised. You could even buy white people by paying off their debts. The debtors then became your property by some cynically twisted process of law.

In 1910 Sir Roger Casement was sent to the Putumayo district of Peru to investigate the atrocities. His report created a sensation, and resulted in an English rubber company being compulsorily wound up. According to travellers who were there at the time, Casement told only a fraction of the ghastly story of what was going on, and no effective steps were ever taken to improve the hideous lot of the unfortunate Indians.

"Slavery, bloodshed and vice reigned supreme on the rivers," said Colonel P. H. Fawcett, "and there was no halt to it until the bottom fell out of the rubber market." Even then, according to other travellers, the atrocities continued.

The Indians were hunted for sport, not being considered human by the depraved white traders and rubber men who ruled districts where there was no law. The native men were slaughtered, or taken to the slave compounds and flogged into submission, the children's brains were dashed out against trees, and any comely girls were raped or taken back to the settlements for the personal harems of the white managers.

Sometimes the Indians got the better of it. An armed party, sent into the forests to find slave labour, were later found in a large dug-out canoe drifting down river. Each man had been chopped up into little pieces.

Things are different today, but nothing has altered the malignant nature of the wild life in the Amazon.

The Image of Fear

Wang-Foo had always longed to become a state official and for years he had worked and studied hoping that one day he might be considered sufficiently promising to enter for the first examination. But learning seemed beyond him and he could not write an essay without making innumerable mistakes. He was constantly chaffed and teased by his fellow-students because of his dull wits. All the same, he persisted with his studies, always hopeful that one day he would achieve some small success.

After his day's work was finished Wang-Foo liked nothing better than to go out in the evenings to meet the other students, with whom he drank and enjoyed himself. Despite all the chaffing about his scholastic incompetence, Wang was popular socially. He was always game for anything, and utterly fearless, and after several cups of wine, no matter what foolhardy act they dared him to do, he had never yet failed to carry it out. He delighted to hear their acclamations for his deeds of daring and to be admired for his courage; it made up for his insufficiencies in other respects.

Wang's fellow students were always thinking out deeds more daring than the one he had previously performed, for they wondered just how far his dull wits would lead him.

It was the ringleader, Chu-Ming, who thought of a blood-curdling escapade for Wang which frightened them out of their wits, and after which Wang, though his courage remained, became a changed man.

"We all know that you are a brave fellow, Wang," said Chu-Ming. "But I bet you dare not visit the Temple at midnight and go to the torture chambers."

The other students applauded such a brilliant idea, for it was said that the screams of the tortured heard in the corridors of the Temple were so terrible that even the stoutest would come out pale as death and shaking with fear.

"If you do this, my friend, we will give you a feast in recognition of your courage," continued Chu-Ming. "But, of course, we will need proof that you have indeed entered the torture chambers."

With several cups of wine inside him, Wang was quite happy to undertake the test his friends demanded, and the promise of a feast was an added incentive.

"What would you like me to bring back from the Temple?" he asked.

His friends were full of suggestions, and at last it was agreed that the effigy of the most fearsome of all the gods, the Judge of the Underworld himself, should be brought back by the fearless one for them all to see.

In the corridors of the Temple stood the carved images of all the gods and devils of the Ten Courts of the Underworld, which looked frighteningly lifelike. None was as horrible to see as the fearsome Judge with his green face, fierce staring eyes and bushy red eyebrows and beard. One could only guess at the retribution which might befall anyone who dared remove an effigy from its place in the Temple, for no one had ever done such a thing.

As midnight struck, Wang entered the dimly-lit chambers of the Temple. The Judge's image was enthroned in the left corridor and Wang quickly made his way there, trying to ignore the screechings and wailings of lost souls in their agonies of torture which seemed to surround him, echoing from every dark corner of the sinister place. The trials had been held under torture and many had been tortured to death.

The carved images looked terribly alive in the half gloom and Wang only glanced at them briefly as he searched for the one of the Judge. He stopped short with a gasp as he at last contemplated the repulsive effigy which he must take to show to his fellow students. He repressed the shudder which went through him as he lifted it on to his shoulder. It was only a wooden carving after all.

Quickly he retraced his steps, anxious to get out of the Temple and away from the nerve-racking cries of the damned which followed him as he plodded along with the fearsome burden.

By the time he got back to his companions his spirits had revived. Nothing unforeseen had happened, and he had carried out his act of bravery to the letter. He set the Judge down where all could see him, and his drinking companions gasped and recoiled as they viewed the hideous image which made their blood run cold.

Wang awaited their acclamations, but at first they seemed to be overcome and turned away from the horrific Judge, pale and ill at ease, wishing that they had never suggested such frightening proof of Wang's courage.

When Wang saw his companions' unease he experienced a feeling of superiority. At least his courage exceeded theirs. The Judge's image did not seem so fearsome to him now, away from the ghostly corridors and the haunted cries of the Temple. He poured himself a cup of wine and also one for the Judge, whom he jestingly invited to join them. He poured the red wine into the carved wooden mouth, and it trickled down on to the floor, looking like a pool of blood at their feet.

Wang's companions were not amused and they begged him to take the effigy back to the Temple immediately. "We all know you are a stout fellow, but it is unwise to invoke the gods. Return the Judge to his rightful place with all possible speed before something terrible happens," begged Chu-Ming, who had never thought that Wang would complete this task.

But Wang was in no hurry. He held his cup of wine towards the Judge's image as though toasting him. "O great Judge," he said, "I am only a simple man, and though I have studied hard for many years, I have acquired no learning. If in your wisdom you would condescend to visit me in my humble home, I would be delighted if you would take a cup of wine with me."

His companions looked on aghast and again entreated their fool-hardy friend to carry the Judge back to the Temple. Wang drained his cup of wine. The party was over. His companions had lost their gaiety. He might as well go home to his wife—that excellent creature whose one drawback was her very plain face. Lifting the Judge on to his shoulders, he retraced his now slightly unsteady steps to the wailing corridors of the dark and sinister Temple, replaced the effigy without mishap, setting it down with extra care, and left it there with a courteous bow.

The promised feast took place the following evening, and as the night progressed all the participants congratulated themselves that the previous night's adventure had ended without mishap. Wang was toasted over and over again, and his companions were by then able to laugh about it, especially Wang's drunken invitation to the Judge to take wine with him in his humble home. They kidded him and asked him what he would really do if the Judge accepted his invitation.

"I should take it as a compliment and accept him as an honoured guest. But that will never happen, my friends."

Wang was wrong in this. Hardly had he settled himself with a final cup of wine before going to bed, when the bamboo curtains were drawn aside and the great Judge himself entered the room. He looked even more fearsome than his effigy. For the first time in his life Wang was really afraid.

He beseeched the red-bearded one not to kill him. "I would not blame Your Honour if you cut off my head, for I must have greatly offended you. But please do not blame me, for I am a simple man, and if you spare my life I will honour you for as long as I live."

Wang was on his knees, and when he dared to look up at his strange visitor he could hardly believe his eyes, for the Judge was grinning at him.

"Have no fear, my friend." His voice was gruff, but not at all frightening. "Never before have I had an invitation from a mortal. I appreciate it. Now get up, my good fellow, and pour me that glass of wine which you promised me."

Wang jumped to his feet and rushed around attending to the Judge's comfort. He built up the fire to warm the jug of wine, and went to order the servants to prepare food for his guest. Wang fetched the food himself when it was ready, for his wife refused to go near their fearsome visitor, of whom she had heard many strange and horrifying stories, and she was sure that if the servants set eyes on him they would all run away in terror.

The Judge was indeed a frightening spectacle with his green complexion, dark-red hair and beard like sprouting fire. But Wang also saw pleasure and amusement in those fiery eyes and he was no longer afraid. The learned Judge discussed the classics and made many quotations. Wang did his best to reply, asking simple questions which were answered with ease by his visitor, who then recited poetry from the Underworld, which Wang agreed was much the same as the poetry of mortals.

Having wined and dined very well at the feast, Wang soon dropped off to sleep while the Judge was still talking and drinking, and when he awoke in the early dawn his guest from the Underworld had gone.

This was the first of many such visits from the spirit Judge who talked and drank with Wang far into the night. Wang's wife was very frightened each time the Judge visited her husband and she could not believe that any good would come of such a friendship.

"You are supping with the Devil," she told him. "Do not encourage him to come any more. Leave him to drink alone, then perhaps he will not return."

But Wang would not hear of it. "If I reject him now, his wrath will surely descend upon me and us all. No, it is much better to remain friends."

The Judge of the Underworld was a Chinese intellectual, and soon found that Wang's limited intelligence was a drawback to their friendship. He tried to help Wang with his studies, but Wang's efforts were very poor and the Judge grew impatient with his mortal friend.

One night the Judge left much earlier than usual and Wang, knowing that his spirit friend was annoyed with him, stayed up drinking alone. Perhaps the Judge would not come any more and that would please his wife, as well as his student friends whom he saw only occasionally these days.

Later, very drunk, he staggered to his room and flopped down on his bed in a stupor. Some time later he was awakened from a deep sleep by a sharp pain. On opening his eyes, he cried out in horror, for the Judge was standing over him with a vicious-looking knife with which he had just cut open Wang's chest. Wang's cries were strangled in his throat as, mesmerized, he watched the bearded one taking out his internal organs and placing them on the table beside him. Wang no longer felt any pain, but he experienced a terrible fear as he watched with horror and waited to die. Eventually it was too much for him and he fainted.

When the Judge had arranged Wang's organs on the table beside him, he drew from his pocket another heart which he proceeded to put in place of Wang's heart. Chuckling with satisfaction, he replaced all Wang's other organs and closed up the wound, fastening it securely with a bandage.

When Wang came to he was light-headed, but he felt no pain. There was no trace of blood and he thought he must have dreamed the horror which had taken place before his eyes. But when he saw his heart on the table beside him, he knew that it had been no nightmare, and he was filled with dread.

The Judge appeared before him at that moment, picked up the heart from the table and put it in his pocket.

"Do not be afraid," he said, looking at Wang's anguished face. "You will not die. I have simply exchanged your inadequate heart for one of higher intelligence. Your heart will be put in the place of the one I took from the Underworld. You, my friend, will become more intelligent and our discussions more rewarding for both of us."

Wang fell asleep in a state of exhaustion and disbelief. In the morning he awoke refreshed, his fears dispelled. He removed the bandage and found no sign of blood, just a thin red line, with the wound perfectly healed. Elated, he told his wife, but she refused to believe him, saying he must have been scratched while in his cups. But she was soon to wonder and to question her husband further, for his studies were no longer a labour to him and he made rapid progress in his work.

The Judge did not over-praise him, but told Wang that he could now enter for the first examination. Wang did and, to the astonishment of everyone, came first. Wang was honest enough to tell his fellow-students the secret of his success, though it was evident that few believed him.

Meanwhile another problem was on Wang's mind. Though greatly indebted to the Judge, he begged the great one to grant him another miraculous favour.

"Tell me what it is you desire, my friend, and I will do my best for you," responded the Judge.

"It is my wife," confessed Wang. "I am fond of her, and she attends to my every need. I was betrothed to her in childhood and obediently followed my parents' wishes. But, though her figure is excellent, her face leaves much to be desired. In fact she is really quite ugly. Would it be possible for you to give her a beautiful face?"

The Judge's eyes flashed fire as he contemplated his mortal friend. He grinned widely, exposing his purple-tinged, uneven teeth. The idea plainly appealed to him. "It may take a little time," he said, "for it will be not so easy to find."

Two weeks later the Judge came to tell Wang that he expected to arrive with his heart's desire that very midnight, and he must make sure that his wife was given a sleeping draught so that she would be unaware of what was happening.

On the stroke of midnight the Judge arrived silently and promptly, and with a thrill of nervous anticipation Wang saw that the Judge had something concealed under his coat.

"I had great trouble in getting it," said the fearsome one. "But I think you will be pleased." He drew the object from its place of concealment, lifting it by its long silken hair.

At first Wang shuddered with horror as he saw that the blood was still wet upon the slender neck, but as he contemplated the beauty of the face, its perfect features, winged eyebrows with long curling lashes resting on rounded cheeks, all he could think of was that beautiful head lying on the pillow beside him each night.

The Judge was impatient to get on with the operation, and he urged Wang to take him to his wife's bedside as quietly as possible so as not to disturb the servants. Wang was given the head to hold while the Judge took out his terrible knife, and Wang preferred to admire the beautiful face and feel the silkiness of the tresses rather than watch the Judge cutting off the head from his wife's body. The Judge took the lovely new face from Wang and fitted it carefully and with supernatural skill to the neck of the inert body on the bed. Wang shuddered as he saw his wife's poor head lying there where it had rolled off under the Judge's knife.

The Judge completed his awful task with mystic passes, and Wang was thrilled and awed to see the lovely new face grow warmly into sleeping life, the lips move, the eyelids flutter. The Judge then gave Wang his wife's old head, telling him to take it and bury it deeply in the garden. After assuring the trembling Wang that all would be well in the morning, the Judge left.

Wang performed his gruesome task and then drank several cups of wine before he went to bed. But sleep would not come easily to him. Twice he crept to his wife's bed and found she looked just the same as when the Judge had left, with her new head propped up with pillows, pale and beautiful.

In the morning he was awoken by a terrified maid telling him that there was a strange woman in his wife's room with blood on her neck. When Wang went into the room he found his now beautiful wife washing away the dried blood. Then she looked at herself in the mirror in dumbfounded amazement. She traced the thin red line around her neck with a delicate finger. There was no bleeding but there was a difference in the colouring of the skin above and below her new face.

The maid fainted and lay on the floor, ignored by husband and wife as they both admired the beautiful features, rosebud mouth, perfect almond-shaped dark eyes and dimpled cheeks. Wang told his wife what had happened to cause this amazing transformation, and though she could not help being pleased to behold her new beauty when she had previously been so plain, she had her misgivings, for she could not hide her fear of the Judge. Now they were so much in his debt she was afraid that a day of terrible reckoning would come.

Where Wang was content to accept the Judge's gift in all good faith, his wife wanted to know from whom she had acquired her beautiful new head, and she told her husband that she would not be happy until she had found out.

Wang was reluctant to ask the Judge such a question, and it required several cups of wine to enable him to pluck up courage to do so at their next meeting.

After expressing his profuse thanks for this new happiness, he said, "I am afraid that my wife is asking many questions. She wants to know whether the head was taken from the dead or from the living."

The Judge's face seemed to turn greener than ever and his eyes glowed like red coals in the pale light of the lamp. Wang wondered if he had gone too far in trying to satisfy his wife's inquisitive fears and doubts.

"Despite my reputation, I would never take from the living, you can assure your wife of that," declared the Judge. "How the poor girl met her death was none of my doing."

Encouraged by the Judge's assurance, Wang said: "It seems as though the girl's death was not a natural one. But how did you come to know of it so quickly? I realized by the still wet blood on her neck that the deed could not long have taken place before you brought the head to my house."

"And you were correct, my friend. Only a short time previously she had been murdered by a villainous character who saw her at the Temple, and, taking a fancy to her, followed her home. She had been mourning the death of her betrothed and he thought that she would welcome his attentions. He entered her room after dark and forced himself upon her. She was a virtuous maid and refused him, fighting him with all her strength, whereupon he became so incensed that he attacked her with his knife and cut off her head."

"What a dreadful tale. But you must have known what was happening. Why did you not try to stop this foul deed?"

"Do not question me further, friend," said the Judge. "You asked for the head of a beautiful maid upon which you can now feast your eyes daily. You must not think of anything else. Certainly your wife must never be told how it came into my hands."

Wang realized only too well the significance of the Judge's remarks, and he could not hide his dismay. His spirit friend left earlier than usual, reminding Wang of the secret they shared.

The tale of the beautiful new face of the wife of Wang-Foo soon spread, and many came to see for themselves, but they never stayed long. The older ones spoke openly of the folly of receiving favours from the Underworld and consorting with the spirits of the Devil. One day Wang and his wife were visited by a high official called Yu-Tang, who on seeing Wang's wife was quite overcome, saying that she was his daughter returned from the dead.

Wang, guessing who the man was, sent his wife away, for she was disturbed by the scene no less than himself. On questioning Yu-Tang, Wang knew that he was the father of the murdered girl, so he tried to explain how it happened that his wife had the face of the official's dead daughter. Whereupon Yu-Tang blamed Wang for his daughter's murder, refusing to believe that another had been the culprit. As he left Wang's house, he threatened to go to the authorities with the story and to accuse Wang of the murder of his daughter.

Wang realized that the time of reckoning had arrived. The Judge had kept away since Wang had questioned him, and even if he came now, how could he help, for no one would believe his story of the fearsome Judge of the Underworld. The servants had never seen him, and in their simple minds had accepted the change in their mistress as being part of their master's new mystic powers since he had acquired knowledge so suddenly and mysteriously. Wang's wife wept bitterly when he told her that he might be taken away by the authorities at any time, for he had been accused of the murder and he had to tell her why.

Under the circumstances he was sure the Judge no longer cared what happened to him. But at dusk that evening the Judge came and he told Wang to send a servant to the house of Yu-Tang with a letter telling him that he could prove his innocence. "Say that he must come to your house immediately and hear the truth from someone who knows the real murderer, whose name will be revealed to him." Wang wrote the letter and told his servant to deliver it with all possible speed.

The Judge said that he would return when darkness fell and when Yu-Tang had partaken of Wang's hospitality.

Wang doubted whether Yu-Tang would accept the invitation, but he did come, and was at first in a belligerent mood, though after several cups of wine both men were in an easier frame of mind.

At the appearance of the Judge, however, Yu-Tang seemed scared to death, for never had he seen anyone who looked so fearsome in the shadows cast by the lamp.

"Do not be afraid of my learned friend," Wang told him. "He cannot help his looks. Have some more wine while he tells you the story of how your dear daughter met her death."

Yu-Tang had more wine, but even after he had heard the Judge's story he refused to believe in Wang's innocence. "I am an important official," he said, "and I cannot accept the word of a spirit from the Underworld. There is no proof that another cut off my daughter's head, and even if it were true, you were the one who instigated the crime. You should have been content with your wife as she was."

Wang refilled the wine-cups and the more they argued the more convinced he became that all was lost, and then as the two mortals became so drunk that they eventually fell asleep the Judge carried out his plan, for it was the only way of saving his friend Wang from arrest by the authorities within a few hours.

Wang was awakened in the early hours by loud bangs on his

door. Still in a half-drunken stupor, he staggered to his feet to open it and to give himself up, but the officials pushed by him asking for the murderer Wang-Foo. He followed them back into the room where Yu-Tang had been sleeping with his head resting in his arms on the table. Yu-Tang was roughly lifted and half-carried out of the house, protesting at his treatment, but to no avail.

Wang could do nothing but watch in stupefied horror and disbelief as he saw that the unfortunate man had a thin red line around his neck.

Wang looked into the mirror, knowing that the Judge had been busy with his knife for the third time.

The face that looked back at him was that of Yu-Tang.

Lullaby for the Dead

If there was one thing Colonel Ewart detested, it was public transport. Perfectly at home on a horse (he had been in India with Hardinge's cavalry at the time of the Sutlej campaign, in which he had distinguished himself), slightly less so in a private carriage, he regarded with incredulous horror those citizens of London who allowed themselves to be herded into omnibuses: on the whole, he would have preferred death to travelling in one. But in these degenerate days, the great coaching times over, even he could not avoid an occasional ordeal by railway train. The only defence was to face it like a soldier, and thank one's stars things had improved since the beginnings: he recollected with a shudder the conditions of open carriages, flying grit, wildly rocking trucks and suffocating, filthy smoke. At least things were better now.

For his long journey from Carlisle to London he had carefully chosen from Bradshaw an unpopular train. It took a little longer than the crack trains, but he hoped it would compensate for this by a reasonable emptiness. Not that Colonel Ewart particularly disliked his fellow-men: it was the state of being herded together with them that he found intolerable.

He was relieved to be shown by the porter into an empty compartment. His luggage disposed on the rack, the man handsomely tipped, the guard greeted, a new volume of military memoirs invitingly placed by his side, together with an unread *Times*, and

the *Illustrated London News*, he prepared for a journey which migh
be tedious but at least would not be horrible.

In his service days the Colonel had been renowned for his capacity
to appreciate a situation rapidly and assess its probable outcome. On
this occasion the gift failed him.

When the whistle blew and the great train began slowly to move
out of Carlisle station he was still alone. Much relieved, he detached
a page of *The Times* containing matter which did not interest him,
and scrupulously laid it on the opposite seat as a barrier between his
feet and the upholstery. Would that all travellers would do the
same, he thought righteously, and prevent that unpleasant experience
of finding oneself sitting on a boot-soiled seat! Stretching out his
long legs in comfort, he opened the paper at the leader page.

Then it occurred to him that his boots were very new and he
would be even more comfortable without them. He removed them,
and his great-coat, and settled to read. But the route was fresh to
him, and after a moment he raised his head and looked out with a
certain pleasure at the fine Cumberland scenery which was rushing
past. Bleak and yet fertile in its way; happily free from the human
figures which so defaced landscape to him: yet how fortunate were
these once remote places to be linked to cities by modern inventions.
What a remarkable number of telegraph poles there were, for
instance. He must have counted twenty in the last couple of minutes.

At this point *The Times* slid to the carriage floor, for Colonel
Ewart was asleep.

He woke with that unpleasant dryness of mouth and discomfort
of the neck which always accompanies a train doze. So acute were
these symptoms that he came to the conclusion that he must have
been asleep for a good hour—possibly more. The rugged fells of
Cumberland had been exchanged for the unmistakable scenery of
Lancashire lakeland. They must have passed Shap Fell long since.

He bent to retrieve his paper and as he did so saw with annoyance that he was no longer alone. In the corner facing the engine on
the opposite side of the carriage sat a woman. She must have got in
at Penrith, confound it: how soundly he had slept not to have felt
the train stop and been aware of her entry! At least she looked like
a lady, not the sort to be a troublesome fellow-passenger. He had
suffered much with eaters of nauseous-smelling picnics, complainers
about draughts or stuffiness, and incorrigible talkers. The woman was

sitting quietly enough, bending forward a little. He never noticed the cut or fashion of women's clothes, but had the impression that the loose dolman which hid her figure was slightly old-fashioned, judging by the sort of thing his wife wore. Her small winged hat had a veil attached to it which concealed, he felt sure, a young face, for the hair that showed was brown and rich.

The Colonel suddenly became aware that he was not correctly dressed to appear in the presence of a lady, lacking as he was both coat and (worse) boots. With something like a blush mantling his campaign-tanned cheeks, he began to apologize, at the same time struggling into his coat and attempting to insert his feet into his boots without the aid of hands—an operation which proved to be quite impossible.

"I really must beg your pardon, madam," he said nervously, "for my state of—ah—undress. I had no idea that you had entered the compartment, or I would not have departed so much from—ah—from . . ."

His apology seemed to be wasted, for the lady did not reply; did not even turn her head towards him. She continued to sit forward, looking down.

The Colonel hemmed and began again. "If I have unintentionally offended you, madam, I apologize sincerely."

Without answering, she began to rock gently, her arms with their falling shawl-sleeves hiding whatever she was cradling—yes, cradling, for now she was humming softly, almost tunelessly, an air which Colonel Ewart recognized from far-off nursery days as one sung by the old Scots nanny who had brought up himself and his sisters. How often he had heard her in the twilight dusk of the night-nursery, crooning it over one of the cots. How did it go? Something about a bairnie, and sleep, and a watching mother . . . Good heavens, was the woman travelling with a baby? The thought made Colonel Ewart's blood run cold, for although a good and affectionate family man, he recoiled from the human young in their earlier stages unless decently confined within cots, playpens or perambulators. The thought that he might be shut up with one for—how many hundred miles?—appalled him utterly.

Or perhaps it was an animal she nursed, though he saw no basket which might have contained cat or puppy. In fact, she appeared to have no luggage at all. Perhaps she was getting out at Kendal. He hoped so, for her behaviour was certainly very strange, productive of the sort of discomfort the brave Colonel was not used to feeling. He wished he could make her speak to him, even if it led to some unthinkable discussion about babies.

"Madam," he tried again, edging a little nearer.

She made no reply to this new overture, but broke off her humming and turned slightly towards him, still concealing her nursling. Through the veil he could just see a pale face and a pair of eyes that looked a little wild. There is nothing like a veil for lending provocativeness to a woman's glance, but this one produced in the Colonel no agreeable sensation of being tantalized. She glanced down at her lap, and held—whatever it was—closer, then glared back, fiercely he thought, at him. She appeared to be protecting her charge against him. Good heavens, she needn't trouble! Now she was crooning again, and he could distinguish a few words.

> Hush ye, my bairnie, my bonny wee dearie—
> Hush ye, my dove—

Colonel Ewart, in spite of his distaste for infants, could not resist out of sheer curiosity a closer look at the baby she was hugging so jealously. It would make an interesting anecdote to tell his wife when they sat at dinner that evening. He crossed to the opposite seat, so that he was sitting on the same side as his fellow-passenger, and moved up almost next to her. At that moment three things happened simultaneously. The woman's mouth opened in an O of soundless horror; though he could not see her face clearly, he would never quite forget it. Her arms rose in defence of what lay on her lap. An appalling crash shook the train and halted it with a violent jerk, throwing the Colonel to the floor.

It took him several moments to collect his thoughts and to realize, with relief, that he was not hurt, only bruised and battered. Stiffly he crawled to his feet among a scattered heap of valises, a soldier's chivalry impelling to offer help to his companion before thinking further of himself.

She was not there. The corner where she had been sitting was quite empty.

Outside the stationary train there was a confused noise of shouts and screams. No doubt, he thought, she had bolted from the carriage at the instant of impact and was somewhere out there among the passengers and crew he could see milling about on the line. He opened the door and climbed out. The train had not been derailed and there was only a short drop to the ground. Barely was he on his feet when he found himself confronted by the guard, to whom he had spoken at Carlisle. The guard was panting, capless and dishevelled.

"All right, sir? Thank God for that."

"What in Heaven's name happened, guard?"

"Don't know yet, sir. A mercy it was no worse, and so few travelling."

The Colonel was reminded of his carriage-mate. "The lady who was in my compartment—I hope she was not too alarmed? I thought she seemed in a rather nervous state of mind before the accident."

"What lady's that, sir?"

The Colonel described her as well as he could. "She got in at Penrith, I believe, when I was dozing."

The guard looked blank. "Nobody like that got in at Penrith, sir. I saw 'em in myself, and went down the carriages afterwards. You were alone in yours, and asleep, like you say."

"Nonsense, man! D'you think I can't believe my own eyes?"

The guard pointed to the disembarked passengers. "See anyone like her there, sir?"

The Colonel could not, but he persisted. "Of course she was in my compartment. You *must* have seen her. Youngish—veiled—with a baby."

"A *baby*, sir?"

"Well, I didn't actually set eyes on it—I was just going to ask her if I might look at it when the crash came: but she was certainly nursing something, and singing to it."

The guard's face turned an unpleasant greenish colour.

"Oh, my God! She's come back."

"Back? What d'you mean? Does she travel on this train often?"

"Often enough, sir. But not for a long time now. We thought she'd gone."

"Gone—where? You're being very mysterious, guard."

The guard looked hunted. "They want me over there, sir, I'll have to leave you." The Colonel detained him with a firm hand.

"Not before you've told me what you mean. Who is this young female?"

"All right, sir, if you must know. Years ago—must be six—there was a young couple travelled by this train, going on their honeymoon to London. There was nobody else in their compartment (for which they were glad enough when they set off, I reckon) but it was clear what happened."

"Well?"

The guard hesitated and went on. "This young man, the bridegroom—he must have been leaning out of the window at speed, watching the scenery; and a goods train came past, with a spike of sharp wire or something like it sticking out. Cut his head clean off, sir."

Colonel Ewart's complexion changed noticeably.

"When the train got into Kendal station the guard found her—praise be it wasn't me—rocking and singing, and nursing the—the body. She'd pulled the—the shoulders up off the floor, into her lap. A terrible sight she was, and mad as a hatter. Died soon after, I heard."

Colonel Ewart had never been so quiet at dinner as his wife found him that night. When he felt able to tell her of his experience, he added that his chief emotion, at the time and after, was one of deep thankfulness that the train collision had occurred *before* he had edged near enough to his companion to see what it was she nursed.

Rose: a Gothick Tale

Old Mrs Catt dexterously arranged the folds of her lace curtain to permit a better view of the goings-on next door, herself remaining invisible. Not but what all Highgate knew that very little occurred in the village without Mrs Catt perceiving it, and reporting any irregular aspect of it to the vicar. A widow in her sixties, her only pleasures lay in the interesting encounters she had while exchanging books at the Literary Institute (her name was down for the new, eagerly awaited novel by Mrs Henry Wood), in zealous attendance at the parish church, and in keen observation of the life that went on in the little High Street.

Her house, Lilac Cottage, was admirably placed close to the road, two doors from an inn. Here, half a century ago, some eighty coaches a day had called on their way from London to the North. Now its bustling days were over, but it still provided Mrs Catt with plenty of visual fuel. On this bright May morning, however, her sharp eyes were fixed on the house that lay between the inn and her own domain. New people were moving in at Maytree Cottage.

Soon after breakfast a cab had decanted at the door a respectable-looking young woman who had marched briskly up to the front door and let herself in, after banging the wicket gate and glancing disparagingly at the tiny overgrown front garden. Thereafter followed sounds of energetic scrubbing and cleaning. Windows were flung up with protesting creaks, buckets of water rushed down the

470

drain in the back garden. Mrs Catt listened approvingly. The last tenants had been none too particular, and certain unpleasant varieties of insect life had found their way next door. Mrs Catt recalled the often-repeated local legend of how, when a group of ancient cottages in Gallows Lane had been pulled down, whole squadrons, regiments, legions of dispossessed bugs had emerged and marched in full military formation across the road, so densely massed that the traffic stopped for them, and one particularly nervous horse took fright and bolted, later being discovered cropping the grass at Friern Barnet.

Within two hours or so of the young servant's arrival came the furniture. Modest but good, Mrs Catt noted, as the draymen transported a pretty occasional table, a chiffonier and some dainty whatnots from wagon to house. Small stuff, too, very suitable for neat rooms and twisting staircases.

"Quite a lot of it new. That means they've not been married long. Perhaps he'll carry her across the threshold. If they *are* married, that is. One reads such shocking things nowadays—gentlemen taking houses for these actresses. Well, they'll not fool *me*. I can always tell."

Mrs Catt was disappointed on both counts. The young man who emerged from a cab just before dinner-time handed out his lady with tender courtesy, but allowed her to enter her new home on her own feet. He looked pleasantly boyish, his youthful complexion belying the luxuriant handlebar moustache; the lady even younger, slight and pretty, and certainly a bride, Mrs Catt decided. Pausing at the gate to look up smilingly at the creeper-clad housefront, the blossoming red may tree, the girl drew off her gloves, and Mrs Catt saw a broad gold band on the wedding finger. On other fingers, she noticed with eager interest, were at least four other rings: the sunshine struck colour from diamonds, dark fire from rubies.

"Well-to-do, then. He's married above him, I shouldn't wonder."

Within twenty-four hours of the couple's arrival, by discreet employment of her small servant, followed up by a neighbourly invitation to take tea, Mrs Catt had discovered that their name was Winterborne, that they had just returned from a honeymoon by Lake Geneva, that Mrs Winterborne was the daughter of a knight who had his own estate in Sussex ("that explains the rings," she thought) and that Mr Winterborne worked for a firm of wineshippers in Eastcheap. Over the second cup of tea, she discovered why they had chosen to live in Highgate.

"My father's town house is in Cavendish Square," said the bride, her modest, gentle manner securing her from any charge of snobbery. "I spent much time there as a child, and I used to look up the streets that run northwards, towards the hills and the green trees and the church tower, and think how lovely it looked and how different from stuffy London."

"I could never breathe there properly, you know, John," she added, turning to her husband.

Her husband looked at her fondly.

"If only Highgate were not so hilly! I'm afraid you will find walks here very tiring, my love."

" Mrs Winterborne is delicate, then?" enquired Mrs Catt.

The bride laughed. "It's nothing—I had scarletina a few years ago and it left me with a silly fluttering of the heart that I get sometimes. Exercise is the very best thing for it, I'm sure."

"You'll get plenty of that in this house," Mrs Catt warned her. "Three staircases, all steep."

"Oh, I don't mind that a little bit! Even if there were four staircases—or six—I should still love this house, oh, *so* much. Just like a cottage in my own Sussex village, yet so near to all the theatres and the shops and the parks."

"And there's even a conservatory at the back, you know," put in her husband. Mrs Catt did know: through the glass roof it was possible to observe, from her back bedroom window, anyone within the conservatory, as fish are observed within an aquarium.

"We shall have geraniums and mignonette and all the things that smell sweet," Mrs Winterborne chattered on. "John can smoke his pipe out there when he comes home from the City, and then do some gardening—it will be *so* good for him."

"And I shall grow some capital roses," added John. "There are some in already. My wife's name is Rose," and he looked at her with a romantic devotion surpassing anything the Literary Institute could supply. Mrs Catt sighed, watching them leave her house, hand in hand. David Copperfield and Dora had been just such a couple (so sad that Mr Dickens had died prematurely, and was not still writing his wonderful books) and they had lived in just such a Highgate cottage.

"Let us hope their story will be happier," thought Mrs Catt. Nice neighbours might be less interesting than the other sort, but all kinds of things might happen to colour her life, with the Winterbornes next door.

A year passed, and the may tree was in bloom again. Mrs Catt saw Rose Winterborne pick an armful of the rich crimson boughs, and leant out of the window to call a warning: for hawthornblossom is notoriously unlucky, a death-bringer, when carried into the house. And in Rose's interesting condition—so soon to be resolved—she should be particularly careful. But the small figure, its new matronliness concealed by a shawl, had vanished into Maytree Cottage bearing its sheaves with it. Mrs Catt shut the window and returned to the preparation of a beautiful pincushion worked in a rosebud design and bearing the legend "Welcome Little Stranger".

John Edward Winterborne came into the world on a starry June night, one of the most exciting of Mrs Catt's life. Straw muffled the cobbles outside the two cottages, the very horses at the inn were reproved for neighing; Dr Talbot's barouche rolled up solemnly to the gate, a monthly nurse flitted in and out on mysterious errands. For all this pageantry, John Edward's arrival was normal and uneventful: mother and child were reported to be as well as could possibly be expected.

Mrs Catt attended the christening, and was enraptured by introductions to Mrs Winterborne's noble relations, not to mention the sending round to her later of a piece of magnificently fruity, sherrysoaked, blue-iced cake, the product of the village bakery. All were well: healthy child, proud father, radiant young mother, with such colour in her cheeks. The legend of the may blossom and its ill-luck must be a parcel of ignorant superstition, Mrs Catt decided, as she deftly arranged her pillows and opened a book by Frances Hodgson Burnett.

A half-hour chime from the school chapel clock awoke her. Or had something else penetrated her sleep before the clock struck? Struggling up from dreams, she listened. It was so. Somebody was pulling insistently on her front door bell, and its jangling was succeeded by a series of knocks. Alarmed, Mrs Catt retreated under the bedclothes.

"Some impudent thief who wants me to open the door to him, so that he can knock my brains out and walk in. Well, he won't catch me that way!"

She waited, listening. Perhaps Bessy in her attic would hear and come down, in which case they could lock themselves in a room together. But Bessy, young, and physically tired out, slept on. Then Mrs Catt became aware of another sound. A voice calling something, and it sounded like her name, faintly reaching her through the aperture of the letter-box.

Resolutely she lit her candle, left her bed, put on wrap and slippers, and went downstairs, candle in hand. Before reaching the door she took the precaution of arming herself with the downstairs parlour poker, a formidable object in the shape of a sword. But now she recognized the voice outside as that of John Winterborne.

"Mrs Catt! Mrs Catt! Please come down! *Please!*"

She unbolted and unchained the door, and saw him there on her garden path, half-dressed and wild-looking.

"Why, Mr Winterborne! Whatever . . ."

"Oh, thank God you heard me! I tried to rouse them at the inn but they sleep like the dead. Mrs Catt, will you come with me at once? It's Rose, my wife. She's ill—very ill, I fear!"

Without hesitation Mrs Catt, who had never before stepped beyond the boundary of her own bedroom other than fully dressed, untied the strings of her nightcap, cast it off, seized her bunch of keys (concealed by night in a vase), and, stepping outside, re-locked the door. John Winterborne hurried her down the path.

"What is Mrs Winterborne's ailment?" asked Mrs Catt, as they went.

"I don't know—it came on, suddenly. She woke me and said she felt ill—oh, she looked so strange, and now she won't speak to me."

They were at the door of the bedroom shared by the Winterbornes.

Somebody had lit a lamp. By the yellow light Mrs Catt saw Rose Winterborne lying across the bed, one plait of brown hair touching the floor, her face upturned. By the bedside Janet, the servant whose capability had impressed Mrs Catt on the day of the moving-in, was standing shuddering convulsively, her hands to her mouth, uttering occasional whimpers of fear. Mrs Catt threw her a contemptuous look and went up to Rose. The hand she raised was cold and fell limply from her own. Cold too was the cheek she touched, and beneath the healthy colour the sun had given it was a greenish pallor.

Mrs Catt gently raised one of the eyelids, then turned to John.

"What have you given her? Brandy? A bed-warmer?"

"Everything we could think of." He pointed to the bottle and glass on the table. "She couldn't drink. It spilt on the pillow—there. We rubbed her hands—we . . ." His voice broke.

"You must go for Dr Talbot. There is nothing I can do. Go now. I'll stay with her. And Janet had better make some tea to sustain us all—if she's capable of it."

Still whimpering, Janet trailed out. John Winterborne, with a last wild look at his wife, rushed from the room, and Mrs Catt heard his running footsteps clatter down the road. She seated herself by the side of the bed, and began to rub the cold hand of the unconscious girl. But already she feared that the doctor, when he came, would pronounce Rose to be something worse than unconscious.

In the nursery upstairs John Edward began to cry.

Rose Winterborne was buried four days later. Dr Talbot had diagnosed a sudden failure of the heart; unexpected in so young a woman, but there had apparently been a history of cardiac symptoms. As he had attended her regularly before and after the birth of her son, no autopsy was considered necessary.

A steady drizzle fell from leaden skies on the hearse and the carriages containing the mourners, as the cortège moved away from the gate of Maytree Cottage. Rose's father had yielded to John Winterborne's plea that Rose should be buried in the churchyard of the village she had chosen as her married home, rather than in Sussex. Here, at least, he could be near what remained of her. Sir Harry glanced anxiously at his son-in-law as they sat side by side in the slow-moving carriage. Since the tragedy John had seemed stupefied with shock, unable to give expression to his grief. He had stood by the open coffin as relatives and neighbours had filed in to pay their last respects to the dead. Mrs Catt, torn between genuine sorrow and irrepressible morbid fascination, saw from behind the handkerchief she held to her eyes his white, stony face, his gaze drawn as though by hypnotic compulsion to the still figure in the coffin. "A beautiful corpse," thought Mrs Catt.

Rose was to be buried in her wedding-dress. It was of white muslin, richly trimmed with points of torchon lace. From the modest high collar a cascade of frills covered her bosom and fell to the tiny waist—"eighteen inches the day I was married," she had loved to tell people, with a pride they readily forgave. John Edward's arrival had hardly increased the waist's dimensions. Her hair had been lovingly built into a tower of curls, and a curling fringe lay on her forehead like the tendrils of sweet peas. In her ears were ruby earrings, and the hands clasped on her breast glittered and shone with jewels.

"Should we not—remove them, perhaps?" Sir Harry had suggested. "They were her mother's, and it might be that when John Edward marries, he would wish to give his bride . . ." His son-in-law's expression stopped him. Silently the undertaker's men entered, heads bowed, and laid in place the coffin-lid.

She was to lie among the monumental splendours of Highgate Cemetery; still fashionable, though the earlier stones, that had been put up forty years before, were beginning to crumble, and grass and weeds already ironically obscured "In Loving Memory" and "Never Forgotten". For quiet neighbour Rose would have Lizzie Rossetti, mouldering among the swathes of her glorious hair that had grown after death and filled her coffin, so that those who had come to take her husband's hastily-buried manuscript poems from her started back in horror. The once rich and honoured lay, row on row, in the mausolea at the top of the hill; and if foxes or wild cats from the Heath slunk in through the broken doors on a winter night, or laired there in spring, the sleepers on their shelves troubled not at all.

One of these temples to death held some members of a branch of Sir Harry's family, and in this Rose's coffin was laid, new and small. The service was said, the mourners filed back to their carriages between tall obelisk and draped urn, weeping angel and sculptured bust. Maytree Cottage was too small, and the widower's grief too great, to permit of a funeral breakfast being held there. Sir Harry had engaged a room at the inn; and John Winterborne went back, alone, to his empty house.

In the days that followed everything was done to comfort him. John Edward was taken away to the family estate in Sussex, in the care of a nurse. The vicar called to offer spiritual consolation; the ladies of the village brought delicacies cooked by their own hands, and more than one mamma of daughters meditated on the desirability of earning the gratitude of a personable young widower. But his thanks were mechanical, his smile only a polite grimace. Dr Talbot shook his head, for there was little medicine could do to heal a shock to the nervous system. And the old wives said, as they had often said before: "It's easy for them as goes quickly—hard for them that's left."

On Saturday evenings the vicar wrote his sermons for the following day. An academic man with a penchant for classical quotation, it was an exercise he much enjoyed, and he was not pleased to be interrupted by his wife with the information that the butcher's youngest daughter had come to the door with a tale about having seen a ghost in the cemetery, and was now having hysterics in the kitchen.

"Nonsense," said the vicar. "Rubbish. All imagination."

"She is a very truthful girl as a rule, dear; I don't think she would say she had seen something if she had not."

"If she did, it was one of those ragamuffin boys from down the Hill. Give her a dose of sal volatile and send her off home."

The butcher's daughter's visit was followed by one from Miss Sims, an elderly and devout spinster of the parish. She had been laying flowers on her mother's grave, as she did on the eve of every Sabbath, when a figure rose from behind a tall headstone, hovered for a moment "in the air", said Miss Sims, and vanished.

By Monday evening the harassed vicar had listened to six different accounts of the supernatural visitant. He preferred spirits to remain in the celestial sphere, and refused to believe that anything but a practical joker haunted the cemetery. The village thought otherwise; strange tales began to spread. There had been only one death lately, and that a mysterious one—a woman cut off in the flower of her youth, and for no sound reason that anyone could tell. It was whispered that Dr Talbot had not been satisfied; that John Winterborne had persuaded or bribed him not to press for an autopsy. Rich, wasn't she—an heiress? Depend on it, that young man's conscience was troubling him, or why should he look so grim and say nothing to nobody? It wasn't natural. No wonder ghosts were seen flitting among the tombs, and young Alice had heard that wild wailing cry come from the cemetery as she was passing the top gate.

Mrs Catt heard these suggestions with eagerness tempered by revulsion. Nourished on novels, her imagination a playground for persecuted females, heartless villains, deathbed agonies and disputed wills, she was on the one hand only too ready to believe that something very ugly had taken place next door, and on the other quite unable to credit it, in the face of what she had seen with her own eyes on the night of Rose Winterborne's death. In public she pronounced that it was all a pack of rubbish, and that she would as soon believe that the Whittington Stone had been seen shopping in the High Street with a basket on its arm. In private she reserved judgement, and kept watch and ward on her neighbour.

Peering from her bedroom window on a mild evening, a few days after the first ghost rumour, she saw him sitting in the small conservatory that adjoined the back of Maytree Cottage. He was smoking a pipe, the first time she had seen him do so since the funeral. She could not help but be glad of it. The tabby kitten Rose had rescued from some persecutors was curled up on his lap. He was happier, then; he was getting over it. One day there would be a new bride next door, and life would be pleasant again.

All evening he sat there, reading or meditating, as dusk fell and birds ceased to twitter in the tall trees between the cottages and the Heath. A new servant had been engaged, as it was not proper for such a young woman as Janet to remain alone with her master. Twice she emerged, the second time with a cup of cocoa. Mrs Catt decided that nothing else was going to happen, and retired across the landing to her first-floor parlour, there to read and enjoy her own supper.

Her peace was interrupted by the creak of the Winterbornes' rusty-hinged back gate. She returned to the bedroom window to reconnoitre, seeing nothing at first but John Winterborne, quiet in his basket chair, seemingly asleep. Then she was aware of a tapping or scratching noise, several times repeated. She moved to the other side of the window, from which she could see round the corner of the conservatory; and a sight met her eyes which remained to the end of her days somewhere behind their retinae, and which wrenched from her a shriek of terror. Outside the glass door of the conservatory, one hand tapping feebly at the panes, stood a dreadful figure, a thing from the country of nightmare. Its light-coloured rags were filthy with mould and stained with great patches of dried blood; long matted grey hair half-hid a skeletal face. The creature stood with drooping head, occasionally rousing itself to another weak tap at the door. Mrs Catt, cold and paralysed with horror, could only stare. So numbed were her senses that she could not utter a sound, let alone a scream, when she saw that the hand with which it was knocking was no hand, but a single bleeding wound.

The man in the conservatory stirred; at last he had heard the summons. Gently displacing the cat, he moved towards the door, and saw the dreadful thing outside. Through the glass they confronted each other. Then, simultaneously, Mrs Catt heard him utter a cry such as she never heard before or since; and, as the figure raised its face to him, recognized in the skull-features, the ghastly form, what had once been the beautiful Rose Winterborne.

Days and weeks passed before the neighbourhood knew more than the bare, incredible fact that Rose had returned from the grave— no apparition, but a living woman, though near-starved, terribly injured, and changed almost beyond recognition. By a merciful Providence her mind had been spared, and in time she was able to talk weakly of her frightful experience. Her "death" had been some form of prolonged catalepsy, the symptoms of which had completely deceived the doctor. She did not know how long she had lain unconscious after the funeral; she was awakened by a terrible pain in her left hand, and the sound of her own voice screaming. It was dark, but there was flickering lantern-light, and she could see the faces of two men bending over her. A knife came swooping towards her face and she felt the same agonizing pain in one of her ears. Then she remembered screaming and screaming, and the men muttering together, and then they were gone, and she was alone in her coffin in the mausoleum, bleeding profusely and terrified out of her wits. She could remember nothing more until she found herself in the twilight on the lonely path at the back of Maytree Cottage, and her senses came back, and she crawled to the back door of her own house.

It was soon discovered that the two undertakers' men who had come to bear her coffin from the house to the cemetery had been seized by greed for the jewels which adorned the "corpse", and had not screwed down the coffin-lid but left it loose—the reason, no doubt, why she did not stifle as she lay in it. For the same reason they left the door of the mausoleum unlocked (it was at best a ramshackle affair) and two nights after the funeral went to carry out their grave-robbery. Their fright at discovering the corpse to be a living woman did not prevent them carrying out their plan before they fled, and in their frantic haste they hacked off three of the fingers that sparkled with rings, and an ear-lobe from which hung a ruby.

How Rose had lived throughout her week of nocturnal wanderings: what she ate, why she did not bleed to death, were always to remain mysteries. Youth and health were on her side, the mausoleum had sheltered her by night, many harmless berries grew on the bushes, which instinctively she must have fed on, and Nature's marvellous urge to her children that they must survive, whatever their privations, had brought her safely home. Her young beauty was gone, the brown hair was now completely grey, and on her left hand she wore a glove until the day when, a serene old lady many times a grandmother, she died.

But John Winterborne never recovered from the double shock of his wife's supposed death and her ghastly return, and within three months Mrs Catt watched from the window another funeral wind its slow way down Highgate Hill.

The Eyes of Thomas Bolter

His real name was not Thomas Bolter. It has been lost over the years, for his strange story was told by a beachcomber of long ago to his friend Andrew Lang, the great teller of tales and collector of supernatural instances. Lang suppressed the name and his friend's, taking, as he said, the common privilege of writers on medicine and psychology.

The Beachcomber was a man of science, utterly materialistic. He believed in no manifestation which he could not see, hear and feel for himself. Ghost, ghoul or goblin had no chance with him. If one appeared before him, gibbering, he would not fear it, for to him it had no existence. This was just as well, as the Beachcomber was a student of anthropology and ethnology, engaged in writing a treatise on the customs and superstitions of the natives of the Pacific Islands and the then almost uncharted territory of New Zealand. In his journeyings he came across some unco' things, as he put it. Whistling for the wind, killing your enemy by remote control, digging up your ancestors once a year to propitiate the spirits who walked in the wild bush: all these the Beachcomber had noted with detached interest. Even for a Lowland Scot he was hard-headed. Darwin (then still alive) was his only God, the *Origin of Species* his only Bible, the theory of natural selection his only superstition.

Until he met Thomas Bolter.

Bolter was a *pakeha*, a white man, one of the few on the island off the New Zealand coast which the Beachcomber happened to be visiting. Unlike the Beachcomber, he was English, though not pure-blooded Saxon, the Scot's sharp eye discerned. There was in Bolter's countenance something of the Oriental: a Jewish strain, perhaps. His face was pale, of an aquiline cast, his eyes remarkable. They were large and as nearly black as eyes can be, with a curious dull, dead lustre that reminded the Beachcomber of something. Yes, now he recalled what it was: the Magic Mirror of Dr Dee, Queen Elizabeth's pet astrologer. The Beachcomber had once been shown this, and had been interested to see that it was not a mirror at all, but a piece of black wood, ebony or the like. Of such might Bolter's eyes have been made.

They were not the only odd thing about him. He was an agent for a firm which imported sheep from the mainland. When they were landed two or three drovers would escort them to the sheep station, six miles away, usually accompanied by the conscientious Bolter. As a general rule the "mob" would arrive early in the day, so that they might reach their destination before dark. It happened one day, however, that the boat came in late in the afternoon. Bolter decided against the advice of the drovers to let them travel straight away. An argument ensued, and the head drover refused to accept responsibility.

"Right," said Bolter. "I'll take them myself with a couple of Maoris."

"You'll lose half of them before you get there," remarked the Beachcomber, who was standing by.

Bolter smiled his characteristic smile, which curled his mouth without reaching his eyes.

"Will I?" was all he replied. And off he went, stick in hand, dog by his side, two Maori boys unwillingly shepherding the fine-wooled merinos bleating and baaing before him. The Beachcomber shook his head.

Next morning, as he sat outside his hut, writing his treatise, one of the Maoris appeared through the trees, wearing a face of alarm.

"That Bolter," he said. "He is a devil!"

The Beachcomber took his pipe out of his mouth. Devils were always worth investigation. "How so?" he asked.

"*He sees at night.* Last night, when dark fell, the sheep ran away here and there, to the left and to the right. Bolter told us where to follow!"

"He heard them, of course," returned the Beachcomber.

"Then why did we not hear them? Are our ears duller than the ears of *pakehas*?"

"Apparently," was the Beachcomber's comment, as he resumed his writing. No devilry, after all.

But when he mentioned the matter to Bolter, the agent told him quite simply that he had not followed the movements of the sheep by hearing, but by sight. The Beachcomber raised his shaggy eyebrows.

"Perhaps you'd tell me how."

"I saw them," Bolter explained unemotionally, "by a dim ring of light surrounding them. Whenever I want to find something in the dark, I fix my thoughts on it and this light begins to glow."

The Beachcomber smiled his incredulity. "That's a fine useful gift," he observed sardonically.

"You don't believe me," said Bolter. "All right, I'll prove it. Shall I tell you what you have in the right-hand pocket of your coat at this moment?"

The Beachcomber glanced down at the pocket. It was deep, and fastened with a button. "Aye, do that," he invited. Bolter's strange eyes swivelled towards the pocket, and fixed their leaden gaze on it. In spite of himself, the Beachcomber felt a slight coldness creep along his spine. After a moment Bolter said:

"It's a photograph. You have not had it very long. It came by mail from over the sea—Scotland, I think."

The Beachcomber made a noncommittal noise that could have meant either no or yes. "Describe it," he said.

"A woman. Not young—grey-haired, I think. Wearing a lace cap, and a dark dress. Some kind of brooch or ornament at the neck. She's sitting in a chair—in a garden. There's a small creature on her knee—a dog. Yes, a dog."

The Beachcomber's jaw had dropped, for the description was perfectly accurate. The photograph had only arrived two days ago: Bolter could not possibly have seen it, and the Beachcomber had not mentioned it to him or to anyone else. He was intrigued, fascinated. Here was, in every sense, one for the book. He began to cultivate Bolter, asking him questions about his background and education, which proved to be extremely ordinary. He was twenty-five and engaged to be married to a young lady of Whangerei, on the North Island coast. Of his ancestry he knew little. There was nothing unusual about him at all, except for his strange gift. The Beachcomber decided that a bountiful Providence had presented him with the perfect subject for experiment. Every evening he would hold what amounted to a séance, with Bolter as medium. At home, he scorned the fashionable interest in spiritualism, the new craze, which he was perfectly sure was all blethers and hoaxing. But with Bolter there could be no possibility of deceit. It was, of course, only a highly developed telepathic gift, such as natives employed when they wished death on a man who was miles away, and the man dropped and died. There were no spirits involved, for spirits did not exist.

The meek Bolter was at first quite willing to demonstrate his powers. He diagnosed the contents of pockets, "read" the address on envelopes, gave the dates of coins. All these tests were carried out on objects carried by the Beachcomber, for the Maoris, having got wind of devilish practices, kept superstitiously away from them both, and the only other white men on the island were uninterested in "conjuring tricks".

At first Bolter seemed unaffected by the experiments. But after a week or so he began to show signs of nervousness; a disinclination to be alone, a tendency to jump at sudden noises and to glance apprehensively over his shoulder when sitting with his back to the door. The Beachcomber put it down to the strain imposed on Bolter's system of exerting his powers too often, and decided to cut down the séance time. Bolter, however, begged to be allowed to spend his evenings in the hut which was the Beachcomber's home.

It was a little inconvenient, for the Beachcomber liked to work quietly after sundown, pipe in mouth, on the voluminous notes he had made during the day. He was, however, basically a kindly man, and resigned himself philosophically enough to working with Bolter in the other chair, reading spasmodically or making occasional unnecessary remarks: as though, the Beachcomber thought, he wanted the reassurance of hearing a human voice.

One night, when they had sat in their usual fashion for two or three hours, and the Beachcomber had begun to yawn in a meaning manner, Bolter suddenly broke into speech.

"I don't want to go back! Can't I stay with you?"

The Beachcomber glanced round the small hut. "Not unless you like sleeping on the floor: I don't care for it myself," he said. "Come on, I'll go with you as far as the door. Have a wee drop of whisky first to settle your nerves."

But Bolter trembled and clutched at his sleeve. "I can't be alone! Don't you understand? I daren't sleep by myself."

"Brace up, laddie," said the Beachcomber kindly, patting Bolter on the shoulder. "You're neither a foolish native nor a bairn. Be a man!"

"You began it!" Bolter was on the edge of hysteria. "If it wasn't for you I wouldn't be like this. You stirred it all up, and now I'm afraid."

"Afraid of what? A person that can see in the dark has no need to fear the night!"

"I don't know what I'm afraid of—at least I don't want to talk about it—but I must have company," Bolter said more calmly. "Won't you come back with me, just tonight? There's plenty of room for us both in my hut. I promise I won't ask you again!"

The Beachcomber sighed. He liked a night's sleep as well as the next man, and the prospect of soothing Bolter's nerves for the next seven or eight hours was not an enticing one. But, he reflected, he had managed to sleep in the most uncomfortable conditions from Skye to the New Hebrides. Bolter's hut and Bolter's snores (if he did snore) could hardly be more disturbing than, say, a hole in the sand of Egypt, with the nearest oasis uncomfortably distant; or a straw pullet in Africa, within earshot of the revels of drunken tribesmen whose reputation for cannibalism the Beachcomber knew to be well founded. He decided to fall in with Bolter's whim, to the agent's pathetic gratification.

Together they walked towards Bolter's hut. The night was dark for a Pacific night, the moon hidden behind clouds. From the nearby pens the bleat of a wakeful sheep broke the silence. A morepork, the owl of New Zealand, uttered the cry which gives it its name, and the Beachcomber beguiled the walk by recalling quotations about owls. "The moping owl does to the moon complain"—poet Gray might have been writing specifically about the morepork, surely the most moping of owls. "They come as a boon and a blessing to men, the Pickwick, the Owl and the Waverley pen." What could Owls possibly have in common with Pickwick and Waverley? Realizing that he was drifting into nonsense, the Beachcomber switched his memory to his national bard, and spoke the lines aloud, in his rich rolling Edinburgh accent.

> *"Is it, sad owl, that Autumn strips the shade,*
> *And leaves thee here, unsheltered and forlorn?*
> *Or fear that Winter will thy nest invade?*
> *Or friendless melancholy bids thee mourn?"*

"I like that," Bolter broke in eagerly. "Do go on!"

There are seven more stanzas to Burns's *Ode to the Owl*, and an unlimited number in his combined works. At two in the morning the Beachcomber was still reciting them, between yawns. It was with keen relief that he saw Bolter's head dropping towards his chest. Pleasant as it is to hear the sound of one's own voice, enough is enough, he reflected; besides, there had been something uneasy about the recital. Bolter's convulsive trembling was unnerving to watch. The Beachcomber knew all about the infective quality of fear: he had seen it often enough among primitive tribes to recognize the symptoms, and he now recognized them in himself. It was an unusual, and disconcerting, experience.

As Bolter's head dropped lower, the Beachcomber gently assisted him to lie down on one side of the wide pallet-bed and covered him with a blanket. Then he extinguished the lamp, not without a wry glance at the framed photograph on the wall. Bolter's bride was going to have some poorish nights, he surmised. He lay down on the far side of the bed, in his clothes, pulled the rough blanket up round his shoulders, and fell instantly asleep.

When he awoke he thought at first that it was broad morning. The room was full of light and movement. As consciousness returned he saw that the light came from the open door. The full moon had emerged and was making the small room brilliant—in fact, he had never seen moonlight so bright: it was as though some extra candle-power had been added. As for the movement, the Beachcomber could not quite believe his eyes. The hut seemed full of great black dogs. Labradors, were they, or some sort of hound? They were romping, leaping on and off the furniture, rolling on the floor, charging and biting one another, like puppies at play. Yet (and the moment of realization was a chilling one) they made no sound at all. Not a growl nor a footfall accompanied their wild sport, not a claw-scratch or jaw-snap could be heard.

The Beachcomber was passionately fond of dogs. If he had not been, the sight before his eyes would have reduced him to a state of abject terror. As it was, he merely stiffened his muscles with apprehension when one of the dogs leaped on to the bed and stood over him. He saw its eyes gleaming red, small pits of fire, and drew his head back into the pillow like an alarmed tortoise receding into its shell. But the thing only lowered its own great head and nuzzled his face. He was curiously relieved to note that he could *feel* the icy coldness of its nose. It jumped down and rejoined its companions, and he found that he was shivering. Perfect love casteth out fear, he told himself—how could a dog-lover possibly be afraid of these apparently harmless, though disquietingly quiet, beasts? And yet, where had they come from, for he had seen no such dogs on the island? He did not care for the trend of his own thoughts. Goading himself to action he flung back the blanket and stood up, a swirling mass of dogs at his feet. Ten? Twenty? It seemed impossible that the hut could hold so many; even more impossible that their number had increased since he awoke, yet so he suspected. However that might be, he must get rid of them.

"Get out!" he yelled. His own voice sounded strange in that silent room. "Be off, the pack of you!" He clapped his hands and made shooing gestures, for somehow he did not care to raise his foot to the dogs. Relief flooded over him as he saw them obediently stop their play, and slink towards the door one by one. When the last thin black tail had vanished into the moonlit path outside, he shut the door and bolted it, and leant against it with all his weight. He was ashamed to feel sweat on his forehead, for he had never thought himself a coward.

For the first time he remembered his companion. Astonishingly, Bolter was still sleeping: he had not stirred at all. The Beachcomber bent over him, and peered curiously at the upturned face, sharp-profiled as the face of a corpse, marble-white in the moonlight.

"Bolter!" he said, though not loudly. He would have liked some human society at that moment, even Bolter's. But the man in the bed neither stirred nor spoke. He lay like one in a trance. The Beachcomber climbed back into the bed, thinking how cold it had grown; how cold, in fact, the whole place was. It might have been somewhere in the Arctic rather than the Pacific regions. He looked at his watch: it was a quarter past four, the hour of remorse, despair, and death-thoughts. He must go to sleep and bring morning nearer.

Sleep came to him quickly. He emerged from it with irritation, mixed with physical discomfort, for the blanket which was his only covering was sliding off. He gave it an angry jerk. It resisted, as though with a life of its own, and continued its descent towards the floor. He grasped it firmly, dragged it up, and held it about his neck. In another moment or two he would have been deep in sleep again. But the blanket was once more at its tricks. It was slipping, slipping downwards, until with a violent jerk it left the bed and lay in a heap on the floor.

The Beachcomber was by this time very frightened. He grasped his companion's shoulder, and shouted his name. But Bolter slept on. His pasty face wore a look of pain, as though he were silently enduring a nightmare.

The Beachcomber once again pulled up the blanket and held it fast. At the other end of it something else, invisible, pulled and tugged. Panting, half-sobbing with fright, the Beachcomber crawled down the bed, pulling the top of the blanket over his head and straining to hold it there.

For a blessed moment he believed he had defeated his opponent in the dreadful tug-of-war. He lay still, a wild creature thinking itself invisible beneath a stone. It was then that he felt a touch on his shoulder, and tensed with renewed terror. The unmistakable pressure of fingers was on him, creeping up the outline of his cheek to grasp the blanket-hem. In a frenzy of fear he flung the blanket off his face and grabbed wildly at the thing that had touched him. Then, with an animal shriek, he flung it away from him. It landed on the floor, and lay clearly visible in the moon's rays.

It was a hand. There was no arm: it had apparently been roughly severed at the wrist. The skin was dark, almost black, and covered with hair, the fingers were short and blunt, with long, dirty nails, like talons. The thumb was missing. Perhaps the nastiest moment of the night was when the Beachcomber realized the reason for its absence. He had always dreaded leprosy.

He must have fainted at that point. Possibly the faint merged into sleep, for when he opened his eyes again the moonlight had given way to the blessed light of day. Beside him Bolter was stirring.

By the time he had told Bolter about the thumbless hand he had begun to believe that he was describing a bad dream, and was about to add, with a deprecatory laugh, "Of course, if one is aye delving about among Maori legends one is inclined to get them on the brain." But Bolter, with a glaze of sleep over his dull black eyes, replied calmly:

"Plenty of people have seen the hand. They wouldn't share a tent in camp with me, because of that. You were lucky you didn't get the big black dogs as well. I'm always afraid I'll see them myself, one night."

It says much for Scottish fortitude and resilience that the Beachcomber was prepared in the interests of science to repeat the ordeal next night. Fortunately, perhaps, for his nervous system, Bolter's fiancée arrived that day on a visit, chaperoned by her aunt, and the pleasure of her company cheered up Bolter so much that he did not require the Beachcomber's and was not prepared to discuss the events of the night.

Strength of character and tact do not always go hand in hand. Before the young lady left the island, the Beachcomber was tactless enough to tell her of her intended's strange gift of optical hyperaesthesia, and of the dogs and the hand. He thought she ought to know, he said. She made no particular comment, but some days later Bolter came raging to the Beachcomber's hut with an open letter in his hand. Mabel had broken it off, he said. She had discovered that after all they were not suited to one another. He was very angry and upset, and blamed the whole thing on the Beachcomber.

Perhaps it served the Beachcomber right that for years afterwards he could not retire to bed without a feeling of insecurity, always making sure that the bedclothes were tucked firmly under the mattress: and like the youthful warlock-haunted Burns, when on nocturnal rambles kept a very sharp look-out in suspicious places.

Index

Alexander, Mrs, 384, 387–9
Allen, Thomas, 43–51
Amazonia, 444–52
Ants, 449–50
Antwerp, 15–22
Arrowsmith, Father Edmund, 31–4, 41
Ashby, Mother, 62–8
Ashuanipi, Joe, 167–8
Ashton-in-Makerfield, 41
Atlantic Ocean, 158–62
Avory, Mr Justice, 296
Ayscliffe House, 132–41

Ball, tunneller, 113–19
Barlow, Joseph, 33
Bartlett, Colonel, 120, 121, 124
Bartlett, Giles, 124–9
Bartlett, Lady, 124–9
Bidel, Anne, 25–6
Bidel, Benoît, 26–9
Bidel, Maria, 25, 27
Blair, Mr and Mrs, 95, 100
Bodneys, John, 133–4, 140–1
Boguet, Grand Juge Henri, 25
Boin, Father Jean, 23
Boscombe, 131
Bourgot, Pierre, 23–5
Bowes-Lyon, Sir David, 110
Boyleston, John, 43
Boyne, Battle of the, 82
Brooks, Edward, 170–8
Brown, Mother Mary, 64–8
Brunel, Isambard Kingdom, 113–19
Bryn Hall, 31, 34–41
Buckland, Dr, 161
Burlin, Arnold H., 360
Burns, Robert, 97

Bute, Dr Andrew, 96, 98–100, 102–103
Byfield, Adoniram, 44–51
Byrne, Michael, 84–7, 94

Caird, Arabella, 100, 103
Cambridge:
    Jesus College, 42–51, 52–60, 274–81
    Peterhouse, 307–19
Camp Cooke, 376, 379
Candiru, 448
Cannibalism, 169–78
Capucci, Maria, 385–8
Cartwright, Constance, 397–407
Cartwright, Major David, 398–407
Casement, Sir Roger, 451
Catalepsy, 470–80
Catherine, Empress, 103
Cats, 42–51, 282–7
Catt, Mrs, 470–80
Charles I, King, 31, 43, 52
Charles II, King, 31, 53
Chase family, 303–4
Cheops, 260
China, 453–63
Chu-Ming, 453–5
Claes, Jan, 17
Collins, Richard, 73–9
Collins, tunneller, 113–19
Cranbrook, Kent, 62–8
Cranswell, Amelia, Edward and Michael, 142–7
Crawley, 353, 359–62
Croglin, 142–7
Cromwell, Oliver, 42–3, 53, 81

Damascus, 241–9
Deal, 69–79

Deane, Goodman, 57-8
D'Arcy, Rosemary, 148-57
De Balsam, Hugh, Bishop of Ely, 307
Dee, Dr John, 276
De Montmartin, Father, 324-7
De Orellana, Francisco, 445
Devil, the, 21-2, 62-8
Donaldson, Kevin, 428-37
Donovan, Marcus, 149-57
Donovan's Drop, 148-57
Dowsing, William, 43
Dresden, 197-207
Drowning, 112-19
Drumkattle, 427-37
Druids, 251
Dublin, 80-94
Dudley, 169-78
Duncan, King of Scotland, 107, 109
Durham, 320-7
Durrand-Deacon, Mrs, 361-2

Eaton, Mark, 189-96
Earnshaw, Lionel, 282-7
Egypt, 197-207, 258-66
Electric eels, 448
Elizabeth I, Queen, 31, 103
Elizabeth, Queen, the Queen Mother, 105-8
Evans, George, 53-4
Exorcism, 320-7
Ewart, Colonel, 464-9

Fairweather, George, 107
Fanaticism, religious, 80-94
Fawcett, Colonel P. H., 451
Fersen, Baron and Baroness, 329-40
Fickling, Joseph George, 376, 379
Fish, flesh-eating, 445-8
Ffryar, Anthony, 275-81
Foley, Lt.-Col. Cyril, 251-6
Foulis, Duncan, 95-103
French, Mrs Vera, 378, 380
Furstenstein, Freiherr zu, 251
Furstenstein Castle, 250-66

Gandillon, Perrenette, 29-30
Garswood Hall, 41
Germyn, Gervase, 54-60
Ghosts, see Hauntings
Gilbert, Ellen, 34, 38-41
Gilbert, Gerard, 34-8
Gilbert, Richard, 34, 38, 40
Gilbert, Sir Robert, 41
Glamis Castle, 105-12
Glasgow, 95-103
Gordon, Matt, Jr., 376, 380
Granville, Dowager Lady, 105
Grave robbing, 341-52
Graunge, Gregory, 278
Gray, Arthur, 275-7
Gray, Thomas, 308
Grey, Elizabeth, 131, 134, 136-7
Grey, Ellen, 131-2, 134-9
Grey, Mary, 131-41
Grimes, Peter, 307-19
Gunn, Horace, 271-3
Gwinett, Ambrose, 69-79

Haigh, John George, 353-63
Hamilton Falls, 167-8
Hansen, Mark, 377
Harcop, Lord, 341-7
Harvey, Reverend M., 162
Hassan, shopkeeper, 241-9
Hauntings, 31-41, 42-51, 52-60, 105-112, 120-30, 131-41, 179-87, 208-17, 229-40, 241-9, 267-73, 274-81, 320-7, 383-96, 427-37, 438-43, 464-9, 480-9
Heart transplantation, 453-63
Heidiger, Schloss, 408-17
Heinz, Georg, 408-17
Heinz, Karl, 408-17
Henderson, Dr Archibald, 359-60
Henderson, Rosalie, 359-60
Hendry, Mary, 259-65
Hendry, Michael, 258-66
Henry XV of Pless, Prince John, 251-2
Hetherington, Margaret, 341-52
Hetherington, Robert, 345-7
Highgate, 470-80
Hobbes, Thomas, 45

Hollywood, California, 374, 376–82
Humphries, Mr Justice, 362

Imprisonment, unlawful, 408–17
Ince Hall, 34
Intolerance, a Satire, 81–82

James VI, King of Scotland (James I of England), 25
Joseph, Croyance, 299–306
Joseph, Ti, 298–306

Kaye, Emily, 288–97
Kemble, John, 109
Kither, James, 63–7
Kotka Veski, Estonia, 328–40
Kraken, the, 160

Labat, Père, 305
Lancaster, 31–2
Laycock, Robert, 279–80
Liana, 450–1
Louisiana, 229–40
Lycanthropy, 23–30, 163–8, 256
Lyon family, 106–7

Macbeth, 105
McSwan, Donald, 353–8
McSwan, Mr and Mrs, 353–8
Mahon, Patrick, 288–97
Malcolm II, King of Scotland, 107, 109
Makepeace, Sir Jeremy, 342
Manley, Robert, 386
Mannington, Dr, 323–7
Martin, Lynn, 376–7
Martyn, Mother Anne, 64–8
Mary, Queen of Scots, 107
Marylebone, 383–96
Medford, Massachusetts, 374–6
Mentot, Philibert, 23–5
Merioneth, 165–8
Merriment, Lieutenant Commander Gerald, 438–43
Minchins, Mrs, 70–8

Monckton, Jack, 190–6
Moncrieff, Alastair, 427–37
Moore, Tom, 81
Morello, Josef and Maria, 219–27
Morgan, Roger, 397–400, 405–7
Morton, Honourable Clive, 342
Mummies, 197–207, 260–6
Murder, 15–22, 69–79, 91–104, 131–41, 179–87, 188–96, 288–97, 353–63, 374–382, 408–17, 418–26, 453–63

Newhurst, Sussex, 208–17
New Zealand, island off coast of, 481–9
Nitokris, Princess, 197–207
Noakes, Arthur, 208–17
Noakes, Edith, 208–9, 212, 216–17

Oakville, Georgia, 267–73
O'Brien, Dermot, 80–94
Osborne, Basil, 133–7
Oxford, 45

Palmer, Freddie, 385–8
Parker, Richard, 169–78
Phantasms, living, 103
Philipson, Nathaniel, 35–41
Piranhas, 445–8
Poley, John, 52
Poligny, 23–5
Premonition, 364–73, 397–407

Rae, William, 97, 99, 102
Reford-Jones, Tony, 315
Reston, Dr, 279, 281
Riley, Mrs, 155–7
Rodes, Lieutenant Martin, 438–43
Rotherhithe tunnel, 113–19

St-Claude, 25–30
Sarret, Georges, 355
Savage, Wullie, 107
Scarabs, 260–6
Schaffer, archaeologist, 260
Scotland, 418–26
    See also Drumkattle; Glamis Castle

Scott, Sir Walter, 109–10
Seabrooke, William, 299
Shawcross, Hartley, 362
Sherman, Dr John, 43–4
Short, Cleo, 374
Short, Elizabeth, 374–82
Simeon, Brother, 320–7
Sinclair, Mona, 365–73
Slater, Mrs, 404–5
Snakes, 448–50
South Kensington, 353–62
Spiders, 318–28
Spilsbury, Sir Bernard, 296, 359
Squando, Norwegian barque, 179–87
Standings, Yorkshire, 398–400, 406
Statham, George, 385–8, 390–6
Stephens, Barbara, 355, 358, 360, 363
Stephens, Edwin, 169–70
Sterne, Richard, 53, 54
Stilton, Hunts., 188–96
Strathmore, Lord, 105, 108–9
Sullivan, John, 80–94
Summers, Montague, 256

Talbot, Dr, 473, 475, 476–7
Tamson, Jessie, 95–103
Thame Park, 342–52
Thomas, Thankfull, 54–9
Thompson, Mary, 213–16
Torture, 328–40, 453–63
Toth, Ann, 377, 379
Townley, William, 34–6
Trains, 364–73, 464–9
Turrell, Mrs, 313–14

Valetta, Malta, 438–43

Vampires, 110–12, 142–7, 250–66, 282–287, 307–19
Vaughan, Eve, 283–7
Vaughan, Jack, 283–7
Verdung, Michel, 23–5
Verrill, Professor A. E., 162
Vermeylen, Anna, 15–22
Vermeylen, Mynheer, 17–19
Von Hochberg, Count, 251
Voodoo, 304–6

Walsingham family, 267–71, 273
Wang-Foo, 453–63
Warburton, Sir Peter, 64
Webb, Inspector Albert, 362
Werewolves, *see* Lycanthropy
West Indies, 298–306
Weyer, Johan, 25
Wheldon House, 120–30
Willems, Margriet, 17
Williams, Maggie, 137–41
Williams, Teresa, 125–9
Wilson, Mother Anne, 64–8
Wilson, Sue, 120–30
Winterborne, John, 471–80
Winterborne, John Edward, 473, 475, 476
Winterborne, Rose, 471–80
Winterton, Mr, 241–9
Witchcraft, 62–8, 148–57, 250–1, 256–7
Wright, Mother Mildred, 64–8

Yu-Tang, 461–3

Zombies, 298–306